The Critics Hail Charles Ingrid's PATTERNS OF CHAOS Novels:

**Books by Charles Ingrid
in DAW Omnibus Editions**

THE PATTERNS OF CHAOS

Volume One
RADIUS OF DOUBT
PATH OF FIRE

Volume Two
THE DOWNFALL MATRIX
SOULFIRE

THE SAND WARS

Volume One
SOLAR KILL
LASERTOWN BLUES
CELESTIAL HIT LIST

Volume Two
ALIEN SALUTE
RETURN FIRE

THE PATTERNS OF CHAOS

Volume One

Radius of Doubt

Path of Fire

CHARLES INGRID

DAW BOOKS, INC.

DONALD A. WOLLHEIM, FOUNDER

375 Hudson Street, New York, NY 10014

ELIZABETH R. WOLLHEIM
SHEILA E. GILBERT
PUBLISHERS

www.dawbooks.com

First Paperback Printing, January 2002
1 2 3 4 5 6 7 8 9

DAW TRADEMARK REGISTERED
U.S. PAT. OFF. AND FOREIGN COUNTRIES
—MARCA REGISTRADA
HECHO EN U.S.A.

PRINTED IN THE U.S.A.

Dedicated to my father,
who flew for his country and loved it,
and to fellow classmate Roy Corrigan,
who flew because he loved it also,
even though it was the death of him.

And to Sheila, for remarkable coolness,
in the face of fire.

RADIUS OF DOUBT

PART 1

The House of Star

Chapter 1

High winds tormented the descent of the incoming shuttle, buffeting it from the moment it entered the atmosphere of the planet called Sorrow. Passengers aboard the vehicle in the freight section clung to their safety webs and harnesses. In the forward cabin, only two first class passengers endured the bad ride. The Choya got to his feet, heedless of the bumps and dodges, and began to pace. His fellow passenger, the Daranian, closed his eyes and began to recite religious verses in a high-pitched hum. Through his thick lashes, however, the Daranian continued to watch the Choya pace. Though both beings were bipedal, like most of the sapient races, the thick, furred body of the Daranian could not compare with that of the Choya. The Choya was tall and slender, yet broad-shouldered, his double-elbowed arms sinewy with grace . . . and there was a natural arrogance to his stride, the self-assurance of one who was a leader among aliens; a role to which a Choya seemed born.

The shuttle vibrated with a high-pitched screech, nearly out of range of their hearing. The Choya stopped in his tracks and looked upward, his thick brown hair cascading backward from the coronet of horn that crowned his head. His attitude of watchful listening held for another second and then the shuttle plunged.

The Daranian fell from his seat and dangled at the end of his safety line, but the Choya kept his feet with little effort as the shuttle leveled off with a tremor. As the Daranian hauled himself back into his webbing, it struck him that the Choya had acted as if he'd known what was coming.

The Choya threw him a glance. "I think," he said, "we've had enough." With economy of movement, he crossed to the "Authorized Only" door locks leading to the control cabin.

The Daranian concealed his grimace of triumph. The

Choya *was* a *tezar;* he'd been correct in his estimation of
his fellow passenger, and the legendary *tezarian* pilots
would no more tolerate this buffeting than cross-marry outside their Houses.

The Choya disappeared beyond the bulkhead. The Daranian closed his third eye in supplication and increased the
fervor of his chanting.

Palaton forced the second bulkhead open. He was exhausted, having come off a year-long contract; and now the
rules of approach to the Halls of the Compact subjected
him to the indignity of being transported by an inferior
pilot. His horn crown prickled with the intuition of something violently wrong in the control cabin, and as the air
lock came open, the hysterical voices within hit him like a
blow to the face.

He hadn't wanted this assignment and wouldn't have
taken it if his elder hadn't ordered him. Two weeks in the
predatory political atmosphere of the Halls was not what
he considered a well-earned vacation. His *bahdur* talent
flickered with fatigue, warning him of a dangerous drain on
his psychic abilities, and then the hysteria of the pilot and
navigator slammed at him. Palaton flinched, gathered his
reserves, and lashed out.

"Who's in charge here?" he said, flexing his arms and
folding them across his chest.

There was an immediate, stunned silence in the cockpit
as the pilot and navigator swung about to face the intruder.
The pilot, a quad-armed brachiator, wrinkled his pelted
face while the navigator, one of the flighty, winged Ivrians,
settled to a perch. The Gorman pulled his lips back from
his canines, snarling, "You're off limits."

"And you're off track. What's going on?"

The Ivrian clacked his flexible beak several times in menace display before sputtering, "Storm center has us. We're
caught in the leading edge."

Storms above Sorrow were no simple matter, but a pro-
fessional should be able to handle it. Compact rules of approach stated that only neutrals could pilot in from the
orbiting stations where the deep space ships berthed, but
Palaton was not going to accept any rules which would
subject him to any more abuse.

"Let me in," he said.

His words were soft, but his dual voices were low with intent.

The shuttle caught another thermal drop and plunged abruptly. Palaton shifted his weight to the balls of his feet and his knees flexed, but the Ivrian went sliding off his perch in a flurry of feathers. The pilot grabbed his webbing with a groan and shook his furry head. Palaton finally caught at the wall to keep his balance, narrowed his eyes, and glared at the control board. There was no automatic pilot here—computer sentience was against the rules of approach to Sorrow, to avoid having drones sent in to wipe out the multiracial city. But it didn't change the fact that a competent automatic pilot could have handled this shuttle.

The Gorman shoved over violently. "Here," he grunted. "Take it." And buried his face in all four of his hands. Palaton would get no prettier invitation. He came forward and sat down in the second's chair. The Gorman's presence felt like a light, greasy film over the controls and he forced back a shudder as he took the guidance system in hand. He sent his *bahdur* spiraling outward, feathering the edges of the storm, with its highs and lows, its turbulent clashes. For a moment, his abilities dimmed, flickered as if lightning had struck, and his heartbeat pounded fiercely in echo.

A *tezar* was nothing without his *bahdur*. It happened to all of them, sooner or later, guttering out like a primitive tallow candle, but he wasn't prepared for it to happen to him. He shook off the icy shock traveling through him and reached again, and this time he found the prescient knowledge he needed.

The shuttle came into his control like a child going to its mother and settled there, in comfort. He, in turn, took it and cradled it, skirting the furious winds which had tossed them about and finding clearer skies. The shuttle answered awkwardly, like a young bird with a crumpled wing.

"You've got mechanicals," Palaton said aloud, as soon as he identified the source of the problem. "Probably a chip gone bad. Anyone would have had difficulties."

Anyone but a *tezar*. He did not say that out loud. He did not have to. The Gorman raised his face. His broad, almost flat nose sniffed.

"I thank you, *tezar* Palaton," he said.

"Think nothing of it," the Choya answered. "I'll bring it on in, if you don't mind, considering the malfunction." He gathered up the shreds of his energy, pushed worry aside, and functioned on pride. He could not possibly have felt his *bahdur* flicker. Not possibly.

"I would be honored."

The Ivrian said nothing, but its wing agitation settled from a furious buzzing to a languid fanning. The second-class passengers in freight knew nothing about the danger they'd been in, and even the Daranian had only his guesses as to what had happened.

There was another violent plunge of the shuttle, then it leveled out once more and the turbulence disappeared. The Choya did not return from the control cabin, but the Daranian rode out the rest of his passage in peace.

Palaton suffered the effusive thanks of the Daranian upon arrival, reminding himself it was the due of a *tezar*. He watched as the Daranian fumbled off about his business, choosing the confined interior of a cabcar to ride the rest of the way into the Halls. He himself felt like a claustrophobic freed and as he turned his head into the wind, where the scattered clouds of a milder storm spit-spattered him, he took a deep, steadying breath. The fear that had lanced him was finally loosening its grip, but Palaton was left unsettled in its wake. Even fatigue had never dimmed his power before. Without his abilities, he was nothing. He was a Choya without lineage—a thing almost unheard of and seldom spoken of publicly—and without his *bahdur,* he had no career, no calling.

Every *tezar* was faced with the inevitability that his talent would one day burn out. That was the nature of psychic ability. But in the Choyan race, psychic abilities were not a come and go talent. They were as steady as any of the five more common senses sentient races shared. They kept the nature of their abilities hidden from other beings, as much to keep the upper hand in galactic politics as to avoid being exploited, but only those abilities needed to pilot the soulfire, or *tezarian,* faster than light drive, carried a debilitating genetic disease with it.

He was too young to be ill. Too new to be used up. He could not be facing the beginning of his end. The high winds of the upper stratosphere that had telegraphed a restlessness to the planet's surface now whipped a chill wind at him. It brought the sting of tears to the corners of his eyes, but he stood on the obsidian plains until his head cleared. The wind spoke of storm and the storm reflected his own inner passion. Standing near the shuttle berths, smelling the burn of the recent landing, listening to the creak of metal as it cooled and settled, the shouts of the multilingual crews working over the berthing cradles, all these soothed and polished and buffered him. When he was ready, he turned to the transportation alcove and defiantly chose a jet sled over the conventional vehicles. He did not like feeling staid.

The crystal canals leading to the massive city known as the Halls of the Compact were empty of traffic in the early morning light. He left the helmet off—one size rarely fit all, particularly not when it came to the Choyan race, whose dual brain pans and horned crowns were of a large and proud size—and a few spattering rain drops dampened his face. Palaton bared his teeth in annoyance at the weather. He would not go gently into the storm, but as the jet sled took him over the canalways, the rain faded.

Sorrow smelled of an early spring. The weather held the edge of a newly tempered sword blade. Palaton enjoyed the passage of winter into spring. He drank the air in now as the rapid glide of the sled along the canals flung it into his face. If he looked down, he would see what was imprisoned in the crystal and recall all too clearly why the planet had been named Sorrow. As he neared the Halls, the canals converged into a solid lake, self-bridged by a separate, flawless arch of quartz, whose glassy interior remained unstained—but the death encapsulated below it was reflected in its mirrorlike surface. All those who wished to enter the Compact had to pass over that bridge—and those resolute enough occasionally looked down.

An entire race of people had died within those crystal confines. Massed together, frozen forever within the canals and lakes of this part of the continent. No member race of the Compact held within its history a clue to who these people had been or what had happened to them, but their death was a stark memorial to the awfulness of the event. Had it been war or suicide? Destruction or preservation, waiting for the day when the crystal could be split and the people offered up again into life? No one could hazard a guess—but the technology of it remained beyond anyone's ability to duplicate or undo. The common theory was that it had been an act of war, and it was in the hope of avoiding another war like that one that the Compact had been woven.

Thus far, in a limited way, the weaving had been successful. There had not yet been another war of such destructive scope. Palaton did not see how there could possibly be. No member race in the Compact knew how to construct a weapon which could do what this one had and he did not think any would even dare try. The view from the bridge was a daunting one. It was the children which bothered him the most.

He took the bridge at an incredible speed, with the sled monitor warning him of reckless endangerment, and the governor kicking in to slow him down. It mattered not. As a *tezar* he knew exactly how fast and far he could go. The sled did what he wished—he came off the arch in a high jump. For a moment his heart soared. Then the sled slammed to the canalway and he braked rapidly as he neared the traffic of the more conventional roadway and then reached the garages. Like the rain clouds which were skittering away, the wind and the speed had purged him. He turned the sled into transportation and passed through the security portals.

"That's him," the Daranian said to the being who stood in the shadows beside him. "I came in with him on the transport. He saved our hides. The turbulence damn near brought us down."

The shadowed being said quietly, sibilantly, "He should have saved me the trouble."

"I don't want to know," the Daranian answered. "I pointed him out to you. My part and obligation in this is done."

"Of course," the shadowed one responded, but the Daranian had already hunched his head into his shoulders and lumbered away. The dark one looked after him through slant eyes accustomed to seeing in the night and smiled. He looked down again from his vantage post as the Choyan prey passed below. Then he sprang out and down, landing effortlessly, and he, too, passed through the security portals, his weapon of hollowed bone perceived as organic and harmless. With a grim quickening of pace, he caught up with his prey and trailed him into the Halls of the Compact, biding the time to strike.

The tongue-lashing he got from the garage officials restored Palaton's cloak of arrogance. He needed it to survive within the Halls, he more than any other Choya who might have been sent here. But there was no ground-tied being who could tell him what to drive or how fast to drive it. He was a *tezar*!

Rejuvenated, the fear of his talents dimming blunted and pushed as far back as he could force it, Palaton readied to pick up his assignments. He registered at the front directory and waited in the lobby until his map could be printed out and his itinerary handed him, but even as he took it, he already knew where he would be going. The contracts wing was easily accessible to the fore of the city complex. He would be among more businessmen than politicians and he preferred it that way.

Moameb's uneasy health had shoved him into this assignment, weary though he was from his last contract, but he would only spend two weeks in this hellhole. There would be a pouch of contracts to pick up and a dozen or so to finish negotiating personally. There were always more jobs than pilots and the *tezars* could pick and choose as they wished. They were the lords of Chaos. They alone could navigate the realm beyond faster than light speed with any degree of accuracy. They were the main commodity of the Choyan people in this butcher shop of a galactic alliance. And no one alive within these Halls would know the shame that Palaton carried within him, a shame far easier to hide among strangers than among his own people.

Palaton found himself smiling grimly as he strode along the walkways to the contracts wing. He had resented Moameb's blatant maneuvering at first, but knew the elder had a reason for everything he did, even now, as disease-racked as he was. The elder's patient leadership by example as well as by haranguing the cadets seemed aimed more and more specifically at Palaton. "Consolidate your position with the Compact," he'd insisted. "You need more than your reputation." He'd ignored Palaton's rebuttal that he was not a politician, that he could not ply the arts of compromise.

"Compromise is nothing more than following thermals. You're a pilot, aren't you? Then, by God-in-all, go with the flow!"

The walkways about him were thronged with bodies, each moving in a pattern and direction known only to itself. Yet there was a deference shown to Palaton. He could not help but sense it. He was a *tezar,* and they gave way to him. He let his guards down a moment to bask in the subtle respect, a childish indulgence but one which his ego needed. The warmth of the touch comforted him. Still, he was no psychic vampire, he would not feed off the unsuspecting, and he prepared to put his guards back up.

A clammy, vile brush of emotion grazed him. Palaton choked as if he'd swallowed wrong and fought to maintain his outer pace. Something wrong, something evil paced him. The enmity followed him, but as his *bahdur* passed over it the feeling slipped away. Palaton felt sudden unease. His talents did not include telepathy or empathy to any great degree, but he had sensed something; he was sure of it. He turned away quickly as the corridors and wingways of the business section grew more crowded.

Once out of the crowd, he was able to appreciate the beauty of the glass and stone building. A view of the nearby snow-capped mountains, amid a dark blue sky so virgin and rich with moisture as to be nearly purple backdropped the Compact buildings. He looked for a reflection behind hint and saw nothing. He scanned the passing beings, most bipedal and walking, a few in adapted carts. Nothing unusual or sinister met his survey. Palaton paused, not liking his inability to trust himself. Alone in non-Choyan territory, he had only himself to trust.

He would have to turn the corner whether he liked it or not. The corridor floors began to separate into business halls and he sought out a lift.

Once inside the lift, he spoke his floor number and conference hall identification code. The lift glided into motion, separating him from the crowd, moving to a final destination. He looked out and downward and saw nothing cut off from its pursuit of him. Palaton clicked his tongue inside his mouth. He was becoming overly cautious. Then, thinking of the hair-raising jump off the bridge, grinned madly at himself for even thinking such a thing. He was still grinning when he emerged from the lift and saw the being waiting for him outside the conference rooms.

The Abdrelik had his back to him, but Palaton's jaws clamped shut and his gorge rose all the same. He hated the amphibians, could not tolerate their personal habits or their worldviews. He almost turned away and left. The Abdrelik had heard him, however, and swung about. He was compact, squat, with a massive body that could survive in land or sea. His purplish green skin had a sheen approximating slime and on his lumpish head, a sluglike creature sat like a sideways hat, or a living wig, busily feasting on the tiny parasites and fungi which Abdrelik skin was prey to. It made sucking noises as it fed.

The Abdrelik facing him opened wide his two lidded eyes. He made a grimace approximating a Choyan smile. "Palaton," he said, his voice booming. "What an unexpected pleasure." Drool escaped from the corners of his mouth as GNask spoke.

Nothing an Abdrelik found pleasurable would please Palaton. He came to a halt. Before he could respond, two figures came between them. He recognized neither, knowing only that they were humankind, small and awkward in their movements, and when they spoke Trade, their accents were stilted.

"A moment, Master Palaton," the taller human said. "We've been waiting . . . we have a contract. . . ."

The interruption was a gross breach of Compact protocol, but there was a desperation in the two that Palaton found he wanted to answer.

The Abdrelik bristled. His voice rumbled outward, a warning of the eruption soon to follow. "Palaton, we have an appointment."

If the humankind annoyed GNask, Palaton would find a need to speak to them. He bowed forward. "A moment, GNask, is all they ask. I am, after all," and his glance flicked over the chronogram, "early." He stepped aside, drawing the two beings with him, out of the Abdrelik's reach. "What can I do for you?" he asked, without taking his eyes off the bulging amphibian.

The Abdrelik's anger was plain. Even the symbiont stopped its feeding, putting out two tiny stalk eyes to look about in disturbed curiosity. Palaton suppressed a shudder as he bent to hear the humankind speak.

Humankind were new in the Compact and he'd never had to deal with them. As he looked down now, his gaze met theirs and Palaton found himself momentarily struck dumb. The eyes, he thought. The eyes were so like a Choya's that he could scarcely look away, large and luminous and expressive, eyes that he'd never thought to see in another species. *Eyes were the window of a people's soul.*

"Master Palaton?"

"I'm sorry," he said, abruptly brought back to an awareness of his surroundings. "Begin again. You have a contract?"

"We've been waiting weeks for a *tezar* to review it for assignment. No one will give us an appointment."

Humankind had no seniority in the Halls, had not yet won true acceptance in the Compact. No one would employ favors to smooth their missions. In the peculiar way of their kind, even their most senior ambassadors were transient, rarely serving more than a handful of years. One scarcely had time to introduce oneself before the humankind was gone and replaced by another. Moameb often complained of the fleeting reliability of such ambassadors. And, as the Abdrelik's expression so keenly conveyed, they were considered one step ahead of the food chain and if that became a misstep, they would be at the mercy of many of the aliens who formed the Compact.

But they had found sympathy in Palaton. He reached for the diplomatic pouch they carried. "You've had your contract evaluated by the Combine?"

The smaller one flinched. His single tone voice rose higher. "What evaluation?"

"Ah." Palaton took his hand from the pouch without retrieving it. "You've missed the most important stage of hiring a pilot. The Combine has to review all contracts and approve them before you can make an appointment for assignment."

The taller man flushed. "No one told us. I beg your pardon, Captain Palaton."

He was unfamiliar with the honorific the humankind used, but he heard the respect in the voice tone. He bowed his head slightly. "I'm glad to have been of some service. When you come before the board in the Combine, tell them you have a Class Zed priority. This means that you come from an underdeveloped system and can claim front line assistance. You'll save yourselves time that way."

They withdrew. ". . . weeks!" the smaller one's pallid voice drifted back to Palaton's hearing.

"Help now . . ." the taller one answered mildly, as they disappeared around the corridor's curve.

GNask said nothing as they passed him, but a string of drool cascaded from the corner of his mouth to the corridor floor. He mopped his lips absently on the back of his hand.

The ambassador looked back and met Palaton's gaze. "And now, *tezar,* if you're finished playing with the lower life-forms. . . ."

"Ambassador." Palaton passed into the conference room. He paused a moment in the doorway and looked back thoughtfully. His horn crown prickled with sensation as though he could hear something normally beyond his range of hearing, but he did not actually hear anything. It merely felt as though he should be able to. He had to let the moment go. Frustration ruffled through him. He could not doubt himself, not in front of the Abdrelik, but he felt a thin edge of desperation. Was he feeling the first symptoms of the disease which would first take his *bahdur* from him, leaving him a burned-out hulk, then slowly cripple the remnant left?

He could not deal with this. But he had to. There was no one else to deal with it. Palaton took a deep breath and pushed onward.

GNask brushed past him. The room security sealed itself. He dropped his diplomatic pouch on a conference stand, thick fingers manipulating the locks, and pulled out the contract documents. The screen lit up as Palaton sat down.

"I have a need," GNask said, "for only your best. That's why I made an appointment with you, specifically, when I heard you were replacing Moameb temporarily."

Apprehension made Palaton circumspect. He stretched a hand out on the tabletop between them. "My presence here does not mean I will be the *tezar* fulfilling your assignment." He looked at the split screen delineating the contract first in Abdrelikan and then in Trade. He kept his expression neutral, wondering if his eyes, like the humankind's, betrayed him. Did they show the disgust and revulsion he held for the kind of work the Abdrelik offered? Did they show his fear?

The split screen offered a wartime contract. The Abdrelik gave him time to view it before commenting.

"Lucrative," GNask said, "for us both."

"You don't need to make FTL jumps to fight a war." Palaton looked away from the screen.

"This one must be. The Kirlians are well armed and defended. We can't neutralize them as the Compact has directed us to without it." GNask paused. "We've been unable to set up a command post within the system from which to strike. We have to come at them from without."

"They're efficient."

"And bloody." GNask pulled his lips into a smile. "I relish the challenge."

"You armed them."

"Of course. They wished to fend off the Ronins."

Palaton's dislike deepened. The Ronins were assassins in the singular and butchers in the plural. The quills that made up their headdresses were far from hollow in their natural state, filled with a deadly toxin that could drop a foe at ten paces. Before a Ronin could go offplanet, it had to be disarmed, but that did nothing for its naturally ferocious nature . . . or its murderous tendencies. The Choya tapped a nail on the tabletop, considering the subtle manipulations of the situation. "I suppose the Ronins cried foul."

GNask's flat, dark eyes sparkled. "Once again, of course. So we will disarm the oversupplied and overzealous Kirlians, and then take contract to defend them against the Ronins who will once more attempt to subjugate the Kirlians if they can avoid getting their paws burnt."

"As you say, a lucrative proposition." Palaton took a deep breath. His scalp crawled with distaste, and he took care to keep his voices pitched neutrally. "The Combine agrees you need the *tezarian* drive, it is not necessary that I agree, and so it will be supplied. I do agree that half a dozen pilots will be necessary and you'll have your assigned *tezars* within three planet spans. Satisfactory?"

"No," replied the ambassador, leaning across the table on forearms nearly as thick as Palaton's thighs. "I want a Choyan of your caliber. And I want you."

"I am not available."

"Squeamish, Palaton? Or up to your neck in local politics?"

"My personal concerns are none of your business." Menace prickled in the air of the conference room. Palaton had felt afraid that GNask would pierce his armor. Now that the Abdrelik was attempting it, rage replaced the fear. Rage was easier for Palaton to deal with. His tone became steely.

The two locked gazes.

"I disagree," said GNask. "I have a vested interest in the fall of the House of Star."

"The Wheel turns," Palaton answered evenly, though the aura about GNask seemed suddenly to flare crimson, obliterating normal vision. "That is life."

"In six hundred years of FTL flight, there has always been a House of Star at the helm." GNask considered his blunt nails. He looked up briefly. "There must be considerable upheaval and concern among your fellows. *Tezars* live a brief but spectacular existence among the Choyan, but Star has ruled since the inception of the *tezarian* drive. You are not only losing an emperor, you are losing an entire ruling House!" GNask's voice sank into a hoarse whisper.

Palaton thrust himself to his feet. "I don't speak to you of egg layers and warm water silt. You don't have the liberty to speak to me of my brethren."

The purple hue of GNask's hide deepened. His two lidded eyes blinked rapidly as he followed Palaton's movement. "I think I do. What I witnessed here this morning intrigues me, combined with the rumors."

Even though he knew he was being baited, Palaton could not help himself. "What rumors?"

"Rumors of illegal traffic between humankind and Choyan. I could scarcely credit it myself. Yet you yourself seemed drawn to them. Perhaps what I've heard is true . . . that the Choyan are culling them out and educating them."

Such a breach of Compact regulations was unthinkable, yet he had also heard intimations, but in-fighting among the Choyan was kept intensely private. What had humankind to do with it? Palaton drew a deep breath. *The eyes,* he thought, *damn those eyes!* "Your contract," he said softly, "is in peril." He heard the undertone of danger in his own voices.

GNask pulled back rapidly. "You threaten me?"

"I warn you only that no contract the Combine puts out is beyond review or appeal."

The Abdrelik smiled grimly. "You can be convincing. I see I tread on boggy ground. You can afford to be arrogant, Palaton, because no one pilots like a *tezar* and no one has a drive as reliable as the *tezarian* drive. But you'd do well to remember this is a yoke which none of us wears willingly and with the House of Star falling . . . none of us may have to much longer." GNask got to his feet and snatched back his diplomatic pouch. "I have taken no offense from your personal remarks."

He lied. But Palaton told the truth as he leaned over the tabletop and said, "But I have taken every offense from yours and if I find your or any other Abdrelik claw meddling in the works of my or any House of the Choyan, I will take your hide off you, GNask, and give it to your heirs for an egg basket."

The amphibian ambassador froze, eyes bulging. His jaws open to reveal tusks that could shred Palaton, horn crown and all. His intent to murder shimmered through the room. Palaton needed no *bahdur* to read it. GNask lifted a shaking hand as if in appeal, but it was fury which trembled in him.

Then the assassin struck.

Chapter 2

Palaton dodged before he heard the *pfft*. GNask moved also, barking out an order for the lights to go dark, and the room plunged into blackness as Palaton hit the floor. He lay still a moment, listening. His *bahdur* augmented senses overwhelmed him with the Abdrelik's fear and anger. The ambassador's perceptions flooded whatever he might have picked up from the assailant. Palaton took a deep breath and concentrated, filtering out the Abdrelik's emotions. Death was in the room, a palpable smell and chill—Palaton took hold of it, though his skin crawled as he did so—and found what he searched for. Above—he was above and moving confidently along the conference room balcony. Palaton could almost taste the assailant's bravado. Darkness did not hamper his perception.

"He can see us," he told GNask urgently and began to move under the shelter of the room's screening. The Abdrelik was on his own and Palaton wasted no more energy tracking him.

The ambassador's abrupt darkening of the room was to the assassin's advantage but Palaton had no intention of signaling his action to reverse the advantage by ordering the lights to glaring intensity. He'd have to do it manually and risk drawing the assassin's fire.

With himself and GNask in the room, Palaton had no idea which of them was the target. If he were a betting Choya, which he was not, he would have bet the Abdrelik ambassador was not a popular man. Still, his *bahdur* had been nagging at him all morning. No, Palaton thought, he himself might well be the target and as such, he would do well to keep moving.

Palaton got to one knee, shifting away from the wall screen, and mentally outlined the room's features in his mind. He knew where the manual lighting controls would be located . . . near the door and at the podium where GNask had displayed the contracts.

Any target could be expected to bolt for the door, breaking the security seal and making for freedom. The assassin would do well to watch the doors. The *tezar* put his cheekbone to the flooring where the marble tiles laved his face with coolness. Palaton took a breath and moved, not quickly, but deliberately, with all the grace and elegance a Choyan body was heir to, and gained the podium. Another *pffft* split the darkness, passing his crown, skimming so close he felt it touch his aura. A comet tail with the stink of poison wafted past his nose.

Light flooded the room again, white light, white hot, so brilliant he thought his sight might be burned from his eyes. He narrowed his glance in reflex even as GNask let out an involuntary yell of surprise and annoyance.

Something fell from the balcony behind him. Palaton swung about, saw the lithe body twist and land supplely on its feet. It was dark, carried about it an aura of evil, and more darkness cloaked it. There was a ripple around its edges where reality shimmered like air off hot pavement. Palaton recognized the distorted effect of illegal shielding.

The assassin had weapons and shielding; they did not. He had *bahdur,* but the facets of his talent were limited, and nothing he wished to reveal in front of the Abdrelik ambassador. The Choyan kept their secrets. He quickly sifted through his options as the assailant made another move across the width of the conference room.

Palaton pitched his voices low, demanding, using control, saying, *"Run."* He gave a mental push as he spoke and looked up to see the being across from him, a dark cloud of menace, focusing on him.

Within that black cloud, he could see a denser outline and knew the assassin had hand and blowgun to its lips. Palaton's mouth went dry. "Run," he husked, voices breaking. It was accented by the faint trill of the security alarm, and Palaton realized it had been going off ever since the action started, and he had not heard it, having filtered it out. Now the noise drilled through him. Patrols would be on their way in response. The being's window of opportunity was closing rapidly.

"Run," he said a third time, and the assassin dropped its hand and weapon from its mouth.

GNask kicked the sundered door open and fresh air swept in. Their stalker's nerve broke entirely.

The assassin answered by way of action, fleeing out the rear doors of the conference hall where the security locks had been broken. The noise of the busy traffic in the outer corridors hooded in. Palaton reached into the podium and turned the lights down to normal.

"You must be a popular being," he said mildly to GNask.

The ambassador rolled heavily to his feet and got up, surprising muscular strength hidden by his bulk. His large lipped jaws worked, without immediate reply. "I owe you nothing," he said finally.

"Nor I, you."

Footfalls pounded down the corridor and Compact security police poured into the room. The patrol leader to the fore snapped out, "There's been a breach of the security locks on this conference hall. For your safety's sake, we will escort you to another meeting room."

"I'm not surprised," Palaton said dryly. He put his booted foot down on the poison dart near him, crushing it to powder. "The doors appear to have been forced open. However," and he swung about to look at GNask. His brow arched. "I believe our appointment has been concluded without incident."

They traded a look for a long moment, then the Abdrelik appeared to make the same decision Palaton had. Neither wanted to face a grueling Compact investigation into the matter. Palaton had no wish for the Compact to know he'd drawn the attention of an assassin and as for the Abdrelik, he would have multiple reasons of his own for avoiding inquiry. GNask retrieved his diplomatic pouch. He stated, "The distinguished *tezar* is correct. We've no need for further conference. Perhaps Palaton has need of your escort to his next appointment, but I do not." He brushed past the patrol and left, the room darkening for a moment as his massive body filled the doorway, shutting off the sunlight outside. It was just a momentary dimness, however, and then the Abdrelik was lost to view.

Mulling over the Abdrelik's remarks, Palaton realized that the ambassador had not made the assumption that he alone could have been the assassin's target. GNask had let Palaton know that he knew the *tezar* could also have been the prey. It bothered Palaton only in that he wondered if GNask could have made him the target.

The security force hesitated, then did a trotting survey of the privacy room. The patrol leader stopped at the door whose seal had been forced. He ran a four-fingered gloved hand along the seal.

"Subtle," he said. "*Tezar* Palaton, did anyone attempt to force entry?"

Palaton smoothed his expression. Too neutral and the patrolman would know he lied. "Not to my knowledge. We had a disagreement and the esteemed ambassador kicked the door. Quite hard. You will probably find traces of the marks from his boot heels. I think the seal may have popped under the blow. However, the integrity of the conference has been maintained and I've no complaints."

The patrolman motioned his force out the door. "Thank you. Do you wish escort . . . ?"

"No. That will be quite unnecessary. And," and the corner of Palaton's mouth quirked, "my next appointment should not be so hot tempered as an Abdrelik." He gathered his map and itinerary from the tabletop and left, the patrolman closing the door behind him. The smoothness of his exit belied his frame of mind.

The assassin had only desired to do bodily harm in an endeavor to take Palaton's or GNask's life.

GNask's guileful maneuvering had been aimed at nothing less than his soul.

He canceled his other appointments, feeling suddenly fragile, although he was certain the assassin had fled the Halls and was probably making his way off planet. His memory of the lithe body within the shielded darkness and the grace with which the assailant had regained his balance despite falling from the balcony led Palaton to the conclusion that the assassin had been one of the Nortons. The feline beings seldom hired out as assassins, but within their own tribes murder was an accepted method for attaining promotion within the ranks. The more he considered the nocturnal sight and sly movement, the more he felt he was right.

But his intuition would not tell him why. Why had he been marked? Or had the Norton been sent to kill the *tezar*, any *tezar*, who'd shown up for the contracts appointment?

And knowing this, had one of his own people sent him to the death trap?

The Wheel turns, he thought. Within the Halls of Compact, he was a *tezar*, a pilot who brought order to the patterns of Chaos, a driver who challenged the limbo of faster than light. Within his House, he was a product of the unthinkable, born of a cross outside his lines, and his mother refused to name his father, leaving Palaton to bear the brunt of her sin. Was he to be a target for her choices?

And how had GNask been able to hint slyly that the Abdrelik had known his secrets? Or had the ambassador merely been plying what he knew of all living nature, that everyone carried secret burdens and guilts? Palaton chided himself for letting the Abdrelik get to him. All the ambassador could possibly know of him was that he was a superb pilot, even among a race of superb pilots, nothing more. He told himself that, and did not believe it. His inner dialogue clenched itself like a fist in his stomach.

He wandered through the conference wing and found himself outside, where the storm-drenched air was laced with a clean scent and the sun shone brilliantly through slate gray wisps. He pivoted on his heel to stare at the roofs of the temple buildings and he found himself suddenly drawn.

He made his way against a current of flesh hurrying the other way. The crowd deferred to him, his passage parting a sea of beings. He took his due as they gave it to him, assuming the mantle of importance being a *tezar* gave him, and used it to shield his rapidly crumbling facade of invulnerability.

The temple wing of the Compact city was no less impressive than the business wings, though the politics here were often far more subtle . . . and mortal. Palaton pulled up— and took a deep breath, then recognized the outline of the Choyan temple, and made his way to the chapel.

Once within the grounds designated for the Choyan sanctuary, he saw only his own people. He dodged the secretaries of the Prelate. There were politics and workings here

that would make the gears that drove the Halls of Compact
look like a child's toy. He had come to rest in the chapel,
certain that he would be alone in his worship.

Across the green lawns, he saw the flagstone A-framed
building, its doors open, a faint glowing light issuing from
within. His stomach eased a bit. Palaton strode inside,
ducking slightly to pass under the door frame and paused
at the interior altar. There he left his boots.

The quiet murmur of water permeated the building. A
bird flew across the high peaked ceiling, driven in earlier
perhaps by the rain, unwilling to leave or perhaps unaware
that there was an exit. The secretaries of the Prelate would
drive it out later, gently, waving palm fronds at it to avoid
injury. For now, both the bird and Palaton were free to
seek sanctuary.

Under the bare soles of his feet, the wood decking felt
highly polished. He padded to the edge of a brook, eyeing
the island it encircled. There were rocks here, meant to be
used as seating, but it was the island he sought, and so he
stepped into the brook to wade across.

The water was chill, invigorating and cleansing. The
brook had been measured, and he took his own measure
within it. Seven strides to the island. Seven steps of contrition. The water warmed as his feet stirred it. He climbed
the island bank and stood, his mind emptied, his heart full.

He sat cross-legged in a hollow lined with dried leaves
and flowers. They gave out a faint aroma as he settled
down. He closed his eyes, thinking of home, his home,
which had been denied to him the day his *bahdur* had been
tested and he had been shown to have the qualities needed
for a *tezar*. Those qualities were the only thing which kept
his life from being a living hell and yet . . . he thought of
his mother and the Household in which he had been raised.

There were three great Houses of Choyan. The Houses
of Star, Sky, and Earth. The House of Star held the predominant number of pilots, though the abilities were also
found in Sky and Earth. Within the Houses were divisions
signifying the different Choyan positions upon the Wheel
of Life. Ascendant, then Right Wheel, Descendant, then
Left Wheel. There were millions of Choyan within the
Houses and their portions of the Wheel. Each knew his
bahdur, each knew his abilities and tendencies from birth.

Each strove to fulfill his potential. That was the lifelong struggle of a Choya.

Alone among *tezars,* Palaton knew only half of his heritage. Marked by bastard birth like the lowliest of the Choyan classes, he knew little of the genetic legacy he had been born to fulfill. Although he was a pilot whose sense of direction was infallible, he himself felt lost. When the *bahdur* failed, he would be lost, without a heritage.

Had that bastard birth marked him for death as well as failure?

The bird inside the sanctuary fluttered from rafter to rafter as Palaton looked up at the noise of its wings. The bird skimmed the top of a floral trellis and came to rest on the flexible branches of an evergreen seedling, bouncing a little on the willowy branch.

Palaton put a hand to his brow, rubbing the base of his horn crown, where the weight he bore sometimes pained him. Water splashed abruptly behind him and the Choya sprang to his feet, heart pumping rapidly.

There was one of the humankind in the stream. He looked ridiculous, stick figure stiff, trousers rolled up to his knees, and he froze in place as Palaton stared at him.

The being smiled tentatively. "Some place, huh?" he said in Trade, his words a little slow as if he thought in his native language and then spoke in rough translations. He did not have the Trade slang exact, but Palaton's *bahdur* augmented the Choya's hearing of the humankind's speech and made up the difference.

Palaton did not move, frozen by shock at the being's trespass.

"Do you come here often?" the humankind offered up, as he crossed the stream of water.

"No," said Palaton mildly, feeling the other's aura. He recognized the aura of the taller humankind who'd appealed to him for help before his appointment with GNask. There was nothing but benevolence approaching him. On a scale of paranormal ability, this being scored only slightly above a stone wall. Humankind reportedly set great store by such abilities, but rarely possessed even an iota of them. He relaxed as he interpreted nothing sinister about the trespasser.

"I do," said the man. "It's quiet and out of the way."

He sat down on a nearby rock, put his head back, and breathed deeply.

Palaton watched as the other partook of the sanctuary's atmosphere of well being. He came to the conclusion that this one had no idea he trespassed, no idea that this was Choyan property, no idea that he was in the heart of a temple. He contemplated sending the being out, but his curiosity kept him from this automatic response. He forced himself to resettle. "There is," he remarked, "a peace about this place."

"I can't take it outside. The canals, the lake . . ." the being's single voice faded. "None of my briefings described it the way it is. Why do you . . . why do you build the Halls here?"

"To remind us. Sorrow was found this way. We crossed its path long after its people reached their sad destiny. We don't know why or how—we only know that we, too, could reach the same destiny if we do not stop to negotiate among ourselves. Perhaps you have something similar in your history?"

"I don't—" the being halted. "Pearl Harbor," he said, "I guess. It's a war memorial. Off an island shore where most of the Pacific fleet went down. After a hundred and some years, the sunken vessels still leak oil and the men aboard are buried within their hulks. It's sobering."

"Sometimes we need to be sobered into making peace."

The man nodded. He rolled his pant legs back down, hiding his pale skin. "You're the *tezar* who helped us earlier, aren't you?"

Palaton smiled wryly. The awe of his office no longer had the being tongue-tied. Perhaps it was because they both sat, wet and barefooted, within the parklike confines of the temple. "I am."

"I want to thank you for your aid. The protocol of the Halls is something I'm still struggling with. I'm John Taylor Thomas and I'm newly elected."

"As are all your people." Forty years was a minute amount of time in the Compact. Palaton did not wonder that the beings were struggling with understanding their place within it and its workings.

The man fell silent. Palaton was struck by the similarity of their hair locks, though the humankind's were far shorter and he had no horn crown to protect his skull casing. The being looked up. "I just met a Quino," he said, "who claimed to have known one of our long dead American presidents. It sort of rocked my sensibilities."

"Don't let it," Palaton replied. "He may well have, though the Quinonan aren't known for their truthfulness. More likely, it was one of his hive which had done so, and he retains the memory. The Quinonan were exploring your system for centuries before they reported your presence to the Compact. Such exploration is illegal and the effects of it will color proceedings for decades yet to come." Palaton personally did not like the insect beings, with their undead white skin, bulging heads, and immense flat eyes, but he most resented the psychic shield they projected, intended to generate abject fear in others. He felt the Quinonan to be compassionless bullies. The hive conscience was not a favorite of his to deal with. He offered a further bit of wisdom. "The politics of the Halls are not confined. They spill out everywhere. It is not wise to let your guard down."

"If not here, where? If not with friends, with whom?" the man answered. He stood. Palaton looked into those remarkable eyes.

"You're aware you trespass?"

The other shrugged with a fluidity of movement Palaton had not expected these angular beings to possess. "And will you ask me to leave?"

Palaton laughed dryly at himself. He should have known no motive was so uncomplicated. "Now you know why Choyan have crowns of bone. Otherwise, it would be easy for an enemy to sneak up and brain us. You are persistent, whoever you are. You have tracked me to ground. What do you want?"

"The stars," the man answered intently, suddenly meeting the Choya's gaze, and the expression on Thomas' face struck a blow to Palaton's soul. "Give us the freedom of the stars."

"It's not mine to give."

"The *tezarian* drive. Surely you can install it in any vessel you wish."

"There is no *tezarian* drive without a *tezar* to pilot it." Inwardly, Palaton felt intense sorrow. Here was another race which would dig at him for his secrets, which would despise him for keeping them.

"Without it, without access to contracts, we're hostage in our own system. The Abdreliks consider us part of the food chain, the Quinonan use us for barter like devalued coins."

"I cannot give what you cannot understand, even if I would break the laws of my people." Palaton spread his hands. "We contract ourselves to your will, insofar as the Combine will allow. I can give you nothing more."

"You mean you will give me nothing more." He ran a hand through his hair, a gesture of futility that Palaton read well. "Now you've seen what all the Compact talks about, a human begging for crumbs of help. You have it all, and we're dying, and none of you will help us. You take our children and give nothing back." The humankind paused, swallowing back what else he might have said.

That pricked sharply at Palaton. Here was another who hinted at what the Abdrelik had insinuated. "What do you mean? What children?"

"My child," said John Taylor Thomas urgently. "I don't want to give her up. Tell them for me."

"We don't take children. You're talking about the grossest kind of exploitation. It's against our laws as well as those of the Compact."

John Taylor Thomas gave him a scathing glance. "I thought," he said slowly, "you were different. A captain among the Choyan, disinterested in political games. Our children leave. Choyan take them. They never come back. All we have in their wake are vague promises of help, of advancement. But even that we don't receive. I want our children back, *tezar*. I thought I could ask you for help." Without further word, the man recrossed the brook and gathered up his shoes.

"What children?" Palaton called after him desperately, but the man kept walking. Palaton read the lines of his stiff stick-figure form and saw nothing of defeat there. Guileless creatures, direct and frank. What had the ambassador meant? What had GNask befouled by mentioning it with his sly innuendo? What had Moameb known that he did not?

Chapter 3

John Taylor Thomas made it back to his compound where security guards stiffly saluted him and watched him enter. He could feel them staring at his back. He wondered if they could hear his heart thumping inside his chest. He slapped his palm over the lock to his private quarters, felt the briefly irritating wash of the retina check pierce his eyesight, then was inside, safe, alone.

He collapsed on the bed, feet dangling over the edge, gaze fastened on the ceiling, and waited for his heartbeat to return to normal. His ears rushed with the *swish* of adrenaline driven pressure. Slowly, he regained control again.

The Choyan had a natural self-assurance that bordered on arrogance. He could accept that. He thought perhaps that he had found one who would level with him, one who would listen and respond in kind, devoid of the political dance that seemed to permeate everything said and done within the Halls of the Compact. Disappointment keened through Thomas that he had not. The *tezar*, though gracious, had been as opaque as any of his race.

Thomas sat up on the bed. He loosened his diplomatic tie from around his neck. His compound window overlooked the rugged purple mountains, a far better view than that commanded by his office window. He stared at the horizon as if it could offer him the advice he most desperately needed.

He'd run for office on a techno-eco cleanup slate and now he was in danger of losing his backing, a volatile constituency if ever there was one. Only the e-t ambassadors were elected, but the reasoning there had been good. No one branch of government, national or international, nor any one country, could then control the fate of the world by mere appointment. Campaigns, however, were financially risky. He could not have done what he did without surreptitious backing. For himself, he had never questioned whether the price was too high. He'd been prepared to pay it. Earth needed technological assistance to clean up its ecological messes, and the aliens could provide that, if they would. It was time to take a stance of strength in the Halls of the Compact and demand assistance. He would demand that assistance. He could show that strength. He would pay the price.

But now his backer had contacted him and told him the debt would be called in and how, and he realized he'd given away his first born child.

Thomas blinked fiercely at the window, his tie clenched and crumpled in his knotted hand. There was no one to rant and rail against. He'd never had a means of contacting them, they contacted him when they wanted him to know something. He'd been warned to maintain silence. He'd broken it today in his overpowering need to save his daughter, and the *tezar* had either feigned ignorance—or Thomas was dealing with a fringe group of Choyan, a splinter group, and there would be no help for him because there was no open knowledge of these activities.

He did not think Palaton had been lying. There had been an intelligent openness in the alien's eyes which had bespoken silently what could never be said aloud. So where did that leave Thomas now? What options had he?

He could fall back on a strategy the Americans had perfected: if a people will not help you, perhaps their enemies will.

Thomas reached for his communications line and signaled his secretary. She answered briskly.

"Betty, get me an appointment with Ambassador GNask. And make sure it's after lunchtime or whenever that thing's eaten."

"Yes, sir," the woman said without missing a beat. Thomas closed off the line. His knotted hand relaxed and the crumpled tie fell to the carpeted floor where it lay, unheeded.

GNask lowered himself into the semi-sludge bath awaiting him. The tepid waters felt both cool and warm as they washed silkily about his body. His legs trembled a moment as the water and the seating took the weighty bulk of his body. He gave a long, breathy sigh. His *tursh* had settled upon his forearm, feeding, and as the bath made it more mellow, it simply lay contentedly. GNask stroked it fondly. His *tursh* was of the family line, a lineage traceable as far back as Abdreliks traced their symbiont, perhaps even to the first partners. An Abdrelik was only as good as his *tursh*, his family liked to quote, and theirs were as prominent as any. He sorrowed for the lesser classes and for the armed forces who could not take their symbionts with them, settling instead for topical creams to keep their skin clean and pure. No. A *tursh* provided more, much more, and he owed much of his success to his. He stroked it a last time and sank back into his bath, resting the heavy folds of his neck against the rim of the soaking tub.

He had been basking for the better part of an hour, water swirling about his bulk from time to time as the tub recirculated and warmed it, when the wall screen illuminated. His heavy-jowled secretary filled the window.

"Your appointment is here, your honor."

GNask positioned himself more solidly upon the podium seat inside the tub. "Admit him," the ambassador droned, rousing from the calm stupor he'd allowed himself to be lulled into. He cooled the water temperature, bringing himself back to alertness.

With a click and a nearly inaudible whoosh, the wall panels opened to admit a small and diffident figure. He frowned and felt a rumble of anger and hunger boiling up from deep within him as the junior ambassador of the humankind stepped in. GNask stifled his reaction and reached for his *tursh*, stroking it to calm himself. He did not occupy the position in the Compact that he did by allowing base emotions to rule his judgment. He would not ruin spans of work in one imprudent moment.

The man looked pale, but then, most of his kind did, even those with skin the color of fine mud. He glanced around the bathing room and then perched upon an upholstered guesting chair without being invited to do so, and GNask felt his jaw tighten. What was it about these beings that so inspired the worst in him?

Perhaps it was their huge eyes and their fearful look, the

look of prey flushed out of the shallows, unable to think of a way to fight free. No sporting game these, but fodder, nothing more and often much less. They had soiled their own waters almost beyond redemption and had the nerve to come whining to the Compact to be saved—they, a race which had achieved space!

His symbiont quivered in agitation under his stroke as it absorbed the humors of his temper. GNask opened his eyes wider, knowing the voluptuous folds of his face would be emphasized and spoke. "Good afternoon, ambassador."

The man nodded, saying, "I understand I owe you an apology, ambassador, and have come to deliver it in person."

GNask's attention was piqued. The being had some spine and sensibility, after all. GNask liked spine. It made the meat easier to pull away from the smaller bones. "Your apology is noted, John Taylor Thomas, and also the admirable point that you have delivered it yourself, in person."

"It seemed the proper protocol." The humankind shifted. He seemed paper thin, but GNask could see a wiry strength in the way he moved. He would be fast, on foot. Flailing, in the water. His guts rumbled a second time. "I don't expect you to sympathize, your honor, but politics on my world are complicated. My predecessor does not care if I disgrace myself or my world. Few rules of protocol, or, indeed, briefings of any kind on procedures, were left for me." A fleeting expression passed over the humankind's face, an expression that unfortunately reminded GNask of a Choyan smile. "I must resort to learning by experience and I regret deeply if any of my clumsy attempts have offended you."

"The matter is forgotten." GNask waved his hand. He found himself fast losing interest in the being. He reached out and retuned the water temperature before dropping his hand back into his bathwater.

"I know your honor has many appointments, but might you indulge me with a question or two before I leave?"

His *tursh* purred slightly on his arm. GNask's gaze flickered over it quickly. The humankind must have enough of a personality to please it. That thought alone brought his attention back to the man. He looked up, meeting the other's expression.

"If I can enlighten you in minor matters, I will do so."

"You are one of the founders of the Compact, are you not? The Abdrelik race and the Choyan race."

"Yes. Not myself personally, but I have lineage going back to those first days."

"Who discovered Sorrow? I've done a little research on it, but the roots are obscure."

GNask felt his face folds crease with irony. "No one is certain. It may have been a Quino explorer, or a Choyan *tezar* or one of our raiders."

"And the . . . people . . . of Sorrow . . . were like that always?"

"From the moment of scouting. A terrible enemy, eh, to have done that to a people and then move on? It is one of the reasons we came together in Compact. There is an enemy out there perhaps greater than any of our petty rivalries."

"But no one knows what happened."

"The quartz which binds them has been difficult to date, to analyze, even to penetrate for core samples. Modulation readings are about all we can get . . . and that is affected by the matter trapped within it."

A fleeting look, a tiny shadow, passed over the man's face. GNask knew nothing of its inner meaning. He wondered if it indicated deception. He would have to take time to study this race's body language. The vocal nuances of Trade would be too difficult to pin down with this one's poor accent. "If you are interested," GNask offered, "I can have my secretary access background material from our archives, material not normally available to general audiences although it is not classified."

"That would be greatly appreciated."

GNask felt a surge, of pleasure. This one might be easy to introduce to the Abdrelik viewpoint, so different, so much purer, than that of the Choyan. Although this man carried no weight in any of the greater committees, a prudent vote here and there, even in lesser decisions, was always a plus. "Why do you ask?"

The man shifted. "A morbid interest on my part. I guess. The interference of discoverers upon new entry worlds . . . the tampering. . . ."

"Tampering? Do you think Sorrow has been tampered with?"

Another shift of weight. Uneasiness, perhaps? GNask leaned forward slightly. His *tursh* put out stalk eyes, reflecting the change of temperament. The humankind said, reluctantly, "My people tend to think of themselves first."

The Abdrelik followed that train of thought swiftly, answering, "The Quinonan behavior on your world is to be regretted. However, you have moved past that. There were sanctions offered as recompense on your behalf, as I recall."

"There are others. . . ." John Taylor Thomas' voice trailed off. He cleared his throat. "My predecessor left a task for me, a task that he was unable to complete, a task that transcends our inherent rivalries for power. If we prove our case, there will be other compensation due us—aid we desperately need. I'm sure you're aware of our plight."

GNask nodded, letting his eyelids fall slightly, looking less alert, more bored, not letting his subject know that he hung on every word, was dissecting all he could from the man's behavior as to the truth and reasoning behind the facade of his words. "There are committees to help your research," GNask prompted.

"The . . . subjects . . . of my research are greatly revered. I have been blocked at every attempt and don't think I'll be getting much more help."

The silted water in the bath surged with GNask's abrupt movement. The man would not have been so bold as to come to him, accusing the Abdrelik of tampering. Therefore, he came aware of the uneasy balance of power forever seesawing between the Abdreliks and the Choyan. Without saying so, he accused the Choyan. No doubt, he hoped the Abdreliks had been keeping a careful watch on their rivals in power . . . which they had. There had been shadowy reports of Choyan in territories where Choyan never ventured, Choyan who could not be traced back to Cho or their predominant Houses. Now here was another nebulous suggestion. He had pondered much over the assassination attempt on the *tezar* Palaton which had posed a threat to himself as well. Perhaps there was a motive here which could be uncovered and used against the Choyan bloc. He did not think the humankind had the courage to order an assassination, but if the Choyan had been tampering, there were other races which would. GNask interrupted the man before he could utter another word.

"This matter will take some thought and consultation on my part. My committees take a great deal of my time, but perhaps there is a member of my junior staff who might be able to give you some insight. I suggest, ambassador, that you make an appointment with my secretary as you leave. Give me some time . . . a day or two . . . we'll see if we can't find some cooperation for you."

John Taylor Thomas stood up. "Thank you, your eminence. I am in your debt."

Their gazes met. As alien to him as the humankind was, GNask felt the sudden surety that this being knew what it was to incur such a debt and to pay it. He nodded. The humankind bowed and left.

GNask sat there, contemplating his next move until his bathwater turned quite cold and his *tursh* climbed to his head, retreating from the chill.

Chapter 4

The dance of manipulation and profit that marked the Halls of the Compact exhausted Palaton by the time he left and made the outward-bound FTL jump for home. A connecting flight brought him closer and he rented a cabcar to finish the journey to Blue Ridge.

There were three main flight schools: the Commons, where those of the general population who were tested and proved talented were trained; the Salt Towers, named for the nearby gigantic salt cliffs and the site where most of the elite scions of the ruling Houses were trained; and Blue Ridge, his destination. Every *tezar* had an affinity for the school which had trained him. Palaton was no different and he found the anticipation building as the conveyance brought him closer to the home he was fondest of. He got out as the cabcar settled to the driveway surface and took a deep breath in relief. A windstorm had swept through, leaving behind its spice-scented fragrance, for the winds had come across the hills where the groves and brush grew wild and abundant with the pungent flower called *tinley*. The aroma almost made up for the damage, swirled banks of fine dust here and there, green feathery branches of the fragile thara trees down everywhere.

Located on the outlying borders of the city holdings, the barracks looked as if Blue Ridge had borne the brunt of the wind's fury, but it had been constructed to do so and the cadets were out sweeping walkways and grafting to limit tree damage. They paid him little attention, though he could almost feel them staring after him as he walked up the drive.

His master was waiting for him at the front doors. The elder smiled broadly. His hair was silvered about his horn crown, and the lines in his face nearly obscured the jewelry he had imprinted under the healthy bloom of his skin, yet his dark eyes flashed with amusement. For an ill Choya, Moameb looked remarkably fit. Palaton felt his brow furrow in irritation as Moameb spoke.

"It must have been a successful trip," he said. "I heard you nearly got yourself killed."

"You're looking well," Palaton answered dryly. He wondered why the other had pleaded invalidity, sending Palaton to the Halls of the Compact in his place.

Moameb had the grace to flush, bringing out the tracing of his facial jewelry in bright contrast. He scratched at the base of his horn crown, above the right temple. It was a quick, diffident gesture, like a twitch. Then he answered, "You'd be surprised how quickly my health returned after they grounded me."

The mildness of the elder's words belied the punch behind them. Palaton felt as though he'd been gutted as he sucked in his breath. Grounded. Never to fly again. His *bahdur* so extinguished that he would never again do what he'd been intended to do. The disease had eaten at him until he was terminal . . . but he might as well already be dead if he could not fly. He got words out past a suddenly contracted throat: "I—"

Moameb cut him off. "I don't want to hear it." There was an edge to his Choyan double voice which told Palaton that the elder didn't lie. He did not want to hear pity or sympathy. He stood aside in the doorway. "Come in and tell me what happened."

Behind them, the soothing strains of a *lindar* recording floated almost inaudibly on the air. The hall smelled of fried bread and Palaton almost smiled, thinking of the cadets' evening meal. He stepped inside and felt the homeliness of the hall wrap about him like a cocoon. Here was where he had been taken in, when his mother's Householding would not have him, and here was his House, if a *tezar* could ever make a barracks a House. But this was not his alone, he'd shared it with eighty cadets and of that eighty, sixty had lived to become *tezars*. Attrition wore at their numbers daily . . . death and burnout, so that there were never enough. The great barracks were never full, but they were never empty either. From this cocoon issued forth beings of incredible ability and terrible destiny. If they did not die of the disease, they died of its consequences, lost in the limbo of an FTL jump, lost in Chaos, drawn into its patterns without hope or end.

Moameb pushed him into a chair by the solar hearth and while he basked in its warmth, which Palaton felt a little too keenly but managed to ignore, knowing that older bones needed more heat, he told his instructor what had happened. He mentioned the ambassador's sly innuendo of collusion with the humankind, but did not tell him of the disturbing trespass in the chapel. He wanted to have Moameb's reactions to the Abdrelik's accusations first.

Moameb looked at him keenly. "As you describe it, the Abdrelik was at least as worried as you."

"I think so."

"Then he could not have sent the assassin."

Palaton's brow quirked.

"Don't discount the ambassador," Moameb warned. "He's as likely a murderer as I've ever met. But neither do I think you have to walk about looking over your shoulders. The chances are that the Norton's target (if it was a Norton which sounds likely, thank your stars it wasn't a Ronin) was the *tezar* who'd come to negotiate the new contracts. It could as likely have been me as you . . . or any Choya."

"And I was flattered."

Moameb laughed. "A jaded response if ever I heard one, which means I would have given anything to have seen the look on your face. You hide yourself well, Palaton. As for Choyan involvement with humankind, there may be some minor meddling—what new race does not intrigue us? But nothing to the extent that the Abdrelik suggests. The Quinonan are infamous for that, not us. How fatigued are you?"

Palaton considered the empty glass of brew in his hand which had helped to lubricate his tale. He was somewhat, although not altogether, satisfied with Moameb's response. He determined not to let the man's last words haunt him. He'd come home, and he needed the respite. "I'm more mellow than tired," he evaluated.

"Then come with me. I've been grounded, but I'm still an observer here. I'm due at the plateau in a few minutes. Come watch a run or two with me. There'll be no one about to do business with before this evening anyway."

Moameb fingered the observation glass hung upon a thong around his neck.

Palaton considered the proposal. The raw edge of excitement and adrenaline a new cadet lived on could be contagious. He needed that feeling, he thought. The newness of flight and all its abilities. He stood up. "Let's go."

They caught a skimcraft to the plateau and then a cog rail up its side to the great, wind flattened mesa, where nothing grew that had not made its peace with that invisible current. The grass and brush were wiry, limber, and tough, growing low and twisted. As the railcars crested the plateau's edge, Palaton felt the wind in his mane. As it had been on Sorrow, it was spring in this hemisphere of his planet, spring just past the edge of winter, and there was a chill to the breeze. He could see the rows of thrust gliders and the cadets milling around them as their instructors sent them about their various duties around the dual launchers.

"First launch?" he asked. He was not empathic, but he could feel their nervousness and excitement clear across the expanse of the plateau. He would have to be as dead and dull as stone not to.

"No . . . this should be their third run."

"Ah." The third run was the flight which separated the *tezars* from the cadets. They'd flown with all their senses as well as their innate talents. Now they would be sensory deprived and their *bahdur* alone would keep them aloft and safe. They would be monitored, but there were always fatalities from here on out in the training. The knowledge was sobering.

Moameb took his elbow. "This should be the largest graduating class since yours," he said.

"The attrition hasn't even started yet."

"But their test scores are high. We hope to lose the smallest percentage ever." The silver-haired Choya lengthened his stride. "They're waiting for us."

Palaton drew salutes and sidelong stares as he joined the class. He could tell from the crimson patches on their sleeves that this was the second wing, the second ranked grouping among the cadets. Blue wing must be flying from the campus in the mountains where crashes were invariably fatal, and it was possible green wing was not yet off the simulators back at the barracks holding.

Thrust gliders were basic: catch a thermal once catapulted, and you were free until landing, and that should not be too difficult from these heights. The more complicated aircraft and shuttles and deep space liners would come seasons down the line. First came your senses, your ability to trust in those genetic, innate talents bred into you . . . then came the machinery invented to give sustained flight.

They looked younger than he remembered. Palaton hid this rueful thought as he paced among them. They moved in waves, first jostling forward to touch him as though he imparted luck, then dropping back out of deference, only to eventually grow bold again. Tall even for a Choya, he looked over the tops of their heads and met Moameb's gaze in amusement.

He looked away as he wondered what role his old mentor could now possibly play in the development of this wing when he had not even the *bahdur* to help keep a cadet aloft if he or she failed. He watched as Moameb bent to the equipment bins, which had been battered by the years and initialed by the various classes until they were beyond repair, and began to issue deprivation helmets.

All the cadets, male and female alike, had worn their hair down, simple and without adornment, because of the helmets. Now they came forward shyly as their names were called and took the gear. The helmets were fierce-looking, dark and hooded. Palaton hid a shudder as he looked at them and remembered how he'd hated them. Not for himself—but for his friends who'd died wearing them. A cadet usually did not wash out of the wing at this stage. He usually died in training.

There were cadet graduates with purple starstrike badges on their shoulders waiting beside the noses of the thrust gliders. There was one graduate for each plane . . . the graduate would be the safety net for the plane's pilot. Their *bahdur* should be strong enough to assist any pilot in trouble. It was a good net in theory, but the reality was sometimes far from it. The graduates had not yet passed their final exams; in fact, part of that exam was working here with the new flights. And, with two catapults loaded and ready, the flights were about to begin.

"Who's up first?"

Palaton turned at the clear, concise voices of the wing instructor. He wasn't mistaken, it was Kedra coming out from behind the catapult where she had been checking the launch mechanism. He thought he might have flushed, for he had once had an affinity for this tall, striking female, her bronzed mane long enough to curl to her waist in the back. She looked at him and smiled fleetingly before turning away with her stylus and automatic pad poised in her hands. "Well?"

The red wing was suddenly mute, their bravado fled. The first launch would be a terrible thing to witness. They stood with their dark helmets tucked under their elbows, the neutral colors of their flight suits stark witness against their skin, highlighting their fear.

"I'll go," Palaton found himself saying. "I haven't blind-flighted in a long while. It's good for the soul."

Moameb gave him a triumphant smile as he tossed out a helmet and now he knew why the elder had brought him up to the plateau.

Learn by example, the elder had always taught him. And he'd been brought up to this wind flattened mesa to give that example. Palaton gripped the helmet between his palms until the material was no longer chill, then he turned and strode to the plane that was held in the catapult launch.

Kedra gave him a leg up onto the wing. The purple star-strike badge of the graduate flashed as he reached up and gripped Palaton's boot as well. The instructor stepped back and let her student say, "I'm here if you need me."

"As a *tezar* will always be for another," Palaton replied automatically, and the young Choya's lips tightened with pride as he nodded and backed away. Palaton settled himself in the pilot's seat. He moved it back for his legs, but there was little he could do about the spread of his hips and shoulders. With a more mature body than most of the glider pilots, he fit in the cockpit as well as he could. He checked the wing flaps and the tail rudder and stick control. Then he picked up the ebony helmet from his lap and secured it over his head.

Instantly, there was no light except the faint spidery red flickering from his own eyes which faded as his sight adjusted to the total darkness. Horn crown obscured by the helmet, he lost his hearing as well. He smelled nothing but old, rank sweat worn into the helmet's lining. Taste gone except for the sudden, dry cottony feeling in his mouth. He tried to lick his lips in surprise. Fear? No . . . surely not. Anticipation, rather.

The thrust glider shuddered. He recognized it as the catapult arm moving into release position. He felt a feather light touch of his guide's *bahdur,* acknowledged it and sealed it away. If and when he needed another's eyes, he would open up for that *bahdur,* but he would not be a *tezar* if he needed it.

The mechanism launched. The thrust glider arced forth with a gut-wrenching suddenness that abruptly shoved his head back against the headrest. He found he'd been holding his breath and as the glider hurtled forward he forced himself to relax.

Palaton opened up his *bahdur.* He did not need to see the ground to sense its aura, but it was the wind he reached for, moving the stick and paddling his feet gently on the controls. He did not care if he was off the mesa's edge or not—the wind was there for him, tamer after the previous windstorm, and he rode it.

There was a purity in glider flight, like sex without any precautions or entanglements of intention. His heart beat faster in exhilaration as he felt the glider take the thermal and soar, far, far above the mesa and the ground below it. The auras bloomed like a rainbow after a tempest.

He wanted to hang glide all day, and he could if he could find the right thermals, but he knew the red wing below was watching him and aching for the freedom he now had. He began to bring the glider down, wafting gently until the dry lake bed at the mesa's base sent him a message of its aura and he came down. Three bounces and he was skidding to a stop.

There were instructors on the lake bed as well, waiting to load the glider onto the railroad and take it back topside, and one of them knocked on the canopy. He took off his helmet and popped it open. The Choya grinned at him. Palaton grinned back foolishly.

They were lined up for their chance when he gained the mesa again. He'd seen three go off after him, as the cog rail cars painstakingly geared their way up the side of the plateau. The first two had gone off achingly pure and fine. The third had wobbled and taken a heart-stopping plunge before settling.

Moameb was waiting for him and took the helmet from his hands. "You set them back on their heels," his mentor said with a fierce pride in his voices. "You should have seen the look on their faces."

"It felt good." He took a bottle of juice from one of the graduates and drank deeply. "What about that third launch?"

"She panicked, but the senior cadet got her straightened out." Moameb's tone dropped into neutral. They both knew the cadet could not afford any more distrust. Either she had the instinct—or she didn't.

Palaton watched as five more launched. Then, his concentration disrupted by a vague sense of unease, his attention was drawn to one of the purple star-strike badges. She stood rigidly, the cords of her slender throat tight, her eyes closed, and he knew she was locked into her talent. But the glider had not yet left the second catapult. It was scheduled to go next.

The thrust glider trembled, mimicking the panicked movements of the pilot within it. Locked in yet trying desperately to get out. He looked to it and saw the cadet clawing at the canopy. The glider shook heavily and he saw the catapult arm react, going back to release it prematurely, while the other plane was still in its airspace. He caught Moameb's arm and yelled, but the catapult shot forward and the glider arced upward. The cadet assigned to it keened aloud, swayed, and dropped.

Chapter 5

The errant plane pitched skyward. There was a heart-stopping moment as the senior cadets broke rank, running to the fallen Choya'i. The crimson wing froze in place, torn between the unconscious female and the two pilots in immediate jeopardy. Palaton took a deep, gulping breath as he flung his chin up and watched the gliders.

He thought for a moment they would collide, but then the second hit the faint backdraft of the first and veered away slightly. He was reminded of fighting hawks as they neared and sculled away. But the pathway of the first had been invaded enough as it plunged off the mesa's edge that it bucked into a thermal, then a wind shear hit it and it tumbled dramatically.

Moameb put his glass to his eye and let out a sound. "He's hit his head. He's unconscious."

Kedra called out, her imperious voice cutting across the panic, "Give it lift!"

The senior cadets had been grouped about their fallen comrade. Now they looked to their instructor. Simple levitation would not keep the glider aloft . . . it would take the combined efforts of those who possessed that talent. It would mean abandoning the other pilot in the runaway glider.

Every instant counted. The second plane had, by good fortune, caught a warm thermal, despite its wing waggling, and rose off the mesa. "I've got it," Palaton said, in spite of himself.

The cadets with the purple star-strike on their shoulders leaned together, clasping hands, and he knew their talent arrowed after the first plane. A joyous shout told him they'd steadied it, they had it cradled, even as he sent his *bahdur* streaming after the panicked pilot. *Bahdur* couldn't feel cold, could it? Yet his mind seemed lanced with ice as he reached after the Choya. He found the cadet still thrashing under the canopy, unable to get his helmet off, clawing at the straps under his chin, his horn crown swelling with the battering and the helmet becoming ever tighter.

The Choya felt Palaton's bright touch. It flared into the darkness surrounding him like a beacon. For a moment, Palaton felt panic himself as the other latched onto him, then he carefully separated himself and the student. That was what he must have done to his observer, leeching away her soulfire, driving her down, and that was what he would do to Palaton if he let him.

A parasite like this deserved to die. Palaton's thought filtered through the battle to reach the other, and he pushed it away. He had no right to judge. Determinedly he reached out with just enough *bahdur* so that the other ought to be able to see the auras and thermals and guide the glider.

But the panicked pilot seemed unable to take those threads. It was all or nothing. Palaton felt the cadet clawing at his mind shield even as he must still be flailing at the glider's restraints. There was real power behind the cadet's desperation, power which frightened Palaton in spite of his experience. He thought of drowning Choyan who could pull their would-be rescuers down with them.

Moameb's hand fell heavily on his shoulder, breaking Palaton's thought, as his mentor said, "Do what you can. The other's down safely."

Palaton blinked. He'd been locked in the other's visual deprivation, in total darkness, as if he once again wore the helmet. Now he could see the glider spiraling downward and knew the cold wind icing across them carried a wind shear at the mesa's edge. Once the plane hit that—

"He's fighting me," Palaton got out, and his throat hurt, and he knew the cords of it were standing out tightly. The base of his crown was stippled with sweat.

"Do what you can," the other repeated.

Palaton took a deep breath and went sightless again as he delved into the other's dilemma. He felt it as the pilot grabbed the stick and oversteered, experiencing the downward plunge, unsure of how to right it, unable to distinguish up from down or even right from left. The glider swooped, its responses set for the slightest touch, overreacting with the terrified cadet's heavy-handedness at its controls.

His *bahdur* flared orange in the darkness. Palaton let as much of it go as he could afford to, giving the desperate pilot whatever he needed and more. He felt himself being swallowed up and knew that drowning sensation again.

Then his *bahdur* went out. He lost it all. His jaws yawned in a shared silent scream with the Choya as the plane went down.

Moameb's touch brought him back. Palaton found himself on his knees in the wiry prairie grass, its bruised scent rising around him. He looked up. Moameb had paled.

"An ugly way to lose a cadet," the elder said, and held out his hand. "There was nothing you could have done. *Bahdur* or not, his actions brought the glider down as surely as the wind shear."

As suddenly as the wind had come up, it dropped away. Palaton looked across the mesa edge where dust rose in a smoky cloud and he could hear the thin shouts of the landing crew. Now there was no wind shear. Another minute or two longer. . . .

Shaken, he got to his feet. Moameb's hand was warm and he kept his clasped inside it for a moment. His *bahdur* had failed. Again. Bile rose inside his throat. And the cadet was dead because of it. He needed to tell the elder of his failure. It must have shown in his eyes.

"There was nothing else you could have done," Moameb said and squeezed his hand tightly before letting it go.

Kedra strode across the plateau. She put a hand to Palaton's temple, brushing back a stray lock of hair and wiping away the perspiration of his effort. "Thank you," she murmured gently, "for trying."

He could not respond at first. How could he tell her of his failure? That his *bahdur* had gone, leaving them both stranded? That he was no more a *tezar* than the dead Choya? "I—" he got out, but no more. Kedra dropped her hand and turned to shout instructions.

"Get the Choya'i down from the mesa. She's in shock." She looked back to Palaton. "That glider downed more than one cadet." She paused as a litter bearing the Choya'i was carried past them, her classmates solemnly encircling it. She waited until they were out of earshot and loading the railroad cars. "She's been paired with him before. She knew he was leeching and told no one. She thought she could handle it. The crash was her failure as well as his death."

"Lovers?" Moameb said.

Kedra shook her head. "No. Not yet. But indications are that she augmented his *bahdur* to help him get by."

Or that he just took it from her, as he'd tried to take Palaton's before Palaton's talent had abruptly abandoned them both. He stood on the mesa and felt like a blackened, flameless, burned-out torch, listening hollowly to them speculate over the accident.

Kedra put her hand on his wrist. "Let's go down," she said. "There's nothing more to be done here." She looked across the plateau, staring off at the horizon. "Perhaps it was for the best," she murmured, thinking aloud.

Palaton feared to correct her.

The heady smells of dinner permeated the barracks by the time they got back down. The skimcraft ran in shifts, taking twelve at a time until all of the crimson wing, the purple star-strikes, and instructors were brought back. Palaton's stomach churned at the odors as he walked into the hall.

He ate because he should, chewing mechanically, seated among diners who kept silent in a way that was unnatural for the cadets' hall. The first death of the new classes always had that effect. He'd forgotten it. Forgotten the honor of the new *tezars* at fulfilling their destiny and the starkness of the reality that even that honor might not always be good enough. Not only had a pilot died, but one of the graduates had failed a portion of her passing exams. It was not enough to be able to fly. A *tezar* had to be able to support his brethren in any way he or she could. This was their strength.

He watched the Choya'i once or twice. She held herself rigid on the bench, picking at the food on her platter, pushing it around with her two-tined fork, not eating, but busying herself so that she would not have to meet the pitying glances of her fellows. He wished he had words to comfort her.

As the long, rough-hewn tables were cleared, the inner doors blew open, carrying in the pungent scent of deep space liners and landing fields where the sands were turned to obsidian by the heat. Instinctively, the pelt hairs rose at the back of Palaton's neck as he turned to see who'd swept in.

Nedar stood in the archway, his black mane wind-tossed between the wings of his horn crown. The gaze of his dark eyes ranged across the immense room. He stripped off his flight jacket and let it drop to the floor. A green wing cadet scurried to pick it up and hang it in the corner.

Nedar was of the House of Sky, a *tezar* with the instincts of a predator, a survivor, one of the best combat pilots the Choyan had ever spawned. He strode forward arrogantly, hailing Moameb.

"Elder! A round of brew to remember the fallen. It's too quiet in here." He straddled a bench.

Kedra pushed herself away from the instructors' table at the head of the hall. The servers were poised, waiting for confirmation of Nedar's order. She frowned a second, then gave a brisk nod. They ran to get kegs and tankards. She crossed the hall.

"Nedar, a pleasure to see you." Her voices communicated that pleasure, with an undertone which reminded exactly who was in charge of the cadets' barrack and who was an interloper. Palaton admired the subtlety, though he thought it would probably be lost on Nedar.

"The pleasure is all mine. The pilots' hall is too empty tonight. I heard Palaton was breaking bread with the cadets and I came to keep him company." Palaton lost his mental bet. Nedar took a foaming tankard and downed it.

More likely the pilot had come to bring Palaton back, anxious to learn what new contracts were being offered. Palaton had not yet posted them. Their eyes met as Nedar thumped his empty mug on the table. Moameb stood. A tress of silvery hair fell into his eyes. "Palaton, you've been gracious for far too long. I detain you from your duties and your rest."

Palaton pushed away from the table. Nedar's voices cut across the growing talk and the clamor of the kegs being uncorked and trays of tankards filled.

"Let him stay, elder! I didn't come to drag him away."

"Nevertheless, it's time we both left. The wings need time alone to salute their fallen."

The two *tezars* stood, eyeing one another. Tradition left

the wings to themselves while they assessed their lives and their losses. The older brethren like himself and Nedar who'd already passed the rite of passage were intruders. Palaton had been waiting until after dinner to excuse himself gracefully, but now Nedar's brashness was carrying him away. Nedar snapped his fingers, and the cadet who'd put away his jacket now bolted to bring it back. His mug had been refilled and he quaffed this one in three long hard gulps. He let himself belch when he thumped it down empty, said, "To tradition!" and took the jacket from the nervous Choya holding it. "Come on, brethren. We've work to discuss." And Nedar led Palaton away from the cadets' barracks.

Nedar paced as Palaton worked on the interlink to post the new contracts. The *tezars'* hall was entirely different from the cadets' barracks. It was not an immense, open hall, but a series of smaller rooms, some for meditation and some for negotiation, many for gaming and entertainment, several smaller dining halls, and rooms such as this where work could be done on the interlink. The walls were studded with memorabilia from famous flights and fliers. Palaton worked under a portrait of Quesan, one of the House of Star, who'd begun as a *tezar* and ended as an emperor.

Nedar paused to read over his shoulder. "A garbage run," he sniffed. "Have we nothing better to do than that?"

Palaton did not answer. He hadn't yet come to GNask's contract and knew the other would seize it the moment it came up on the reading board. Across the planet, the interlinks would post the same contracts at other *tezar* halls, though this was their main holding. The emperor's staff would receive notification and from thence it would go subspace on Choyan interlinks for those *tezars* already on contract but interested in transfer or just in the latest news.

A *tezar* generally knew when and where a war was going to start before its participants did.

Another pilot entered the room. He was chestnut-maned, chunky, and short, the epitome of the House of Earth, which ran to shortness and solidity. He grinned widely as he saw Nedar hovering over Palaton.

"Nedar! When did you get in?"

"And since when do I answer to you?" Nedar thumped

the other on hefty shoulders. "This afternoon, if you must know."

"And when are you going out again?"

"As soon as I can."

Burly Hathord stopped at Palaton's elbow. "That's a mess of contracts you're posting. Rumor has it that Panshinea is going to request all contracts be reviewed by him prior to posting." Only the name of the emperor drew reverence out of Hat's voices. All else was game to be made fun of.

Palaton's fingers paused over the keypad. He looked up. "Seriously, Hat?"

"Dead serious. The emperor doesn't want his best *tezars* off and unavailable if he has to defend the throne."

Nedar's expression became speculative. "Where did you hear this?"

"And when?" Palaton added.

"Yestereve, from my sister."

Hathord's sister was an administrative diplomat. His source was impeccable, for she was a somber Earthan, not give to humor or flights of fancy. Palaton would believe anything she said, even if she declared the sky to be yellow and the grass white. Nedar had filled a small glass goblet with hard liquor. He swirled the amber liquid about the bowl.

Nedar did not have to think aloud for Palaton to guess his thoughts. If the emperor imposed such control, the reaction of the *tezars,* whose independence was both legendary and necessary, would be split. Panshinea might well find himself immersed in the civil war his weakening powers invited. It was not up to the *tezars* to defend a ruler whose time to abdicate had come.

Nedar took a sip of the liquor instead of speaking. Hat added carelessly, as if unaware of the charged atmosphere in the room, "I've never heard of a Descendant Wheel so determined to hang on."

"We don't know that he's Descendant. He could be Right Wheel," Palaton said. He returned to his processing, but his fingers moved slowly so he could talk with Hathord as well.

Nedar cleared his throat. "His actions speak for themselves, Palaton. The House of Star is far from what it was.

The Wheel has turned, it's that clear. The throne must . . . evolve."

Hat let out a short bark of a laugh. "And it's a Sky who'll push it every time." He squelched his humor as Nedar swung around to look at him. He cleared his throat. For an Earthan, he was remarkably inept at balancing.

Palaton hid his smile as he turned his attention to the Abdrelik contract, which he was now setting up to feed to the interlink. As he'd predicted, Nedar's attention was riveted on the screen.

"That looks promising."

Hat was half a beat behind him, eyes squinting in his furrowed face. "God-in-all, but those Droolers love a fight."

"It keeps us employed," Nedar replied absently. "It keeps me *alive*." He finished his drink. "What do you say, Hat? Join me in battle."

"Not me. Look at that set up. Disarming an overarmed Class Zed system . . . they could take your head off your shoulders coming in." Hat shuddered. His whole squat body vibrated. "I like freight runs. Nice commission and nice dull expectations."

"Ummm." Nedar spread a hand open across the top of Palaton's, halting his processing. "Put my name up for that when you've finished inputting."

"You've just come off contract," Palaton said mildly.

"Never mind. This is what I like to do. It's like honey to children."

"You'll burn out."

Nedar's dark eyes narrowed. "Do you live in my head? No? Then I'll choose what I do."

Hat sensed the enmity. He sputtered, "It won't be final, Nedar. Not until the panel authorizes it."

"They'll authorize it. The Abdreliks need seven fliers. How many do you think will put in for this contract? The panel will fall all over themselves okaying the volunteers and grit their teeth assigning brethren to fill the remaining posts. Put my name in, Palaton." There was a blaze deep in his dark eyes that reminded Palaton of what his unseeable *bahdur* felt like to him. The Choya tilted his head defiantly, black mane of hair tossing back through his horn crown.

"It's a slaughter."

"It's a contract."

"You'll not be able to Household. You'll be wherever the Abdreliks staff you."

"And you'll miss my tender company, eh, Palaton?" Nedar showed white teeth in a smile. "The Droolers pay well."

He kept protesting. "The work is intense. You've just come off a contract without leave. You've not had your medicals yet—"

"Lay off." The hand overspreading his grew tense. The veins stood up tightly through the back of Nedar's skin. Palaton could count a pulse rate through their throbbing if he wished. "I am not you, nor you me. My *bahdur* burns brightly. Don't cozen me, brethren," and he said the last with an ugly twist that told Palaton they were not, nor could ever be, brothers, but they were most definitely and eternally enemies. He had often thought Nedar held a hatred for him. Now he knew. *We hate what we fear most.*

Palaton stared down at the back of Nedar's hand until the Choya moved it away and he could continue processing. When the contract had been fed in and was accepted, he entered Nedar's name as requested.

"My thanks," Nedar said smoothly. His breath smelled faintly of the liquor he'd imbibed.

Palaton closed down his posting to the interlinks. "Don't mention it," he answered.

Hat shuddered again. He looked from one to the other, fighting his inborn Earthan tendency to make peace. Palaton put a hand on his shoulder. "Reviews will be in the morning."

"Who's reviewing?"

"Moameb, for one, I imagine. He's been grounded."

Flying *tezars* were not allowed to review or make assignments because of possible conflicts of interest. Nedar's brow went up in surprise and Palaton felt a stab of gratification. Evidently Nedar had not known that Moameb's affliction had progressed to that stage. Palaton dropped his hand from his friend's shoulder.

"It's been a long day, brethren, and I intend to put an end to mine."

He left the posting room for his quarters in the sunset wing.

* * *

His old rooms had been sealed while he was gone these last three seasons on assignment. They smelled slightly stale as he opened them up, despite the herbal potpourri he'd left behind to keep both moths and staleness out. His flight bag had been left leaning against the closed door and he kicked it across the now open threshold. He did not like what he'd seen in Nedar's eyes and he walked now to the small oval reflective hanging over the bureau. He leaned forward and looked closely.

As he'd suspected, he had the same driven look. The compulsion to fly, no matter what the cost. The terror that the day when that could be taken away might be closer than ever dreamed before. Did Nedar have secrets he feared known? Palaton closed his eyes tightly for a second, then he opened them, took a deep breath, and ordered his quarters' door closed behind him.

There was a message posted on his private interlink. Palaton sat down and massaged the back of his neck before opening the comlink.

It was dated several days ago, though it was in Moameb's voices. Palaton listened and read the printout confirmation, then sat back in stunned silence.

His mother had died. His only hope of learning the truth about his genetic destiny had fled with her. How could he honor his destiny without full knowledge? And why had Moameb said nothing to him about the tragedy?

Chapter 6

He dreamed of Sorrow. Of figures cast in crystalline coffins, of a planet vein-shot with canals and lakes of the dead. Of their silent message, which he tried to hear and could not.

He woke, covers twisted about his horn crown and face, lips dewy with sweat, and lay for a moment in the darkness. He thought of Kedra and that it would have been sweeter to have gone to bed with her, but it had not been offered and he had not asked.

He drifted to sleep a second time. Like a stray wisp of cloud, he dreamed of entering his mother's Householding and came to ground, and walked, searching for her.

Or perhaps he *was* her, the dead, for there was nothing living as he walked. The auras had gone out of everything he passed, colors faded to sepia. The potted trees weeping in the courtyard might have been synthetic for all the lifeglow he caught from them, but he knew they were not when one bud opened and bloomed before his eyes as he walked slowly past.

His footsteps brought no ring from stone or wood. His touch was ice. His heart thudded heavily in his chest with the fear that he might be trapped here forever, but Palaton told himself he dreamed and hoped for the best. The Choyan spoke of other races, other beings as "the walking dead," for most of them had not the sensitivity to know what was living and what was not. They could not sense the God-in-all. Perhaps he walked as one of them, alien, among his mother's rooms.

A door swung open before he could put the palm of his hand to it as though the wood, once living and still vibrant, could not bear his touch upon it. As he ducked below the lower archway of a Choya'i's quarters, he could hear his mother's voice. Tresa sat, curled on a large sedan pillow, embroidery in her lap, and spoke to an unknown Choya. Neither of them sensed his entry.

Her artistry in embroidery had been well known and Palaton recognized in the half-finished canvas across her lap a wall hanging that now resided in Emperor Panshinea's palace. She had pricked a finger and now sat, contemplating letting the blood stain the thread and canvas, a seal of the artist's suffering, or sucking away the crimson drop and keeping her work free of blemish.

She decided on sucking up the drop. She looked up from her finger to say, "I do not want him tested."

Palaton knew without being told they discussed him. The Choya sitting across from her was massive across the shoulders and even inside his loose shirt, muscles visibly bulged and shifted with his movement. "There will be only the singular consequence and none other."

Her facial expression was stubborn. "But you *will* try, regardless. If I will not tell you who his father is, you'll try to find out however you can."

"The testing is only for his talents," the Choya persisted just as stubbornly, and a surprised Palaton realized this was his grandfather, a Choya he had always perceived of as elderly. But this Choya was still in his prime, his voices rumbling with low thunder. "If he's accepted as a *tezar* candidate, he has some hope even if you keep your silence."

His mother took three deft stitches. When she looked up, her sadness had been gathered back and only her eyes reflected it. "I have no choice," she said. "Silence is my only recourse. And if you think his *bahdur* is his only recourse, then so be it. He's so young. . . ."

"We'll not send him out until he's older, but to even know if he has a place among the cadets will aid in his education."

"I wanted him to be a priest. I wanted a chance for him to do some good in the world," she said, as if not hearing her father's reassurance. She put down her canvas a second time.

Palaton listened in amazement. In all the years he'd lived with his mother in the Householding, and in the brief returns he'd had after entering school, she'd never spoken of her hopes for him. She rarely spoke to him at all. He started forward to force his presence upon them, dreamsmoke or not, but his grandfather thrust himself to his feet and began a diatribe against the priesthood and Palaton felt himself jerked away. The silver cord of sleep yanked him abruptly out of the room, out of the past, out of hope.

Palaton woke panting. He threw his mangled covers aside, damp with sweat, and stared upward at the ceiling.

He was not dead, she was. He was not bereft of hope, she had been. And he knew then, though no one had informed him, that his mother's sudden death had been a suicide. As for the rest of the dream, he had no way of knowing if he had manufactured it from a childhood memory of eavesdropping, or if it had been a farewell sending from his mother, or if it had sprung full-blown out of his own restless desires.

It was with relief that he sensed the faint bloom of life from the wooden bureau across the room, the aura of his own figure lying in the bed, the dim auras of reality that surrounded him. At least outwardly, he was no longer alien among his own people.

He slept past review. Moameb left word for him to join him in the east dining room, a small, intimate room glowing with antiques burnished with polish and attention over the hundreds of years the school had been open. The tables were small, scarcely bigger than writing desks. Perhaps that was what they had been at one time, before the interlinks. The tray between them held mugs of steaming *bren*, flier's juice the cadets called, it because of the many pots of *bren* all of them consumed. The *bren* had been brewed strong, its aromatic steam welcoming, its color dark as poet's ink. Palaton pulled up a chair and palmed a mug gratefully.

"I'm sorry," Moameb said. "I couldn't find the words to tell you face-to-face. I thought once upon the mesa, but—"

"It's all right," Palaton told him. And it was, and the silver-maned Choya relaxed. "What did I miss in review briefing?"

"Nothing much. Nedar has already left to fulfill GNask's contract. We felt that there would be little to gain by denying him."

"And the other six?"

"Four volunteers and two assignees."

Palaton thought of burly Hathord. "What about Hat?"

"He's going to stay here at the school. I'm training him to replace me."

Palaton did not have to feign pleasure. Hat would be perfect taking in the young fledglings. He sipped cautiously at his mug. "And me?"

"A combat contract, but not for the Abdreliks."

Palaton balanced the mug in front of his face, leaning on his elbows on the small tabletop. "Where?"

"A small system, one you're probably not familiar with. A chance to go exploring, and do some good in the worlds."

The echo of familiar words stung Palaton and he hid his startlement behind the mug of *bren*. "I'll be leaving soon, then."

"A week or so to rest. You booked for some retreat time at the temple, you'll get that, and a few days to pursue whatever other, ah, interests you have." Moameb got a slightly foxed look on his face.

Palaton ignored it. He took a strong draught and let the *bren* burn its way down his throat and into his stomach, the aromatic oils rolling off the back of his throat and rising into his sinuses. There was a mild rush. He savored it. He set the mug down. "How long is my stay?"

"Six seasons, our time." Moameb paused. "It's a civil war. Could be longer, could be less."

"And I'm on the side of the good guys," Palaton said dryly.

His mentor's face wrinkled thoughtfully. "I hope so," Moameb answered. "I certainly hope so."

The seven steps across the temple brook at Sorrow represented the seven senses purified by those who attended to the God-in-all. There were the five senses of sight, hearing, taste, scent, and touch, the sixth sense of paranormal ability and the seventh of the soul.

All those who were *tezars* knew that there was no purification of the sixth sense for them, that once the neuropathy began, there was no turning back, but that had never stopped Palaton from being religious. There were rituals within the temple that both lifted and comforted him. The brook had been only a temporary rite, now he sought the full services of the temple.

The temple on the school grounds had probably been there before the school, from the looks of it, granite cut blocks fit into one another so solidly a knife blade could not be slipped between, yet the raw wind off the plateaus could find its way through. The underground mineral springs and natural mud baths within lent a warmth that would be stolen away the moment a bather rose out of the basins and the wind could get at him.

For days, Palaton did all that was required of him. He meditated, fasted, bathed, composed a new melody for the *lindar,* edited a book another acolyte had written on a mathematical analysis and played five-team kickdown, a process which chipped a tooth which he had capped, but that did not matter because he'd gotten one of the winning goals. When he was ready, finally, completely ready, he went to talk to the Voices of the God-in-all.

The chamber was dimmed, as it was supposed to be, and Palaton entered cautiously, using his aura sense to tell him where the low benches were, found one to his liking and lay down upon it. The sense that this bench had been worn down through the centuries by those who had lain upon it touched him. He had been settled and still only a moment when the whisper of the Voices entering swept across the stonework, flooding his senses: the hem of a robe touching the ground, the pad of a slipper, the scent of herb soap and a faint, sweet smell. Palaton smiled to himself. This Voices had a sweet tooth and had eaten a candy before coming in.

The Voices of the God-in-all shifted about for a moment, seeking a comfortable position. It might be one of the acolytes or the Prelate himself or any of the other religious officers in between. It mattered not, though Palaton wondered briefly whether it was the Choya who'd wrestled to block him on that final goal. The Choya had walked somewhat stiffly. From age or athletic contest? He could not ask, of course, and knew he would not be told. He let go of the wonderment. It fluttered away like a dry leaf in the wind.

The Voices spoke, a Choya, tenor and high baritone, the sounds of his voices pleasing and soothing. He gave the ritual invocation and Palaton responded and they slipped into the rite of Voices and Listener which was somewhat of a misnomer because the guidance of the Voices would be to listen when Palaton opened up. He wanted to talk of his fears of losing his *bahdur* and knew that he could not, because even in the confidence of this ritual, the incident would be reported. He lay trapped in uncertainty. The Voices grew still.

Then, gently, "What do you think of when you prepare to sleep?"

Palaton felt his face warm, then knew the Voices did not ask about sexual fantasies or accounting worries. "You mean when I need to sleep and can't?"

"Yes."

"Pure flight." The words left his mouth before he'd considered, but he knew the rightness of them.

"Pure flight?"

"Flight without cost or exploitation, without mechanical augmentation." Without the torchlike burning of *bahdur*.

"Like one of the thrust gliders, or do you mean levitation?"

"Not levitation." Palaton spoke slowly. "I'm in a plane. But there is no fuel expense or the hum of motors—yet it's not a glider. It's as though *I* drive the plane. I pilot it and it's only a shell, a second skin. It's like a glider, but not dependent on thermals. I can cut across wind currents, through storms, whatever is necessary. And the glory of it is—I know where I've been, where I'm going, and *why*. I know what the destiny of my flight will be and all its consequences."

"Omnipotence?" suggested the Voices.

Palaton felt uneasy at the interpretation. "Perhaps."

"If not, then . . . enlightenment?"

"Enlightenment." Palaton felt the stone bench under his hips, cupping them, pillowing his shoulders. He felt the press of his horn crown against the rock, his hair a thin mattress underneath it. He had had a dull headache earlier. It had gone and he had only noticed the change now. He repeated a second time, "Enlightenment. Maybe."

"And why do you seek this pure flight?"

"Because that's the way it's supposed to be," Palaton said, and was surprised to hear his words edged with impatience.

There was a noise, as if the Voices closed a notepad at his knee. "Child," the Voices said. "Do you know what you search for?"

"I'm not searching," Palaton answered slowly. He amazed himself again. "When I dream. . . ." He paused again remembering the dream when it came to him. "I've already found whatever it is. I'm complete. Fulfilled. Pure."

"Then you are fortunate. Most of us know only that we must search." The Voices moved a little closer, and Palaton smelled the faint sweet haze of his breath again. "You probably need us less than we need you. You dream of journey's end while most of us dream of the hazards of the journey. You must ask yourself if this is because you. wish to avoid the journey—or if this is because you know your destiny already and know the journey will be successful. Most of us live day by day coping with our failures. Have you already learned this difficult lesson or have you acknowledged this weakness within yourself?"

"I don't know," Palaton answered uneasily.

There was a feather light touch upon his brow, a benediction. "You must search. Palaton, you have completed the Purification. You're free to leave the retreat whenever you wish. I understand your contractors are awaiting you. Goodbye."

Palaton felt unfinished. Did this dream interpretation mean the priest knew of his difficulty with his talents. Or perhaps that he would outlive his *bahdur*? Or even that he might be that rarest of *tezars* and not contract the disease? It had been known to happen once or twice. He sat up in the dim cave. "But how do I know?"

"By making the journey. Only at journey's end will you know."

"Wait—" and Palaton groped outward, grasping for the Voices, hoping to catch an arm or a bit of robe. There was only emptiness beside him. The cave was totally empty save for himself. There was no faint aura of warmth or presence beyond his own. He sat up. He told himself the Voices had merely teleported out, even though the normal implosion of air which would follow such an event had not occurred.

"God-in-all," Palaton muttered. "Who in the dark aura was I talking to?" He brushed his hair off his forehead and back into the swoop of the natural tiara of his horns. He left the cave dissatisfied, not knowing if it was for the lack in himself the Voices had hinted at or the listener's ignorance of the answers he needed.

Chapter 7

GNask ordered the room sealed until they three were alone, the humankind ambassador, his squirming get, and himself. The ambassador's child looked like a pallid, plump grub and fought determinedly to remain at large, running around the room on legs that seemed too frail to propel it at such a speed. The Abdrelik watched with the fascination of the hunter for prey, knowing he could not strike.

John Taylor Thomas said nervously, "I'm taking a great risk in meeting you alone like this."

GNask answered, "The risk is mine. There is no other way to accomplish what we must."

"Why do you need to see my child?"

The Abdrelik could not take his eyes away from the glistening, darting movements of the toddler. He said heavily, "My sources have been drained. I cannot find the information we need to secure her future. Therefore, in the interest of our alliance, we need to make adjustments in our plans."

Thomas had put a hand out as the toddler careened about the small room, but she eluded him with a squeal and kept running, her fine halo of hair standing on end. He drew back his hand and looked fearfully at GNask. "Adjustments?"

"If the Choyan want her, they will take her. However, we can take steps—"

"No. That wasn't what you told me. That wasn't what we agreed upon, ambassador."

GNask shifted his muscular bulk. He was taller than the man and nearly three times as broad. He feared nothing from the being although the other's tone spoke of stress and a great effort to maintain control. "We agreed that I would help you. I am helping you. My tracers upon Choyan activity show that there is a circumspect line of traffic which we cannot pinpoint as to origin or destination, traffic which does not seem to be related to any of the three major branches of Choyan society. However, the planet of Cho has been kept veiled for many centuries and, try as we can, we are not as expert as we'd like to be."

"They're not taking my daughter!"

"They *will* take her, ambassador. That seems reasonably inevitable, for they are a cunning and capable people. Since we cannot prevent their action, we can only take steps to ensure her traceability. A simple implant—"

Thomas' complexion blanched. He ran a hand through his hair. "They'd detect it. They'd dispose of her before they'd allow it through the system."

The Abdrelik puffed in distaste for the rampant emotionalism of the humankind. Then GNask caught himself and said, "An ordinary implant, yes. But not this. It's organic. It does not transmit. All it will do is stimulate the subject itself to reveal its whereabouts. The Choyan will have no control over your daughter's behavior, over her innate desires, however they may wish to indoctrinate her, because we will have been here first."

The room's austere interior held only the three sentient life-forms and a small, sterile table. GNask now reached out to that table. The slug symbiont resting on his wrist began to slither downward, tracks glistening, undulating toward the tabletop. John Taylor Thomas watched in fascination, mouth half-open.

Finally, he uttered, "What are you going to do?"

GNask said only, "Bring the youngling here."

Thomas hesitated, but the toddler had run out of steam and came staggering over to her father and sagged against his trouser leg as she embraced him knee-high. GNask patted down his waist pouch until he found the instrument he wanted and withdrew it.

Thomas looked at the compact, precise laser knife. "What are you going to do?" he repeated tensely.

"Imbue her with what she needs to assure her survival and the success of our alliance. You need her returned. The Compact needs the Choyan to cease and desist subversive activities." GNask showed his tusks. "We do what we must." The laser's tip glowed and, as the symbiont rested on the tabletop, the Abdrelik sliced down, quickly, cleanly, so unexpectedly that the *tursh* hardly quivered at all with the movement. A finger-length segment curled away and lay heaving with a life of its own.

GNask reached out and took the child away from her father. She gasped as he swung her into the air and sat her down upon the tabletop. Before she could scream or scramble away, the Abdrelik had lifted her mane of hair away from the nape of her neck and made a quick, cutaneous incision. He placed the *tursh* segment upon it.

"God," Thomas cried helplessly as the slug segment thinned and disappeared within the slice on his daughter's neck.

"A year at the most," GNask told him. "Your kind is not a sufficient host for longer. But the *tursh* will do its work. There will be no scarring when this heals and the *tursh* will assimilate itself further into the body. When it begins to die, it will return to this area and an abscess will form. That will have to be treated carefully. Do not call on your doctor. Contact my office. Once the abscess is healed, the indoctrination will be imperceptible by any means. This is not a psychological indoctrination that can be detected by testing. Her entire makeup is being altered. The Choyan would have to read her mind to know what we've done."

"And when they take her, she'll . . . she'll want to come back?"

"Want is not strong enough. She'll not rest until she is reunited with us. She will betray the Choyan conspiracy by any means she can and return to you." GNask watched the man closely. With his *tursh* attempting regeneration in her body, she would also be imbued with those basic memories and drives that were of his lineage. Even though the symbiont would eventually die rather than propagate, the links would be permanently forged for a symbiotic relationship. He wondered how that would affect the radically different humankind.

How, for example, would she curb her desire for the taste of human flesh?

GNask turned away in his musing. "It's done. I will leave you to your daughter. Enjoy her in the time you've left. Enjoy the great enterprise we've begun together. Her lifetime will bring to fruition the efforts of more than just the three of us." He picked up his *tursh,* made soothing sounds of apology to it, and returned it to his scalp.

The toddler sat stunned into quietude on the table. Her father stood uncertainly, arms open, unable to reach for her as if repelled by what his daughter had suddenly become. He cast a last look at GNask. The Abdrelik thought darkly of Choyan eyes, which he detested.

"We are allies," the Abdrelik said. "We will not let one another down. To the end."

The expression on John Taylor Thomas' face was unreadable and he did not make a sound until the Abdrelik had unsealed the room and left, fresh air flooding inward in his wake, filling a vacuum of sourness and hatred. "The end has begun," he murmured and reluctantly took his daughter into his embrace.

She neither cried nor welcomed his touch. Her too bright eyes seemed turned inward, to other stimulations.

What had he done?

Chapter 8

The smell of the mechanics' bays leaked into the wardroom. The air was permeated with the din of the robotic arms at work, the staccato of metal being drilled and polished and refitted, the *whirr* of instruments, the smell of burning plastics, the sludge of oils and lubricants, and the pungent sting of fuels. Palaton had grown wearily used to it and found it as necessary a part of his morning as a steaming mug of *bren*. It was more irritating to hear silence and smell the solvents used to clean idle bays.

He sat at a table with his bare feet propped up—he'd not yet put his boots on—the obligatory cup of *bren* in front of him. It left little brown rings on the tabletop and some of the liquid had soaked into the edge of the charts he was reading over. He absently put a finger down and mopped the rings into another direction on the sloping and warped tabletop and sucked a tooth for a moment, the capped tooth, and thought of where his best entrance window to the system would be. He made a stylus mark at a possibility.

There would be satellite mines along the approaches and other deterrents, but that would not be his worry. He was to pilot through Chaos from this station to that system and then open up the belly of the mother ship and deliver his load of attack vessels. Then he would pull back, out of range, until recall and swoop back to gather them up. He and five others were going in, delivering a wing of nearly five hundred vessels, yet even that would not win this war. It had not these five seasons past and there was little hope it would in the future.

He saw the specter of defeat more clearly than he did the chart he narrowed his eyes at.

Palaton sat back in his chair with a sigh. The wardroom

was empty. He was up early with his habitual Choyan restlessness, and he savored the solitude. He wrapped his hand around the mug and drew it to him, warmth spreading through his palm.

He had not discussed the possibility with his contractors nor they with him, but he knew the course had been run and they had lost the risk they'd taken. It saddened him.

It had been a racial war, the Threlks and the Gurans, with the Gurans scrambling to avoid genocide, and the Compact maintaining a neutral position. Palaton did not pretend to understand the politics that would dictate neutrality in one situation and meddling in another, but he knew he did not wish to see the Gurans wiped out. They were a generally cheerful, ingenuous little people, and he held a respect for them that had nothing to do with his contract.

Moameb had promised him he might make a difference and he was deeply troubled that he had not. Not in the long run.

Palaton stared at the charts in front of him, charts showing the webwork of the planet's defenses over strategic holdings, particularly over the shieldings and mine nets that kept the Gurans from utilizing their surface strongholds effectively. Early morning fuzziness obscured his vision. He rubbed his eyes.

Their run that day was strictly defensive, opening an escape window that would allow as many evacuees to flee their home planet as could board the ships. Across the regions of Chaos, in the Gurans' system, hundreds of people were loading their ships in a misty morning and saying good-bye to their heritage. Many of them would not make it out despite their escort. But a few would, and the Threlks' dream of total genocide would not be realized. Such a small difference.

There was a step behind him. He shifted in his seat and turned. Nedar stood in the wardroom, a visitor's badge winking upon the frayed collar of his flight suit. He looked exhausted, battered, the whites too wide about his dark eyes. But he gave an arrogant smile.

"I heard you were flying from this station. I thought you had no taste for war."

"I take the contract I'm assigned to, the same as you do.

I don't go looking for it." His voices sounded wary, taut, and he hated the way they betrayed his ambivalence toward a fellow *tezar*. He mellowed his tones. "Sit a while. I'm just looking over the day's flight charts."

"No." Nedar shifted weight. "I'm just off-contract and headed home." His eyes scanned the table in front of Palaton. "I've heard about your war.

"Have you?"

The Sky lifted his chin defiantly, his ebony hair tousled from the helmet he now carried by one strap. "Cutting your losses?"

"Not if I can help it."

Nedar paused. He put up his free hand and rubbed the base of his horn crown as if something pained him there. "You tried to warn me once, Palaton. Let me return the favor. It's easier to fulfill a contract when you stop trying to be a hero." He turned away abruptly and left the wardroom, the bulkhead hissing shut behind him.

He left a distinct vacuum in his wake, his missing presence a chill in the air. Palaton stared after in mild surprise, wondering what all that had been about. He turned his attention back to his charts, half-expecting Nedar to return and explain himself. He found himself staring without sight and rubbed his eyes again.

Palaton widened his eyes and refocused. The offensive sites marked seasons ago suddenly came into clear definition. The continent of Fimarl, where the Threlks were most strongly banded, was practically impregnable due to the shielding of their satellite nets and warning systems. But as Palaton looked at Fimarl now, his *bahdur* blazed within him as though he'd swallowed a hot pepper, and the netting showed transparent, then disappeared from his charts.

The system would fail. How or why he did not know, only that it *would,* leaving an opportunity for attack and the placement of offensive satellites within that window that would give the Gurans a much stronger position.

Palaton tapped his fingers upon the tabletop. If the netting did not fail, he and all his pilots would be annihilated if they attempted to go in. And his vessel was not meant for the intricacies of atmospheric warfare, being strictly outfitted for deep space.

But if the netting did go down, even for a handful of

hours, it could turn defeat and retreat about. The Gurans would have the Threlks' complete attention. A grudging respect, even, perhaps, a respect that could lead to negotiation.

The charts wavered again under his vision and then they were as they had originally been with the defensive net of Fimarl firmly in place. To do as Nedar suggested would be to overlook this opportunity and he could not do that, no matter what the consequences.

Palaton spread his hand across the continent. One mother vessel detoured on a separate mission to Fimarl. What more losses could they incur? Would it be worth it? Whiffet, the Guran commandant-in-chief, would think him insane. But he would propose what he had to propose and then let the Guran mull it over.

He reached for his *bren* and took a sip. It had gone icy cold. The fugue state of intuition had left him sitting trance-like while his drink cooled. Palaton made a face, shoved his chair back, and went for fresh *bren*. When he returned, Whiffet was standing at the table, looking over the charts, a tired expression etched into his octagonal face. He touched the charts with his great arm. His Trade lingo held a charming accent.

"Working so early? And I would think you had these memorized by now?"

"I got the new weather charts in."

The commandant said, not unkindly, "There is no need to apologize to me."

"It was not an apology."

The Guran looked closely at him, then forced a facial grimace approximating a Choyan smile. "No, I see it was not. Well, *tezar,* your contract draws to an end."

"But not a desirable ending. Commandant, I have a change of action I'd like to discuss with you. Can you reach your sympathizers on Fimarl?"

"Possibly." The Guran's wide, amber eyes regarded him gloomily. "It matters little. We have our survival to think about, not an offensive."

"The Threlks' attention will be concentrated on taking out your evacuating wing."

The Guran shifted uncomfortably as if the Choya criticized him. "We're aware of that."

"Now is the time for your sympathizers to strike and take down the net over Fimarl. It can be done. It will be done, and I intend to be there to take advantage of it."

"What?" The sable pupils within those amber eyes grew huge in disbelief. "What are you thinking of?"

Palaton told him, swiftly and succinctly, omitting only his precognitive abilities. The little commandant sat down abruptly when he'd finished. He rested his great arm upon the table. His lesser arm he curled in his lap where his fingers twitched in agitation.

Whiffet sighed. "I'm loath to risk the sympathizers. I have some hopes they may yet persuade the rest of the Threlks to accept us. And these actions you propose will jeopardize the evacuees.

"Scarcely more than they are already in jeopardy." Palaton did not press. He could see the Guran mulling over the options he'd been presented with. Palaton could offer nothing further to persuade him.

Whiffet looked up. His furry brow wrinkled. "If the net does not go down, you will be destroyed. Your carrier and the wing you transport."

"It will have to be a volunteer mission, but I don't think I'll have a problem getting them." His pilots would not hesitate to go with him under the circumstances. The risk Whiffet anticipated was not the risk Palaton was preparing to take.

The Guran continued to weigh the matter. Palaton held his silence. The commandant placed both hands upon the table, great arm and lesser arm. Palaton knew, the motion had cultural and religious significance, but he couldn't remember what it was. Whiffet's next words told him. "For the good of my people," the commandant said heavily, "I cannot order you to do such a thing. Nor can I order our sympathizers . . . however, this is our world. We will never be able to flourish as well elsewhere and we know that we are not guaranteed a homeland by the Compact." Whiffet looked up. The expression in his eyes was intense. "We do not want to leave. We will be forever grateful for whatever hope you can give us."

"Then, commandant, you have your first and foremost volunteer. Contact your sympathizers. Ask them to do what they can. I'll handle the rest. Only my carrier will go in. The others still have their primary function of evacuation."

Whiffet nodded briskly. "I understand." He hesitated. "And thank you, *tezar*."

Palaton's voices had carried well in the massive bay holding his carrier and the wing of attack crafts. He had the robotics halted and the other mechanics ceased their activities to listen. His pilots had gathered slowly, but all of them were in attendance by the end of his speech, and dead silence greeted it.

He had not guaranteed that the net would be down. But they knew if he felt it, if he had confidence, that the chances were great it would go down. If such a thing had been possible seasons ago, this war would have been over. There was no reason to think it possible now, except that Palaton felt it possible.

He scanned their faces and expressions. He could see them weighing their choices much as Whiffet had weighed them.

The oldest ace among them took his flight helmet from under an elbow and examined it as he held it in his hands. "I'm in," he said diffidently, as if he'd read an answer reflected in its battered surface.

The others did not even hesitate as long. Palaton felt exhilaration as they gathered close and decided how to refit the planes going in and began to re-matrix the robotic handlers accordingly.

Whiffet met him before he entered his carrier for launch. The other ships had been loaded into its belly and all was quiet in the massive bay. But this quiet was different from the earlier silence. This held anticipation, like that of a stalking predator before it strikes an unwary prey. This held readiness, not fear and consternation. Palaton halted for the Guran commandant, felt impatience, and curbed it.

Whiffet took the Choya's hand with his greater hand. "The sympathizers were reached. They, too, volunteered their aid."

Palaton wondered if it would be their efforts which would bring the net down. In all probability. He did not worry. "Thank you, commandant. If all goes well, I'll see you in about forty-eight hours."

"I pray," the Guran said. "For us all." He stepped back,

a whimsical, lopsided looking creature, with all the worries of the world strapped upon his back.

Palaton carried that vision with him as he stepped onto the carrier deck and ordered the lift to take him. to the con. His crew cleared the bridge as soon as he stepped onto it. *Tezars* pilot alone. He waited until the lock sealed behind them, then dropped into the control chair and, smiling, reached toward his instrument panel.

The launch was routine. As the carrier thrust into deep space, Palaton settled his shoulders against the padded chair, considering what he would do when they breached Chaos. Normally, they would emerge in-system, but a considerable flight outside the planet itself. He felt like cutting it closer. Much closer.

The carrier accelerated solidly and lights came on all over the panel, warning of FTL approach. Palaton did nothing. His pilots were ready. He was ready.

The moment of entering Chaos was always unique. Sound, sight, color washed past. Nothing was as it seemed. Palaton reached into his *bahdur* for the truth. The carrier seemed to hesitate for a moment, then steady on. He made his calculations swiftly, fought the controls to do as he ordered, rather than as the sensors indicated, and brought the carrier about on course.

Then he sat back and enjoyed the view, the view of a cosmos in complete and utter random movement, a view as soothing as the falling droplets of a fountain. A view as treacherous as it was lovely, if one got lost in it forever. He liked to think of it as the cutting edge of death itself.

When the time came, he brought the carrier out just beyond the planet's second moon, coming on-line to his pilots as they decelerated. Their speed would have them on approach within a matter of hours. The other carriers would be coming out behind them.

"No decoys to blunt any attack on us," Palaton reminded his pilots after he gave them their real space position so they could check their tracking systems. "Get ready for your drop."

His instrument panel lit up with the gridwork of the defensive and offensive systems down below. They'd emerged on the dark side, opposite Fimarl, but he'd no doubt that

that continent was equally well protected. The small island chains and smaller continent that was the Gurans' beleaguered home base showed under a different gridwork, one not as solid or impenetrable.

"I have blips, sir," one of his pilots called out.

Palaton blinked, then swiveled in his chair to view the screen. Incoming showed, but from the size and speed, they were the rest of the carriers coming out of subspace behind him. "On track," Palaton replied flatly. He signaled his intent to break away to the rest of the fleet. It was received with surprise but swift understanding. Palaton put his hands on the control board and communicated to his vessel what it was he wanted it to do.

They banked sharply right, cruising swiftly through the moon-shadowed darkness of night over the planet's surface, winging toward the dawn and Fimarl.

Automatic defenses began to go off. The instrument screens lit up as the defenses began to zero in on them, firing.

Palaton felt his intuition burn in the pit of his stomach. Or perhaps it was the result of too much *bren* in the early morning. He did not see the network falter over the Threlkian continents. What if he had misinterpreted what he had seen?

False *bahdur* was as deadly as no *bahdur* at all.

He sat, tension bunching in his shoulder muscles and the weight of his horn crown pressing upon his skull until his neck felt as though it could not hold his head in place. He stared, unblinking, at the control grids and various view screens. Something should give. If it did not, they were headed into deadly cross fire which he could not pilot through safely.

The gridwork glowed. He looked at the satellite mines, the configuration of their fire imprinting in his vision. If he closed his eyes, he would retain that webbing across the darkness. Death waited inside that grid.

He had known the network would go down. Not how or exactly when, but that it would. It was foolish to wait on the actions of others. He let his *bahdur* flare out over the screens, discerning points of maximum coverage and firepower and those areas where there would be weak spots of coverage. There had to be weak spots. All he had to do was find them.

A golden line flared out in the corner of his vision. He turned his head slightly and eyed it. Yes. There was a quadrant with minimal coverage at the edge of the field. They could possibly slip through there. It would be a tight and perilous squeeze and they would draw fire. No doubt about it. But the cross fire would be at a minimum. Palaton plotted the course and the carrier began to arc across the shadow, across the fading edge of night and into the dawn, over Fimarl. Somewhere below, the Threlkian war alarms would begin to sound.

The carrier did not respond well to the handling he required of it. It turned sluggishly and did not hold the coordinate line as precisely as he wished. He let out a string of Choyan curses and hastily tapped in course changes to right the vehicle. It plowed rather than soared into the stratosphere.

The carrier shuddered as a strafing line caught it. It shook like a trapped animal, then righted.

Palaton put himself on-line, prepared to stay there until he opened the doors to drop the wing out. "We're going in," he said by way of explanation. "Expect turbulence."

The network hadn't gone down. They were drawing fire and Palaton knew it would get heavier. The panels showed him laser fire streaking after them, missing, but barely, the crossovers getting closer and closer. They could expect worse.

Sweat trickled down his brow and alongside his nose. He didn't have a free hand to wipe it away.

They took a hit. He could almost hear the metal scream. The shield bucklers held but one of them disintegrated so badly he could see the glowing crumbs of it shedding into space behind them. Another hit would take his rear flank out. The carrier heeled hard but answered to him at the helm as he righted it.

Next time it would not.

On the open com, he could hear the pilots and robotics reporting damage assessments. One plane had come loose from all the jarring. Other than that, all was well in the hold.

Next time though it would be a different story.

Palaton swallowed, his mouth gone dust-dry. He shook his head vigorously. Droplets of sweat spattered across the cabin. An instrument keened, telling him they were being targeted.

He veered the carrier. It came about sluggishly, too heavy for the atmosphere and gravity that pulled at it, too vast for the split second timing he needed out of it. He was piloting it as though it was one of the needle nose planes down in the hold awaiting release.

Palaton eased back. He had to decide whether to go on or turn back.

The carrier shuddered again as a beam sheared across a fin, doing little damage but buffeting the whole ship, a warning of the death awaiting them.

Reluctantly, he put a hand out.

Suddenly, his grid lights went out. The instruments went dead. Palaton froze. Then his face cracked in a grin.

No. The circuitry was not dead. The network had gone *down,* just as he'd foreseen.

"Get ready for launch drop," Palaton ordered, and he steered the carrier down into the quadrant.

The Gurans made a ceremony out of contract's end. Their fortress was filled with decorated, celebrating aliens and the air was rich with the smell of food. Palaton wandered the hall, uncomfortable in his full dress uniform. Whiffet was as excited as he'd ever seen the Guran. Palaton contained his own humor as the commandant took him aside.

"A stand-off," the commandant said, "as you called it. Our satellites within their network. Brilliant. They must admit we exist. They have agreed to negotiate settlements with us. *Tezar* Palaton, there will be victory in this compromise yet."

"You have a lot to span."

The Guran nodded. "We know that." He paused. He put out his great hand. "I have never ended a contract with more satisfaction."

Nor I, thought Palaton. He took the Guran's hand. "Thank you," he said.

"And I have a message for you from your Householding. It asks that you report to your emperor's House as soon as possible." The Guran wrinkled his octagon face in an approximation of a smile. "It seems he has need of you, as well."

Chapter 9

He had not been in the imperial district since he had officially been commissioned as a *tezar*. The district was ancient, filled with the history and memories of the Choyan people. Neutral ground, it had never been under attack. It seemed God-in-all had even spared it from the vagaries of the weather and the acts of nature the rest of the planet was heir to. As Palaton gazed through the window of the skimcraft, he felt the pressure of ages upon him.

When the skimcraft came to the debarkation port, he hung back, getting a jacket against the chill of late fall, for the season here held a bitter bite to it. It had rained and the gray stonework about him had soaked it up in black, uneven fractal streaks. The streets were begrimed with black puddles.

Palaton shrugged into his jacket. His luggage had gone on ahead of him. He swung about, reading the portals, chose the one for the palace, and stepped inward. The glidewalk took him into the bowels of the inner district. His stomach churned with hunger and he wondered if he would simply have an audience with the emperor or if he would be required to check into the hostel there until Panshinea found some time to see him. Other than the directive bringing him to the district, he'd had no communication with the emperor.

He doubted that Panshinea had need of a hero, if he even filled that qualification. Or for a *tezar,* for that matter. And though he couldn't deny the prickle of unease at the back of his head, nothing had hinted at the emperor's purposes.

But Palaton felt a need to be wary. An emperor under siege, an emperor's House under siege, provoked nothing less.

The House of Star had taken the Choyan people far.
Though it was the technology-oriented House of Sky which
had given them spaceflight, it was the House of Star which
had given them standing among other races who had also
reached beyond the galaxies. It was the House of Star
which had foreseen that their abilities to pilot FTL would
keep them afloat in an interstellar stew of rivalries. The
Choyan was one of the few races never to have colonized
beyond their home planet. One of the few not to have
billions of members to use for fodder in warfare. One of
the few to be able to stand on equal footing with any other
alien and not have to back down.

The House of Star had done this, and now it was collapsing under its own entropy as Houses did, and the Choyan
people could only wonder what would happen next. The
House of Earth was next on the Wheel, but it had become
an uneven Wheel ever since the level of technology offset
paranormal advantage, and no one knew for sure that Sky
would not try to usurp Earth's place.

Or even if Earth had among its members anyone bold
and canny enough to try for the emperor's throne. Hat was
typical of an Earthan. Palaton himself did not know of any
Earthan strong enough to come forward and wrest the elec-
tions away from either Star or Sky. But unlike other
Choyan, he did not ask himself if Star was descendant on
its Wheel. He *knew,* as did Panshinea. The mighty powers
wielded by the House of Star had begun a fiery fall from
the heavens.

He only wondered if civil war would take the rest of the
Choyan with it.

He did not air his opinion among his brethren. Politics
was a chancy topic these days. All feared the consequences
of the future, for they had not only fellow Choyan to dread,
but the Abdreliks and the Ronin and the other predators
of the Compact.

The topic was as forbidden as talk of marriage outside
Houses, the kind of genetic matings which had once produced erratic and dangerous talents, and had left thousands
of Choyan dead as a result. Perhaps that was why he had
felt duty-bound to assist the Gurans. Genocide was a terrible thing.

The glidewalk bumped as it entered the tunnels leading

into the palace access. He could hear the faint buzz of scanners moving over him. He turned and peered into one surface which was certain to be a two-way viewport and stared solemnly at his reflection. He looked as though he'd come in out of a storm. He made a wry face and glanced away, anticipating the glidewalk's end.

An armed escort awaited him. They snapped to as he stepped off the walk.

"Your luggage has been picked up, sir," the lieutenant said, her voices carrying just the right blend of authority and respect. She had not shaved down her crown in vanity and its proud Star scalloped edges bordered her mass of bronze hair. She wore the emperor's sapphire and gold, with the Star badge of her House clipped to her shoulders. Her cheek was mosaiced with fine traceries of gold and silver under its translucent skin. The jewelry cleverly enhanced an already beautiful face.

The second with her seemed drab by comparison. His stocky body was also clothed in sapphire and gold, but he wore the badge of the Prelate instead of a House emblem. He did not need to proclaim himself as an Earthan, his squat form did that. His hair was fringed with silver, its natural color a mousy nothing that the silver merely drew attention to. He seemed resigned that other, younger, and more ambitious officers would always outrank him.

Palaton wondered why the Prelate had guards among the emperor's security. He stepped into their brace formation without hesitation. "Where to?"

"Himself is waiting for you. We'll take you in the atrium entrance, less fuss that way."

Palaton hid his reaction to being secreted in. He lengthened his stride to keep in step with the lieutenant, and the Earthan guard puffed alongside beside, then behind them. As they passed beyond the tunnels and into the open, a light rain began pattering down. His guards put their chins down and quickened their steps. Palaton kept up with them, blinking against the droplets lining his eyelashes. He could see the throngs of administrators break into a run across the palace steps. Many wore the peculiar helmet thought to protect the wearer against having his mind read. Palaton smiled grimly. Scant protection against the House of Star, whose *bahdur* in telepathy flamed brightly.

The palace looked much as it had once been, a fortress, a vault of mighty wealth, rather than an architecture of lofty inspirations and rule. When and if the throne passed from the House of Star, this bastion would remain in Star's hands. The bureaucracy would pull out, following the administrators to the new Householding, wherever it might be. Palaton looked at the Charolon, as it was named, and tried to envision a different capitol complex. He could not. This had been the hub of Choyan rule and politics for over four hundred years, and it had been ancient even before that.

His guards ducked down a side path, and through a garden gate of clever stonework, and under twisted, knobby vines bared for the winter, their stick fingers holding them in place along a trellis. As he dipped his head under, a last, dried brown leaf drifted past, slid off his cheek and wafted to the ground. The leaf was star-shaped.

The rain began to pelt them. The Earthan guard let out a grunt of distaste and began to run heavily, his boots thudding in the garden mud. The lieutenant led them through the winter garden, into the atrium where a lofty roof protected them, and there they waited. Palaton paused next to a fountain, which was still, its waters drained away, and he heard the faint strains of *lindar* music drifting toward them. The interior of the palace was lit against the gloom of the rain and it glowed warmly. He looked down at his boots, saw mud splatters along his cuffs, and made a face.

There was a straining, grinding noise, and then the fountain base moved aside, revealing an arched door. The lieutenant went ahead and the second came at Palaton's heels as they took him through it.

The *lindar* music swelled louder as they stepped into the study, fronting the atrium, and he saw Panshinea seated at the stringed keyboard. The emperor's large hands roamed freely yet precisely over the instrument and the melody grew stronger.

The room was filled with the color and warmth of the hearth and the abundant glowing Lanterns. Heavy pelted rugs littered the tiled floor and small tables encouraged one to sit or lie upon the pelts near the hearth. Volumes cluttered the built-in shelves of one massive wall and a library ladder hung from its tracks in the corner. Potted plants and hanging baskets from the atrium had also invaded here and their cool scent brought the rain in with them.

The lieutenant and her second came to a halt, listening solemnly as the emperor finished playing the *lindar*. The hammered strings swelled forth a final note and then faded.

Panshinea was dressed for winter, though it was the dead of fall outside. His sable coat was fur cuffed at the sleeves and collar, his boots were heavy, and his trousers thick. Palaton thought of an elder Choya, bundled against the cold of age, and held that thought as the emperor rose from the *lindar*.

Panshinea wrung his hands as he approached and their gazes met, and Palaton was instantly aware that the emperor knew what he thought. Telepathy or no, the Choya had read his mind as easily as he'd read the scroll of music he'd just played.

"Winter seeps into Charolon earlier every year," Panshinea said, and held out his hand to Palaton.

"Emperor," Palaton said, bowing over their gripped hands.

"I trust my lieutenant and her second treated you well." Panshinea stepped back. He eyed Palaton. "They brought you tromping through the garden loam."

The lieutenant flushed, her skin darkening to a rosy color. "My apologies, your majesty—"

He waved. "Think nothing of it, Jorana. It's good for a *tezar* to come down to earth now and then." Panshinea reached forward again and drew Palaton out from the brace of his escort. Jorana and the Earthan guard stepped back to the hidden doorway and fell into a stance they could hold for days, if need be.

Panshinea was the epitome of a Choya of the House of Star. They tended to be lighter in complexion, their skin more translucent, their crowns fuller and heavier, though blunter, their locks of hair tending to hold the reds and yellows of the sunlight in their hues, their eyes lighter as well, blue or green or hazel. His double-elbowed grace in playing the *lindar* was what could be expected of a Star, his body sinewy and well-corded but tall and wiry in its strength. He was not quite Palaton's height, and a little heavier, and there were humor lines about his luminous eyes. His hair was light brown with a red shine to it, and a tiny spattering of gray right where his horn crown held the mane back. His eyes, were pale green, with a darker rim of forest green like a faint aurora. His nose flared well and his jaws had not yet gone to the jowls of a prosperous merchant, the only disagreeable feature of the House of Star.

The emperor drew him across the wide study and sat him down on a well-padded couch near the hearth. He lowered himself to a large, flared chair at its corner. The jade eyes considered Palaton. "I remember you from your commissioning," Panshinea said.

Palaton was flattered. "Thank you, sire."

"You're surprised? Don't be. We graduate some five hundred *tezars* a year, and the number of Stars among them steadily dwindles. I see the fierce faces of Skies growing in your ranks, and I worry."

The emperor's frank words startled Palaton more than the recognition. It was true that the number of Sky pilots grew at an astronomical rate in comparison to the other Houses—more proof, if one looked for it, that the House of Star was in its descendancy, though the overall number of pilots was steadily decreasing. But there were more than ten thousand on the current rolls of pilots and that he should be known among them did surprise Palaton.

The emperor twisted in his great chair. Flames from the fireplace illuminated his profile. He seemed on the verge of saying something else when there was a noise at the proper entrance to the study, and a Choya entered, with a com at his side.

"I beg your pardon, Panshinea," the Choya said, his dark eyes creased with years and wisdom, his black ebony hair streaked with yellow white. "Trouble," he added, handing over the com unit. He looked at Palaton and assessed the situation. "If you'd care to come with me, *tezar,* I can make you comfortable while—"

"No," interrupted Panshinea. "He can stay. This news will be old before too much longer anyway." He adjusted the unit to his forehead and brought the microphone down for speaking.

The elder Choya gave Palaton a look, and in that look, Palaton saw himself as trespasser and unwanted, a look he had not seen since he'd become a *tezar.* He also recognized the elder as the emperor's chief adviser, Gathon, Minister of Resource. Gathon's lips pursed, but he held his silence, dark eyes boring into Palaton.

"What's wrong?" the emperor asked softly, his voices quiet with menace. He listened intently. "How many rioters and where did you hold them? All right . . . all right. Send me a briefing. But you convene a meeting and inform them once again that there is no choice in this. It's time for Relocation and what needs to be done will be done."

Relocation. Palaton tried not to listen and yet he heard, and he knew what had happened. The resources of their planet were thin, delicately balanced, the population of two hundred million Choyan kept in check so that the planet might bear their presence without too much strain. But after thousands upon thousands of years of civilization, there would inevitably be strain. Pollution. Soils too depleted for further agriculture. Whole counties had to be uprooted periodically and forced to relocate, to migrate to another section of the continent which had lain bare, resting, awaiting its turn in the cycle.

Householdings were stripped bare and left behind. Centuries of family graves and history forcibly abandoned. Charolon itself might be emptied someday. Protests and riots seemed inevitable. Sometimes bloody.

Palaton, lost in his thoughts, looked up and saw that the call had been finished. Panshinea had removed the com and was watching him with a neutral expression.

"Relocation," the emperor said, "is only desirable for the other Choyan."

Palaton smiled wryly. The homily seemed apt. Gathon stood, the com unit dangling from one broad-palmed hand. "May I be of further service, majesty?"

"No. But have cook send in afternoon *bren* and some sandwiches, if you would." Panshinea sat back with a heavy sigh as the minister left. "Tell me," he ventured, "about the Gurans and the Threlks."

Palaton told him what he could without breaching the security dictates of his contract. The emperor listened keenly and asked discerning questions, his mind quick and his knowledge already fairly complete. When the *bren* and food arrived, Palaton gulped what he could between the rapid-fire interrogation as Panshinea moved to fill in what he did not know of the story.

Panshinea sat back in his chair. "Evacuation had been decided upon before you came to contract, however," he said, finally.

"Yes. With great reluctance."

"Do you know where the Compact had agreed to resettle them?"

"No." G-flesh planets were not particularly abundant and most of them already held a population which could not be supplanted. Not legally or morally, anyway.

"If I asked you to, Palaton, if your emperor commanded you to, could you determine where?"

Palaton grasped for an answer, his mind whirling away with the why of it. Why would the emperor want to know? What good would it do for him to know? "I . . . could try," he got out.

"Then do it. I will not send you into this blindly," Panshinea said. He stood up. "We've resisted the inevitable for centuries, but if it is the last act of the House of Star, I intend to see us begin colonization. Cho's resources are too thin for us to continue our balancing act. We must expand. We must grow. We must allow our population to rejuvenate. We've no choice but to emigrate."

Despite the hearth's reflected heat, Palaton went cold. The Choyan belonged on Cho where the God-in-all could be learned and perceived by all of them. To leave was to leave the God-in-all, to search for Him anew . . . and possibly find false gods on false worlds. The Choya'i would bear differently, if they could bear at all. The children would mutate to adapt to the new planet however compatible it might be. They would change beyond knowing. They had been temperate for centuries, fighting to preserve the balance of their homelands. The House of Sky would fight him claw and horn about this. Did Panshinea want to bring down his House before its time?

He looked up and saw the jade eyes locked onto his face and knew that the emperor had read every thought tumbling in his mind.

Chapter 10

" 'Oh, but thou would wrest this heavy crown from mine brow before my eyes are closed in sleep,' " Panshinea quoted in irony. He reached out for a poker and stoked the fire as the sudden beat of rain drummed loudly on the roof, sounding as if the heavens had opened up. Outside the windows everything darkened to premature night. "No, *tezar,* I did not read your mind, but I did not need to. Your shocked expression is an open book."

"There must be other options." Palaton felt as though the couch he sat upon rested on unstable ground, on a treacherous bog. He listened to the rain thundering down on the ancient roof and wondered what rain on another world would sound like on another Householding. It was ridiculous to think such thoughts—as a pilot he'd spent most of his adult life on other worlds. He already knew that rain sounded differently, depending upon the building material of the roof and the weather pattern of the world.

"There are. To continue as we have always done is one. But it is not one I feel is in our best interest. Do birds always nest in the same nest generation after generation, despite the crowding and the lack of forage? No, they spread their wings and fly, unafraid, to the next tree and the next and the next. But we Choyan do not fly, because we are afraid of becoming less Choyan than we are now and we do not consider that we might become more." Panshinea kept his grip on the poker but waved it slightly as though he kept beat to a melody Palaton could not hear. "Before you think me seditious, understand that I have spent most of my years upon this throne considering the conclusion I've come to. Ask yourself why, among all thinking people, we alone can master Chaos. Were we not intended to fly beyond our nests? *Were we not?*"

Palaton looked up. "I can't say." He paused. "But if you wish me to inquire whether there was a planet set aside for the Gurans, there are others who are more discreet and experienced at this sort of inquiry than I."

"You refuse me?"

"I suggest that there are others more adept. I am a pilot, Emperor, not a diplomat."

"Your present demeanor suggests otherwise." Panshinea drew his feet under him. His wiry body tensed.

"We serve Cho and the Choyan as best we can," stated Palaton calmly, but his heart kept pace with the thundering rain still pelting the rooftops. His throat closed as he sensed the sudden swelling of *bahdur* toward him, emanating from the emperor like a lightning strike. The air stank of power.

But nothing touched him. Panshinea sank back in his chair, shrunken with pain, and Palaton watched, his throat muscles relaxing slowly, as the emperor writhed.

He knew then, as few in the world must know, that the emperor was dying of neuropathy, like a *tezar,* the degenerative disease burning away his nerve paths. The question was not whether Panshinea would die on the throne. It was when . . . if the Skies or the disease would bring him down first. Palaton reached forward instinctively to soothe the pain. "Sire. . . ."

The emperor took a shuddering breath. "You are honest," he said as he gathered his composure. "I must ask myself if I can trust an honest being. Have Jorana take you to your quarters. We'll talk again in the morning."

Palaton stood. Jorana was already striding across the library, her bronze hair flowing back with the swiftness of her movement, as if she had been listening for the emperor's faint voices. She stopped just short of securing his arm and Palaton knew he had been dismissed and that she would see he left.

They took a step away.

"And Jorana."

She swung around to the emperor.

"Hurry back to me," Panshinea said, a glitter deep in his eyes.

She flushed slightly. "Yes, Majesty," she answered. She would not meet Palaton's eyes as she turned back to him.

Gathon was waiting outside the study doors, his lips still

pursed in that expression of his. Jorana halted, allowing
Palaton to exchange words with the minister.

"Anything said within Charolon is confidential," the minister said.

"I understand."

"See that you do." Gathon jerked his chin and Jorana
marched forward again. Palaton moved past, but he felt the
minister's dark glare upon his back until the hallway
turned, bearing them out of view.

Palaton wondered what a Sky was doing as a minister to
the House of Star. He wondered if the Choya's innate abilities and devotion to Cho mired him in a job he hated.

The intricacies of Charolon were vast. Without a guide,
Palaton would never have found the apartments he had been
given unless he consulted his *bahdur*. Jorana led him there
and left him. He entered the rooms, found he'd been given
an exterior view, and that the rain had dwindled to a thin
drizzle once more. The darkness had lightened to a foglike
gray that hung over the park and grounds. Palaton threw
open the windows and took a deep breath. He began to feel
the fatigue of the journey that had brought him here and sat
down on the edge of a bed. There was an aura about Charolon he had never seen before and he could not define it.

He had not asked to be in the emperor's confidence, but
now he bore the burden of it. The emperor would not release him unscathed. The only question was what would be
required of him, and was it an act he could perform and
still live with himself?

With a taste in his mouth like ashes from the burning fire
below, Palaton lay back on the bed and drifted into sleep.

He awoke to a soft knock on the door. He blinked, for-
getting his dream as it drifted away from him, sat up and
looked out the still open window. The room was icy, the
sky outside the pitch of deepest night. The knock sounded
again and he rolled to his feet.

Jorana stood inside the doorway as he opened it, framed
by the softest of lighting from the corridor. It set her mane
into a golden aura.

"I thought it would be easier for me to find you than for
you to find me," she said gently. She put an open hand
out tentatively.

He took it and drew her in. She filled his arms nicely. "I thought the emperor waited for you."

"Panshinea has other amusements," she said, her voices low and warm. She fit her curves neatly to his leanness and did not complain about the chill in the room.

Soon he did not feel it either as her heat thawed him.

She left his bed in early dawn. He lay with one eye open, watching her dress, his nostrils filled with her scent, musky and perfumed and hinting of the sex they had shared. She stood and fastened her collar, one hand going to her House badges to make sure they were in place. Then she leaned down to give him a swift, fleeting caress.

"Trust no one," she said. She closed his eyes with a touch of her fingertip.

He waited until the door closed before snuggling into the warm hollow in the bedcovers. Her words sealed him back into an uneasy sleep. When he awoke again, the bleak sunlight was streaming through clouds and the birds were chortling in noisy clamor.

Breakfast was a public affair, buffet lines for those doing business with the throne that day. He found credit chits upon the bureau in his quarters and cashed those in for a breakfast of *bren,* weak and watery looking, fresh baked rolls, stewed *aprins* with nectar sprinkled upon them, and braised eggs. The food was good and hot, the *aprins* sweet and juicy though their season was summer and Charolon stood on the brink of winter. He savored the tastes of home.

He listened obliquely to the conversations going on around him, not endeavoring to pick up talk, but doing it anyway. There was a lot of concern about the relocation riots—Panshinea had been right in saying that it would soon be old news. Troops were being sent in force to evacuate the county of Danbe and bloodshed was expected.

Palaton knew about the Danbeans. Superstitious folk, as rooted in their river valley as the stone mountains surrounding them were rooted in the earth. He also knew the river waters were strained greatly by the population and that Panshinea had probably waited as long as he could before ordering Relocation. Strange that a population would stay and completely destroy the ecological balance before moving voluntarily, he thought as he ate his braised eggs.

Even stranger that they would add to their own destruction by warfare.

He found the Earthan second waiting for him when he cleared his dishes. The Choya stood with a resigned look etched into his heavy face.

"*Tezar* Palaton, please accompany me."

The summons did not surprise Palaton. What did startle him was the view across the massive dining hall, crowded with Choyan and alien visitors, of a *tezar* moving with an arrogance he thought he recognized. He froze in place and felt his gaze narrow.

The Choya was in one-quarter profile and Palaton stared a moment longer until he identified the aura as Nedar's. He wondered what purpose Nedar had at Charolon, and then wondered if it was the same as his own. Had Panshinea summoned him as well? And if so, why?

The Earthan guard touched his sleeve. "*Tezar*," he repeated patiently.

"Coming," Palaton answered absently and followed the guard, pondering the paradox of Nedar's presence. What need had Panshinea of the best of the current pilots off contract?

Panshinea stood in his formal offices. He smiled widely as Palaton entered. "Brethren. Minister Gathon has convinced me that your instinctive reticence is invariably correct, and that you will be most unsuited to the task I suggested last night. However, I'm hoping you'll attend me for a season or two. I'm in need of a personal pilot and an honest Choya."

Palaton decided he must remember to thank the disapproving minister. He gave a correct smile. "My leisure time as a pilot is not always available."

"I'm the emperor," Panshinea said brusquely. "Something can and will be arranged." His eyes went hard. He turned sideways. "May I introduce you to the Prelate of the House of Star, Magi Rindalan."

In the rear of the oval office, ensconced amid upholstered pillows and rich, antique carved woods, the head Prelate of the God-in-all rested, his eyes gleaming like pale lights in the corner of the room. Palaton felt a pulsing at the base of his throat. Of the three Prelates of the three Houses, Rindalan was without dispute the most powerful.

The Prelate stood, large hand held out in greeting, his robes rustling about his gaunt body. His horn crown was the largest Palaton had ever seen, and his sparse fringe of chestnut hair barely covered his domed skull. He had pale blue eyes of the first water and his grip engulfed Palaton's own.

"*Tezar* Palaton," the magi enthused. "I am pleased to be meeting you. Your fame proceeds you and does Cho proud."

There was a glow beyond the warmth of flesh touching flesh as their hands met. Palaton had never encountered anyone with such a forceful aura. Their meeting practically sparked, and there was an answering flash in the Prelate's light blue eyes. An expression of satisfaction passed over the holy one's face before he turned away and Palaton wondered what he had done to please the Prelate.

"I am proud to be one with Cho," Palaton answered. "But I'm afraid whatever reputation I have has been greatly exaggerated."

"Nonsense," countered Panshinea. "You carried out your contract with the Gurans brilliantly."

"I took advantage of Choyan talents," Palaton murmured. He felt ill-at-ease. "And I did nothing but drop the wing. It was my pilots who delivered the payload."

"As modest as an Earthan," said the Prelate heartily. He stalked about the edges of the room, his robes rustling noisily about his ankles. "Are you sure this fellow is one of ours?"

A long, slow second passed. Palaton found himself holding his breath, unsure of what the emperor's Householding knew about him. Did Rindalan know of his dubious parentage—and if he did, was he challenging the emperor with it? Palaton hesitated, uncertain of what to answer. Panshinea filled the silence with laughter.

"Rindalan has a ribald sense of humor, does he not?" the emperor said, before sitting down with a thump. He added, "We'll be needing a sense of humor. The Danbeans have vowed to fill their river with blood before they can be forced to leave."

The Prelate raised a lanky finger in warning, a digit as thin and knobby as his entire body, and looked toward Palaton, who suddenly felt extremely uncomfortable. "*Tezars* are divorced from Choyan politics, Highness," Rindalan said mildly.

"It matters not," said Panshinea. "He'll be flying me over tomorrow."

Palaton felt his eyebrow raise before he could control it. He turned slightly away from both the Prelate and the emperor to hide his expression, embarrassed at his lack of restraint.

"And do you think," said Rindalan dryly, "that taking a hero with you will protect you from public opinion?"

"It couldn't hurt. Besides, I'll need the best piloting skills. Intelligence says they'll have their shields up in case we send in drones to dislodge them. They're an agro-community and their shielding won't hold against someone like Palaton here."

"You're defying them," Rindalan warned. "Even an emperor hasn't the right to mock his people."

"By the fading aura, someone has to knock some sense into their thick, horned skulls! The Danbe is dying. They're not thriving there, the population is doing little more than surviving. The laws of relocation were set up with a purpose in mind and must be obeyed. There is no right or wrong here, there is only *necessity*."

Rindalan examined a bit of fluff on his sleeve, but his voices filtered up strongly from his bent face. "I'm told there are those who say Charolon itself is overdue for relocation, and that those who must move and those who can stay are decided . . . politically."

Heat blazed up on Panshinea's face. The grimace of anger accompanying his words distorted his handsomeness. "They'll flee Charolon like plague-ridden rodents when I die. That'll be soon enough for my critics. Relocate carrying my ashes with you!"

Rindalan had not looked up, but he responded soothingly, "Now, now, my emperor. You are a Choya in your prime. Thoughts of death are beyond you. We can't afford to be melancholy. There's work to be done and you alone can do it."

"Do you hear that, *tezar*? The High Prelate has conceded a realm of Cho is under my rule rather than his."

Palaton, standing to one side, ignored till that moment, felt keenly that he had no right to be there, nor did he understand why the two of them tolerated his presence. He did not want to know the workings of the throne. He did not want to be privy to Panshinea's flaws or the Prelate's ambitions. "With your permission," he got out, "if I'm to fly, I'd like to oversee the plane's preparation."

Panshinea's gaze flew to his face. The emperor stared, while his color paled to normal and his distorted features reverted to normal. Palaton had the distinct feeling that the Choya had forgotten who he was and why he was there. The Prelate, too, looked at him, and though his face was half-hidden by the line of Panshinea's hunched shoulder, there was a wariness about his stance.

"Of course you wish to fly," the emperor said, his voices vibrating with patronization. "Like birds on the wing, let loose your *tezars* to the sky!"

"Another play, majesty? Or is it poetry this time? Your reference eludes me," Rindalan remarked smoothly, as if aware Palaton was suddenly floundering.

The emperor hunched, as if in pain. His walk crabbed. He crossed the room to the Prelate. He put out his hand. Rindalan countered. There was a flare of auras as they touched, a burst that made Palaton's eyes water with its brightness.

Panshinea took a deep, shuddering breath. His *bahdur* shone thinly. "Well," he responded. "If you need a plane, Gathon will order you one. And what would you recommend?"

"Nothing less than a stinger if you intend to make a fly-over through shielding." Palaton could hardly talk, but the warning remained on Rindalan's face to say nothing untoward. He had just witnessed a parasitism of talent, but the Prelate acted as if nothing unusual had happened, as if Panshinea had not stolen from him. Palaton thought of the parasitic pilot who'd died the last time he'd been to Blue Ridge. It had been a just fate for that Choya. What, then, should he think of his own emperor?

Palaton had no idea. The Prelate stayed half-hidden, his purposes his own.

"Do you know why I intend to go to Danbe personally?" asked Panshinea keenly.

"I suppose," Palaton answered slowly, "I would do it to show them their vulnerability. I would show them that I was willing to risk my blood first to save them the bloodshed that might follow if rioting continued and force had to be brought in. But I wouldn't settle for a fly-over. I'd land and tell them face-to-face."

"Let them know that no one is safe or above the law, not even their emperor?" Triumph colored the emperor's voices. His eyes looked brighter.

"That approximates it."

Panshinea smiled gently. "Then we're of a mind. I will not place my life in the hands of someone I suspect. I'll have Jorana take you to the airstrip. Gathon will send a commission ahead of you. Take whatever plane you see fit. I want to leave this afternoon, after my luncheon conferences." He turned to Rindalan.

Palaton was halfway out the door when the emperor said, "GNask has a most interesting proposition. He has offered to lend me mercenaries to save me the agony of sending Choyan after Choyan. What do you think, Prelate, of hiring the Abdreliks?"

"I think it absurd."

"As do I. The ambassador surprises me with his knowledge of the Danbe situation, but I won't let an Abdrelik set foot on Cho. Their intelligence is accurate enough." Mercifully, the closing door muffled the rest of the conversation.

Palaton stopped in the hallway, sickened by what he'd seen, and he took a deep breath to cleanse away the aroma of Panshinea's illness.

Chapter 11

His mouth had gone dry. He had felt both Panshinea's *bahdur* and his sanity flicker in and out, burn hotly and then gutter. Was he the only one who sensed it? He could not have been . . . the Prelate Rindalan flamed with aura. By his very position which bespoke extreme closeness with the God-in-all, he could not fail to sense Panshinea's illness. Rindalan must know what Panshinea stole from him. As for Gathon . . . the Sky minister might serve purposes of his own, but being taken down with Panshinea could hardly be one of them.

But Panshinea would fall. It was inevitable and the more erratic his behavior became, the quicker the downfall. Palaton guessed that Rindalan and Gathon must be praying for the time needed to consolidate their own futures. And when that time came, he would not give a gold piece for the length of Panshinea's life. The emperor would die.

He'd not seen such a thing in his lifetime. The old emperor, Panshinea's uncle Clibern, had died in his sleep, at an advanced age, a steady if unspectacular ruler. His boyhood memories of the funeral processions in each city's streets and the feasts of farewell were dim, as was his memory of Panshinea's ascension.

The palms of his hands itched as though he should be gripping something and could not. The only destiny he could control was that of the plane he'd be taking out as soon as it was serviced and the emperor was ready to leave. But the consequences of that flight would either serve Panshinea well . . . or aid his enemies. Palaton would be riding treacherous winds and thermals which could downdraft or shear off without warning, bringing him tumbling down. With a feeling in his gut vaguely like hungriness, Palaton turned to the corridor that would take him to his rooms where he'd await Jorana's escort to the airstrip.

Two floors up, the Earthan second met him coming off the lift. He wore his winter uniform buckled against the outside weather. The guardsman's smile was tight.

"*Tezar* Palaton," he said in welcome. "My lieutenant is delayed. May I convey you to the airstrip?"

Disappointment pricked him, but he had no right to expect Jorana's personal attention. He inclined his head. "Let me get a coat against the wind and I'll be right with you, Second."

"Call me Darb," the Earthan told him, and took up position outside the door as Palaton entered.

Palaton scouted through his gear quickly. He took an all-weather coat and his flight suit as well, thinking that he might not come back to his rooms. He changed into flight boots, packed a small duffel, and stepped out of the room, his *bahdur* flickering about him, raising the hair on the back of his neck, his horn crown throbbing briefly. This suite was not his home—he had not stayed here for more than a day's span, yet he had to resist the urge to look it over with a sweeping glance of farewell as if he might never return. He shut the door firmly on his superstition and stepped out to join Darb.

They left the palatial estate by way of a circuitous route and Palaton thought of times far back in Choyan history when barons fled rival armies through such back routes. Charolon was old enough to have stood through warfare like that. Its stained rock walls held flickering auras that he might have read, if he'd had the talent for it. It occurred to him, as he echoed Darb's footfalls, that no one other than the emperor's staff and Nedar knew he was there. He could disappear from the face of Cho and no one would know what had happened, unless they stopped to read yet another anguished aura splashed like blood upon the walls of this cavernous tunnel. A chill worked its way down the collar of his flight jacket.

The tunnel mouth opened up and a stray beam of light arced down from splitting clouds to illuminate the conveyance waiting for them. Darb settled in the driver's seat, stating, "The emperor does not always like a public departure."

"I guessed as much," Palaton answered dryly, seating himself. "How far are we from the hangar?"

"Another twenty minutes or so." Darb punched in coordinates and started the vehicle. It hummed into power and lurched away.

They drove through a newer section of the city, its lines cleaner, straighter, its direction driving upward, stacking inhabitants efficiently, if not as grandly. Darb piloted the vehicle through the passways, shadow lines of the buildings dappling them and Palaton thought of his cadet days when he raced planes down blind canyon walls, his *bahdur* pinging like a fire alarm.

The Houseless lived in these areas, the Choyan who had no extrasensory talents, or at least none that were reliable and measurable. They were God-blind, this massive part of the population, dependent upon the guidance of the Houses. Palaton looked out of the window and wondered, for the hundredth time, what it would be like when his *bahdur* burned out. How would it be not to know the living from the dead, not to feel the vibrations of the God-in-all which ran through every organic part of Cho, not to feel connected to the balance of nature of his own world?

Palaton stared at the faces of the Choyan they passed, those walking in the streets, those glimpsed through storefronts, those whose faces were mirrored in the windows of other vehicles—none seemed particularly anguished. They did not seem bereft. It was not true that you did not miss what you had never had—there were yearly riots between the Housed and the Houseless. He wondered if the settlement at Danbe was Housed or if it was generally a God-blind population. A settlement which had a Householding had enough talent running through its gene pool to be sensitive, if not totally aware. If otherwise populated, then their resistance to Relocation might be easier to understand. Other than through scientific testing, they could not see or feel the damage they inflicted upon their surroundings. Without that inner sight, they could not truly believe.

Darb did not need to keep his full attention on driving. Letting the vehicle do its automated work, he turned fullface when Palaton spoke.

"What's Danbe like? Is it God-blind?"

"It's not Householded, if that's what you're driving at."

Darb's thin lips tightened further. Palaton saw the distaste on his face, his frown distorting the facial tracing under the fine layer of his left cheek. Plain onyx lines, rather than more expensive jewelry, and Palaton speculated as to what the second's background was.

"I was wondering," Palaton said mildly, "why the Danbeans refused to move."

"You don't have to be Housed to have a love for your home." Darb returned his attention to his driving and his expression settled into sullenness.

Palaton could see that the Earthan would not be pressed into further conversation. There were ripples here he could sense, but he had no way of discovering all the ramifications and he knew better than to stir such waters. He sat back and formulated flight plans while watching the canyons of apartments give way to service factories and manufacturers and then to reclaimed fields.

A windbreak stand of trees stood stark and bare along the line of a runway that had seen better times, but was still more than sufficient for their needs, with a hulk of bays and hangars hugging the far end of it. The vehicle turned in and came to a halt inside the wide flung doors of the foremost bay.

Palaton got out and stretched before reaching back in for his bag. Darb remained seated, keyboarding in an entry to his duty journal, and Palaton left him in the vehicle, anxious to see the plane. He moved deeper into the hangar, alert for the noises of the robotic crew serving the stinger, but a great, empty building greeted him. Palaton cast about, thinking the small, sleek plane might be hidden in the shadowy recesses of the hangar, but he saw nothing. He heard Darb shuffle up behind him and turned, saying with mild irritation and disappointment, "The stinger's not been brought in yet."

"Nor will it be, not to this location," Darb answered quietly. "This field's been abandoned for several years." His voices echoed in the cavernous building.

Palaton dropped his bag to show his empty hands, but Darb had pulled his enforcer and stood steady, barrel trained on the *tezar*. There was a quaver to the Earthan's voices which screamed out the second's instability, and Palaton fought to hold himself still and calm.

"What is this? Have I offended the emperor?"

"Panshinea? No. Him you have not offended." Darb looked old and tired. The enforcer wavered slightly in his hand and he wrapped his second hand about his first to steady it. "Turn around, *tezar*, so that I don't have to see my disgrace reflected in your eyes."

"You're not disgraced yet. Turn back from this."

Darb's nostrils flared as he gave a cynical snort. "My House orders this. I have no choice." He took a side step. "Surprised? You have a short memory for a *tezar*. You've faced assassins before."

He could not keep his amazement inside, but he masked it with sarcasm. "Calling yourself an assassin is rank flattery." Palaton gathered his *bahdur* as he spoke, readying to move before Darb could shoot. He fought to hold his aura even, before he could flare it out and leave it burning behind him creating the illusion of himself frozen in immobility while he moved out of harm's way. He'd never done it before and was not even sure it was within his talents' range, but it was the only chance he had with Darb facing him at point-blank range. His thoughts raced ahead of his words and he could feel his aura gaining strength.

"I don't deserve the attention."

"My House disagrees."

"The Earthans are not killers. Leave that to the Skies."

"We do what we have to for the greater good. The Wheel turns—you'd deny us our ascendancy, all of you! We are not adequate, they say, to the challenges that face us." Darb's lip curled back. "We'll take what should be freely given."

"I don't stand in your way."

"If you think that, then you're more of a fool than I thought you." Darb's voices hardened and Palaton could empathize with the squeeze of muscles that accompanied it. His finger would be contracting along the trigger.

Now, and only now. Palaton let his aura blaze, flaring with a heat that scorched as it left his body, and he threw himself to the left, skidding across the dusty, broken concrete flooring of the hangar as Darb fired at the illusion left in his wake. The weapon discharged, blinding them both, leaping in Darb's shaking hands.

Palaton got to his hands and knees. He bolted upward,

racing across the building even as Darb let out a cry of dismay.

Palaton had never faced an enforcer before. He had no idea what kind of charge they carried but knew it had to be considerable. He took a running leap to catch a machinery crane, snagged the hook, and let it carry him swooping into the shadows. The enforcer spat again. Its heat seared across the back of his head and Darb cried out a second time.

Fear settled in Palaton's gut, cold and greasy. He kicked out with his heels and caught the high catwalk stretching across the hangar's eaves. He hung upside down by his knees for a second as he let go of the crane's hook. He had a blurred view of Darb searching wildly, then he righted himself with a grunt and perched overhead on the catwalk. He watched Darb flounder about below.

The second had called him a fool, and a fool he was. The world, he thought, was far bigger and more devious than he'd given it credit for being. He was a baron, and a rival's army had come to wipe him out. The reasoning behind it could be figured out once he had survived.

Palaton stood up cautiously. The catwalk gave no metallic moan beneath his weight to betray him. He did not think he could walk along it silently and if noise did not reveal him then dust surely would. He looked up into the darkened eaves of the building and saw utility cables which had come loose from their mooring and hung downward like vines.

They might loosen further . . . or not. Secure, they would take him to the rooftop and out the ventilation gratings. He might even make it back to the vehicle before Darb.

Palaton flexed his hands to work his nerve up. Then, with a short bound, he leapt up and caught the cable. He hung, dangling in the air for a moment, before the cable came loose with a tremendous whine and he plunged groundward.

Darb looked up and shouted. The barrel of the enforcer pointed upward, discharging magma-like into the dim recesses of the hangar, as Palaton swung downward. The flare missed. Palaton knew he was a target and that Darb could not possibly miss again. His *bahdur* smoldered, but for what purpose, he did not know. He only knew that he wished the Earthan motionless. Palaton lost his sight briefly and felt, before his eyes cleared, the impact of their two bodies colliding.

The impact jarred him to his teeth. He let go, the cable snaking about him like netting, and Darb rolling away with a loud grunt and an audible snap. Palaton slid to a halt on the flooring, trying to catch his breath, fighting to get back on his feet before the second could come after him again.

Gasping, Palaton rolled to his knees. Darb never moved. He lay stretched out on the broken pavement, his hand curled tightly about the enforcer, his uniform besmirched with dust and filth. His neck was twisted at an impossible angle. Palaton sucked in a breath as he realized that the impact had broken the Earthan's neck.

Choyan had incredibly strong necks because of the weight of their crowns, yet that same strength was treacherous just below the skull case at the apex of the neck itself, where the crown weight rested. There was that one small area of neck where the crown overwhelmed it, where a solid chop would snap the vertebrae despite the musculature.

There was the imprint of a heel in the flesh of Darb's neck at the nape. Palaton could not have hit him more solidly if he had planned to come swinging down from the eaves.

Gorge rose at the back of his throat, hot and burning. He got shakily to his feet and spat it out. He had done Darb a favor. His House would have treated the second much worse for his failure. He told himself that and knew it was true, and regretted the death anyway, and not simply because Darb could give him no answers now.

Quiet voices said, "Palaton."

He looked up and hesitated. Jorana stood in the hangar door. Her face creased in distress. "I saw," she said. "I would never have believed it if I had not seen it. I couldn't get a clean shot. I couldn't save you. . . ."

"He's dead," Palaton said lamely.

She strode across the hangar floor and knelt by the body. She touched him and shrank back. It astonished Palaton that she would react so to death. Surely she'd seen more of it more intimately than he had. "He's stone cold," she said. "But I saw him die. What did you do to him?"

"Nothing. I gave him an illusion aura to get out of range. His neck broke when we collided—"

Jorana swung about on her heels. She stayed kneeling at Darb's side. "He wasn't capable of this. Even for an Earthan, he wasn't capable."

"But he did."

Her expressive eyes watched him closely. "Who are you, what are you?"

"A *tezar*, nothing more."

She turned away from him, ran her hand over the body again. She shook her head, baffled. "The why and how of his death tells me that, even if you don't know it, there is more." She stood, slowly. "A Choyan who does not know himself is a mystery in itself."

Palaton's mouth felt like dust. He could not know himself, not without knowing his parentage. But he knew himself well enough to predict his behavior and reactions, and no one outside his House had ever come this close to unmasking him.

"I did nothing." He shook his head for emphasis. "He brought me here. He turned the enforcer on me. I ran for my life. What would you have done differently?"

"Nothing." Jorana tilted her head in consideration. "He probably would have killed me. I thought I knew Darb well." She halted abruptly. "I'll take care of the body. Can you go on without me?"

"If I have to."

"You have to. The emperor is making preparations for the flight you've promised him. You'd better hurry." She turned her back on him and he left the hangar to let her mourn in private and then do whatever she had to do.

He picked up his duffel near the doors and headed back to the vehicle he'd arrived in. Jorana's skimcar stood off to the side. The on-screen readout showed him that Darb had doctored the vehicle destination and driver. According to the information, Palaton had driven it alone.

He climbed in the driver's seat. He sat for a moment, door open, listening to the wind keen, thinking about what to do.

Palaton reached out and closed the conveyance's door. He found the emperor's airfield in its stored memory and keyed it in. Let them think he'd gotten lost and wandered. Darb had doctored the destination journal and it would never lead to this location.

Jorana came out of the hangar. She paused by the window. "I've erased the auras. If and when his body is found, they'll think salvagers did it. This area is due for demolition and redevelopment soon. The pickers will be swarming over it. From the condition of his body . . . the time of death will be dubious anyway. I've changed my duty log to show that I sent him on perimeter patrol."

This could not be free. "What do you want from me?"

She was close enough to caress him. But she did not. Her lips curved slightly. "I have a career," she said softly. "I worked hard to become Housed. I wanted to pilot the skies and the Chaos beyond, but I wasn't that good. But my child. . . ."

What she suggested lanced through him, piercing the shock of Darb's attack and death. "I'm a stranger here. I was told not to trust anyone but I've made the mistake of doing it three times." Rindalan, he thought, and the emperor and the Earthan second. No more.

"And you'll trust no more. You're learning," she said, and her voices trembled with regret. She moved away from the vehicle.

Palaton eased the brake off and the conveyance jolted forward. He had a flight ahead of him and now he let its importance overwhelm everything else. It seemed the one rock solid event in a swiftly changing world.

Chapter 12

"No flight plans," Panshinea said, rocking back on his heels.

"Your highness, I must. It's regulation and with good reason. If we should go down, it's the fastest way to trace us—"

"If we go down, *tezar*, the House of Sky will start a generation-long celebration and there'll be no one out looking for us." The emperor looked out the plane window with a melancholy air. "And I don't want the communicators knowing where we're going. I'm having enough damn trouble with the media."

Tezars did not need flight plans, they were for the lesser talented and instrument tracked, but Palaton had been well-instructed and Panshinea's whims went against the grain. Rindalan looked away as Palaton glanced at him and he knew that no help was forthcoming from the Prelate. "Very well, your highness," he answered. "Then we're ready."

The emperor looked back at him. "Have you ever, Palaton, not been ready?"

He did not need much time to think about it. "Not for flying," he answered briefly, went up front, shut the door between them, and sat down at his console.

The windshield revealed a flying lane cleared for their exclusive use. The crew walked away from the plane, ducking temporarily out of his line of sight and reappearing near the hangar. Only the flagman remained, red banners filling his hands. He directed Palaton out onto the lane. The sky had gone bleaker, and it looked as though it might begin to empty out its tears soon. He thought briefly of Darb lying undiscovered, unmourned, where he and Jorana had left him in an abandoned building under that bleak sky. He brushed the thought from his head and ignited the engines for warm-up.

The plane thrilled under his touch. Its instruments were honed for lightning reflexes. He dried the palms of his hands on his pant legs. Then he began to key in targets, coordinates, thermals, and a destination that he simply *knew* lay where he said it did, because that was what he was. The console cued him when the plane was ready, and he eased it out onto the flight lane. When the flagman signaled, he pushed the throttle forward, the plane rushing to take off.

Then he was airborne, free, balancing between gravity and wind lift, the machine answering his wish, his hope. He leaned over the console, feeling like an aircraft himself, balancing between instrumentation and *bahdur*. The geographical and meteorological patterns of the world could be read by instrumentation, but there were other patterns affecting flight and those he searched after now. There was a topography of spiritualism that surrounded Cho, a topography that constantly changed, was being carved out and rebuilt, sculpted and let fall, nurtured and destroyed, and it affected the physical world in ways which only the talented could perceive.

He had not flown Cho in over two years, and as he did so now, he grasped for its essence, held it ribboning in his fingers, silken, then harsh, fresh, then corrupt, and he wondered.

There was a rattle behind him and Panshinea leaned into the control room.

"How long before arrival?"

Palaton brought himself back to the instrumentation. "Two hours," he gauged.

"Time for a nap," the emperor grunted, and stumbled back to the lounge of the plane. Like the plane itself, the passenger area was sleek and dynamic. Panshinea would have to lie lengthwise if he wished to nap. Palaton smiled to himself.

He felt himself slowly losing that expression as Cho reared up at him, demanding to be perceived and understood. He caught a sense like that he felt when skimming Sorrow, that here was a mystery he must divine, that his own personal mystery depended upon its revelation. Flying into the low ceiling and a late autumn storm front made the plane buck and pitch, and yet below this reality was another layer just as storm-tossed and demanding.

Palaton's sense of well-being disintegrated into anxious watchfulness as the war plane skimmed over the continental divide, chasing the shadow of the sun, barely seen through clouds boiling in the sky.

He'd been wrapped in silence for a considerable while when the cabin pressure changed subtly, incense whiffed inward, and he knew the Prelate had entered. There was a creak in the gunner's chair behind him. Palaton checked to make sure the firing console was inactive before swiveling his head toward his companion.

Rindalan folded his hands over his robed lap. "Do you ever think of the God-in-all as your copilot, *tezar?*"

"No. More like the wind beneath my wings."

"Ah." Rindalan looked out the windshield. "Perhaps that is more suitable."

"And desirable," added Palaton without thinking. Rindalan gave him a dry laugh.

"There were auditions for this position," he informed Palaton. "And I'm still not sure His Highness made the best choice."

"I'm not political."

"No. I can see that. Nedar is, but he's far too aggressive. Actually, I favored a pilot who is not a *tezar*, but Panshinea likes to bask in the adulation the commons give you."

That settled the unanswered question in Palaton's mind about why Nedar had been at Charolon. It had been buried behind all the other questions needing answers, but it had been niggling at him.

Palaton did not ask why the emperor didn't pilot himself: they both knew why. His *bahdur* could not possibly be reliable enough any longer. He did not divert much of his attention from the panorama before him, busy avoiding thermal drops which would waken the emperor if they hit a pocket, but he said, "If your eminence would enlighten me, perhaps I could adjust my attitude."

Rindalan leaned forward. Palaton could only glimpse the Choya's profile from the edge of his vision, but the Prelate looked almost predatory. "If you did," Rindalan said, "I'd not trust you the way I do now."

"Then," and the corner of Palaton's mouth quirked slightly, "I'll settle for being second best and first chosen."

"You may pray we had not," reflected the Prelate. "Your instruments show shielding."

"We're nearing the Danbe. Is the emperor awake?"

"Not yet. I'll take care of it." Rindalan rose from the gunner's chair. "And thank you, my child. You may not be political, but you are astute."

The cabin wheezed with slight pressure again as Rindalan left. Palaton splayed his fingers over his console, wondering what the Prelate would have said if told of Darb's attempted assassination. And hadn't the holy one just given him a vote of confidence? *Or had he?*

He turned on the main cabin comlink and display so that Panshinea would have full access to what Palaton was doing. He did not wish the gunner's seat reoccupied. He scanned the console.

"Coming into the Danbe River basin, Your Highness. Full shielding is up and instruments show that return fire is being readied."

"Identify us," Panshinea answered. Palaton imagined the emperor sitting on the edge of his seat by the side viewing window, the sunlight setting his hair ablaze.

"Doing so." Palaton keyed out their id, and his own as well. Recognition came back so quickly he half-wondered if they had a precog among their commons. The response denied access. He told the emperor even as he sculpted out a point of entry despite their crude shielding.

"Take us in anyway," Panshinea snapped.

It wouldn't be easy. The shielding had blinds for those with *bahdur,* diversions of aura and instinct. And he couldn't know that they wouldn't fire, so he built in evasive action, and sat back to look at the webbing they'd strung and what he needed to do to pierce it without being caught. As aura blazed into his vision, he knew that few *tezars* would attempt what he was going to try. But he thought he could do it, and knew he had to, if the Danbeans were to survive Relocation.

He made his choices and keyed them in quickly. The plane trembled in answer, surging forward. He took the controls manually, with the computer backup for assistance. "Gentlemen," Palaton said grimly. "I hope you're wearing your restraints." He banked the plane sharply and took it down.

It was like unweaving a delicate tapestry. The shield was built in layers, and he peeled them away, slicing through them, never coming in directly because that was how shields defended. The plane skimmed delicately under his handling and it bucked twice as ground to air fire erupted near them.

"Those are automatic shots from the system," Palaton said. Some shields were fully automated, while some relied on partial automation and self-determination, and the remainder were manually called shots.

He could hear Panshinea muttering, "And is that supposed to calm me?" He was too busy to answer.

The seventh pass brought them under the shielding, clear of all but ground to air fire, a deliberate act to bring them down.

Palaton called for a landing lane. The response came back reluctantly, giving him the west to east lane.

"I have landing clearance," he informed the emperor.

"Get it down before they change their minds."

Palaton nodded absently, banked a turn and brought the plane in, knowing there would be no other air traffic to bother him, and hoping that they would not now be fired upon. He waggled the wings on the pass and came into line with the runway.

The Danbean air was acrid, dry despite the river, warm and windy. He had taken crosswinds into account, but as he stepped out onto the airfield, Palaton thought that he hadn't done so enough. Part of the turbulence had to be accounted for by high winds. He looked across the ground and saw crews on the run, conveyances pulling up behind the security fencing, and general havoc awaiting them.

He remarked to Panshinea, who was right behind him, "I believe we surprised them."

"We by God-in-all had better have impressed them."

Rindalan muffled a sound behind the emperor. It was made inaudible by the growing noise behind the security gates as Choyan poured out of buildings and onto the airfield. They were shouting something.

"What is that?" Panshinea asked.

Palaton didn't answer, but the High Prelate did. "It sounds, Your Highness, as if they're shouting '*tezar.*'"

The luminary of Danbe sat across from Panshinea at the conference table. He was a massive Choya, broad across the shoulders, with an elaborate horn crown, and dark, ebony hair streaking down his head and back. He was not one Palaton would have liked to lock horns with, and even Panshinea spoke with a circumspect look on his face. The luminary was a commons, but he radiated confidence and charisma, and knew his city-state backed him.

A timid Choya'i entered, as if knowing she interrupted matters of import, and scurried across the tiled flooring. The luminary's aide took her whispered request and frowned. He looked across the table.

Malahki paused, even as his finger stabbed out a point to Panshinea. "What is it?"

"I'm sorry, your honor. The Secondary Education Level has come in with busloads of children. They want to greet *tezar* Palaton. I can't disperse the crowds until they do."

Rindalan muttered an aside to Palaton. "That's your third bow."

Palaton did not answer. He was used to welcomes, although never one this tumultuous. He stood. Panshinea said, without looking up, "I give you leave to go."

He had not thought of asking leave. "The God-blind ask for me."

Panshinea waved him off.

The luminary watched him, weighing him with eyes of brilliant gold and brown. Some commons chose not to be tested after a disappointing childhood. Palaton wondered just how much talent was buried behind that shrewd gaze. Rindalan stood up between them, smoothing down his robes. "I think I could use a breath of fresh air, Palaton. May I accompany you?"

Palaton let him by. By the time the holy one had passed, Malahki's gaze had already dropped to the tabletop where the Choya studied the notes he had been taking.

The Choya'i aide waited for him, her hands tucked nervously inside the sleeves of her jacket. She smiled as he drew near. "The children," she explained, "have been driven a long way to see you."

"I won't disappoint them," Palaton said. "Do you test often in this area?"

"No," she answered abruptly, with no further explanation, and he followed her out the door to the balcony of the civic hall.

Choyan filled the courtyard. He could see the smaller figures being led to the front, and the adults stepping back. Eyes brilliant, flashing in the late afternoon sun as they looked up at him, the young of his world crowded under the balcony. They could not sense his aura, but they devoured the sight of him as hungrily as if they could. Palaton raised a hand to them.

"Tezar." Spoken in a roar. The sound of it sent a chill down the back of his neck. He could do what they could not yet there was no spite or jealousy in their voices. They adored him for his talents.

The aide handed him an amplifier. It was country-standard, technologically modest, and as he took it, he wondered if those to the rear of the massive courtyard would even be able to hear him. "Thank you," he said, his voices modulated. The crowd hushed to listen.

"The Choyan of Danbe have shown great courage, and there are even more days of courage ahead. It was my pleasure to bring your emperor here. He made a request of me because he is concerned about your welfare and your future. But my pleasure is also my pain because I had to cross your shielding to do so. Still, it was done because I am a *tezar* and have the ability to do it. There are others who can follow. Remember that. There is courage in compromise as well."

Palaton looked down to the eager faces of the young. He smiled. "I hope to see some of you after the next Choosing. Thank you." He handed the amplifier back, suddenly becoming aware Rindalan stood at his elbow, so close he might almost have shared the amplifier with him. But the Prelate hadn't spoken.

The crowd roared again, their voices filling the air, until their words became indistinct thunder. He stood until he could stand no longer because the Choya'i tugged on his cuff, taking him away. He answered her insistent demand.

The balcony door shut behind them, dimming the sounds of adulation. Rindalan smoothed his hair back from his crown and very quietly said, "Listen to that. A *tezar* garners more shouts than even an emperor—yet even an emperor cannot bear to lose that noise. That is something for you to remember, *tezar*."

Chapter 13

Panshinea retreated with a sunken look to his eyes, Rindalan murmured a few vague apologies, and the talks broke
off abruptly in midevening with the emperor leaving for
the secured rooms prepared for him. Palaton hesitated as
Malahki called him back. He looked to Rindalan for guidance. The Prelate smiled. "Remember," was all he said
before disappearing after Panshinea.

Malahki smiled. "Don't worry," he said. "I've been told
that you're merely the pilot. A drink in the rear courtyard?
It's been a long day."

Palaton followed in curiosity. The luminary strode out of
doors, where a fog could be seen rolling in from the river
as the dry night air coaxed it upward. A small table had
already been set with cups and a carafe of wine, and a
hand-*lindar* against the balcony wall. Malahki grabbed it
up before sitting.

"Do you play?" he asked.

"No. But I enjoy its music. Shall I pour?"

"You honor me," said Malahki by way of permission and
leaned over the instrument, cradling it in his arms. He began
to stroke its strings vigorously, as if releasing pent up energy.
The melody was a common folk dance, lively and strong, and
sweat dappled the luminary's brow before he finished.

He drained his wineglass in one gulp. He held the empty
glass to the light and looked through it at the wine stained
walls. They were a pale yellow in the night.

"Do I convince you of my appetites?" asked Malahki
abruptly.

If Palaton hadn't cadeted with a few commons, he would
have been startled. The commons hated the stereotype of
coarse, gutter mentality even as they embraced it for its
shock value. But he merely smiled.

"Each Choya to his own," he answered and saluted with his half-empty glass. He would not drink any more for the rest of this meeting, not knowing when he would be called upon to fly. He watched Malahki.

"What was our flaw?"

"Ah, now. That would be telling."

Malahki leaned over his hand-*lindar* to pour himself another glass of wine. "And the flaw was nothing the God-blind could see anyway."

"Partially. Partially it was skill. And partially it was because, no matter how challenged, none of you had made your minds up yet to fire at your own emperor."

"No guts, eh?" Malahki took a deep drink. If the pale amber wine affected him, he didn't show it. He brushed back a stray lock of his deep black hair. "Was the fly-in your idea or Panshinea's?"

"Does it matter?"

"It does. If I knew that Panshinea had suggested it, I might develop some respect for the Fallen Star." Malahki ran a quick bridge across the *lindar* strings. He looked up, catching a flash of something in Palaton's eyes. "Now that surprises you. You've been away, *tezar*, doing heroic things for other worlds. While you've been gone, our emperor has lost a considerable amount of esteem."

Palaton kept his voices smooth. "The Wheel turns. We all know that. Sometimes it seems to creep, at other times to spin."

"Shall I pour you another cup?"

Palaton quickly covered the mouth of his glass. "No, thank you. I've had enough."

"Yes," said Malahki sitting back so quickly the strings of his instrument pinged, "I suppose you think you have." He looked out across the night-darkened courtyard, a much smaller one than where an audience had greeted Palaton earlier. "But we haven't had enough. This is our river, our valley, our land, our homes. We haven't had enough."

"Tell the emperor."

"I have been. All day. I may be just a common, but I sense that Panshinea isn't listening. Relocation is as much a political maneuver as it is an ecological one. We're to be made an example of, to show that he still has his authoritarian grip. Well, *tezar,* that remains to be seen." And Malahki launched into another vigorous musical rendition, punctuating the melody with boot stomps and slaps of his hand against the belly of the instrument.

Palaton listened, hearing the power and the dream and the frustration in the song. He did not dare excuse himself until it was finished lest he miss a nuance or anger the luminary. The wine lingered until only a last, shimmering drop, like a yellow diamond, gleamed at the bottom of his glass.

Rindalan woke him in the morning. The elder Choya gave him a critical look, peered at the whites of his eyes, then said, "You look fit enough to fly."

"Of course I am." He swung his feet off the bed, dressing automatically. "When do we leave?"

"As soon as possible. His Highness and Malahki have been at it since dawn. Panshinea has issued an ultimatum. Now we leave and then we wait."

Palaton paused with one flight boot on and the other dangling from his hand. He heard disapproval in the holy one's voices. "Trouble?"

"Not for you, no. Unless, of course," and Rindalan cleared his throat, "you drank too much last night."

"And you've already given me my preflight clearance on that one." Palaton tugged his boot on. He hefted his flight bag. "I'm ready."

The Prelate led the way, swaying within his robes with the stride of a stately yet careful walker, wary in case his body should suddenly fail him. Palaton followed, shortening his own steps, trying not to overtake the older Choya.

They had no farewell committee. Panshinea waited impatiently with only two of the luminary's aides to protect him, his cheeks flushed with the chill of the morning. The wind had tousled his brilliant hair, nearly obscuring his horn crown. His eyes fixed on Palaton.

"Fit to fly?"

"Always," Rindalan answered for him. "Why such an early start? Are we being kicked out of town?" He held his robes with two fisted hands, a beanpole in the wind, his only belonging the humplike pack on his back.

"In a manner of speaking. Malahki asked for seventy-two

hours, I wanted twenty-four, but I gave him forty-eight."
Panshinea's gleam brightened, with his awareness that the
aides listened to them despite the biting wind. Palaton gave
him half his attention, the other half watching as the crew
fueled and readied the plane. "Forty-eight hours," the emperor repeated, "or I'll declare martial law and Relocation
will be forced."

Palaton never took his eyes from the maintenance crew.
"We'll be ready in moments," he said.

"Good." Panshinea turned, eyeing the panoramic foothills of the river basin valley, ignoring the quiet leave taking
of the two aides. In seconds, they were alone on the airfield.
Palaton waved the crew off. He went over the plane himself
for a last check.

Then he pulled down the small stair and helped Rindalan
mount it. Panshinea sprinted up the steps as if in a hurry
to leave Danbe, and Palaton followed.

The holy one took his seat, breathing heavily. Palaton
looked toward him and raised a brow at his emperor.

"Don't worry," Panshinea said. "Age affects us all." He
followed Palaton into the control pit but did not speak until
he'd ignited the engines for warm-up.

"Can you land this anywhere?"

Palaton looked curiously at his ruler. "It's a war vehicle,"
he said. "It requires quite a length of lane. But if it were
flat enough and long enough. . . ."

"Good. Circle around when you get up. The shields are
off for the moment. I'm betting Malahki will put them up
as soon as our exhaust trail shows. But I want you to
come back. There's a site I want you to put down by, if
you can."

The shield went up almost before they were clear of it.
Palaton climbed, then banked, leaving the vapor trail Panshinea had requested. Then he set up jamming frequencies
and took the plane down, hopefully out of range of the
facilities and instruments of Danbe.

The emperor leaned over his shoulder. "Down there.
See."

Palaton brought his targeting grid up for a closer look.
"It's an industrial complex. Possibly even a crematorium.
It appears deserted."

"Can you get us down there? The abandonment, I'm sure, is temporary."

Gone was the erratic, paranoid emperor. In his stead was a decisive leader. Palaton did not hesitate as the lane swept close. There was a grassy length along the river, possibly muddy, long enough for the plane to land and turn about again for takeoff. He could do the maneuver, though he wasn't entirely sure he wanted to.

"I can do it if it's necessary."

"It's necessary," answered Panshinea. He left the control room for his seat, whistling a classical air, as Palaton took the stinger firmly in hand.

The plane and the river nearly betrayed him. The grassy strip was boggier than he'd anticipated and as the hard brakes came into play, the stinger struggled to spin sideways and down into the river. Palaton fought and kept the plane straight, but his arms were trembling with the effort when it finally stopped. He could hear Panshinea and the Prelate get to their feet, but he called out, "Wait till I've turned about."

"Good idea," Panshinea returned. "We may have to leave in a hurry."

Palaton had enough fuel to leave the engines idling, so he did, but he blocked the wheels before trailing after the emperor and Rindalan. Panshinea bounded across the yard like a child. He headed, not for the complex, but for the crematorium Palaton had targeted earlier. He squatted down, rooting among the ashes and incomplete waste with a river stick.

Rindalan said mildly, "What are you doing, Highness?" His pale blue eyes watered slightly in the chill wind.

"Gathon gathered this bit of intelligence for me." Panshinea looked up from his squat. "This crematorium is illegal and, sadly, inadequate for industrial waste. But we asked ourselves, why did they have it? Why did they want it? What were they attempting to destroy so completely we would never know of it?" The emperor dug up an empty vial which hung to the tip of the stick. "Whatever it was, they shut this down quickly when we flew in. They didn't finish burning. Have we anything for samples?"

The two of them stood there at a loss. Palaton could see even more waste beyond the emperor.

"Rindy, toss out your pills and give me that massive vial you carry about with you. I can get soil and ash samples, at least."

"Majesty, my medicine—I'm at risk without it.

"Palaton will have you back to Charolon in a twitch. Take one now, just in case, and we'll get you more. Come on, Magi. Where's your trust in the God-in-all?"

Rindalan looked sour as he pulled a good-sized bottle from his inner vestment. "The God-in-all helps those who assist themselves," he muttered. He put a tablet under his tongue and then emptied the bottle in a muddy hole before Palaton could offer to keep some of the pills for him. He toed the ash and silt over the tablets before handing the bottle to Panshinea, who promptly filled it.

Palaton pulled his transcripts out of his inner breast pocket and took the protective pouch off them. He returned his private transcriptions to the pocket, took the pouch, and filled it with vials, sediment, and what looked like half-charred computer memory bits. He zipped the pouch shut and pushed it into Panshinea's hand. "This should do it. I suggest we leave, Majesty, before we risk contamination."

Rindalan said heartily, "And I second the suggestion." His lips were pale.

Panshinea took it and stood up. "You don't question me?"

They stood silently. He tilted his head. "Perhaps you do. Ask yourselves why they do not come to the Choosing yet show a *tezar* as much adulation as any Householding. Perhaps they haven't given up on being talented—perhaps they've chosen other methods of achieving it."

"Remnants of the Lost House," Palaton murmured.

"No. Nothing so simple. Genetic experimentation, if Gathon's theory is correct." He lifted the bottle and pouch. "If this shows waste tissue or serum, we'll know why they refuse to abandon Danbe. They're conducting experiments here they cannot leave and cannot reveal."

Rindalan sneezed.

The emperor lost his obsessed expression then, the lines of his face softening. "Come on, Rindy. Let's get you out of the wind." He took the Prelate's arm and led him to the plane.

Palaton trailed after thoughtfully. Genetic experimentation had been outlawed centuries ago, long after the Lost House had destroyed itself with aberrations too horrible to contemplate. Even commons could not be so fearless of the consequences . . . could they? He thought of Malahki's fierce gold eyes and wondered. And then he considered the method within Panshinea's madness and wondered some more.

Chapter 14

Nedar was waiting for them at the airfield. Palaton instantly spotted him among the maintenance crew, just from the arrogant stance, before any other difference set him off. He throttled down for his landing, found his jaw clenched, and forced himself to calmness even as his plane touched the air lane, wheels burning.

The weather at Charolon had taken another turn toward winter. There had been ice on the runway, but the crew had sanded it, and he controlled the minor skid, bringing the stinger in just where he wanted it. He finessed the taxi, shut the plane down, and barreled into the main fuselage. The windows had been curtained and the lounge darkened.

Rindalan lay prone, Panshinea leaning over him, reading a bound text of classic plays, his voices rolling with timber and emotion. The gaunt Prelate looked past the emperor. "Home?"

"At last," Panshinea answered, setting aside his book. "Now you go partake of your medicine and rest in peace."

"God forbid," the holy one said. "I've indigestion from that dose you made me take. Never fix what isn't broken. Still," and his bleared eyes focused on Palaton, "it's good to be home."

Palaton opened the lock and put the stairway down. He waited until the two had gone ahead, did a quick sweep about the cabin to make sure no belongings were left behind, and trotted down.

Nedar had greeted the emperor and the priest and moved on, his palm hovering over the skin of the stinger, just about to stroke it when Palaton grabbed his wrist. The two paused, almost in a dance move, animosity more chill than the dropping air temperature.

"No one," Palaton said, "touches my plane but me."

Nedar smiled widely. "A careful Choya. Still, one wonders why." He twisted his arm quickly, breaking Palaton's hold, and dropped his hand to his side. "A stinger," he commented, looking over the plane. "Nice. The emperor called me out and asked me to be waiting for him."

Palaton didn't answer. He knew what Nedar was doing, using *discernment* to determine where they'd been, and he didn't like it.

Nedar's smile grew more brittle. "There are other ways," he said, and turned away. He quick-marched to catch up with Panshinea, offering to carry his pack and the specimen pouch. If his skills were great enough, that alone would tell him they'd been to Danbe—but not how Palaton had broken the barrier. It was important to Palaton, for a reason he could not explain, that Nedar not know that much about their flight.

A shuttle took them back to Charolon. The two pilots did not talk. Rindalan sagged, his spare figure within his robes looking as if it could fly into pieces at any moment, and Panshinea wore an odd little smile of triumph on his face.

Jorana met them at the side entrance, saying the media communicators had been hounding the palace since late evening and that Gathon advised a statement be made, whether Panshinea wanted to or not.

The emperor said, "Open the conference room, then, and I'll be there as soon as I've talked with Gathon." The lieutenant nodded. Her gaze lingered on Palaton's face as she turned away.

Panshinea dismissed Nedar, then said to Palaton, "The rest of the day is your own. Talk to no one, please, even if the opportunity should arise."

"I understand."

"I wonder," Panshinea returned, tapping a finger against his elegant lips, "if you do." He offered an arm to Rindalan and escorted the Prelate up the public walkway into the palace, leaving Palaton at the mouth of the hidden ingress.

It was cold at the tunnel entrance. The streaked stonework sparkled with the bite of frost here and there, where the morning sun had not touched it. Winter had the capitol building in its ever firming grip. Palaton shrugged into his jacket and went up the secret passageway. Jorana's and Nedar's auras still tarried, marking the trail for him.

He retired to his rooms, found a new pouch for his transcriptions, and made his latest additions. He did not describe Malahki well and did not wonder that it wasn't within his skill to do so. He made a visit to the palace chapel and took a perfunctory seven-step cleansing, but did not feel absolved.

He took dinner alone, watching the rebroadcast of Panshinea's statement. Little was said beyond the fact that representatives of the emperor had met with representatives of Danbe and that a forty-eight hour ultimatum had eventually been declared. Palaton turned the broadcast off, mulling over the ultimatum.

If Malahki's city-state had done the unthinkable, would forty-eight hours be long enough in which to destroy all the evidence before Relocation? Or would they want total destruction? What had they to hide and what might they have accomplished? Younglings who no longer had to attend the Choosing to measure their talents and see if they could be aligned with a House was a matter which could change the entire society of Cho as he knew it. Commons who were no longer God-blind, yet totally uninstructed and unprincipled in their use of their *bahdur* . . . Palaton contemplated chaos. There was no foreseeable way to navigate this future.

What did Malahki see when he looked into it?

Palaton stood restlessly. He went to his windows and saw that the capital city had quieted, stunned by winter's first real blow—snowflakes skirled past the window, muffling all sound and light. Streetlights illumined the clouds of snow drifting into the city. It hadn't been snowing long—the dirty black stonework shone through its cloaking. Palaton watched the storm. It should snow most of the night. He felt its chill and shrugged into a fleecy pullover.

He did not feel like sleeping. Palaton consulted the palace directory and found what he was looking for. He left his apartment to begin what looked to be a long convoluted walk. He found his thoughts haunted by children—those of Danbe, and those of the humankind who'd once asked for his help, and the one which Jorana said she'd wanted from him.

Children were the future. Children without heritage or knowledge of their potential and without the training to

help them achieve that potential . . . His own issue would
not know its destiny, and he could not conceive with Jorana
without revealing his own lost past. Sexual liaisons were
one sweetness, bonding to reproduce another, and one
which he'd denied himself. It hadn't been difficult earlier
but now he was in his prime and others about him were
making that commitment. He owed it to his House and to
the *tezar*s, for his line bred strongly, and fresh talent for
his strenuous profession was always needed. Always.

But even though Jorana spoke of releasing her fertility,
he didn't think he could release his. He did not have the
love and trust in her that he needed before he could reveal
himself. Her beauty did not hide her ambition. Her advice
to trust no one, he feared, applied to herself as well.

With Darb's death between them, he didn't know how
long he could deny her. The more hidden the second's
death remained, the more doubt there would be to cloud
the issue. He had done something which he couldn't undo
and which shrouded his own future. Perhaps today it was
still not too late. Perhaps.

Palaton stumbled within his thoughts, looked up, and
found himself at the private exhibition galleries of Charolon, the end of his journey. Inside the palace security system, the gallery remained unlocked, though the doors were
closed. Security scans did not track his progress.

He asked admittance and it was given him.

The artwork was incredible. He stood inside the threshold, the night suddenly given light and depth by the works
displayed for his viewing. After long moments, he wove his
way through the sculptures and mobiles, past the pictures
and projections, until he reached the tapestries and wall
hangings. There, the tapestry his mother had woven drew
him inexorably.

He marveled at the detail, at the threadings, woven and
then embroidered over. The panorama drew him in until
he found himself examining it minutely—and then knew
what it was he searched for.

He had dreamed, or been sent, that moment. A single
drop of blood glistening on her slender fingers. Would
Tresa allow it to mar the work, signifying an artist's pain
and struggle, or would she not? In his dream, she had put
her finger to her lips . . . but now, as he drew close and

looked, he saw the rusty-brown stain, as transparent as a teardrop, marring the threads.

In the years since her death, he'd thought his dream was only memory reawakened, surfacing out of his grief. Now he was riveted to the spot, unaware of where he stood or what he knew. The incident had to have been a sending and in it the artist had changed her mind and not allowed her work to be stained. A second chance. Palaton put a fingertip to it in wonder.

That portion of the embroidery showed the Great Wheel in Chaos above Cho, balanced upon its threaded turning the three Houses of Sky, Star, and Earth, depicted both in ethereal terms and with the more concrete symbols of each stitched in. The Wheel hung above Cho, rising.

Or, as he looked at it, perhaps crashing, diving into the flames of Cho which had birthed it.

Palaton stared for a long time. What had flames to do with the Houses of his people? This was not a classical representation of the birth of the Houses and he was not of a mind to understand his mother's artistic interpretation. And yet that tiny bloodstain upon the Wheel had captured his attention. Was there a message written here that only he might see and understand? Had she yet things to tell to him, to reveal?

"I'm incomplete, Mother," he whispered to the hanging. "You left me that way and because of it, I can't hear what you're trying to tell me." He dropped his hand to his side.

The staccato of bootheels upon the flooring outside the gallery caught his attention. Palaton turned, made his way to the open door, and slid it nearly shut, unwilling to be seen. His horn crown prickled with intuition.

The gallery lights dimmed. He watched through his narrow avenue of sight as the walkers came his way, one brisk, the other stumbling, slurred or reluctant. They came into view and Palaton caught his breath.

Jorana, and a young Choya, barely out of his childhood, eyes glazed, hanging upon her escort. Palaton felt his nose flare slightly, but he could detect no drug or alcohol upon the youth. From the coarseness of his horn crown, Palaton guessed him to be a common.

The Choya gave a convulsive jerk, pulling out of the lieutenant's hold, and he fell, taking her with him. Drool splattered the floor beneath his head and he stayed down, mumbling into the tiles. Jorana cursed, got to her knees and tried to shoulder lift him up. His weight was too much for her.

Palaton stepped out of the gallery. "Can I help you?"

Startled, her eyes went wide, then narrowed. "Of all wrong places for you to be in. Get out of here, Palaton."

He bent to bring the youth to his feet anyway. The Choya appeared stupefied. His mouth stayed slack and he had no idea where he was, or with whom. "What happened?"

"No questions. None." Jorana shouldered the limp form. "Please."

He knew then, for he could suddenly feel the aura taint. This youth had none of his own, sucked out of him like a dried fruit, but an oily overcoating slicked him and Palaton knew whose it was.

Panshinea.

The emperor has his own diversions, she'd told him. Like stealing the *bahdur* from the innocent and defenseless? The rape of a soul unable to defend itself? She saw his eyes and said, "God-in-all. You *know.* How could you?"

"How could I not? Where are we going?"

"I'm getting him out of here and you're going back to your apartment. It's your life. Get out of here while you can."

He hesitated a moment longer. He lifted a stray tress of hair from her eyes, so that she could see better. It was soft beneath his fingers. "How could you let him do this?"

Her lips tightened. "It keeps him going," she said. "A small evil weighed against many . . . I don't know. Now get out of here before you're found. I'll come to you later." Struggling to balance the youth's weight she brushed past him.

Palaton looked up. He'd noticed the corridors had no immediate scans. Now he knew why.

It was more important to protect the emperor's secrecy than hundreds of years of artwork.

He took a deep breath and left.

True to her word, she came to him in those last, still hours before dawn, when all Choyan slept deeply and the souls of the weak often slipped quietly away.

But he was not weak, and he did not sleep, and he was on his feet the moment the door began to open.

The gold and silver traceries under the translucence of her face underscored bruises of fatigue. Her gray-blue eyes held the traces of tears recently shed. She carried a carafe of fresh-brewed *bren* in one hand and two mugs in the other.

He drew her in and shut the door firmly.

"For your information," she whispered, "the security recording of this sector has been temporarily disabled."

She trembled with weariness as she sat down at the small round table by the window. She drew the curtaining back. "It's finally stopped snowing," she said.

Her hands were chill when she handed him his drink. She'd obviously been out in it.

Palaton mulled over the various things he could say to her, but before he could voice them, she said, "Darb's body was found earlier tonight. It's been established that salvagers killed him. The cold snap froze his body down and exact time of death couldn't be established." She sipped at her *bren*. "You're lucky."

"And I shouldn't press the fates."

"No. I don't think you should."

"Then I won't ask what you did with the Choya."

"Good." She looked back out the window. There were damp streaks in her bronze hair where snow had melted. "I couldn't tell you anyway, except that he'll be all right. His talents . . . what there were of them . . . have been bled. He was, and still is, a common."

"But talented enough to infuse our emperor. How close to being Housed was he? Were any of them?"

Her gaze flickered. "Close," she said. "It was Gathon's idea. I think if Rindalan found out, he'd break all ties with Panshinea. That, in itself, might bring the throne down. We can't afford that now. We can't afford for the failings of one Star to be interpreted as the failing of the entire House." She rested her mug on the table.

He reached across and cupped her hand. "How long has your family been Housed?"

"I'm the first." A certain fierceness and pride underlined her voices.

He should have been surprised, but wasn't. Some of the

new converts fought more fiercely to preserve their birthright than the old, established lines. He could sympathize with her, but not with the emperor. "Panshinea has to be stopped."

"No! He has to be cured."

"There's no cure for the neuropathy. It can be slowed or even remitted, but there's no going back."

"He doesn't think so—" Jorana stopped abruptly. She drew her hands out of his reach "The more I tell you, the more danger I put you in."

"All right." Palaton rocked back in his chair. The *bren* felt good in his throat, warming as it sank to his stomach. "I've enough for balance."

"Balance? Oh . . . Darb." Jorana half-smiled. "How quickly you fit into palace politics."

"No," he said. "How quickly a pilot learns about updrafts and downdrafts."

"How to stay aloft."

He shook his head slightly. "Not quite." He watched her shiver despite her warm drink. He put his cup down and extended his hand once again. "I've a better way to warm you."

Sudden hope arrowed through her expression, then dimmed as she read the look in his eyes. "No promises," she said for him.

"No promises."

Jorana rose, taking his hand and pressing it to her throat. Her pulse drummed wildly under his touch. "For the moment, that's good enough." She came to him a second time.

Chapter 15

Sun streaming in the window woke him. Palaton blinked at its brightness, then realized that it was near noonday, and the light reflected from the snowfields about Charolon. He rubbed a watering eye and sat up, sheets tangling about his hips.

Jorana murmured and moved away from him, settling into the warm hollow he'd left behind. Her face had gone soft with sleep, peaceful and content. He put out the back of his hand to caress her cheek, then froze in mid-movement.

She shouldn't still be in his bed.

Palaton paused, thinking. She slept with abandonment, without worry over duty or work. Either she was off-duty . . . or part of her duty was to be with him.

He didn't think she would have revealed seeing him last night before meeting him. No, she'd been too genuinely worried about that. Therefore, that incident did not affect her coming to him. If it had, if she'd worried about implications, she would not have seen him last night.

Palaton pulled his hand back. He got out of bed carefully so as not to disturb her and went in to bathe quickly. He dressed in his high altitude flights, warm even in this winter aftermath, and pulled on his boots. The image of Nedar meeting him at the airfield, attempting to discern their whereabouts, and the knowledge that the emperor had called him out, nagged at Palaton.

There was no need for Nedar if Palaton had been chosen as Panshinea's pilot. Unless there were jobs that Nedar would do that Palaton would not.

Such as leading in a military force through Danbe's shields before the forty-eight hour ultimatum had expired.

Palaton snatched his jacket off its hook. He left his apartment at a run. He'd known he wouldn't be privy to whatever the labs had found in the samples they'd brought back, any more than he'd be privy to Panshinea's economic councils. He was a pilot, nothing more.

But if he'd been used to thread the needle, to find the fatal flaw in Danbe's shielding so that Nedar could later destroy it, that was his business. It was his skill which was being perverted, skill that Nedar couldn't quite match. Not only was Panshinea making a mistake, he was compounding it by using the ambitious Sky to do it. Whatever public opinion would later review these actions, Nedar would twist to his advantage.

He left through the public entrance, wide steps sanded so that the snow and ice would not prove a danger. Media communicators littered the vast staircase, muttering about the emperor canceling public meetings again. Where was Panshinea this noon?

At the airfield, watching his police enforcers take off. Palaton snagged an empty conveyance, programmed it, and skimmed off with no one noticing him.

The abandoned airfield was abandoned no longer, a hub of activity, the winter day streaked with vapor trails from the planes taking off, the air whining with their propulsion. Nedar must already have been gone, spearheading the flights.

He found Panshinea alone at the edge of the air lane, his furred coat flapping about him. He left the conveyance and approached the emperor.

Panshinea's green eyes widened at his approach. The emperor smiled wryly.

"Gathon told me you would know."

"I should have known sooner." Palaton breathed deeply in regret.

"And you would have stopped me?"

"Yes."

The emperor hummed to himself. He shoved his hands deep into pockets. "You can't save me from myself, *tezar*."

"Somebody should."

Their attention was drawn by a stinger screaming to become airborne overhead and winging away. Palaton's horn crown still rang with the noise when Panshinea said, "We found genetic waste. All we feared was in those samples we took. I won't use that as an excuse, of course. Too much panic if we revealed it. We'll call it toxic industrial contamination, necessitating immediate removal and Relocation. It's for their own good. Malahki will fight at first, and when he's lost, he'll have saved face. He won't reveal it either. And he'll have to bury his experiments even deeper underground next time. We'll add years to his schedule, perhaps even discourage him altogether."

"Should he be discouraged?"

Panshinea looked away from the sky, meeting his gaze face to face. "Let me tell you something you won't have learned as a child from your history books. Let me tell you something most Choyan don't admit under any circumstances. There is no Lost House. We destroyed it, we Stars, Skies, and Earthans. The House of Flame, it was thought to have birthed all of us, but we destroyed it. Why? For doing much as Malahki was doing for the commons. We gave back the talents of healing, because a Flame could poison as well as heal. They meddled where no one, not even the God-in-all, should meddle. And there's not an emperor along the way who regretted the decision. Not even me. Not even if a Flame could have healed me." Panshinea shrugged defiantly into the wind.

It tasted of afterburn. Palaton looked around, then back at the emperor. He thought of his mother's artwork. The Great Wheel . . . descending or ascending . . . from a bed of flames on Cho. Had she known of the annihilation? "How . . . long ago?"

"Centuries. Before modern civilization. Oh, I don't doubt there's a stray or two out there—even the commons have talents there's no accounting for—but they'll not come back. We scourge them if we find one. We don't miss them much. Science makes up for miracles. But we've strict ethics for our technological community, rules which Malahki has chosen to ignore. He'll pay for that. Maybe enough that he'll hesitate to do it again. If not, he'll go the way of the Lost House. You've my word on that."

Panshinea looked up sharply. He must have felt Palaton's slight wince. The emperor showed his teeth in a half-smile. "My word not good enough for you?"

"I said nothing."

"An honest Choya doesn't need to. It's etched all over

you, my Palaton. I can't keep you, now. You refuse too steadfastly to be corrupted by me. You would destroy yourself trying to save me. Not physically, as the others are doing, but morally. I'm not worth it. An incorruptible *tezar* is worth far more than a corrupted emperor. We've contacted Moameb at Blue Ridge. He's got a contract for you. You'll take it, of course."

"And if I don't?"

Panshinea studied him. "You would give up flying."

"Not voluntarily."

"That doesn't matter to me. The *bahdur* flickers in every *tezar* sooner or later. No one would dispute our word that you're done for, burned out, dying."

"Blue Ridge would."

The chill of the winter morn had brought a harsh flush to the emperor's handsome face. He half-turned from Palaton. "You cannot fight me." His breath fogged in the air. "There is always some secret, some price too high to pay. Don't make me search for yours, Palaton."

But as yet his secret remained hidden, or Panshinea would have revealed it to him. Given the choice of flying or not, he would fly. At least he was being given that option. He did not show the relief he felt. "All right, Highness. If you wish it."

"I wish it." Something gleamed deep in his green eyes. "Or do you wish to stay and save me?"

"I'd save you . . . if I could."

"Then look and listen, *tezar*. Not even Gathon knows this, nor my devoted Rindy. Somewhere out there, someone knows how to renew *bahdur*. Not my poor, perverted way, but someone who knows what they do. The last emperor had begun to track them down, but they've grown canny. Find them for me, Palaton. Find them for me and save us all. Even yourself," and the emperor put a hand out and grasped his wrist, a chill band of iron. "It flickers in you as well. I know it. I've seen it in your eyes. Save yourself as well as me. Find out how they do it. Promise me."

His touch chilled Palaton to the bone, and he was struck speechless, unable to answer. Finally, he was able to force a single nod.

* * *

Jorana never suggested she should go with him. She watched him pack, his luggage as spare as always.

"I'll try to get him to bring you back."

"I don't want to come back." Palaton fastened a strap. He paused. "I want to fly Chaos."

"He's given you a garbage run!"

"For now. He could have had me killed for what I know. It wouldn't be the first time someone has tried."

Jorana blushed faintly. She put a hand on her hip. "It may be seasons before we meet again . . ."

"And maybe then I'll be ready to give what I can't today." He offered her that slim hope.

"Crumbs?" she said, her voices light.

"No. Not for you." Palaton hoisted his duffel. "Perhaps Nedar—"

She struck him. Not hard, but his cheek stung. His eyes blurred with sympathetic pain, then cleared.

Jorana hissed, "If the emperor's not good enough for me, why would you offer Nedar?"

Slowly, he said, "You've got high standards."

Jorana collected herself. She opened the door and paused in the threshold. "You could lose yourself, if you tried."

"Should I try?"

Her eyes sparkled too brightly. "No. Please."

"Then I won't. I'll come back to Cho, to my home at Blue Ridge. You'll be able to find me if you want to." He passed by her.

She whispered, "Thank you."

Palaton was waiting for shuttle assignment to Blue Ridge, looking forward to seeing Moameb, when he noticed a security crowd forming. At the end of the port, he saw diplomatic signs being flashed and then a large conveyance pulled up. Through the scanwalls, an Abdrelik could be seen moving with that odd, lumbering grace that defied gravity.

Palaton thought wryly that GNask had fallen from Panshinea's grace at about the same time he had. He ignored the furor in the Charolon port and turned back to what he had in hand, reading.

GNask cast a large shadow over him. He smelled boggy and his symbiont made a litany of slurping noises before lapsing into sudden silence as if the Abdrelik had somehow hushed a noisy watch animal. His guards, Choyan and Abdrelik alike, remained a discreet distance away.

"Well. Shipping out, *tezar*?"

Palaton looked up. The Abdrelik showed his tusky smile. "Ambassador. It appears so. But I'm going cross-country while you're outbound."

"Too bad we can't share accommodations, eh?" GNask laughed. His bulk jellied in response. "I hear you turned down Panshinea's generous offer of employment."

"I prefer deep space. Most *tezars* do."

"That's what you're bred and trained for. Or so I hear." GNask lowered himself onto a table instead of a chair, his weight being more suited for it. "Myself, I abhor the travel. I am thankful my job rarely calls for it."

"Going home?"

"Back to Sorrow. Regrettably, not home. And you?"

"I've a new assignment." Palaton watched the ambassador mildly, feeling the probes in his questions.

"Nasty business in Danbe."

"So I hear."

GNask scratched his whiskery, rubbery underchin. "Colonization would ease the strain of such incidences. You Choyan manage your population admirably, but the land does wear out. A new planet, new lands—the future could be vast."

Palaton made no comment. He knew the Abdrelik was aware of the Choyan position on colonization. He said, "I wish you a comfortable trip."

"And I wish you a fulfilled destiny," GNask replied ironically in passable Choyan. "You saved my life once. I am disposed to thank you for it. My security force has given me a small parcel. It would be . . . awkward . . . to try to remove it through outbound customs. However, I think it might be appropriate to leave it to you. I am done with the material." He took a pouch and gave it to Palaton before rising and making his way down the terminal, security force in tow like some nebulous train of fabric trailing behind him. Palaton watched him go.

The ambassador knew, or shrewdly guessed, of the dissent over Danbe. Perhaps Gathon, Rindalan, and even Jorana did best to keep Panshinea in power. A civil war on

Cho would bring the Abdreliks swooping in like carrion scavengers, eager to pick the Choyan apart for their secrets.

He went to a privacy cubicle before opening the pouch. It was diplomatically sealed and Palaton knew that probably the Abdrelik would not have been challenged on its contents. Whatever awkwardness there would be in carrying it through was in GNask's imagination.

The first item in his hand froze his heart in mid-beat. Palaton stood and looked at the missive. It had been reconstructed from partially burned paper and Palaton knew why the Abdrelik hadn't kept it—it was not admissible as evidence in any court. Reconstructions were too dubious, to subject to forgery. But this was Choyan in a way the Abdrelik probably wouldn't even be able to recognize and so Palaton didn't doubt its authenticity.

It was the Earthan directive to Darb to have him killed. It was from his House and his Householding, brief and simple and without explanation other than that it was work which had to be done for the greater good of all Cho. Palaton's heart stumbled back into a normal rhythm. He steeled himself to empty the rest of the pouch's contents onto the viewing vestibule.

There was a tiny, crystal vial of poison, a single injection. The tag on it was in Abdrelikan, but the label was in Choyan. It was, he saw, addressed to him. With it was a small note, bearing the crest of his Householding. It said: "Save yourself. Deal with Panshinea."

Palaton handled the fragile vial gingerly. If it had been sent to him, he'd never gotten it. He fingered the note with his grandfather's embossed seal. The aura was too faint, too corrupted by Abdrelik stink, to read. How, by the God-in-all, had the Abdreliks gotten it? And what did it mean? Had it been meant for him, or merely been rigged to appear as though it had been meant for him?

The last item was another bottle, small and intricate. He curled his fingers around it, caught by the perfumed memory, the aura too powerful for even the Abdreliks to muddy it. Jorana. Runes were etched into the glass, naming it, with instructions on how to employ it. He placed it on the vestibule tabletop next to the poison, for it was as insidious. He'd heard about such concoctions, had often wondered if they existed, and now he had the proof before him.

It was an aphrodisiac. If he had not left, if he had still insisted on not releasing his fertility, she would have stolen it from him.

He didn't know if such drugs worked, but Jorana had evidently been willing to take the chance. He put a fingertip to the bottle, rolling it along its side. The faintly purple liquid inside foamed a little as it stirred. He wondered only if the Abdreliks had retrieved this from its hiding place in her room—or in his.

The dual fertility of Choyan partners made accidental pregnancies and sexual politics damn near impossible. Had his mother been so compromised or had she planned what she had done to give birth to him? Was he crossed outside his House or perhaps even with commons blood . . . or had he been stolen from her body, though she never gave him up to the thief who had conceived him with her?

Trust no one. Palaton activated the incinerator in the vestibule and, one by one, he destroyed the three items with all their implications. What motive the Abdrelik had in giving them to him, he couldn't be sure. He was only certain it hadn't been gratitude. He also knew that when he left Cho this time, he couldn't look back. The emperor had given him temporary exile. Palaton would be wise to flee as far as he could.

A call for boarding his shuttle flashed, repeated in audio. Palaton hoisted his duffel and crossed the terminal in answer. He looked forward to the peace of Chaos.

PART II
Burnout

Chapter 16

"We're being tracked," the Ivrian said, hovering about his sling in agitation, wings blurring, his eyes all pupil, iris a bright ring about a well of darkness.

"I've got it," Palaton answered smoothly. He watched his screen. "Ronin or maybe even Abdrelik. They're waiting." He sat back in his chair. The control room illumination cut sharp planes into his face. "This is a strange region to be playing these games in."

Both knew the tracker was attempting to plot the workings of the *tezarian* drive, even if on a very limited basis. Palaton had not had a tracker in years. His palms itched now, before he placed them over the control board. It would do no good for the tracker to trail them into Chaos, but they never learned. Even the Ivrian navigator/copilot at his side would be banished from the control room before he pulsed the engines into FTL, and once into Chaos, only another *tezar* would have the remotest chance of finding them.

Palaton licked dry lips. "They're anxious to lose another ship."

Rainbow left his hammock chair and advanced to Palaton's flank. "He wishes secrets," the Ivrian hissed.

"And you don't," Palaton answered wryly. He looked over his shoulder in amusement.

Rainbow stretched his back in discomfort. His pupils pinpointed. "Nevertheless," the alien said.

The Ivrians had achieved a limited short run success in Chaos piloting, the best of any of the other races. Rainbow had been the thorn in his side as well as his copilot for the duration of this contract, spying as much as aiding, and both knew the Ivrian's purposes. If there were a secret to be found here, Rainbow undoubtedly felt he'd earned it, and he resented the usurper plotting their present course.

"It doesn't matter."

"To you, perhaps," Rainbow said sulkily. He withdrew to his acceleration sling over his control board and moodily watched the screens.

Palaton laid in his final course before he reached the sector where he would complete acceleration into Chaos. When that moment came, the Ivrian would be banished from the room as well. It did not matter how trivial, how unimportant the run—and this one was just to release several barges of toxic waste into the sun of the nearby system—he would not ignore his procedures.

The tracker grew bold, came close, and knew it must surely have been picked up by their instruments. Palaton watched it, knowing he would lead the vehicle to its death, and wondering how to discourage it.

Rainbow continued to pout. "Tell them to go away," the alien muttered.

The idea had merit. Palaton opened a comline, searched around for a suitable frequency, then hailed the vehicle.

The answer came back swiftly and smoothly. "*Tezar* Nedar, it is our pleasure to meet again."

Palaton paused carefully. Chaos patterns did not often intersect, but Nedar must be in the region somewhere. He hadn't had a meeting with his fellow pilot for years. Nedar had been in the emperor's graces little longer than Palaton. He looked to Rainbow. "Is there a war nearby?"

The Ivrian shrugged. A few gauzy feathers drifted down from the gesture. "Always. Somewhere."

Palaton put himself on-line again. "I beg your pardon, but you are not communicating with *Tezar* Nedar. This is *Tezar* Palaton. Please keep your distance. I'm on a waste run and contamination is possible."

A static of confusion followed his information. The link cut off sharply. He watched his grid, saw the ship rapidly gaining ground, all coyness gone. Were they approaching to confirm contact . . . or to eliminate an awkward witness? Or worse, were they on a covert capture mission, an attempt to take apart a ship with *tezarian* drive just to find out what made it tick? Such subterfuges were usually done in wartime runs, where lost ships could be explained more easily. If so, that also explained why they thought they were contacting Nedar. These were games no Choyan could afford to play.

"Rainbow, go secure in the secondary cabin."

"But Palaton—"

"Get out of here. We're going into FTL now."

The Ivrian flew from the control room, leaving a trail of dust motes and fine feathers swirling in his wake. Palaton swung about only long enough to determine that the Ivrian had indeed left.

The ship vibrated in answer to his abrupt demands on it. The barges in tow pulled dully in response, dragging them down.

The Ivrian's shrill voice came over the intercom. "Palaton, they're arming."

"I see it."

"We're well within range."

"I see that, too." His eyes, his hands were busy, playing the ship for all it was worth. The instrument augmentation had only one real advantage over conventional FTL drives—it was incredibly responsive. He set it up now and then waited for the final kick into FTL.

It came with a blur of color and a ringing of noise. He sat back in his chair and watched the aura-light of relativity go momentarily haywire, then collect itself again. Before he blacked the view screen down, he stared out a moment and let the sight of Chaos make his senses reel like the most heady of wines. Then the shield went dark, protecting him.

Rainbow's voice jarred. "We've lost them."

"No," murmured Palaton quietly, too low for the intercom to pick up. "They've lost themselves."

If they'd enough sense, they could pull back and drop out of Chaos, emerging in a region of space they could not chart for, but most likely emerging clear. They would probably even emerge in known space, although at some distance from where Chaos had been entered. But the longer they remained in Chaos, the more likelihood there was of destruction. Palaton felt sadness but not remorse. They had known what they were doing, though why they had hailed him as Nedar. . . .

The run through this brew of Chaos would be short. Palaton set a timer, pulled out a book of poetry and began to read, ignoring the Ivrian's attempt to plot random motion, voicing frustration over the intercom.

He had nearly finished the volume when his timer sounded. His panel surged back into life, flashing with color. The instruments gave him a confusion of readings, unable to cope with what they attempted to measure by normal methods. He looked instead at the Choyan panel, saw a few more coherent readings, and took a deep breath. Instead, he looked for the diffuseness within Chaos, the pattern that was not a pattern called the Butterfly, and one he likened to the Singing Choya'i. His *bahdur* burned when he called on it, giving him the sight to see with, the hands to steer with. He sought the sun which would act as the attractor within this random shape, found it and, with reluctance, left the spaceway of the Singing Choya'i, her neck in a graceful stretch as she no doubt sang the praises of the God-in-all.

He decelled the ship rapidly, not wanting to lose his advantage, and as the normal instrumentation leapt into valid readings free of Chaos' confusion, he saw he'd done well. He pulled the ship into alignment with the sun and said to Rainbow, "Find me a trajectory to drop the barges off. I don't want to go in too far."

"Just drop them and run, eh?" Rainbow answered.

"I'm tired," said Palaton and suddenly knew he was. He closed his volume of poetry, returning it to the recessed bookcase in the cabin, and sat back in his chair. His brow ached just below his horn crown and he put a hand up, massaging it absently as he leaned over the large grid-panel control board. Rainbow read back a decaying orbit passage to him and he okayed it. There was nothing to endanger here, this was a barren solar system, and the sun would annihilate the cargo he delivered to it.

Rainbow confirmed the release of the barges and Palaton banked the ship out of their pathway. He felt, rather than saw, their journey past, large, shadowy, indeterminately evil things looming and then gone. He stretched his hands over his control board again. "Let's go home," he said.

He would be bored but for the danger. Chaos challenged him now. The more he piloted the more complicated it grew, gathering offenses from his past mistakes, it seemed, all minor and yet gathering momentum until the day he would make that miscalculation which he could not save or undo. Pilot paranoia, the *tezars* called it, and anyone who flew enough had it. Unfortunately, it was not an imaginary paranoia. Sooner or later Chaos would claim any without sufficient *bahdur* to traverse it . . . claim them or drive them out of its turmoil forever.

It was a bottomless grave into which he would some-day sink.

Palaton blinked, found his hands shaking, and clenched them quickly. "FTL acceleration on my mark," he got out to the Ivrian in the secondary control room.

Rainbow acknowledged. Palaton signaled the engines, felt the swoop of response to acceleration and, just as his horn crown began to ache with the speed, they entered Chaos.

The moment his shield went dark, he knew they were not alone. He thought of the Ronin tracker, but the aura approaching him was entirely different. Palaton wavered in confusion, then steeled himself.

He'd caught the edge of it; a psychic backlash of confusion and pain and hopelessness. He wondered if perhaps it had bled out of Chaos into the barren solar system, for it mirrored the dark feelings he'd had just before accelera-tion. He was intersecting paths with another *tezar*, a Choyan in crisis.

Palaton made whatever course adjustments he could, then sat back and opened his mind, scanning, reaching out to the pilot-in distress. His *bahdur* scattered sparks of hope into the darkness like a crown of fire radiating from his core. *Come to me . . . center on me . . . reach out . . .*

The miasma sucked it in, greedily, as though the darkness itself fed on his energy, but he knew it did not. But it was frenetic energy that diffused his own. He redoubled his efforts, throwing out a psychic lifeline. Behind his closed eyelids, he could see it, a golden rope that, caught by the maelstrom of Chaos, spiraled and then convoluted into pat-terns he could no longer watch.

The effort left him open to the backlash of despair from the lost one. Palaton caught his breath sharply as it lanced through him, leaving a yawning gap as though it had clawed his insides out. It left him panting in pain, sweat stippling his face as it ran down.

He thought, for a split-second, of saving himself and abandoning the Choya in trouble. He rejected that thought as soon as it emerged, knew a fleeting second of shame for having birthed it, and then shoved that out as well. He had no time for self-doubt. Still in pain, he loosened another burst of *bahdur*, felt it staining the universe as it washed out of him, and prayed it would find the soul he searched for.

A willow wisp of a touch. Brazen, Palaton extended himself again. It was like a fleeting vision at the edge of his range. Smoky, indistinct. He wondered now if it were indeed another Choya he endeavored to help. Could it be the Ronin ship he'd misled earlier? But those thoughts didn't matter even as Palaton thought them. He would give whatever aid he could to the lost. He unraveled his talent again and tossed it forth, watching it disappear into Chaos faster than a spider drops webbing strands. It wove into a gossamer pattern, then disappeared from sight.

His face and neck were now drenched in sweat. Focused within himself as he was, he could feel the warm stream running across the planes of his cheekbones, his chin. His hands trembled where they rested over his knees. His heartbeat felt enlarged, vibrating his sternum as it pulsed. He forced himself to breathe steadily before he looked back into the void.

Contact! The other grasped at him, gulping down *bahdur* as though it were a hot cup of *bren*, sucking it out of him so quickly Palaton gasped. His fingers knuckled into his legs in reaction. The other would strip him dry and they'd both be lost! Palaton anchored himself. He put up blocks the other hammered away, desperately, a drowning Choya like some cadet in a deprivation helmet. He fought to keep himself from being turned inside out.

The lost one slowed, weakening again, and then Palaton had it, his aura, knew who the Choya was. *Nedar.*

He realized he'd known it all along—that the Ronin had tipped him to Nedar's presence in the sector and that no one else could have been expected—but the shock chilled through him anyway. Nedar, burned out and adrift in Chaos.

Nedar. Follow me.

There was an angry strike of recognition as Nedar realized who his feeder was. Then Nedar pushed away, a rejection, as physical as a violent shove. But Palaton could no more leave the Choya adrift then he could have Moameb or Hat. He entreated, baiting the plea with *bahdur* aura, knowing the other would bolt toward it instinctively before he could think or react otherwise. Survival would draw him after.

And Nedar did come, reluctantly, taking the bait, the bright energy extended to him, hungrily, like a starving man, hating himself for doing it and unable to stop himself.

The Ivrian interrupted his silent struggle. "*Tezar* Palaton. Are you all right?"

A struggle to speak. The cords of his neck extended. The weight of his horn crown felt oppressive, as though he could not hold it. He mopped his slick face. "I'm fine, Rainbow. But I'm busy."

"Yes," the Ivrian answered, his affirmative sounding apologetic. "It's just that I thought—I thought it was time to emerge."

Palaton quickly spun out a second inquiry, of discernment, finding their location in Chaos. The Ivrian was right—he'd overshot his exit window, but that mattered little in Chaos. He could repattern to double back and did so, panting again from the exertion, as though he ran through the void instead of flew. He found a new window and headed the plane toward it, Nedar still in tow.

Suddenly Nedar blazed, his *bahdur* rekindled, and Palaton felt him peel away in confidence, surging deeper into Chaos and out of touch.

Palaton felt emptied, alone, abandoned, used. He shook himself, knowing that it was the other's nature. He said to Rainbow, "Prepare for decel," and, found himself aching in every fiber, as he came fully back to himself, and wondered how close Nedar had come to draining him. He should leave it alone but knew he would not. He could not.

He found Nedar at base, sitting in one of the quiet bars that only Choyan frequented, being more like a chapel in its solemnity than a public house. The Choya looked up as he entered. His dark eyes smoldered.

Nedar wasn't quartered at this base, but he'd had no choice about where to land. He probably couldn't have flown much further. Palaton had known that Nedar, for the moment, couldn't get out of his reach. He approached the table.

Before Palaton could sit, his classmate said, "I won't hear it from you."

"From Moameb? Would you hear it from Moameb?"

Nedar stabbed a finger at him. His complexion had paled, setting off his facial jewelry in harsh tracings. "I overflew my boundaries. It happens." There were tiny lines about his eyes, harsh ones at the corners of his mouth, etched in by age, making his expression severe as well as handsome.

"The pain . . ."

"There is none. I haven't got it yet. I just overstepped my bounds." Nedar curled his hand back around his glass. He looked into the depths of his drink as if he could divine the future in it. Being a Choya, perhaps he could.

Palaton pulled a chair out and sat. "A visit home. A cleansing at Blue Ridge. . . ."

"Where you'd have Moameb waiting for me, waiting to counsel me, telling me being grounded isn't so difficult?" Nedar let out a single harsh laugh. "When's the last time you were home, Palaton? Have you seen the wasted rack you took flying lessons from?" Nedar leaned intently over the table. "For now, *flying is all I've got*. I won't let you or anyone take it away."

"Any time you contract, you represent all of Cho, all of the *tezars* who pilot."

"Any time I contract, I'm fulfilling my destiny. I move forward. You should try it." Nedar tossed back the rest of his drink. He signaled the automatic innkeep for a refill. His breath hazed in the air between them. "If you want thanks, I give them to you. Thanks, my Palaton, for coming to my rescue during a moment of extreme fatigue. Now go away and leave me. There is no cleansing for the likes of us." Nedar pinned him with his intense gaze. "For any of us."

Palaton blinked. The vague memory of Panshinea gripping him at the airfield, telling lies for absolution, held him. Someone, somewhere, knows what they do. They know how to renew *bahdur*. How many *tezars* had the emperor driven into exhaustion and into the void, looking for miracles that did not exist? He was amazed that Nedar would have listened.

He still felt the yawning emptiness feeding power to Nedar had given him, but unlike the other, he did not seek to numb it. He stood up.

"What did the emperor say to you?"

Nedar's gaze sharpened. "What did he say to you?"

"He told me to leave."

Nedar laughed again, bitterly. "He begged me to stay. He begged me to stay so that he could break me, see the look in my eyes as year after year I grew no closer to the throne I coveted." He threw his chin up. "Do you know what you are called at home? The 'hero in exile.' The word got around that you tried to stop the massacre at Danbe, that you stood up against the emperor himself. No one talks about the fact that you laid down a *bahdur* trail so that I could follow it in and annihilate their shields. No one murmurs that you were used by the emperor. No one knows the truth."

Palaton felt his jaws tighten. "And neither, it appears, do you."

"I know a lie when I hear one. Perhaps you haven't listened to enough lies. There is a mockery holding the throne at Charolon. If I find a cure, I won't be extending it to him."

"We do what we do because we are driven by our own desires. If Panshinea sent you out and you went, you're the fool. You keep saying boundaries to me, and I wonder what you know of limits. I intersected a Ronin ship which was lying in wait for you. If it had found you in this condition, we would have lost both the ship and a pilot. I don't need to tell you what the Ronin do to pilots if they can, do I?"

Nedar cupped his refilled glass. "The Ronin have been vivisecting Choyan for decades. They still don't know what we are or what we can do."

"All it takes is one, Nedar. One craven coward who talks instead. One coward who has already reached his limits and hasn't the strength to resist."

"I'm not a coward!" Nedar shoved himself to his feet.

"Neither are you a realist." Palaton held steady. "Get some rest. Go back to base. Abort your contract and go home. We can't stop the disease once it starts, but we do know excessive fatigue kicks it off. I look at you and I see a shadow of the Choya I beat for wing leader."

Nedar shoved his glass viciously across the tabletop. Amber drink spilled over Palaton in a spray. He took his hand and contemptuously wiped himself down, then left without another word. Behind him, he could hear Nedar fall back into his chair and order yet another drink. He did not see the shadowy Choya emerge from a secluded corner and approach the surly pilot who, after a few whispered words, sat up abruptly and listened closely.

Palaton returned to his quarters at base. The hall was on downtime, shadowed and still. He checked his chronometer and knew he would have a full night's sleep if he turned in now. His message light blinked, so he went to retrieve them first.

The first was from Jorana. He would acknowledge it later. She kept in touch with him, briefly, from contract to contract. She was now a captain of the guard and also one of Panshinea's cabinet members. The higher she rose, the harder she would fall when Panshinea finally stumbled once and for all. The thought filled him with mixed emotions. He still did not know how he felt about Jorana.

The second was from his grandfather. The visual transmission was occluded by sunspot interference, which was just as well, for the spine straight elder facing the viewing screen was no one Palaton recognized easily. But the voices were the same, though there were quavery pauses for breath here and there.

"Palaton. I thought it my duty to inform you. Our Householding is being Relocated. Not by imperial order, but by financial decree. We are bankrupted. You are our line's only current *tezar*. Your cousin has been killed on contract and your two nephews washed out of Salt Towers. The expense of maintaining our home here has become a burden I cannot shoulder on your tithes alone. Your mother's grave . . ." and here his grandfather's voices faded so he was almost inaudible. The visual showed him visibly getting a hold of himself. "Your mother's grave will remain with the Householding. I'm sorry, Palaton. You still have your home at Blue Ridge." The transmission recording ended.

He sat in stunned silence. Not that he had ever had much of a home in his grandfather's Householding—Blue Ridge had been his, in his heart and in his destiny from the moment he'd crossed its threshold.

But that his line should have suddenly grown so weak. And why had his nephews, half-nephews, actually, been sent to the Salt Towers instead of Blue Ridge? He found himself unaccepting of the transmission and wondered if Panshinea had not now, years later, found a way to vent his spleen. Only death washed members of Palaton's Householding out of *tezar* school once accepted. Only death. Yet no deaths had been mentioned for his nephews. They had proved unacceptable for one reason or another once under trial. He found it hard to believe.

As for his cousin, Palaton bowed his head and breathed a remembrance to God-in-all for her passing. Dying on contract meant she'd suffered a work accident . . . or been lost in Chaos. He hardly knew her, she'd been older and already a *tezar* at his birth, but it was in her footsteps he'd first followed.

His mind in turmoil, he lay down to sleep. Thinking of Blue Ridge and Hat and arrogant Nedar, he closed his eyes. The cadets used a meditation ritual to purify their thoughts and discipline their fears. Mechanically he fell into it now, for it was the only way sleep would come. Sometime during that drill, he slept.

The intercom woke him. *"Tezar Palaton."*

He was on his feet before he spoke. "I'm here." His mind cleared, thoughts separating into distinct images of reality from dreams. He cleared his throat. "I'm here," he repeated.

"We have an emergency and desperate need for a pilot. Are you available?"

Besides Nedar, he knew of no one in downtime at the base presently, although someone could have come in while he slept. But he knew that if they had, or if there had been a fresh pilot available, he wouldn't be getting the call. And Nedar was in no shape to fly, whether using the patterns or on straight duty. He rubbed his eyes awake. To fly and to serve, the motto of Blue Ridge. "I'm available," he said, and moved forward to answer the call.

Chapter 17

He took no secondary navigator or copilot on the run. He watched silently in the bays as the hospital ships were tractor linked to the main ship he was to pilot. The crews and troops of the hospital ships loaded with a quick efficiency that surprised him. Order out of cacophony and disaster. He was to tow in three of the immense medical facilities. It was important work, far from the garbage runs he'd been doing, for various contracts over the years. As he watched the preparations, he pondered Nedar's accusation.

Only those who know their destiny fully can charge forward into it, achieving it or failing. Only those who know what their bloodlines have prepared them for—Palaton knew he was meant to be a *tezar*. That, at least, would not escape him. For him, it was enough.

Moameb seriously ill now, the neuropathy advanced enough to waste him . . . that was an image he could not erase from his mind. It was time, he thought, to return to Blue Ridge in spite of the emperor's wrath. After this contract, it was time to go home for a little while and catch his breath. Perhaps make a last visit to his mother's grave before the Householding lost all rights to the land. Time to say good-bye.

And time to greet Jorana again, perhaps. He felt a tightening in his throat.

Slender fingers trailed across his flank and went to the small of his back, kneading gently. "You're too tense," Faba said, her voices soft and low, for his hearing alone.

Palaton turned his head. The Choya'i mechanic gave him a smile. She'd gotten out of bed to ready the vessel, her dark mass of curly hair still uncombed within her scalloped crown. She knew where his body knotted up, and when to leave him alone. He welcomed her presence for the moment though their liaisons had never been intended to entangle either of them in anything permanent. Her fingers continued to roam his back, seeking out the knots.

"Are you flying this morning?"

There were no real mornings on base, simply uptime and downtime, thanks to the deep space shielding surrounding the facility, but old habits made the artificial environment homier. He looked out across the deep velvet. "Yes."

"They're lucky you were logged in." Her fingers left his back. They brushed his jawline briefly. "I'll make sure you have a safe flight." Smelling of perfume and machinery, she sidled past him and went down into the bays to work.

He watched her tiny-waisted, yet otherwise full-bodied form go down into the berthing pits. Her voices echoed back up to him as she began to check the fitness of the vessel he would pilot. Palaton smiled slightly in response. First she'd checked him out, now she was checking the ship out.

The medical emergency which had precipitated the activity had sounded severe. The Compact had just voted to send in the hospital ships and supplies to a system ravaged by natural disaster and plague, a system just out of Class Zed status, like an infant learning to walk, unprepared for the havoc its own internal strife would engender. There was also some rumor of alien contamination, that the plague would destroy the majority of the population of this twin-planet system, that the viruses had been introduced by the intrusion of the Compact itself. The natives could not combat the ravaging which had begun. The Terran system, he thought briefly, had been more deserving of reclassification. But he had no say in Compact politics unless Blue Ridge sent him there, and certainly not in the councils which decided matters such as these. At least a decision had been made and would be carried out swiftly.

Cargo holds filled, the medical personnel entered the hospital ships, troops at their heels. The ships would stay in orbit and temporary hospitals would be prefabbed dirtside, the troops to provide manpower for construction as well as security. Palaton waited until the "all clear" sounded. Even Faba left the bays.

He walked through all four ships and then his own vessel, as Choyan did, knowing that all five were in his hands alone. He would be the final authority on whether they would space, or not. He found a leaking fuel cap, gasket rings twisted, ordered a replacement, and went on. Nothing else seemed amiss.

He rubbed sleep out of the corner of one eye and walked the ramp of the Compact escort which would be his vessel for this run, the *tezarian* black box drive in his free hand. It took him three minutes to install it and then he felt the berth cradles begin to shift the vessels into position for launch. He sat down and secured himself.

The tiny hairs at the nape of his neck prickled in anticipation. Palaton looked about his cabin, searching with a vague uneasiness, saw nothing, discerned nothing, then turned to his job as the base launched him and then the four hospital ships in his wake. He reached under the control console and found a Compact tracer, stretched his lips wryly at the feeble attempt to track him, destroyed it and knew that, even if there were others, they would do no good. Only he could betray himself and his methods.

He spent his free hours until FTL acceleration could be reached plotting their pathway, keeping in mind the size difference between the sleek escort and the massive hospital ships following. Their course had already been set, but Palaton liked to manipulate the numbers. He monitored their sector to see if he drew any Ronin, but if there was other traffic it kept clear.

As they neared FTL acceleration, he notified the hospital ships to prepare for Chaos flight. Because reality bent in Chaos, it was disconcerting, even terrifying, to the senses of the uninitiated. Tranquilizers and confinement combated the effects. The Choyan were not particularly susceptible to it, although he'd seen a few cases of stark, raving terror of colors that bled, time that bubbled, solid material that appeared to become nonexistent.

"Thank you, *tezar*."

Palaton looked to his rear screens. The cable that stretched between them, like an umbilical cord, was just as necessary to preserve their lives. It stretched lazily across the expanse, waiting to be dropped when he launched them on their own. The pilot of the transports was doing a good job, keeping the cable stretched but not taut. He wondered who it was—a Quinonan perhaps, or an Ivrian, or perhaps a Norton. Someone who burned, no doubt, to know his secrets.

He took them into Chaos with a majestic sweep, grinning at the sheer power of it, at the wonder of it, feeling like a dark sorcerer. He bypassed the Singing Choya'i and searched for the Falling Tree instead, going deep into the patterns, making haste with caution as Moameb would say. The escort responded with hair-trigger quickness, but the four transports lagged behind, sluggishly, and the cable drew tight. He adjusted the escort to match the transports' ability.

Chaos took away the hull of his ship. He felt as though he rode a chair suspended in space, its currents whirling with light and sound and fury, the console a keyboard in front of him to strike and coax celestial music from. Palaton liked this effect although it did not strike him often and made most pilots uneasy, especially those with a fear of falling, for it seemed he sat on the brink of eternity, about to plunge into it as the starship hurled forward.

After a few heady moments, the hull and shielding re-formed, and he was once more inside their protection. He mourned the loss of sensation, then scouted for the peaks that were so like those beyond Blue Ridge. Nothing met his search.

Palaton rubbed his eyes and sent his discernment arching out, looking for the Mountains of Sunrise. The configuration eluded him, as though he'd gone blind, and then he realized his *bahdur* guttered like a candle burning out.

Panic closed his throat. He'd been sitting back in his chair, at ease. He slammed forward on its edge, the console digging into the flat of his stomach as he leaned over it, peering into the shielding which mirrored only his anguished face back at him. Chaos was right there, patterns laid open for him to read—and he saw none of it.

He took a gasping breath and knew keen empathy with what Nedar must have felt. He did a quick meditation pattern to open himself, letting the *bahdur* well up, like a fountain.

Emptiness met him. There was nothing secreted inside him, no wellspring of reserve, nothing. His soul was dead, empty, as quiet as stone. He clawed at it as if he could scrape enough power together to save himself—to save the four hospital ships he took with him to certain death—and found not even scrapings.

Then it blazed briefly, illuminating his world, filling it with a sky bowl of fireworks, showing him they were about to plunge over the rim of the pattern called the Waterfall . . . a plunge as mystical and dangerous as a real life drop over an immense falls. His comlines came on, all four ships, and he knew they were taking a rough ride.

He forced his voices steady. "A mild disruption. Keep everybody buckled in. I'm taking shortcuts and hitting a few rough spots."

The escort dropped, plunged, his stomach going with it, the four ships following as the cable jerked taut and drew them down. It was like hitting a ten-thousand-foot air pocket drop. He clenched his teeth, wondering when they were going to hit bottom.

Darkness came when the descent ended. Palaton chewed on his lips, found them flaking and chapped as he did so, his mouth gone unutterably dry. Where had he taken them? How mired in Chaos were they?

He found one trembling hand laid over the black box of the *tezarian* drive. He looked at his instrumentation. He abandoned *bahdur* and grabbed the keypad he'd been doing calculations on. He knew where they'd been heading—he knew they'd just left the Waterfall. He wasn't completely adrift. Yet. . . .

From the feel of the ride, he could tell the swirls and eddies which took them. He let Chaos control them, keeping track of the journey, making corrections to keep them on course. Then, Palaton sat back and looked at what he had done.

They were close enough so that he could bring them out if he could *discern*. If he cut loose the cable, he could slingshot them away from the escort, giving them the impetus to make that exit window—even though it meant he himself could not go. It was possible.

If he had any *bahdur* left at all.

If he was willing to sacrifice himself to deliver them.

There was no question about that last. He licked his lips. "Transport One, I'm going to cut you loose and slingshot you through. You'll have to send for another pilot when your mission is done."

A silence. Then, "Are you having trouble, *tezar*?"

There was no easy way to answer it. All pilots knew the

danger, even those who did not face Chaos. He fought denial. This couldn't be happening to him. He'd had very few episodes. But it could be happening. It was happening. He smelled his own fear, rank in the control cabin. He forced himself to respond. "Yes," answered Palaton. "But I can get you through safely."

There was a muffled exclamation at the other end, cut off, and the voice resumed, "I'm with you. Ready to slingshot at your mark."

"I want you to accelerate for . . . six clics only. Then decel to leave Chaos. Do you have that?"

"Six clics. I have it."

Palaton took a deep breath. His lungs ached, as if he had not been breathing, or had drowned and had the water squeezed from them, bruising him. He felt a certain headiness as new air flooded into him. He closed his eyes and searched for any tiny spark of talent he might have left.

It answered him feebly. Pain shot through his right arm, arcing over his collarbone and into his sternum. *Neuropathy.* The beginning of his end. If he had ever thought otherwise, the disease lanced certainty into him. A nerve at a time would burn its agonizing way to death. He had seen *tezars* beg for their end. He bit his lip against the stabbing, burning sharpness of it and looked through Chaos, willing the curtains to open and reveal his destination.

He found it. He aimed the escort toward it, bucking across random currents wishing to carry him otherwise. Then he steered into the currents, readying for the slingshot that would bring the transport out safely.

"*Tezar* . . ." The voice of doubt.

"Stay with me, Pilot One. On my mark."

"There is disagreement here. Four hundred lives, highly trained physicians and technicians—"

"Pilot One! On my mark! I'll lose you otherwise." Rear screens showed him the cable vibrating. They sought to cast themselves without his guidance.

"A Choya in burnout . . ." Another voice, overriding the pilot. An administrator? A general of Compact troops? Whatever the title, he heard authority and skepticism in the other's voice. The cable bounced. The escort slewed in response as the heavier transports dragged slightly on it.

He drew on his talents and threw back his own voices of

command. "Stay with me!" He had no idea whether the comline transmitted him faithfully, but there was momentary silence in response. Alternating between sight and blindness, he calculated wildly. Then, "Mark!" And he freed the cable as he sheared the escort off violently, accelerating rapidly.

But the escort did not respond properly, and he knew that quite possibly the transports had released the cable before he did—slinging them into nowhere.

The transports arced away into Chaos. His *bahdur* arrowed a golden blaze across their pathway and charred into the nothingness of the God-blind. His breath sobbed to a halt in his throat. Had he done it? He could not see! He looked to the black box and saw their fate being calculated, their courses set in numbers too awful to read. Palaton slammed his fist across the screen in fear and loathing. "No! No! *No!*"

Darkness descended like a blinding blow to the back of his head.

Chapter 18

GNask enjoyed the company of the Chinese junior ambassador. He smacked his lips as the rotund humankind prepared a freshly caught fish and presented it in a skillet redolent with exotic herbs and spices, the fish still gasping with life, its body seared by the cooking.

"My dear ambassador," the Abdrelik said, picking up an eating utensil. "Diplomatic skills and a chef, as well. Does Thomas appreciate you?"

"Perhaps," the moon-faced man said. "And perhaps not. We should discuss it sometime, Ambassador GNask."

GNask smiled as he cut away a portion. He and Thomas had arrangements that the junior ambassador could not breach no matter what he tried, but his efforts were occasionally rewarding. GNask decided to lead him on.

"I had not known your planet to be so . . . fragmented," he commented.

The Chinese humankind's skill at the Trade dialect was slightly limited. He frowned over the observation, then smiled. "Not fragmented. Just independent. And self-concerned to some extent. We have hopes in the area of computerization that the Class Zed act might be applied to our advantage—"

GNask's com chimed. The Abdrelik paused in irritation. His secretary knew better than to interrupt him at mealtimes.

He opened the comlink. "What is it?"

"An urgent communique."

GNask thought. Then he said, "I'll be in in a moment." To the junior ambassador, he apologized. "But you know how these things can be."

The round yellow eyelids shuttered. "Yes, Ambassador. I know." He reached for a portion of fish himself as GNask swayed his bulk past him.

His secretary had sealed the office when he arrived. "What is it?" His annoyance smacked with every syllable. His symbiont, which had been sleeping placidly, began to stir upon the side of his head.

"Ambassador Thomas, sir, on the private com."

"Ah." GNask seated himself, feeling more civil. He mopped his wet chin. The flat screen came to life.

The sticklike figure of the man had been moving in agitation. GNask watched it with the avid fascination of the hunter, attracted despite himself. Then Thomas saw that the flatscreen had been activated and came to a halt before it.

"Ambassador," GNask crooned. "How kind of you to call. I have your junior here, cooking me lunch."

"I don't have time for pleasantries, GNask. They've taken her."

"Really? So soon?" GNask put a hand up and tickled his *tursh*. The slug began an inaudible purring that vibrated comfortingly into the Abdrelik' hide. "We weren't expecting this. What happened?"

John Taylor Thomas had bleary, red-rimmed eyes. His hands trembled as he pulled out a linen cloth and touched at them. "Skimcraft accident. My wife was injured slightly, but they reported my daughter's death. The skimmer burned . . . the remains were almost impossible to identify. We went through hell . . . then I got a call. 'Don't worry,' they said. 'We've got your daughter. It's time.' "

"Interesting," GNask murmured. His eyes hooded slightly in pleasure. Ruthless of the Choyan, who would have thought it of them? But admirable. Yes, very admirable. And if not their subject, then who had died? Not his worry, of course, and the Choyan were absolute masters in genetics . . . the replacement would match the original in almost every way perceptible. "Thomas, we prepared for this."

The symbiont culturing had been most successful. That was years ago, now, but GNask still slitted his eyes in thoughtful remembrance. He had wanted to reabsorb the symbiont so that he could experience the manchild in the ways she had undoubtedly experienced him, but the *tursh* offspring had not survived the induction. Something in humankind chemistry had made it weaken and die, though not before it had done its task. The child would be, what, fifteen years old as the humankind reckoned themselves. Yes. Old enough to have some power in the world. Able to reach and utilize tools. Able to manipulate, to think, to respond, to operate covertly.

"We'll find her soon, Thomas," GNask said. "They operated callously. We'll find her and stop them."

"They let me think she was dead!" John Taylor Thomas caught his breath, on the edge of a sob.

GNask leaned very close to the flatscreen. "Now," he said intensely, "we find her and we take our vengeance."

The man looked up. "Not until we have our children back."

"Naturally," GNask reassured. "They are our evidence. Now, if you'll excuse me, Ambassador, lunch is waiting. Like vengeance, it's better served hot." He terminated the call and hefted himself up.

The Choyan had overplayed their hand at last. He would have proof of species interference. He might even have insight as to the *tezarian* drive. At the very least, he would further disrupt the power of the erratic Panshinea. *Good news was always the best appetizer,* he thought, as he waddled back to the Chinese underambassador. He wondered what the Choyan did with all those children.

The streets of Sao Paulo teemed with life, life broken, dirty, struggling, filled with potential, yet seldom achieving it, drowning beneath the toxins of waste and poor air, poverty and the utter cheapness of its regard for human flesh. The church grounds overlooked a neighborhood which balanced between middle class and ghetto, neither fish nor fowl, its buildings squat and ugly. Father Lombardi looked out his begrimed window and issued a call for Bevan. His desk was cluttered, his equipment old and obsolete, his fax nearly four decades old, though Lombardi thought it worked better than the new instatrans machines. An apostle of Mother Theresa, who was on the brink of achieving sainthood, he felt that all he could do was be a small island of comfort and sanity in Sao Paulo. All he could offer was a modicum of healing and a lot of faith while the doomed met their fate. He could teach the dream of a better tomorrow, but it was his lot to struggle with the overwhelmingly undermet needs of today.

He pulled at his white plastic collar. The fabric scratched. Pools of sweat runneled down from his armpits staining the dark cloth coat of his Catholic uniform. He waited for Bevan.

From the moment Lombardi had reached down into the cholera-ridden gutters and pulled the child up, he had been different. The father knew it and most certainly Bevan had. He'd rarely been sick a day since being taken into sanctuary. He had seemed to know his lot among the Theresites was destined to be different and so, when the Choyan had come, neither Lombardi nor the child had hesitated to make a deal. Otherwise Bevan would languish here, too vibrant to be comforted about dying, too vital to be wasted.

A chancy hope for the future was preferable, no matter how shadowy it seemed. Lombardi had only given three or four of his children away to the aliens in the past. He had never heard from any of them again, but he didn't feel uneasy in his dealings. These were a deeply religious people, he knew, from having spoken with them. They offered quiet support of the massive financial strain of the sanctuary. They received promising children as students from time to time. Father Lombardi gave no one away who did not wish to go.

Quiet as his thoughts, Bevan had entered and stood waiting when Lombardi looked up a second time. The slender youth had snapping dark eyes, a nose overly large for a fine-boned face, luxurious hair that maned down to his shoulders, thin quick fingers. He perched now on the crowded corner of Lombardi's desk.

"You sent for me, Father?" he asked in the native tongue of Brazil, though he knew Compact Trade fairly well, and English fluently. Also he spoke a smattering of Japanese and Italian. He picked up a fax and read it idly.

"It is time," Father Lombardi said with dignity.

Bevan dropped the paper. His obsidian eyes reflected excitement, though his carefully schooled face did not. "Time?"

"It is time for you to leave us, Bevan, as you and I agreed."

The youth looked about the office as if expecting to see aliens in the corners. "Where are they?"

"You'll not see them here. I will have you sleep in solitary tonight. Their common procedure is to come while you're asleep. I don't know if . . ." Lombardi cleared his throat uneasily. "I don't know when you'll wake. Off-planet, most likely. Take nothing with you. Destroy all your personal belongings. Give nothing away."

They looked at one another, sagging Caucasian Catholic priest and dark-skinned, uncertain lineaged street child.

"You never lived here," Lombardi said gently. "You never existed. That is the only way I could give you a future."

"Then," said Bevan brightly, "that's the only way I can take it." He slid off the desk and snapped his fingers. "Don't worry about me, Father Lombardi." He slipped lithely out the office door before the priest had dismissed him, but Lombardi let him go.

He rocked back in his chair with a sigh. If there were only some way of knowing what he did was right.

The old fax began to hum, another missive coming in. It was an offer of black market medicine, if he had the monies available.

Thanks to the Choyan visitation that morning, he did. He wondered if prayers were being answered.

A man and a young man stalked the corridors of the space station, watching the cloud cover shift over the blue planet below. The father had the look of an impoverished businessman, a common class in the Americas of the day, but his son was dressed in a flight suit, the new material still sharply creased from its packaging. They paused at the view window.

"It doesn't look so bad from here," the boy murmured. He was already as tall as his father. He was fair, with wide turquoise eyes and a dark shock of hair that continually fell into his eyes, though nothing could hide his earnest expression. He would never be handsome, but he would always be honest and intense.

"No," answered his father. He was not so much looking at the view as searching for the invisible personnel of the way station, the aliens who came and went here so freely.

The boy's hands knuckled over the safety rail. "I want to pilot, Dad," he said suddenly. "So badly I can taste it."

The businessman looked aside at his son in surprise. "Do you?"

"Always." The boy looked up. "So don't feel bad about giving me away."

The man's jaw dropped. "Randall, I didn't—I didn't give you away—"

"Traded then. Me for new methods of waste removal and purification. It'll save your business. It'll help Earth, and I'll have a chance for what I want."

The trade had never been as concrete as that, but the father couldn't bear to disillusion his child. Still, he hesitated. "I don't know . . . I don't know what they want of you. They spoke of college, but—"

Randall gave a slow, strong smile. It illuminated his entire body. The businessman thought of his wife when his son did so. For her, he would have moved the sun and earth itself. "It's not what they want of me," the youth said. "It's what I want of them: Nothing less than all the stars and suns and planets they can offer up. Nothing less." He went back to staring at his world below.

After a long moment, the father slipped an arm about his son's shoulders and they stood in quiet, unmentioned farewell.

Chapter 19

Sharp insistent sound pierced his unconsciousness. Palaton forced himself out of dreams as deep as dark water, drowning him, pulling him down. He struggled to surface and came awake in the escort control cabin. He lay for a moment, cheek upon the instrument panel, uncomprehending. Then the sound, the fuel alarm, registered.

He clawed his eyes open. The noise reverberated through his skull and he pawed at the panel, fumbling to shut it down. Then the significance of the signal brought him erect in his chair, and he stared at the controls.

He was alive, and happy for it, despite the searing pain that ran from his wrist into his shoulder and chest. He was alive, and ashamed of it, because of the four hundred he had led into death. By the God-in-all, he should not struggle to survive now, but he had to. If only to tell the Compact of the mission's failure, so that new crews could be sent out.

To do that, he had to leave Chaos. He had to pull out, regardless of what destiny lay ahead, and send his message out. Then he faced drifting until the escort's systems ran down, or he might emerge in solid rock, though it was more likely he would be in open space, completely at a loss as to where he was or whether any system was within reach of the escort. And if he were going to pull out, he had to do it now, while there was any fuel left for maneuvering at all.

His right hand crippled by pain, he fingered the black box, locked in decel commands and triggered them. The escort answered promptly, its surge pushing him deep into his chair, where he sat, panting for breath and wanting not to die.

It was funny, he thought, that flying had been foremost

in his mind until it came to making a choice between flying and living.

The shields went up as the escort veered out of Chaos and came back into real-time space and he found himself staring into black velvet on the outer edges of a system with a G type star. His panels lit with a transmitted frequency.

Not only was he somewhere, he was somewhere which supported life—and which transmitted for incoming space flights. He had the luck of a child, as the Choyan said. Over Compact frequencies, he fumbled to send out a message of the disaster. He locked it in so that it would repeat, sealing his own fate. His failure would be broadcast for any with ears to hear. If he did survive, he would be grounded unless he could be recertified.

With neuropathy, that hope was gone, seared out, like the nerves which created and transmitted his *bahdur.* Palaton could be a *tezar* no longer. But at least he was alive.

The homing beacon came from the fourth planet out. Readings showed that it was inhabited, though it was more likely to be a colonized planet than a planet with its own native civilization. Palaton took a deep breath and, over a regular hailing frequency, broadcast his incapacity, detailing a low fuel emergency, and asked for permission to come in. He eyed the fuel gauge. The escort could make it in under its current momentum but not much farther. He sat back to wait for permission.

Side screens nagged for his attention. Palaton turned his head and saw, on the outer edge of the system, a ship coming in fast. The computer brought it up on grid and ID'd it for him.

Ronin.

Palaton knew it must be coincidence, unless he was approaching a Ronin colony. The ship could not have traced him through Chaos. But the quilled aliens were opportunists of the first water. They'd take him out if they knew he was nearly disabled. The fate he'd warned Nedar of was about to become his own.

Palaton slapped his hand down, heedless of the pain, cutting off both the Compact signal and the emergency broadcast. He swiveled in his chair, hit the console's arming controls and brought up his weapons systems. The power lights answered feebly. He didn't have much to fight with.

"Hailing Compact Escort One, we have received distress call and need confirmation."

The Ronin voice corning over his open line left no doubt in his mind. Palaton steadied his own voices in response. "Ronin answer back, I've had some trouble, but it's in hand now and I'm tracking a homing beacon." He wanted desperately to ask where he was and whether he encroached in their territory, but knew he dared not reveal any weakness before the Ronin. He waited for the Ronin comeback.

Silence met his statement. The target grid showed the other ship bearing away. Palaton watched it warily.

It turned on him almost faster than his instruments could track it. Palaton bit off a curse as his hand failed him in his first attempt to lock in the targeting grid. He fired a warning shot. He had nothing to lose by engaging with them. Their actions declared their intentions.

The Ronin ship curved in evasive action, his shot going wild and destructing. Palaton smiled grimly. At least they knew he meant business. They must be frantically wondering just how disabled he was—and how much of a fight he could put up.

He was either in Ronin territory or so far out that no one would hear of the incident. There was nothing holding them back.

The ship rocked as the Ronin returned fire. Sensors told him that damage was slight—one of the rear conning towers—and Palaton reluctantly put the ship into defensive maneuvers. The fuel sensors dipped alarmingly. The Ronin fired again. The torpedo sped past harmlessly, exploding aft, and the craft cut through the wake of it, scattering debris.

He could not lead them on. Palaton made a decision and abruptly cut engines back. The ship coasted. He knew that Ronin sensors would pick up the abrupt cessation of the drive. He watched them bearing down. They would not blow him out of the sky—they wanted him.

That was the difference between him and them.

They loomed on his rear screens. Palaton shut his jaws firmly, took a reading, and fired everything he had. An orange burst answered.

The escort vessel rocked and shimmied violently when the aftershock of the blast reached him. Palaton brought the escort around and assessed the damage.

There was little more than wreckage left. It could have been called an act of war—if there had been anyone to know of it. With grim satisfaction, he plotted course into the system, hoping he could make it in before everything shut down. The cadets talked often about flying on a wing and a prayer, and that was exactly what he was doing now.

Shaking, he put a hand to his brow. Fever burned it. Pain so ravaged his right arm that both elbows bent in, muscles standing out in rigid cords. He curled it to his flank, cradling it. He stared at the tiny speck on the view screens calling him to safety. He hoped the colony had a decent spaceport, and he prayed that it wasn't a Ronin colony. The control room's lights flickered out, replaced by the dimmer glow of auxiliary lighting as systems started to fail. The ship fell into a spiraling descent toward the yellow sun.

He began to pray. He was not aware of it when he fell into a pain-racked stupor.

The God-in-all looked him over. His magnificent horn crown cupped a bowl of silver curls, and his eyes were dark and bright. "Well," he said, his voices full of the same laughter that creased lines about his eyes and mouth. "You've come a long way." His Choyan was oddly accented, as if grown rusty with disuse. He put a hand under Palaton's head, taking the weight of the *tezar*'s too heavy skull into his palm, and bolstering him. "Have a drink of this now. When you crash, you do it in style. Most of that escort can still be flown out of here."

Palaton struggled to speak, to tell him. Every bone in his body hurt and his eyes were almost too heavy to keep open. "I failed," he got out. "Lost in Chaos, four hundred. I . . . failed."

"We've heard enough of that," the God-in-all said. "Whatever tales you've got to tell, we can hear later." In Trade, he added, "Cleo, woman, bring those soaking rags over here."

And damp, cooling rags were laid over his limbs, relaxing his convulsive cramps bit by bit, until he could tell he lay on a crude cot stuffed with leaves and herbs, their scent being bruised out of the ticking by the pressure of his weight. Another figure came into his line of sight—it was a humankind, a woman, bulky and with laugh lines of her own around luminous blue eyes. Palaton put up a hand. "Those eyes," he said.

The woman smiled broadly. "My," she answered. "Compliments already. It's the fever. You'll come to your senses soon enough. A *Tezar* complimenting a human. What's the world coming to!" She laughed warmly, and he knew she teased him.

The hands supporting his head let go, easing him back onto a pillow that had been meant for a Choya. Palaton blinked.

"You're not . . . God-in-all."

"By the great wheel's turn, no! Nor did I ever claim to be. No, my child, I'm an old *tezar* and you're in good hands. Now rest, for that's all you need to know and all I'll be telling you." Dry, callused fingers closed his eyes firmly and held them so for a second.

That second was all it took to put Palaton back into a deep, healing sleep.

"I should be dead," Palaton said, his voices falling unnaturally loud into the silence. A cooling rag lay over his brow and he could not see who he spoke to, so he spoke Trade, out of courtesy.

"Wait a bit," the woman answered. He could hear her now, rustling about the room. "You can probably accomplish that yet." The rag was whisked off his forehead and replaced, giving him only a blur of sight, and she dominated that vision. "Of course, I'd be wondering why I was wasting all this time on a corpse."

He listened to her move about the room. She hadn't the grace of a Choya'i, but few alien races did. "How long have I been here?"

"Four days or so." A pause. "I've been listening to you rave most of that time, but you sound fairly sane now."

"Only fairly," answered Palaton.

"Good. Then I'll get Daman. He's been waiting for you."

Palaton heard and felt the pressure change of a recycler as she left. Bad air outside? Or just an inadequate atmosphere? Where was he? And into whose hands had he fallen? He turned his cheek and found his own hands bound loosely at his sides. He tossed his head and the compress slid into a soggy lump beside his forehead as he stared upward, blinking, until he could see.

The room was prefab and sterile, uninteresting and unrevealing. Geodesic dome style, it might almost have been a unit knocked together just to house him. His bed was a matting laid on the floor, and he'd been in it long enough that the herbal fragrance had mostly dissipated. He worked his wrists inside the trussing. Was he guest or captive?

The recycler wheezed faintly again, and a massive, burly Choya filled the room. It was he Palaton had mistaken for the God-in-all—silver curls and all. The elder had brought a stool with him. He now dropped it in place and sat down. "I'll speak in Trade, for the benefit of my *durah*," the Choya said, confusing Palaton. A *durah* was a lifemate, a bonded partner, and Palaton had not seen or heard any Choya'i treating him.

The humankind came in behind Daman and sat as well. He saw an unconscious imitated grace in her posture, an echo of Daman's. She wore her chestnut hair shoulder length, and long silvery locks of gray streaked it along her brow. Her smile was crooked, tight at one corner, as though she shared a confidence which pleased her sense of irony. The Choya wore an old flight suit, somewhat frayed at collar and cuffs. She wore fuller clothes somewhat akin to the robes of an Earthan priest. Something native to her people, Palaton guessed, and his attention flickered back to the elder Choya. A *tezar* himself, Palaton remembered.

"Can you send a transmission?"

"No," the Choya said flatly. He held up a broad, work-stained hand. "There is no longer any need. What's done is done. What's lost is . . . lost."

"No." His heart twisted.

Daman stared sternly at him. "You've been here for days in the throes of first stage burnout fever, and you deny me? I've been away a long, long time, but I've never missed the arrogance of a *tezar*."

"A failure cannot afford arrogance," said Palaton.

"Too true. Had you only thought it before this tragedy might have been averted."

He clenched a hand. "If I lived, they might have, too! If you can get word out—"

"Our facilities are primitive, and, at any rate, our outgoing broadcasts were shut down when you chose to duel the

Ronin. We don't need that kind of trouble," the humankind said. Her eyes flashed.

"They'll not come here. . . ."

"They might," argued the Choya. "They've been known to do it before. However, they're not my immediate concern. You are. I am Daman, of the house of Sky from the Salt Towers, and you are, unless lineage mistakes me, a Star. This is Cleo. How turns the Great Wheel on Cho?"

The woman laughed. "He would refer to me as his *durah*, but you already look stunned. What we are is not what you suspect, but there's no word to describe our bonding."

Fever began to build in his body again. He felt the ripples of involuntary chills shake him. He clenched his teeth. "Your matters are private," he said in answer. "But tell me, where are we, and why would the Ronin haunt you—and why won't you help me?"

"The Ronin haunt us because they want me for the same reason they wanted you—a lone, forgotten *tezar* is fair game. I won't help you because I can't help you. What's done is done. I can't give you back your transports just as I can't regenerate the nerve damage. And as for where we are—we are so far out on the frontier even the Compact has no inkling of where you've fallen. So if you want to hide, *tezar*, you've come to the right place."

Palaton's frame began to thump helplessly on the cot. Cleo rose quickly. "The fever's hit him again."

Daman got to his feet. "Take care of him as best you can." He vanished from Palaton's blurring vision.

He saw the woman raising a hand to his brow. With great effort, he asked, "What are you to him? Why does he call you *durah*?"

The crooked smile drew tighter. "As if you could ever understand. He's a *tezar*," she said, "because I gave him back his *bahdur*." A compress descended on his brow, curtaining away his vision.

Palaton awoke, feeling weak and drained. The pain in his right arm had numbed, but he felt like a newborn, and though he swung his legs over the side of the cot, he didn't think he could stand. He got to his feet though, driven by the need to void his bladder, and stayed up, bolstered by the framework of the room. He found the conveniences, primitive as they were, and used them. Then he staggered back to the cot and sat down heavily, his head reeling.

He could remember Moameb dealing with burn-out fever like a massive hangover. It came and went, leaving disaster in its wake, and pilots coping as best they could. He had hoped he would lose his talent spark by spark, quietly, almost unknowingly, instead of by this massive blow. He was still alive, but was it worth it?

"Is that arrogance boiling down to self-pity I hear?"

Palaton turned around achingly, slowly, to see Daman in the far corner, rocking back and balancing his chair. He had evidently spoken aloud. "Probably," he admitted.

"Ah. I wondered. Is this a common trait at Blue Ridge?"

"Actually," Palaton said slowly, "I think it began as a tradition at Salt Towers."

"Hmmm." Daman brought the legs of his chair to earth. "You can't be so close to death with that sense of humor."

"Truly?"

"Truly." The Choya stood. "Now we must decide what to do with you."

"I haven't *bahdur* enough to get back to base, even if we could launch the escort—and I don't remember you telling me how badly it was damaged."

"I doubt that. You practically aura-blinded me at the peak of your fever. But you've lost control, the ability to access what remains." The silver-haired Choya paced beside his cot, dark eyes smoldering with thought. "As far as the ship goes, it's serviceable enough."

"You could take me in."

"No." Daman stopped in his tracks, an unreadable expression on his broad, creased face. "No, that's not a possibility."

"Why?"

"Because I don't touch Compact lands anymore. I've reason for it, and the less you know, the better." Daman rubbed his hands together. "Do you feel well enough for a hike after dinner?"

His knees felt like rubber. "I could . . . try."

"Then I'll take you out to see the escort yourself. And you can make a decision there. You can go back, or you can bury yourself alive here."

Palaton looked at him. "Like you did?"

Daman's head jerked back as if Palaton had clipped his jaw. His eyes narrowed slightly. "I stay for Cleo's sake. If we left, they would take her away from me. I don't think either of us would survive that. Again, you seek to know that which would jeopardize you. Don't ask me again."

He wouldn't ask. Like his own failure, they must seek to hide secrets of their own. His guts clenched, out of both self-hatred and hunger. Hunger he could deal with. Palaton stood up, locking his limbs and staying up from sheer determination. "Which way is the kitchen?"

Chapter 20

The escort was more than serviceable. It was, reflected Palaton, in far better shape than he was after hiking out to take a look at the crash site. He'd brought it in over a saltwater lake and back bay flats, then let it skid to solid ground. They would have to build a launch cradle for any kind of a lift-off, but Daman was confident there was enough fuel left to get to the trading port which serviced the planet and would have off-planet launching berths.

"Then," he said, with a broad grin, "they'll take your back teeth for payment if you let 'em."

"I'd prefer to keep my teeth a little longer. Will they take Compact credit?"

"It's possible. Always possible. Are you that eager, my friend, to face disgrace?"

An emotion butterflied around inside of him. It took Palaton a moment to identify it as fear. He sat down on a deadwood stump and looked at the escort vehicle, its side tiles scraped with salt and weed. "No," he said finally. "But I can't stay here."

Daman crossed his arms over his broad chest. "Rumors are the Great Wheel is descending for the House of Star. Who's up next . . . refresh my exile's memory."

"The Earthans, supposedly, but everyone knows they can't handle the intricacies of the Compact and its policies. Star feels it doesn't have to let go, and Sky is waiting to wrest the throne away."

"Then little has changed since I left, except that Panshinea has come to the throne and grown old."

"Old?" Palaton found it difficult to reconcile his impressions of the emperor with becoming an elder. Rindalan, now, must be almost rickety, but Panshinea would still be holding to the edge of his prime and maturity. Unless his illness had bested him, he would still be vigorous and as erratically brilliant as ever. "Not him."

"You think not?" Daman's brow arched. He wore no facial jewelry . . . in fact there were no tracings or tattoos anywhere on his exposed skin that Palaton could see. Only the faint tubings of the oxygen mask they both wore to augment the thin air of this poor world. "Well, you've seen the ship. It's best we get back before dark."

Palaton stood. He hesitated. "I want . . . to transmit."

A sharp glance from the other. "It will do no good, and it may well bring the Ronin on our necks."

"I have a duty."

Daman sighed. He uncrossed his broad arms and gestured. "And I a conscience. To fly and to serve, eh, *tezar*? We have a quarter hour. Set it on a pulse trans, and we'll shut it down before we leave. Otherwise, you'll have a power drain as well."

Palaton smiled wryly. "You're a good compromiser. Maybe you should go home and vie for the throne."

Daman's face became stone. "Cho is no home of mine." And he stood impassively as Palaton brushed past him to enter the ship's emergency lock.

Cleo met them at the stead's front locks, wiping her large capable hands on a lab apron. "It's after dark. I was worried," she said. The top of her head barely reached Daman's shoulder. He put an arm about her comfortingly. Palaton turned his head away quickly, unnerved by the show of affection between the two. As he looked away, the walls and ceilings of the buildings swapped gravity, and he hit the floor.

Cleo knelt beside him, putting the back of her smooth hand to his forehead. "Relapse," she said to Daman. "It's going to hit him hard."

"Ummmm. My fault. I should have known a pilot never walks when he can fly. Hold his head up, I'll get him."

Palaton, weak as a wrung out rag, lay on the floor and listened to the two discuss him. He could not even protest when Daman hefted him up like a child and carried him over his broad yet bony shoulder. Cleo swam, upside down, in and out of his view. Palaton was just about to retch despite his empty stomach when Daman dropped him onto the cot.

Palaton clenched his jaws and thought better of the idea for a moment. Cleo leaned over him. The cup of broth in her hands smelled delicious. She hesitated, spoon in hand, looking to Daman. "Perhaps I could do for him what I do for you . . ."

A private thing. Daman gave her a look with a thousand expressions and not one of them did Palaton understand. But the answer was clear. "No."

She nodded and knelt by him, offering the soup. It seemed to keep the worst of the fever at bay for a while, but eventually Palaton succumbed to the joint-rattling shakes and lapsed into dark dreams of Sorrow where a thousand young stared accusingly at him from their crystal coffin.

He ran from the look in their eyes and found himself at the Householding of his youth, his grandfather's estates, the House of Volan, but the buildings were empty, old papers rattling along with his footsteps like dry leaves on a barren riverbed. Gone, all his people, all his kin, all his past. He walked his mother's wing, saw the dust marks on the walls where her embroideries had hung and been taken down. He traced the designs left behind in cobweb, faded stone, and hanging pegs. He walked through the wing, with its studio and atrium additions, to a back door which led to the gardens and, inevitably, to her tomb.

He'd never seen it, but still knew where he stood. One of her few sculptures, a broken pitcher fountain, adorned it, and water still ran from the pitcher's spout into a pool of reflections at the monument's base. It mirrored a serenity he thought his mother had never known in real life. He thought it basest irony that death would give her what had been needed most and now could never be appreciated. The broken pitcher seemed to represent the view Tresa had held of herself. He put a hand out and let the cooling water run over it.

The actual engraving on the tomb held her House, her Householding, her birth and death dates, and a sentiment which she must have constructed herself. "DO YOU REMEMBER ME?"

Both command and question, a charge and a plea, the duality of her voices, and her life. Appropriate, he thought. I do remember you, and I do not . . . because you would not lend me your secrets, and I've no place else to go. He had not been brave enough to ask the questions of himself that had been placed before him. Now he had no recourse, the Householding he'd been raised in taken from him as well.

And as he stood, time changed, and he remembered the garden without the fountain, himself hanging on to his mother's tunic, quiet, triumphant, and afraid, his grandfather towering over the two of them, his voices trumpeting.

"He will be a tezar," his grandfather Volan shouted, *"and you will let him go."*

"No," Tresa said. *He could feel her trembling within his hold. "I saw the test results just as you did. They must be buried, destroyed! Or they will destroy him."*

"My name, my money, is good for something," his grandfather returned. *"I've hidden him as well as I can. But you . . . you betrayed me, your destiny, and this Householding. I thought you dallied with a common. . . . I hoped our blood would run true. But his* bahdur *burns the way no one in our line has ever burned. What House did you sleep with? What fates have you knotted and tangled?"* And Volan bore down on them, his face dark with anger.

Palaton remembered his mother shrinking back, turning her cheek, saying, "I don't remember!"

Not that she would not tell, but that she did not remember.

He broke into a cold sweat at the revelation of dream memory, shaking. Who was he that the House of Earth would send assassins? Who was he that the children of Sorrow and Earth haunted him? Who was he that *bahdur* could burn so brightly and then so suddenly abandon him?

He woke in the night, and saw Daman bowed by the cot, chin on his chest, snoring, voices rumbling deeply. It was a wonder Palaton or Cleo or anything else could sleep with that thunder. He thought of his grandfather for an odd moment, then knew the head of his Householding would never have sat up with him. Tresa had, doing her quiet embroidery. He eyed the Choya. He did not understand the relationship with the woman. It was not sexual, exactly, nor was it equality—but there was something undefinable between them which both attracted and repelled Palaton.

He felt as though he were a voyeur, viewing an unspeakable act which was both profane and holy. He knew without being told that it was because of this relationship that Daman had forsaken Cho and would never return.

It had to be. Humankind was not a member of the Compact yet, and any close contact of this kind was strictly forbidden. Therefore, Daman had removed himself from his race and Cleo from hers. Even those who knew of burnout associated it with the regimen of maintaining the mechanics of the FTL drive. What was their relationship that Daman would have betrayed himself to her?

"Slept enough and thought enough?" asked Daman quietly. It took Palaton aback for a second until he realized that, at some point during his musing, Daman had stopped snoring. The Choya put his callused hand out and caressed the air around Palaton, outlining his aura. He was, Palaton knew instinctively, outlining his aura.

"You look well tonight."

"I feel better. Have you ever had burn-out fever?"

"No. I know what it's like to have the talent leave you, tease you, like waves rushing in and then retreating from the shoreline. I know what it's like to be yawning empty one second and then bursting the next. But I never got the disease like you have. I had it treated at the onset."

"Treated?" Palaton sat up on his cot. It molded with his movement and he bolstered it behind his shoulders against the wall.

Daman hesitated. "Cleo thinks I should tell you," he offered. "She has no children and never will. But she has maternal feelings which well out of her. I sometimes forget she's not Choya'i."

"I don't want to know your secrets," Palaton said hastily, suddenly feeling as if he could bear no more burdens.

Daman's eyes crinkled. " 'Twould be a help to you, I think. But I'll abide by your wishes—" The two suddenly froze.

Daman undoubtedly felt it more clearly, but even Palaton could sense the sudden change in atmosphere. The massive Choya lurched to his feet. "Damn it all."

Then Palaton heard what they'd sensed. Starship, coming in, like a comet streaming into the atmosphere, sizzling with its heat and speed. His heart sank as he realized what he'd done.

"I've drawn them here."

The big Choya shook his head. Moonlight glinted amid his silver curls. "Take Cleo. Tell her I said to get underground. I've a single rider jet sled. My best weapons are aboard that ship." He bolted from the room.

Palaton got up unsteadily. He cast about. Used to senses beyond his ordinary ones, he wavered across the room. By the time he was through the lock, Cleo had the lights on and was joining him in the main room, pulling on her oddly styled clothing.

"What is it?"

"Incoming," Palaton answered reluctantly. "Daman said for us to go underground."

He was not used to her reactions. Her face grayed suddenly and she swayed. He put a hand out to catch her. Her luminous eyes brimmed with unshed water. "Oh God," she muttered. "They've come after us."

"After me." His mouth went dry. "What did Daman mean by underground?"

"This way." Cleo hesitated. "Can't you go with him?"

"I'm useless this way. If they're Ronin, well, the Ronin are not brave. A good defense will change their minds fairly quickly. He's gone to the ship to use the on-board weaponry."

The woman put a hand to her mouth, her gesture stilted because of her lack of Choyan joints. Her gray-streaked hair looked disheveled. She hesitated.

"He said to go underground," Palaton repeated mildly. She yielded. "Follow me."

The steading had been cleverly built for just such a siege. Palaton joined her in a lift that went down at least sixty feet before it opened onto a solidly lined tunnel. There were cots, privies, a water course, and an older recycler generator to keep the oxygen level up and pure. The shelter had been made for air strikes. She sealed off the shaft and led him into the tunnel.

Cleo lay down on one of the cots. She rolled into a crescent, her face blank, as if she could follow Daman in her thoughts. Palaton did not interrupt her trance, if that was what it was, although he thought it odd. He'd had no inkling that humankind had any kind of talent whatsoever.

After long moments, it was not necessary to depend on

talent. The very land surrounding them shook, reverberating with bomb attacks. Cleo looked up wildly, water streaming down her face. Palaton could feel the tension in his hands as though he played the console board, keying on the weaponry, and he knew that his *bahdur*, faintly as it had returned, transient as it might prove to be, gave him this empathy.

Then, darkness.

Cleo let out a shriek and collapsed sobbing upon the cot. Palaton went to her instantly, smoothed her hair back from her forehead, talking constantly, small nonsenses, to quiet her.

The sobbing stilled to a moan. Then Cleo lifted her face from the cradle of her hands.

"He's dead," she said. "It's over."

Palaton agreed, but he said, "He's a Choya and a *tezar*. Don't underestimate him."

Cleo looked at him. Her chin dimpled and trembled. "In the morning," she asked, "will you take me to him?"

If there was a morning. If Daman had taken the Ronin to death with him. Palaton nodded. "In the morning."

Morning illuminated the charred and still burning wreckage. The wind from it stank of death and saltwater bog. Palaton stood in it as long as he could bear it. From a sandy knoll nearby, he had seen the scarring where the attacker had come down as well, a wide swath carved into the earth, and a fiery charred cavern at its end. Thin gray smoke curled into the air above it.

He watched the woman pacing the wreckage as though she wished to comb through it and yet knowing that nothing remained in that twisted ingot which had once been a proud starship and was now a slowly cooling molten coffin for a Choya. She kept her hand to her mouth, muffling her cries. At long last, she turned away from the wreck and came back to him.

"You'll take me to the spaceport."

"If you wish." He had brought this on her. He would undo it if he could. It did not seem possible Daman's vibrancy could be so suddenly wiped from the face of the world. "I'll help however I can."

"No," she said. "I'll help you. I'm going to take you to

the only other place we could have called home. I'm going to take you to the College. No matter what it costs you."

Palaton stared at the crazed woman. He agreed because he had no choice. He could go no lower. He had murdered out of ignorance and denial and last night, he had murdered out of selfishness. He owed her his life and his soul.

A tiny spark of *badhur* had been rekindled within him. He had no inkling of what a humankind would do with it. "I'll take you," he said, "wherever you want to go."

Chapter 21

They helped each other make the journey. They took the hover sledge, a slow, clumsy vehicle modified to transport supplies in bulk, to the spaceport. It was, by Palaton's standards, an extremely primitive facility. They had only three launching berths, two of which were serviceable and the third of which was being used as a dry dock repair bay. There was no distress homing beacon, which, though he had no memory of it, explained to Palaton why he had brought the escort in on a crash-landing basis—because there had been no other way to bring the vehicle in.

The primary occupants of this world were saurian, lazy at midday, scurrying about busily in the morning and evening hours when their body warmth found activity more conducive. Cleo told him they had been a servile race to the Quinonans; he did not remember any such, but knew the Compact had forced the Quinonans to divest themselves of imperialistic activities several centuries ago. This resettled planet might be the result of Compact action.

Cleo did not speak much of the saurian tongue. She had neither the physical attributes to do so nor the tutoring, but Palaton watched in bemusement as the saurians attempted Trade along with a hand-sign language complicated by how spindly their fingers were compared to those of the humankind. Whatever communication needed to be made went through speedily, however, for Daman had evidently been a respected member of the community and Cleo had no trouble spending the credit of his estate. Daman also had his own starship. She ordered it fueled and berth-loaded. She backed up her orders with no nonsense body language, unmistakable in any speech.

She turned around, her face pinked by a day in the sun on the unshielded hover sledge; and fanned herself with a reed-woven hat. "It will take a while, and there'll be a noonday break, but we should be able to board by dusk."

Palaton held himself very tall. He looked down at the woman. His voices sounded faint to him when he spoke, and he hated himself for showing weakness. "I need to rest."

She put a hand out, catching him by the wrist. "Of course you do. They've a center not far from here. How about a cup of hot *bren*?"

"That sounds agreeable."

"Daman made the hotelier order a private stock and keep it for him. Come with me," and Cleo, who towered over these saurian people much as he towered over her, led the way through the bustle of the port.

The hotelier poured real *bren*, hot, dark, its bittersweet aroma pungent in the private booth he'd led them to. Palaton sagged gratefully onto cushions and watched as the obsequious innkeeper, his girth well rounded for one of these saurian folk, bowed and left them.

Momentarily, a look of amusement veiled the expression of regret masking Cleo's face. She circled her hands about the cup, her single elbows resting on the table. She looked awkward, Palaton thought. The amusement fled, her sorrow returned. "Will the Ronin return for them?"

"Probably not. They'll send in spies this time. Daman taught them caution, if nothing else. And, finding nothing, they'll leave." Every word was an effort. His chest ached when he finished speaking and he drowned his pain with the hot *bren*, draining his cup. Cleo refilled it automatically from the silvery urn the saurian had left for them.

"You've asked no questions about where I'm taking you."

"It would do me no good to."

She fanned herself again with her homemade hat. "The answers would do you good."

He sipped cautiously at his second cup, this time feeling the tongue-numbing heat, as the aroma wafted along his palate and curled into his senses, giving him the familiar, soothing taste and, with it, a sense of well-being. "Whatever I have to give is yours. I cannot possibly repay the debt I owe you." *Or the Compact.* He sat watching her, knowing again the yawning ache of his power fled, unreliable, smoldering into gray ashes from what had once been a bonfire of possibility.

"It's not what you have to give me, it's what we can give you." Cleo lifted her cup, but he had the impression it was to hide her face rather than to drink, as it remained motionless at her lips. "If you're not too proud to take it."

She knew little of the Choyan, for all the years she'd spent in companionship with Daman. He had no pride left. She sat and watched a shell performing movements, struggling to maintain a balance, a norm, without imploding under the emptiness. "There's nothing you can do for me. The *bahdur* goes with the neuropathy. The disease progresses at its own rate for each Choya. I have no idea have much time I have left," he answered slowly.

"How do your hand and arm feel?"

"A slight numbness here," and he pinched two fingers together. "The telegraphing pain is gone."

"Minor neuropathy then. You've hundreds of nerves in your hands. You can afford to lose one pathway."

She pricked his anger. "Woman, I'm familiar with my own composition. I know what I face. You do not. How can you know what *bahdur*, or its loss, is?"

"You'd be surprised what I know," Cleo answered enigmatically. She stood up. "I'm going to close the booth off for privacy. I suggest you lie down and wait. We've a credit line here, too. If you're hungry, order something. Just do it before noonday break. And don't leave without me."

He shot her a look. "I've nowhere to go."

Cleo laughed. "You'd be surprised about that, too. If the general folk around here learn a Choya is in their midst, you'll be pestered to death. They think your touch is a talisman. You'd spend the day blessing babies. The hotelier is ensuring our privacy now, but if you wandered . . . you'd be theirs until they brought you back." She set her hat on her gray-streaked hair. And stood waiting for his response.

"I'll stay," he said grudgingly and settled back on the booth cushions. The *bren* was already warming his interior. Sleep sounded like a welcome alternative to arguing with this creature.

"I'll be back." Cleo turned and left the cubicle. It closed off and dimmed in her wake. Palaton shut his eyes wearily.

He awoke to the distinct feeling of being watched. The

hotelier stood inside the booth, two young saurians hiding under the shadow of his girth. Palaton thought that Cleo had not left him as well guarded as she thought. He sat up.

"Master *Tezar*," the innkeep got out in acceptably spoken Trade. "My get. I implore you, for their well-being. . . ."

Palaton put a hand out and the younglings crowded in, each getting a blessing. They hissed with pleasure and scampered out of the booth.

The hotelier beamed through wide lizard jaws. "Thank you."

"It's nothing." He ordered food as Cleo had suggested, picking and choosing carefully, unaware of the differences between his diet and hers. "You can bring it after noonday break," he added, whereat the hotelier who had been looking distressed, relaxed again. He waddled out of the booth after his young.

The disturbance had allowed the heat of the day to penetrate and it lulled him back to sleep. When he woke again, Cleo sat across the table, picking through food the hotelier had quietly left.

He roused as she said, "Our ship's been berthloaded. Fueling's nearly done."

"Have you finished your business?"

"Yes." Her eyes brimmed suddenly. "I wanted to dispose of the homestead and our goods."

"You won't be coming back?"

"No." Cleo shook her head emphatically. "Not this way."

"Then we'll board as soon as we've eaten. I don't fly a ship I haven't inspected."

The brimming in her eyes intensified suddenly, and he knew without her answering that he'd said something that reminded her of Daman. He looked away, unable to bear the additional pain he'd inflicted.

Daman's ship was a standard class cruiser, old, but he'd flown older, and it had been modified with the black box *tezarian* drive, so it was more responsive than he expected. He brought it off-planet in an ungainly move, a sheer triumph of brute force over gravity. Cleo sat in the navigator sling, her face drawn by the strain as they broke free.

"I'd forgotten," she said. "How hard it can be."

He did not answer her, lost in his own thoughts about the job before him. He brought the engines up so that they might enter Chaos as soon as possible. He'd never entered Chaos before without an inkling of where he wanted to go.

Cleo put her hand out again, touching him. A peculiar habit of these humankind, he thought, but did not move away. "When you're ready," she murmured, "I will show you where to go. Daman left it with me."

He looked at her in surprise, then. "You've talent?"

"Oh, no. But I've memory. And Daman knew we would—that is, you could—retrieve it."

The thought of such an intimacy with an alien shocked him into silence. He sat looking at her, ignoring the flashes and beeps of the instrument console which warned him of the approach of the void.

Cleo whispered, "You must do it quickly. It's been a long time since I've faced Chaos. I'm not sure how well I'll be able to take it. It's been tougher than I thought."

He realized then that, like Daman, she was no longer young. Nor could she be expected to look into the face of Chaos like a Choya. He took her fingers off his arm gently and, extending his own hand, cradled the side of her face carefully.

"Look into my eyes."

She did. Beautiful eyes, he thought, before ripping aside the curtain of her thoughts and reaching inward.

Daman's sending burned crystal clear. He took it and left, so swiftly he might have been a lancet piercing a wound, pain induced and then removed. Cleo let out a gasp and her eyes fluttered as he left her. Then she sobbed and buried her face in her cupped hands.

He drew back in shock. "Have I hurt you?"

"No." More sobs. Then, "Oh, God. I thought you'd take it all. I thought . . . I thought I'd have nothing left of him with me." Cleo mopped her face on the back of her hands and sniffed. "Thank you."

Baffled, he returned, "Do not thank me until I have brought us to journey's end." And he prepared for Chaos to take them, praying to the God-in-all that the splinters of *bahdur* he held up to light their way would be bright enough.

Part III

Arizar

Chapter 22

Spring bells bloomed over the south wall of the lower campus. Cleo trained her eyes on them as they clung ivylike to the red brick administration building, the Arizarian sky a vibrant blue backdrop to the plateaus which held the college. She rubbed her arms against a chill she didn't remember from her youth, listening to the murmurs of the upset Choyan behind her, deliberately not looking back to the waiting room with its one-way viewing door which showed the haggard Palaton slouched upon a couch, eyes sunk in weary thought. Two Choyan stood guard over him. The welcome had been far from what she'd expected.

She spoke up, over the agitated muttering. "He brought us in on a mere flicker of *bahdur,* alone, without one of you to guide him, with only my human memory (she did not mention the final visions given her by Daman, nor would she ever). He was incredible. And he will be brilliant again, if you aid him. How can you think of turning him away?"

The Choyan in this room dominated her in a way Daman never had, not even in their first days as Brethren, and she reacted in spite of herself, biting her lip at her boldness of speech.

"You haven't come through our gates in thirty years since we gave you away to be bonded. *Tezar* Daman broke our trust then. How do we know you haven't returned to break our trust again? Circumstances have changed."

"*You* haven't changed, Reeve Bryad." And the Choya who faced her with hair of ebony and eyes of rainwater blue had not. He had aged imperceptibly. Perhaps there was a new line in his face, perhaps not. He carried the weight of authority as easily as his horn crown, but he was still the tutor she remembered, though now he was the

Reeve in charge of the entire campus. "I don't know why
Daman left. I do know that we never set foot on Compact
lands. He vowed he would never do that, and he didn't.
No one knew who he was, what he did. He was a technician
and a trader. If he broke a trust with the College, I don't
know how he could have done it."

Provost Ferson said bluntly, "He left and took you with
him." Ferson had had a stroke since the days when she had
known him as secretary to the old Reeve. Perhaps that was
why Bryad had taken up the succession instead. The Choya
held himself cupped protectively, favoring his left side, the
left side of his mouth slack, his eye drooping slightly, his
arm in a cast. His white hair had that yellow sheen of age.
He carried a wicked looking cane. She somehow imagined
him slinging it at impetuous students.

Cleo blinked. She brought her mind back to the matter
at hand. Were they telling her Choyan never left with their
Brethren? "Was this never done?"

Bryad moved a pace nearer the one-way screen. He ignored her question. "He's one of the House of Star?"

"Daman said so. I've talked very little with him. He's
recovering from a terrible round of burn-out fever." She
would let Palaton speak for himself of the rest.

Provost Gracet had remained seated, saying very little
in her soft voices. She wore her dark hair in short curls,
beribboned among her horn scallops. She said now, "The
greater the talent. . . ." Her eyes were quicksilver gray,
like lies.

A thin, wiry Choya with dark hair and hazel eyes sat at
the desk. He kept bringing up information on his data
screen. He looked up briskly. "There's been no contact
from here." He looked at the Reeve. He seemed nervous
and his voices had been among the tenser tones she'd been
listening to when they talked among themselves.

"He won't be in our data base, then," the Reeve mused.
"It will take some time to access what we need to know,
without being found out. Won't it, Ferson?"

The thin Choya nodded energetically.

"Give us the name again, Cleo."

"Palaton," she said slowly, and spelled it.

The Reeve abruptly put his hand up. "I know the name."
He swung about and stared intently now at the failed pilot

in the waiting room. "Are you sure? That's him. . . . Four hundred went to their deaths because of him?"

Cleo answered reluctantly, knowing she could not protect Palaton's privacy any longer. "Yes."

"We picked up the emergency transmission he put out. It was almost a *sending*, it was so strong." The Reeve mused.

"Another Fallen Star," Gracet said, once again letting the full meaning of her sentence trail away, catching the Reeve's glance. They traded a look.

The Reeve seemed to make up his mind. "Ferson, get Dr. Ligo up here. Our guest will need some downtime before he's ready to talk about the College and what we can do for him. By then, we should have records accessed. As for you, Cleo," and the Choya looked at her down a long, thin nose. "What do you want of us?"

She spread her hands uncertainly. She knew what she'd intended to ask, but the Reeve was correct. Things had changed since she'd left. She wasn't at all sure what the changes were, or if she liked them. But she had nowhere else to go, and this was where she had found Daman. "I'd like to stay here. I can work with the new students."

The Reeve caught up one of her work-creased hands. "You know the greater portion of the lower campus is a biosphere. We can use a skillful gardener as well as a dorm mother." He smiled at her.

Cleo returned the expression hesitantly. She put her other hand in his, determined to use him just as she knew he was determined to use her.

The Reeve waited until he and Gracet were alone in his office. He looked at the data filling the screen which Ferson had left on for him. "Such a one," he said, "would never have come to us on his own."

"Only because we have to be very circumspect in our recruiting."

"No. Not this one."

Gracet stirred, her lips pursing much as they did when students gave her an argument. She did not like being crossed. Her stern expression was at odds with her beribboned hair, but Bryad knew which was the real Gracet. She had never been dainty or pliable and would not be now. "It's too risky. We expect Nedar of Sky. Our contact was sure of his response. That one is desperate. Our information shows them to be classmates and rivals, of a sort. One or the other, Bryad, you must choose."

"We can't afford to choose! We need all the new blood we can get. And Cleo, in her bonded way, senses what is most important to us. He has *talent,* all the bounty a *tezar* is subject to. We can't overlook him or turn him away. We have the advantage, he doesn't. We know the course of the disease. We know his talent will return nearly intact after this initial bout, he doesn't. We have him at his most vulnerable."

"And if he proves a liability?"

Bryad smiled. "According to the records, he's been presumed lost. We've no risk."

"Not unless he himself turns on us." Gracet got up to leave the Reeve's office. She paused at the doorway. "Remember that," she said.

"I didn't inherit this office on the merits of faulty judgment."

"Just remember." She opened the door and left.

Bryad returned to his chair. The information Ferson had accessed so far had been sketchy but intriguing. "So, my Choya," he murmured to himself as he stretched his fingers over the keyboard and made private records. "You think yourself responsible for disaster. I wonder how long I can keep you in the dark?"

It was dark in the ground shuttle. Most of the windows were shuttered against the violent squall which had hit them after leaving the port. Randall stubbornly kept his open as the shuttle rocked and bumped through dark swirling clouds. He saw a sheet of lightning flash, gone so quickly he could barely see it, except that when he closed his eyes, it was emblazoned on his inner sight.

Most of the others were quiet, shocked by the stormy weather and rough flight, still in the grip of the tranquilizer which had been given them for the first deep space leg of the trip. He had only taken half his medicine—he wanted to savor the experience. Now his stomach finally began to unclench and the sour taste at the back of his throat receded, and he could see without experiencing that terrible vertigo. He'd only had one look at one of the infamous Choyan pilots but it was a sight he wouldn't forget.

He kept his cheek to the window. The chill of the insulated pane helped his head clear. The darkness boiling about them made him wonder what kind of storm it was they flew into. Was the Choya who'd piloted them this far still at the controls? If so, he had no fear. If not . . . this was a storm that could bring all but the mightiest down.

The girl sitting next to him pressed her leg against his. He looked down uncomfortably, wondering whether she'd done it on purpose. She looked up at the same time. She smiled quickly. He had only a moment to see that the smile did not make her eyes happy when the shuttle pitched and the youth across the aisle fell from his seat, landing on their feet.

The fallen youth cursed softly. He sat up, a broken strap of webbing hanging over his shoulder. His eyes were dark, his hair a luxurious mop, and he flashed a white-toothed smile that said he knew the worth of his roguish looks. Randall felt a twinge as the girl leaned down quickly to help him up. She squeezed him onto the seat between the two of them.

"Who are you?" she asked softly as he lashed himself in for a second time.

"Bevan," the young man answered. His voice was full of the rhythms of the South Americas even though they all spoke Trade. "And you?"

"Alexa. And this is. . . ."

"Randall," he said quickly.

"Ah," laughed Bevan. "Your name is too serious. It makes you serious, too. I'll call you Rand."

The shuttle lurched again. They were thrown together still more tightly. Even across Bevan's wiry body, Randall could smell Alexa's subtle aroma, the slightly musky-rose scent of a perfume that had been popular at home. His stomach gave a peculiar twist of homesickness. She looked at him as if she knew his thoughts. She wet her lips quickly and looked away.

The nine other students talked little. One girl shrieked every time the shuttle dropped or rolled until her voice went hoarse and then silent. Randall went to sleep thinking of her open mouth gasping to produce sound.

He woke with his ears popping, his body straining against the safety web. Bevan put a hand on his shoulder. The cabin air smelled very acrid.

"I think, my friend, this is it. I overheard some chatter up front. Our guardians are nervous."

As Randall understood it, a second leg of deep space flight was not necessary. Once into Chaos, one could pilot anywhere with a Choya at the helm. But they'd been told they were being moved in stages. Two deep space legs. This shuttle was taking them to a second port. He wondered if they were being followed.

Alexa's face was very pale in the dim light of the cabin. "Are we landing?"

"No." Rand shook his head sharply. "This is no approach." His glance met Bevan's. "This feels like evasion action."

Bevan said, "They want no followers. In space or through Chaos. It's going to be a rough ride."

"Looks like it."

Alexa laughed harshly. "I'm dead already. What does it matter?"

"What?"

"Never mind. How do we survive this?"

Bevan answered. "I think we follow crash procedures."

They stood up, kicking the seats down into their recessed placements and relying strictly on their safety webbing. Hung in their stable yet resilient hammocks, they waited. In the orange-washed light, they could see others get to their feet, snap themselves into the hammocks and do the same.

Alexa wrinkled her nose. "I feel like a fly in a spider's web."

"If it keeps us in one piece, that's okay," said Bevan with his soft accent.

Randall tried to calculate the angle of descent. He swiveled his head about, looking out his window. Black mountain pierced gray cloud. He saw the vessel pacing them. "Oh, God," he said. "That's an Abdrelik ship." The aggressiveness of the Abdreliks scared him. The aliens were unpredictable. And he was off-world now, in territories where they could bend the rules.

Alexa kicked her feet, twirling lazily in the hammock, so she could look out. "Is that it? We're being followed?"

They all knew secrecy was of the utmost importance. They had been told that when they were recruited and it had been reiterated when they'd been collected. Now the revelation of their secret was about to obliterate the adventure they'd begun.

Then the shuttle hit, bounced, and hit again, and the force of the shock sent them spinning through air.

Chapter 23

Rand had been wrong about a landing approach. Light flooded the cabin and the crew entered quickly, disentangling the students from their slings.

"Come on, kids, let's move!"

He dug his toes into the floor for purchase and began unfastening himself as the crew wove their way through.

"Who told you to put the crash webs on?"

"We did," Rand and Bevan said simultaneously.

The crew chief paused. He was a beefy man of florid complexion whose chunky body made folds in a suit never designed to contain his kind of structure. "Good thinking," the man said softly, and worked his way past the three of them. "Get out of here as quick as you can and make for the launching berth."

Rand had to help Bevan down—the slender youth gave an impression of tallness, but although slightly older, was actually an inch or two shorter than Rand—and they both disentangled Alexa. Her form came into their hands, warm and supple, and Rand started, suddenly aware of how different she felt compared to Bevan's lean wiriness. Bevan flashed him a grin as if aware of the same difference. Randall swallowed.

"Let's get out of here."

Up front, the most sedated students were being awakened roughly, gotten on their feet, and force-marched. The hoarse screamer was carried out over a crewwoman's shoulder, slung upside down, her face contorted with the effort to scream.

The sharp, thin air of a desert plateau hit Rand as they moved out of the shuttle. A quick search of the sky showed a building storm front on the leading edge of a range. He could see the dull lights of the berthing cradle and began to move toward it instinctively.

"What's going on?" the girl behind him asked. Bevan made a noncommittal sound, but Rand answered, "They're trying to keep our movements hidden."

Bevan snapped his fingers. "That's why we're going on a two-leg jump."

"Probably."

Alexa stumbled in the dark and bent over to massage her ankle. Her curly hair bounced around her face as she did so. "I don't understand." Her posture muffled her voice.

"We're trying to shake off trackers. That's why they strip-searched us before we boarded the first ship in case we wore homers, and that's why we're pulling some of the tactics we're pulling now."

Alexa stood up. In the desert night, her face seemed pale. She met Randall's. gaze squarely. "Wasn't that an Abdrelik ship?"

"Looked like one. We either lost it in the cloud cover coming in or—" Rand's glance flickered to Bevan. He had a suspicion they'd traded shots.

Bevan shrugged fluidly. "He thinks, my lady," the young man said with his accented words, "we shot them down."

"What?"

Rand took a breath. "We lost 'em somehow. Come on. I have a feeling they're not going to wait for us—they're in a hurry." He took Alexa's elbow and coaxed her toward the berthing cradle. They had exited first, but now the others had outstripped them.

A tall, graceful, yet wrongly angled figure loped past them. He carried a caselike object with him. Rand spotted him out of the corner of his eyes and stumbled himself, drawing up against Alexa's compliant form, as the alien passed and made his way into the starship. It was their Choya pilot. The sight of him made Rand's stomach drop and his chest tighten.

"What is it?" Bevan asked, curious.

"The pilot," Rand said. They looked at him as if waiting for more. He shook his head, urging, "Come on!"

As they entered the loading tunnel ramp, Alexa reached out and gripped each of them by the arm. "Let's stay together," she urged.

That would be difficult as the crew had kept the students divided by sex. Bevan gave Rand another look, shrugged again, and said, "We shall try, my lady."

Relief washed over the girl's face. She stayed sandwiched between the two taller boys as they entered the belly of the starship. The crew counted them off, handing out paper cups with tiny pills in them.

"Take your meds and find your couches. Keep your safety webs on—we're making the jump immediately."

There was no time to separate the three of them. Randall made a rueful face and took all of his medication this time. He wanted to be aware and alert when they reached the College instead of sick with vertigo.

Alexa lay down, fastened her harness, and then put each of her hands out. Bevan took one and Rand, after a moment's hesitation, took the other. Her palm was warm and dry in his. He grew sleepy wondering how long he would have to hold her hand and if his would get sticky and sweaty, embarrassing him. The starship vibrated with power, thrusting them deep into their couches. Just before he lost consciousness completely, her slight voice said, "I want both of you to be my lovers."

He woke alone, his ears ringing, his eyes crusted. He knew the keen disappointment of having missed the flight, the eerie sense of reality twisted inside out, the awesome feeling of walking a corridor which might or might not exist in the same time-frame, all the sensations which toyed with human sanity. Most of all he mourned his inability to take part in the piloting, to understand what it was about the *tezarian* drive which transcended flight. He wanted to be at the helm, piercing Chaos, taking the starship down unimaginable pathways. He lay wrapped in half awake thoughts.

The burly crew men came through. "Wake up, sleepyhead. Breakfast is on and then we're disembarking."

The thought of food brought him out of his safety harness and to his feet. There was a new world outside the skin of this starship. Rand hurried to meet it.

The Zarites at the port reminded him of walking hamsters, though sleeker, with big, round, transparent ears which flicked and blushed with emotion, and furred tails to give them balance. They worked to unload the starship, showing deference to both Choyan and human, their whiskers laid flat against their cheeks, their six-fingered, capable hands deftly working the equipment.

Rand caught one of them watching him surreptitiously. He grinned at the Zarite, watched the blush spread throughout its/his/her ears, and the piebald colored creature spun around in distress.

He caught it watching them again as they climbed into the shuttle which would take them to the College. Other sharp-muzzled, curious faces watched as well. Alexa laughed as she pressed her nose against the portal window when he pointed them out.

She turned her head sharply and their faces almost bumped. Randall drew back. She laughed again, her breath sweet with the aroma of the vegetable casserole they'd had for breakfast.

"They're beautiful." Her eyelashes lowered and rose, and she raised a hand idly to the curve of her neck, where she scratched a minor irritation.

The burly crewmaster had been striding past. He stopped, leaned past them, and saw what they were looking at. He laughed sharply. "Them? The Zarites are fast-fingered, grubby land workers. They'll have the flight suits off you and salvaged before you can blink. Watch 'em. You two settle in or Provost Gracet'll have my head for bringing you all in late." He brushed through.

Bevan leaned out of his seat and drew Alexa in beside him. Rand knew a certain sense of relief as well as irritation as he found an empty flight chair and sat down. Almost there. The goal he and his father had spent years working toward was almost within his grasp.

He was still woozy when they took the shuttle from the Arizarite port to the mountains where the upper and lower campuses of the College of the Brethren were located. He got an impression of a wilderness as varied and unpredictable as old North America used to be only perhaps a bit more lush and river-tracked. They were served mugs of something called *bren*, hot, thick, smoky tasting, like coffee or roasted malt . . . he wasn't sure. It woke him up and sat comfortingly in his stomach like a glowing ember.

Then the hills and mountains of the College rose before them. They were green up to the timberline, then purple and sheer, broken off as if whole cliffs had sloughed away under the pressure of reaching for the sky. Only the purest and sharpest, made it. White clouds billowed in a sky of clearest blue. He could see the hilltop which had been leveled for the campus, and the biosphere units scattered across it. Rand sucked in his breath. The dream was real.

The Choya known as Provost Gracet met them at the front gates. Beyond her, Rand could see the faces of other students, young men and young women, most a little older, some a little younger, all on the threshold of their adult life, looking curiously at the new arrivals. Gracet arrivals. Gracet bore herself with great dignity, towering over the humankind. She looked once, over her shoulder, at the gate. Faces disappeared, then reappeared as soon as she had turned around again. Randall was reminded of the Zarites.

A great deal of the College was built of blue stone and red brick, except for the massive dome-halls which housed the biosphere's gardens, ponds, and aviaries. It looked as if it had been carved out of the mountains. Randall thought of Nepal, in the Himalayas, the Rooftop of the World. His world. This, he thought, was the rooftop of Arizar.

Gracet spoke in Trade, a language which he had spoken exclusively since leaving his home in preparation for this, but he still followed her laboriously.

"Twelve students," she said. "Hoping to become Brethren. We will lose at least four of you in the first few weeks. Over the next few spans, another two of you will leave us. Six then . . . six graduates. Look at one another. Remember your faces and dreams. Either the one on your left hand or your right hand will fail."

Bevan stood to his left and Alexa flanked his right. They looked at him. Bevan shook his head and rolled his eyes. He was not going to be frightened.

"Only the successful will know what it means to become a Brethren." Gracet opened her arms, sinuous and graceful with their double elbows, beckoning them through the gates.

Rand found his duffel in a pile next to the gatepost and hoisted it over his shoulder. He was one of the last to enter. The gate swung shut almost on his heels with a heavy bang, closing away the rest of the world. The bars quivered with a sinister clang.

He was reminded that every dream carries a bit of nightmare within it.

Cleo stood like a mountain, not taller, but vaster, deeper and broader than he was. She kept her chestnut brown hair bound back, the gray streak over her right brow making her look like a thunderbolt had struck her. She moved gracefully despite her heft and embraced the four children put into her dorm by Gracet. Rand found an instant liking for her, though he was unsure of what to say or do, she was so unlike his mother, who wandered palely through his memories of the days before she had left.

Cleo pointed at Alexa. "A loft room for you, with a window seat, where you can curl up at night and read and write poetry."

The girl blushed, her lips half-opened in soft protest, then she hung her head, her curly fringe of hair curtaining her eyes.

Cleo continued briskly. "A separate room for you as well, Master Bevan. I recognize a charmer when I see one and I think you need to be kept alone if the others are to retain anything of theirs."

Bevan murmured half an objection which died softly on his lips. He shrugged in answer. "Your request, my lady."

Rand feared her look when she faced him, but her face softened. "Ah. The clear eyes of a seeker of truth. I'll put you in with Ahmad . . . no. Zain. Yes. That should do."

The fourth student who'd come in with them was another girl, dreadfully thin, freckled, with deep red hair. She had an astonishing birth-mark on the nape of her neck, like a crescent sienna moon. Megan brightened as Cleo called her name. "I have a room, you might not like it, mind you, Stella is bossy and brassy . . ."

"I won't faint away," Megan said. Her voice, unlike her mannerisms, was coarse and deep.

"Good. Well, then, here are your maroons. There are two classes of students here, beginners in maroons, and those about to become Brethren, in the blues. Age doesn't earn you the blues. Going the course earns you that. Any questions?" Cleo held jumpsuits out, with zippers and buckles on them to take up, let out or lengthen almost any seam.

Bevan took his with a sigh, holding it up. He would have to adjust the leg length. He laughed as Rand held his up.

"Who wore that last? An elephant?"

Cleo narrowed her gaze. "Mind your manners, boy. That was mine when I was a student here."

Bevan's mouth snapped shut. He blinked a few times as if checking her credibility, then laughing softly at himself as her eyes crinkled.

The other students headed up the household hallways. Rand held back. "I have a question," he said hesitantly.

"Ask away." Cleo paused, her body quivering slightly, as if holding her back from motion took a great deal of effort.

"When will I meet a . . . a pilot?"

"A *tezar*? Well, my boy, you might never. The ones who come stay at the upper campus. You've got to earn the right." Her eyes misted slightly.

"Did you know one?"

"Ah, yes. I was bonded for . . . many years." Cleo's lips whitened. "Trust you to ask the hard questions. I can't give you those answers now. Maybe later."

"How much later?"

Cleo patted the suit over his arm. "When you've earned your blues." She looked up, saw a head peering over the banister. "Zain, get down here and collect your new lamb."

Zain was a dark-skinned man with cocoa eyes that slanted at the corners and an easy grin. He was tall, with long, gangly arms that reminded Rand of the Choyan he'd seen. Zain wore blue. The third floor room was cozy, two beds, two dresser compartments, two closet/bookcases. Zain's was neat, though obviously lived in, and he had books and manuals strewn all over the pull down desktop. Rand's half of the room did not look as if it had been occupied for some time.

Zain perched on Rand's bed. "Get into your maroons. There'll be a hazing muster any second now. You'll lose points if you're not dressed."

Rand skinned out of his clothes in response. The suit's zippers and buckles nearly defeated him until the darker boy came to his rescue.

"What hazing?"

Zain rolled his eyes. "You'll see." He stepped back. "Now you be good to our Cleo, hear? She's new, just come back to the College after a long, long time, but we like her."

His voice was full of island color. The deep rich sound of it filled the room. Rand grinned in spite of himself. Zain chucked his chin.

"You just a new kid," he said. "You'll see." His voice dropped. "You want to see a *tezar,* I know where there's one. He's been sick . . . he's staying at Dr. Ligo's. We won't go tonight, but if you're good and study hard. . . ." Zain rolled his eyes again, this time in promise.

A pounding at the door interrupted them. A gang of male and female students, myriad in their colors and races, pressed in, grabbed Rand up, and swept him out despite the fact he still had one bare foot, his shoe clutched in his hand. At the fringe of the gang, he spotted Bevan, who had his suit half-on, clutched around his waist, a white cotton shirt over his lean torso. Alexa was dressed, her thick, curling hair pulled back in combs. She waved at him as the mob swept along.

The spring night was cold, crisp, its air rich with a hundred scents he could not identify. Some of it might have come from the kitchen hall, but most from the makeup of Arizar and the campus itself. Bird whistles and calls stilled as the students mobbed into a large, concrete square, surrounded by buildings, and overlooking the biosphere dome. It stayed dark in the early evening, though he saw light sensor units. He wondered why. The students in blue carried an electricity, an excitement, with them.

Once in the square they began to sing. Rand recognized the ancient song from old videos. "We're poor little sheep who've lost our way, bah, bah, bah!"

Rand tried to sing while he jumped on one foot and put his other shoe on. The voices rose in volume, making up for lack of singing talent. Lights went on in the massive stone fortress they faced, and a tall, grave looking Choya came out.

As his gaze swept over them, the crowd quelled instantly. Zain had shouldered next to Rand and elbowed him. "That's the Reeve. He runs everything."

He raised a hand. The silence grew so still, a blade of grass could be heard growing through a crack in the cement, Rand thought. His own heart seemed to thunder in his chest.

"A new class has come in and you rejoice because it is naming night."

Zain gave a little tremor next to Rand.

"Say hello and good-bye to your classmates. The following will report to upper campus in the morning."

Zain held himself tightly. His shoulder brushed Rand. If he were a cable, he would snap. Rand tore his stare from the Reeve and looked at the young man who'd been assigned as his roommate. "What is it?"

Zain shushed him, eyes never leaving the Reeve.

Upper campus meant meeting the pilots, Rand realized. He, too, held his breath.

"Listen: Darcy Fontiene, Hector Delrio, Uwe Luserne and Mitsu Tokagawa." The Reeve paused. "To the rest of you, congratulations in your studies." He turned and left, stalking away with that elegant grace indicative of his alienness.

Cheers and whistles broke out, with the exception of Zain, who stood in shocked silence. He looked to Rand.

"Noooo. . . ." It was more a moan than a word.

Rand knew then why Cleo had chosen Zain as his roommate. She had known the young man would not be moving up. Not yet. Maybe never.

Tears glistening on his face, Zain again cried, "No," then turned and bolted, shoving students out of his way.

Instinctively, Rand raced after him.

Zain showed the fleetness of foot of a natural athlete. Rand's muscles cramped as he pounded after, stiff from the journey, from the medications, from days of lying in relative inactivity. His breath began to husk in his lungs almost immediately.

But he knew he could not let Zain out of his sight. Behind him, he could hear students shouting in alarm. Someone gave a high-pitched scream, a plea, "Zain!"

It did not slow him one bit.

They rounded a Zarite gardener, whose ears went up, then flattened in startlement. Rand skidded on a patch of mud, weeding thrown out on the walkway, nearly went to his knee, caught his balance and righted himself. Zain charged even farther ahead.

The thin mountain air, purer than he was used to, but

thinner at the same time, burned in Rand's lungs. He began to wheeze as if he could not breathe deeply enough. He opened his mouth. Sweat poured down his forehead. He could hear Zain moaning with every hard footfall.

"Zain, wait! I don't know . . . where we're . . . going."

The dark student had begun to slow, but he did not respond. Then, suddenly, he leapt.

Rand could not see what it was. But he counted and then leapt, too, body straining in midair. He hit the rim of a massive ditch, clawed over it and staggered after Zain, who'd gone to his knees for a second but was up again.

Another broken horizon of tall buildings. One was massive, its floors stretching high over the campus, its roof pitched steeply. Zain raced for it.

Suddenly afraid as well as weary, Randall followed. They burst into the interior of the building where the brightness of the lights stunned him a moment. Zain threw himself into an elevator. Rand jumped at its twin.

They paced one another in the transparent lifts. Zain would not look at him. He leaned against the glass wall, his chest heaving, his face wet with tears. Rand pounded on the glass between them, but the other student ignored him.

They got out on the rooftop. Rand nearly broke through the door before it released him, so certain was he of Zain's course. Zain jumped before he could reach him.

Rand lunged as well, and caught him by the sleeve. They both went sliding off the rooftop and down the steep pitch of the roof, stopping at the very edge of the eaves only by Rand's desperate efforts to slow them.

Rand's pulse thundered in his head. His arm stretched until he was certain it was coming out of its socket, every joint pulling, stretching, holding Zain's weight—for Zain seemed determined not to hold himself, but strained for the edge and the plunge to earth which would follow.

"Hold on," Rand pleaded. "Try holding on."

"It's no use any longer," Zain said. His arm slipped a little in Rand's hold. Fabric tore. Rand tightened his grip on the other's wrist, easier to hold than his forearm, but closer to the end. Zain gulped down a sob.

"Tell me," said Rand, "about the *tezars*."

Zain now dangled over the edge of the roof. The cords

in his neck stood out as he looked up at Rand. "Let me go before I take you with me."

Randall countered. "I know it hurts. Don't let go. Don't make me drop you." He swallowed for breath. His chest stabbed with pain. "Tell me about the *tezars*."

Zain grimaced. "When you're a blue, you'll know. They come for you when they want you. They name you. You become Brethren." His voice disintegrated into tears. "There's nothing else I want to be." He opened his hand and began to twist, to wrench, within Rand's grip.

"No!" Rand began to slide forward on his stomach, over the eave, trying to catch Zain's sleeve with his free hand. He could feel his fingers going numb, coming open.

"Zain, stay with me!"

The other gave a violent lurch, tearing himself free. Rand plunged forward to recapture him and found himself yanked back in midair as Zain fell without a scream. His body made a heavy thud when it hit.

Rand began to shake. "Oh, God. Oh, God."

A deep voice said in his ear, "It's all right. I have you."

Rand felt himself embraced. He looked up. A Choya held him.

Palaton looked at the distressed youth within his arms. In the faint light from the steeple tower, he saw brilliant turquoise eyes, stunned by the tragedy they'd just witnessed, innocent in the ways of the worlds. Humankind, he thought. One of the children. Tragedy in his eyes echoed Palaton's memory of the children of Sorrow. The boy did not yet seem to realize he would have joined the other in death but for Palaton's intervention. His voices rumbled with unshed emotion as he repeated, "It's all right. I have you."

Chapter 24

"The boy is no longer your concern," the Reeve said. He sat back in his chair. He tilted his chin up as if to listen to whatever argument Palaton might make.

"He was subjected to an incredible shock."

"Which would have been far more injurious if Dr. Ligo hadn't sent you up to see who was tramping on his roof. The boy has been counseled and is back among friends."

The subtle undertone of the Reeve's voices were pitched to remind Palaton that he was not necessarily among friends. Palaton shifted his weight. "I'm aware that I'm a guest here, but even that caution can't keep me from asking—what drove the student to kill himself?"

Bryad examined a report on his desk. Without looking back up to meet Palaton's eyes, he said, "The process our students go through to become Brethren is arduous. One of the things we do is instill a great deal of pride in the accomplishment. Zain Ardoff had already been refused once in being moved to the upper campus. He could not take being refused a second time. Perhaps it's just as well. If the early courses are arduous, the balance of their duties are nothing less than an ordeal. You're not familiar with what we do, *tezar* Palaton, nor do I feel further explanations are possible at this point. If you wish to become committed to our program, then I can continue this discussion."

The Choya'i in the corner had not till now taken part in their debate. Gracet stirred now, drawing both Palaton's and Bryad's attention. She smiled briefly. "Perhaps our guest is asking questions so that he can make a decision."

Palaton answered, "It's difficult to make any decision blindfolded. What can you do for me . . . and what price do you ask in return?"

The Reeve said emotionlessly, "We can give you back

your *bahdur, tezar.* We can restore it to you for a nearly infinite number of years. The process, once learned, can be repeated whenever your talent grows weary. As for the price we ask that you renounce your House."

"You what?" The shock of the second outweighed the first.

The Reeve folded his hands on his desk. The confidence of the gesture was at odds with the tension in his body as he leaned forward. "Within Cho, the *tezars* operate almost outside the law, indeed, outside of society itself. They answer only to their flight schools and the emperor—and, historically, have even defied the throne. Your talents are what make space endurable. You and you alone keep Cho from being swallowed up. As a *tezar,* you don't need to be answerable to any authority but that of your peers.

Palaton could not sit. He got to his feet, paced a few steps, saw Gracet watching him closely, turned, and looked back at Reeve Bryad. "You're asking for treason."

"No. I'm asking for realism. You've already crossed the boundary. Your loyalties war with the emperor who currently sits the throne." Bryad stood up as well. "We have no quarrel with him. We seek only to consolidate a House which should have been, and isn't."

"And what position on the Great Wheel would you take?"

"A position that is rightfully ours, when we're ready." Bryad stepped to the window, which offered a view of the campus. "We've much to offer Cho. We can't cure the neuropathy *yet,* but we can tame it so that it no longer cuts short the lives of our most talented." Bryad looked back shrewdly at Palaton. "I'm trusting you with this, I think I can, if for no other reason than that if you were to leave, you would leave as a murderer of four hundred. If you stay, you would stay as a hero, as a founder of new talent and possibilities. You would know that the Wheel turns for you, as it does for everyone."

Palaton swallowed tightly. He had no answer to give the Reeve. "What about the children?"

"They," said Gracet triumphantly, "are part of the process."

"But they can't know that. They surely cannot be aware of our *bahdur* and how we function."

"There are rules," answered Bryad, "that even we dare not break. And once partnered, once made Brethren, the children won't either. What I offer you, I'll only offer once. Our resources are limited and there are other *tezars* who don't suffer the qualms you do."

Palaton restrained himself. Gracet's wide, calm eyes considered him as he said, "I have to think about this."

"Do that. Walk about the campus. Attend a few classes, if you would. Watch the children of another world. Then come back to me." The Reeve showed his teeth in a smile.

Palaton left the office.

Gracet stood as soon as the building monitors showed that the *tezar* had gone. Bryad said to her, "What do you think?"

"I think we have a case of natural bonding. We know such things do occur . . . that's how Dr. Nuncia discovered the process. But there's nothing in her writings that tells us how he'll react."

"Then we have him."

"Maybe." She reached up and tugged on one of her hair ribbons, loosening a silky mane. She ran her fingers through it. "If we don't, he could be quite dangerous."

Bryad put an arm out to draw her closer. "One Choya can't bring us down. We've worked too hard and come too far to fall again."

Gracet arched her back in pleasure. She dragged a fingertip across Bryad's desk. Her voices partially muffled by Bryad's actions, she said, "We should have an answer soon. I don't think he can wait."

"Neither," answered Bryad, "can I."

Palaton strode across the campus, aware of the stir among the students. The population wasn't large, although the campus was. It had been made to house thousands where it now held dozens. He could tell by looking at it that it was meant to be the start of a House, of a colony independent of Cho, of all the things which Panshinea had hoped for and yet, if it occurred here, could be the death of him.

With his *bahdur* returned, his life once again held a realm of possibilities. One of those possibilities would surely be that he could redeem himself. He came to a halt under the large, spreading boughs of an immense tree at the corner of the quad. A group of children wandered past, gently herding a youth in the center wearing a deprivation helmet emblazoned with the Blue Ridge insignia. As he stood, astounded by the helmet, the blinded youth stumbled his way. The students parted and let him fumble toward Palaton. The student stopped just short and then removed his helmet.

He grinned to see who blocked his path. "I'm sorry, Provost," the humankind said. "Sensory deprivation class."

"So I see," answered Palaton with a certain irony. He watched as the helmet was handed over and the group made their way off in a different direction. They had mistaken him for a Choyan teacher and he was not about to correct their misperception. Why would the God-blind practice at being even blinder?

He left the shade of the tree. He also wondered how much time the Reeve would give him to make his decision.

Alexa came into the room quietly and shut the door behind her. Half the room looked incredibly sterile, where nothing remained but furniture and a bed.

Randall saw where her glance went and shrugged deeper into the covers of his own bed. He had gone cold and seemed unable to warm himself. Shock, the Choyan had told him. Dr. Ligo, a Choyan with a double horn crown and crisp chestnut fringe hanging from it, had told him so solemnly. He felt numb.

"You look better," the girl said softly.

"I don't feel better."

She sat on the floor next to him. "It sounded awful. I just wanted you to know I'm sorry."

Bevan had already been in. The Brazilian's skin had smelled faintly of her musky rose perfume, imprinted with her scent.

"Will you come to classes tomorrow? They've already started."

His dream of piloting nudged at him. He had left his parents, his home world, and his race behind to capture that dream. He'd been told he would make sacrifices and he'd expected to. But he'd never expected this. His silence woke something in Alexa's face.

She put her hand out and traced his jawline. Then she smiled broadly. "You're going to have to shave soon."

Rand grabbed his jaw where she'd touched it. Stubbly prickles met his touch and he could feel his face grow hot. He snatched her hand away.

But she did not let go of his fingers, catching them up, saying, "You're like ice!"

"I can't get warm. I keep thinking . . . I should have held on!"

"You tried." Alexa held his hand in both of hers, cradling it. She looked up at him, a distant look in her eyes, as if focusing inward even though she looked at him. The moment passed and she smiled again. "Let me help."

She stood up and touched her fasteners, opening up the maroon suit. Randall closed his eyes in instinctive embarrassment, and when he opened them, she was sliding out of the garment and kicking it aside. She wore precious little underneath and quickly removed that. "Move over," she told him, picking up the corner of his blanket.

He did.

She slipped in beside him. Her curves were warm and supple, where his were angular and bony. She wrapped a leg around him and put her palm on the flat of his stomach. He could not help his reaction to her, nor did he want to. Since her first touch days ago, he felt as if this moment would have to happen or he would burst. Her fingers encircled his hardness.

"Is this your first time?" she asked as she moved closer.

"No." The intensity of feeling brought heat gushing through him. His mouth half-opened in voiceless, response.

Alexa smiled again. "Good." She pulled the blankets over their heads. "Then you'll know how to kiss me."

When they were done, she curled up like a kitten and went to sleep, taking up more than half the narrow bed, forcing him to sleep on his side. She'd been right, Rand reflected. She'd warmed him up. He listened to her deep breathing, knowing she'd been with Bevan during the night, thinking about how he felt about her.

Everything was too new to him. He still felt a certain numbness.

A curl of her hair tickled his nose. He moved it away carefully. The bed smelled of their lovemaking and his

sweat and her perfume. He settled down into the nest their
activity had made and slept.

Alexa woke, as she usually did, sudden and hard, gasping, eyes wide and staring as if they had opened before her
conscious mind roused. She felt the lean body behind her and
gathered her thoughts quickly. The darkness of her dreams
receded as she forced them back.

She dreamed of hunting, and the kill, and even, God help
her, the sweetness of human flesh. She dreamed of eating
the helpless and reveling in it. A hot tear stained her cheek.
She brushed it quickly away, determined not to let her
dreams defeat her.

The small scar on the back of her neck, where her shoulder curved into it and then met her back, itched again. She
rubbed it pensively. The moments of sexual passion and
love pushed back her darker thoughts, but only temporarily, and now she wrestled with them again.

She wanted to go home. Her father would make a place
for her, even though the Choyan had told her she'd been
reported as deceased. She knew it was only to take her
cleanly. Her father would know and his position and money
would smooth the way.

And then she and the other would meet together and
feast with the success of their hunt—

Alexa let out a sharp cry, then covered her mouth in
dismay at the sound she'd let out. Her teeth felt sharp
against her skin. She thought of biting deep, deeper, until
the hot sweet metallic blood seeped out. . . .

The girl threw herself out of the bed and went to his
bathroom. She ran water until it was as ice cold as Rand's
hands had been and soaked her face. Then, as the dorm
room darkened the shadows of dusk, she returned and
dressed. She woke Randall, told him that the dinner bell
would be sounding soon, and left him as soon as she could
see he'd awakened. She would have to find another way to
hold the darkness at bay.

Bevan pounded on the door at sunrise. "Classes, sleepyhead," he announced. His dark, thick hair was uncombed,
looking as if he had just run his fingers through it. He had
a shoulder pack slung over his back. "And goodies."

The Trade lingo did not translate quite properly. It came out as "barter bait." Rand walked out of the toilet, a towel around his hips, bare feet slapping on the cold floor, with shaving cream and razor to his face as Bevan opened his pack upon the unmade bed.

"What have you got?"

"This, my friend, is how a student survives." Bevan mulled over the loot. "A pot for grinding and brewing *bren*."

Rand shuddered. He was still not sure if he was going to develop a taste for that or not. He finished shaving—it was not a process requiring a great deal of precision for him yet—and wiped his face dry. Bevan tossed him a pair of shorts and the maroons. "What else have you got?"

"Waterproof styluses, pocket computers and various assortments of homeworld luxuries I don't think we'll be finding here." He held up a colorfully wrapped bar.

"Chocolate!"

Bevan snatched it out of Rand's reach. "Maybe later," he said with a flashing white grin. "But not now. You stole my lady yesterday."

Rand paused, jumpsuit half on, hanging about his hips. "She came to me."

Bevan shrugged. "I do not think she is the type of woman one can capture." Again, Trade did not quite translate the meaning, but Randall thought he knew what Bevan had in mind.

"I'm sorry," Rand added. The other plied his attention to the goods strewn on the bed. He looked up, dark eyes intent. "Did she sleep well?"

"I don't know. *I* slept like the dead." Then Rand gulped, thinking of Zain. "That is—"

"Forget it. I know what you mean." Bevan began sweeping the goods back into the pack. "Stick with me, my friend, and you and I will earn our blues in record time."

"Are you in that much of a hurry?"

"Oh, yes. I have things to do and places to go." Bevan fastened the last two clips at his jawline and grinned at Randall. "Let's go."

Palaton watched the children of humankind. He became aware over days that most of them thought of themselves as grown, though they had height and maturity yet to be reached, that their temperaments ran like quicksilver, their tears almost as quick to surface as their smiles, that they had no real concept of the responsibilities that would face them as adults, though they thought they did. He found himself drawn to the tall, earnest boy with the turquoise eyes, watching him when he did not know he was being watched, thinking of the wrenching moment when their lives had collided with death.

He watched and considered, and he ached. They were alien to him, Arizar was unfamiliar, the Choyan of the College estranged and aloof and yet . . . the most alien of all he saw was himself. He had no place in any of it, not even among his own people.

Chapter 25

Vihtirne of Sky drew herself up from the small throne of her Householding, a throne that was an exact duplicate of the much larger and grander one in Charolon. She was still stunningly beautiful, despite the stress of wielding power for Sky, and her looks held Nedar still, very still, in awe.

The corner of her mouth quirked, an indication that she was aware she held this power over him.

"Nedar," she said, her voices rich with welcome. "Thank you for answering my summons."

If he reckoned relationships, Vihtirne was probably a cousin three or four times removed. If he reckoned power, there was no one in Sky more powerful. She had been a Prelate, but her scientific papers had propelled her into industry and from there into patent ownership and from there into a position of wealth and influence. Choyan died for her love, hoping to prove themselves worthy of marriage, attempting terrible trials. Her love life was a thing of scandal and yet, oddly loyal, in that when she did marry, she never abandoned the Choya until his death. He had been much older. Nedar remembered, as he watched Vihtirne, that it was rumored she currently favored younger Choya.

She held out her hand and he helped her step down from the petite footstool at the throne's base. "You look well."

Nedar nodded. "I am, thank you." Although he had held out his hand to her she kept it, and now led him to a small table, offering intimacy in a shadowed corner of the audience hall.

He had no doubt that any recording devices were wired on her body, for her own private use, as his gaze swept the seemingly innocuous corner. She sat down. He sat across from her, feeling her sexual power as well as her worldly power. It struck him that she was radiating, enticing him, and then he realized that she was fertile, and wasting little subtlety in telling him so.

Nedar sat back in his chair and considered his options.

Two crystal goblets flanked the center course. Their pale pink liquids swirled as the Choya'i leaned over them. Viht-irne lifted the cover off an antique, etched gold plate. He'd expected dinner, instead, his gaze met an empty plate.

Vihtirne laughed at his expression. "Nedar! Would you feast on empty portions?"

"It seems not." He hung an elbow over the back of his chair as he relaxed into it.

"Yet I would give this plate to you if I could. Do you recognize it?"

He shook his head. His horn crown throbbed, but he did not reveal his weakness by raising his hand to his brow and massaging the base of it. Vihtirne was sharp. If she suspected any unwellness about him at all, there would be hell to pay.

"This," she said and stroked the golden platter, "was the dinner plate of Emperor Chasden, of the House of Sky."

He straightened then. Chasden was the last of the Skies to hold the throne.

Her eyes glittered as she looked back at him. "Need I say more?"

"Mistress. You honor me." His heart thumped a few times before he got it steadied, and he knew a tic in his jawline pulsed in sympathy. She offered him the prime candidacy of his House for the throne when it came time to force Panshinea down!

She smiled at the realization visible on his face. She replaced the domed cover. It clanged softly as she did so. "I trust you burn as brightly as ever. Cho cannot withstand another weak emperor. The Abdreliks and the Ronin wait to consume us, and the Quinonan and the Ivrians to lick up the crumbs."

He did not, but he would. Ah, but he would! "I'll serve the House well."

"You will have to. It's not enough to be a *tezar* any more. You need financial acumen and cunning. I will tutor you."

Nedar lifted a crystal goblet. "Then I cannot fail."

"We should both hope not." Vihtirne lifted her goblet, at the same time making an elegant movement and letting her gown fall from her shoulders, revealing a body that marriage and time had not yet diminished.

Bevan bounced on the bed, upsetting a pile of books that went thudding to the floor. He did not seem contrite as Rand swiveled around at his study desk and glared.

"Your Choya has been following you again."

"*My* Choya. What are you talking about?"

Their voices echoed in the still half-empty room. The extra bed had been pushed across it side by side to Rand's. Sometimes Alexa occupied it and at times Bevan joined them in sleep, the three of them curled up together "like a pile of puppies," Cleo said, having caught them at it once, heads pillowed on stomachs, study manuals in their tired hands.

"Don't tell me you don't know."

Rand mopped his sweating forehead. It was deep summer on campus and even though he had his window propped open, the afternoon breeze had not yet picked up and given relief to the sweltering dorms. "It's too hot for this." He turned back to the manual spread out on his desk.

Bevan said, "He follows you everywhere. Not all the time, but I've seen him. And so has our lady."

But Alexa wouldn't have mentioned it, used to secrets as she was, Rand thought. She would no more divulge his than her own. He wagged a stylus between his fingers. "I haven't seen him."

"Ummmm. Well, work as hard as I might, you'll be getting the blues before I will."

Rand cradled his chin in his hands. "I don't know. I can't get this."

Bevan got up and stood over him. "Your Braille?"

"Yes."

In the weeks they'd been there, Bevan had grown more quickly than Rand in height. He said it was because the food was better and more plentiful than he'd gotten in Sao Paulo. Alexa, with a giggle, said it was the loving. Rand had no opinion except that now he could look the other right in his snapping, dark eyes.

"It's easy. We had to learn this at the Theresite. Because

many of us would go blind from disease or deficiencies."
Bevan reached out and shut the book loudly. "What does
this have to do with the Choyan?"

"A pilot has to be able to deal with sensory deprivation."

Bevan curled his lip. "I didn't come here to be a pilot."

"I did."

"Nobody pilots but the *tezars*."

"I will." Quiet determination rang in Randall's steady
answer.

Bevan waved a hand in the air. "Me? I want to rule
Earth's finances. There's a real power."

"And never be poor again, eh?"

"And never be *sold* again," Bevan returned sharply.
They looked at one another. Then Bevan raised and let
drop his shoulders. "There's more to this than we were
told." He summoned another mood out of thin air. "We
need a carnival!"

"Oh, no." Rand raised his hands. "I've got studying."

"Nonsense, my friend. I'll have Alexa teach you Braille
by anatomy, eh? In the meantime . . . it's too hot. I think
a hike up the falls to the cooler climes of the upper campus
is in order."

"What? Are you crazy? Maroons aren't allowed up
there."

Bevan's teeth flashed. "I have not yet had time to read
my rules book. So I don't know anything about this." His
accent became honied. "Let's find Alexa and go."

The girl sat on her window seat, looking over the campus
from her window, her hands in her lap, a faraway vision
dazzling her. She visibly started when they crashed the
door.

"Carnival," Bevan told her.

"What on earth?"

He pointed a finger. "Come, come, my lady. Having fun
is serious business: get dressed for the wilderness. We'll
meet you downstairs. We have a guardian to distract." His
eyebrows quirked, he threw back his head and Rand, with
an embarrassed glance over his shoulder at her, followed
their flamboyant friend out the door.

He not only got them off campus without anyone noticing, but stole a laundry sledge, a drudge hover, to carry them. It was made for weight not speed and slugged its way along the winding hillside pathways, the three of them riding its back as if it were a mythical flying carpet. In honor of the occasion, Bevan wrapped a scarf turban style about his dark hair.

"How will we get there?" Alexa asked breathlessly into the hot summer day.

"Believe it or not, the sledge knows the way. It was used at the upper campus before it was sent down here and repaired. It retains the directional memory."

Rand listened with a new respect for Bevan who ordinarily showed more inclination to sleight of hand than to mechanical acuity. He had to duck quickly as a low-slung branch came his way.

The trees grew sparse and the smell of their bruised needles faint as the sledge wheezed up the final incline, and they saw the upper campus, a massive, gray stone fortress carved out of a mountainside.

It looked like something out of King Arthur or some ancient feudal legend. Rand let out a whistling breath.

"It's going to be tough getting in there."

"On the other hand," Bevan said, "they probably aren't worried much about security. I doubt even the Zarites come up here."

Alexa had a hand up to her brow, shadowing her face. "It must encompass a couple of hundred acres, at least."

"Self-sufficient. It would have to be. Winters are tough this much higher up." Bevan abruptly unwound his scarf, keyed the sledge to a halt and slid off the hover. "I think we should walk the rest of the way."

"And keep to cover." Rand exchanged glances with Bevan. Both looked to Alexa.

She bristled. "Don't even say one word about my staying here."

"All right." Rand put his shoulder to the idling sledge. "How about helping push?"

They shoved the hover to the side and then killed the motors completely. It settled into the bracken with a heavy thump. Alexa dusted her hands on her hips. "I think we've reached the hiking part," she said, and strode off.

*   *   *

Deep purple shadows as cutting as blades were falling across the rock by the time they reached the lower foundation along the pathway the drudge had been following. They came upon a carven gate which was evidently used by service drones. Wheels had deeply rutted the immediate area. Bevan looked it over. The entranceway seemed to baffle him.

Alexa ran her fingers over the etched doorway. "Sensor operated. And none of us probably has the equipment it takes to trigger it."

Rand shouldered her aside. "There has to be a manual release in case of emergencies." He ran his fingers along the ridges. He found a niche. His nail broke with a nasty twinge, but as the pain jarred him, he felt something click even as it tore into the quick of his finger. He pulled back with a sharp word.

Bevan grabbed his hand just before he put it into his mouth to suck away the pain and welling blood. The other shook his head. "Tsk, my friend." He tore a ragged strip off his scarf and bound the finger. With a crooked grin, he added, "Pray they don't consider poison as an alternative security device."

Rand stared numbly as the two then walked past him into the opening grinding wide.

Down morbid stone hallways littered with the carcasses of failed machinery they walked. Rand caught up with them. Their steps whispered on the mossy flagstones. Alexa slipped once. Both boys caught her as she fell and she hung in midair between them. They set her down gently.

They passed a communications room, old, forgotten, its backup systems still blinking with power. Alexa turned to watch it as they passed, as if afraid it would sound an alarm. Then they climbed a back flight of stairs and found themselves at the outer corridor of a building which baked with heat. The smoke issuing from its vents choked them.

Bevan's eyes watered. He took Alexa's hand and drew her past, saying, "Crematorium."

"What?"

Rand had to run to catch up with them, upwind, out of the heat and stench.

"An oven for the dead," Bevan said. "It's hard to bury someone in the rocks." He went on without looking back.

"What dead?" Alexa said to Randall.

He shook his head, uncertain. Everybody died some-place, somewhere. But he wondered now why he had never asked what the College had done with Zain's body.

Bevan stayed in the shadows, in what was clearly an older part of the fortress. It was quiet and the stones showed little disturbance of the moss which coated them. They mounted a winding stair which took them onto a sec-ond thickly walled level. The rock left white powder as their maroons brushed it.

Alexa stopped, suddenly. "I don't want to go any farther."

Bevan urged her. "Come on. It's our only chance to see what the blues do."

She ran her fingers through her thick, curling hair. Then she shook her head. "I don't like this. If we're caught. . . ."

"I've never been caught on an open street yet." Bevan looked hurt.

Rand stood, torn between caution and curiosity. Finally he said, "Come on, Alexa. We're with you."

She turned wide eyes on him, deep in thought. She licked her lips, a furtive motion, then ducked her chin down, look-ing away. "All right. But not much farther in."

They drew her with them, hidden by the gloom cast by the massive wall, until they came to a break and boosted themselves up to a parapet of sorts. It was an outer balcony wall and they faced a bank of windows. Now the late after-noon sun was at their backs, still hot, clear, bright. It pierced the polarization of the windows and they looked in.

Alexa gasped and Randall stared dumbly, uncompre-hending. It was Bevan who said, "This is an asylum."

Humankind occupied the solarium. From the aged to the young, blues and maroons faded with time and disuse, the mentally disturbed rocked, walked, lay in the room. Slack faces with spittle drooling from their lips, or faces contorted with rage as they rocked violently, bang, bang, banging their forms against the chairs which confined them, to faces which alternated between knowing and blankness.

Alexa spun around, put her back to the wall, and took several deep breaths.

Rand could not challenge Bevan who had always had a knowledge of the darker side of life and poverty. These people were clearly not sane or functional. He could not tear his eyes away. As he watched, a Choya entered and came through the room, checking on several occupants, putting a hand out kindly and stroking brows. Bevan took his elbow and pulled him away from the window.

Someone inside let out a howl. It started up those who could still speak. Alexa shook, then bolted.

"Alexa!" Bevan called hoarsely after her. He turned to follow.

Someone caught Rand from behind. He felt hot breath graze his scalp as one hand slid about his waist and another around his neck, lifting him to his toes, pulling him back.

"Bevan!" He kicked and flailed but whatever had caught him up grunted and tightened its grip. The arm about his waist pulled up into his diaphragm and it was all Rand could do to breathe.

Bevan faced him. He put a hand up, saying, "Put him down."

Rand was dragged back another foot. He sensed that his captor was taking him back inside, like dragging meat into a lair. He kicked again, hard, but his captor merely grunted again.

Bevan drew a step closer. He forced a smile. Rand could only imagine what held him. Whatever it was, it was big. He could not drop his chin to see the arms. It could be a Choya, or a good-sized human. The youth waved a hand gently in the air. "You don't want to do this. You want to be good. Put him down."

The hand on his throat grew hard, each finger like a steel band. Rand choked and knew panic. Whatever held him could kill him. Possibly meant to. Possibly did not know the morality of its actions.

Bevan put a hand in his jumpsuit thigh pockets. He came up with half a bar of chocolate—chocolate again!—and held it out. "I've something good for you, if you're good for me."

The grip on his throat and stomach loosened.

"Put him down." Bevan waved the bar intriguingly.

Rand was freed. Bevan dropped the candy to the walk and bolted over the parapet side. With a gasp, Rand joined him. They ran until they found their escape corridor.

Alexa crouched inside the doorway which led to the old

communications center, chewing on her fingernails. She surged to her feet as they pounded into the corridor. "Thank God!"

"Let's get out of here. We've been seen."

Her face paled further. "No—"

"It won't matter," Rand said. "I don't think anybody would believe it. We have to save them."

Bevan's eyes narrowed. "No. We have to save ourselves." The two faced off for a moment and Rand knew a thrill of challenge. Then Bevan flashed a smile. "We've got to get downhill before we're missed."

As they raced to the outside, Rand wondered what he himself believed.

Later that night, he could study no more, and he could not sleep. He padded quietly upstairs to Alexa's room and let himself in. The silhouettes limned by moonlight had not heard him. He stopped, seeing their outlines in movement and rhythm against the window's framework, knowing what he interrupted.

Alexa murmured throatily, while she traced kisses down Bevan's torso. "So good, so good. I could eat you. . . ."

His friend let out a groan and Rand hastily retreated out of the room, closing the door softly behind him, not wishing to be noticed.

He returned to his room and sat at his study desk, knowing he was a floor or two below Alexa's window, and knowing as he looked outward that he saw an entirely different sight, and that he was all alone.

Chapter 26

John Taylor Thomas fielded the late night call from his bedroom within the Ambassadorial offices. Since his daughter's taking, his wife had left, and his personal life had fallen into ruin. There was nothing left to sustain his existence except his work. He slept there and rarely left except to function as a diplomat.

The comline opened up through his private channels. GNask's low, gravelly, and smacking voice woke him up.

"Thomas. We've heard from your daughter."

He leapt up from the rumpled bed. "What?"

"We've heard from your daughter. I beg your pardon for the lateness of the call, but I knew you'd want to know."

"Is she all right? What did she say?"

"We haven't time to discuss that. She appears to be well. She wishes to be retrieved, but we knew that. The signal was weak. It will take some time for us to track it. However, we will locate it, and you will have her back."

Gratitude surged in his throat. He swallowed in order to respond. "What about the others?"

"She had little time to send much information. But, I think, ambassador, we will have our tampering charges substantiated. I think we finally have our Choyan in a trap of their own making."

Thomas' hand trembled. "Good," he whispered hoarsely. "And thank you."

GNask rumbled. "Thank you, Mr. Ambassador. We work together."

The comline went dead.

Thomas paced nervously, trying to absorb what he'd heard. The implications of it would sink in later. For now, Alexa was alive and well. He could not ask for more. He would never have the child returned to him that he had given GNask. But even a remnant of her would be welcome to him. Even that small, strange part.

Nedar left the auspices of his patron to seek out that which had been offered him so clandestinely. His *bahdur* continued to flicker, but he could control its burn by his own usage. Palaton had warned him and taught him an invaluable lesson. Ironic that it had been Palaton who'd disappeared, lost, gallantly sacrificing his own life to deliver four hundred medics out of Chaos to their destination. He had brought them through while losing himself.

But, reflected Nedar grimly, that left one less hero for him to conquer on his way to the throne.

He'd been offered hope, and healing, should he ever decide to pay the price. He would pay the price, his way. The secrecy served him well and intrigued him. He did not know who this splinter group of Choyan were, or what outlawed genetic experimentation they did, but they held out possibilities and he determined to snatch them up. Once he was rejuvenated, nothing could stop him. He journeyed to a base on the frontier fringes of the Compact and put in a call. He was answered promptly and told to wait.

Nedar would wait only for fortune and destiny.

Alexa did not come to him again in those days of summer following their discovery. She found shelter in Bevan's company, and he in turn found strength from her, shutting Rand out. In classrooms they sat across from one another and as the provosts lectured on the wonder, the opportunity, the loyalty of companionship with the *tezars,* Bevan sometimes turned his handsome face to Randall and mouthed, *"Lies."*

The word pierced his chest like a physical wound. As they were taught more and more and yet learned nothing about the role awaiting them, Rand felt the wound deepen. Days passed. He sat in class, balancing his dream of piloting with the uncertainty that the Choyan would ever offer it to him. What was a Brethren? Were all the insane they had discovered the end result?

He could ask no one. If he did, he risked losing all that he'd worked for. And his uncertainties found no solace from his friends, for they had closed their circle, shutting him out. Bevan grew darker, more cynical, and Alexa withdrew into the shadow he cast.

On a hot day, when the thin mountain air seemed unable to slow the arrow rays of the sun, Randall snapped his book shut, threw his pocket computer in his pack, and left class. The provost stopped his lecture a moment in surprise, but said nothing as Rand hurried out the door.

Outside, he took a deep breath. The stifling feeling did not go away. Perhaps it was not caused by the weather. Perhaps it lay deeper. He hoisted his pack and trudged across campus.

Cleo was not in her dorm office, an informal corner of the building's kitchen. That meant she was down at the biosphere, working in the organic gardens. Rand hesitated at the threshold of the kitchen. Finally, with nowhere else to go, he went to his room.

There was a sense of trespass when he opened the door. He couldn't place it until he saw the suit of blues laid neatly across his bed.

Rand put a hand to his chest as his heart began to race. He dropped his pack on the floor and hiked to Bevan's room. The suit of blues across his rumpled mattress was the only item of neatness within.

He took the stairs slowly to Alexa's. The door there was unlocked, slightly ajar. He nudged it open.

Blues hung from a peg on her closet door.

Rand backed out in confusion. What previously he had wanted most now frightened him. He went back to his room and stared at the uniform.

He was still staring at it when someone rapped at the door. Cleo put her weathered face in.

"Ah," she said. "You've come back early and discovered my surprise."

Rand turned to her. "It's the b-blues." He clamped his teeth shut on the unexpected stammer.

"What did you expect? You were made to wear them." Cleo beamed. "All four of you from this dorm were passed into blues. Unheard of, so quickly. But you've worked hard and earned them."

"Did I? And do I want them?"

Cleo looked puzzled. Then she nodded. "Boy, I think you should come down to my kitchen. I have tea brewing."

He followed her obediently, needing someone to talk to.

The tea was a welcome change from the *bren,* whose strongness occasionally turned his stomach. He sat, nursing his cup, while watching her prepare peanut butter sandwiches to accompany it. The smell made him breathe deeply, savoring it. He hadn't realized how much he'd missed peanut butter.

"It's hard for me to digest at my age," Cleo said, lowering her bulk into a chair opposite him. "But I like the reminder of home."

He gulped down his first sandwich in agreement. The tea was sweet and scalding. He sipped at it cautiously.

Cleo rubbed her mug between her work-worn hands. Garden dirt was still embedded in her nails and cuticles. "Now tell me why it is that the sight of blues turns a healthy lad like you pale."

He shook his head.

"I blame myself," the dorm mother said. "I should never have bunked you with Zain. But I was fairly new myself and didn't know his mind like I thought I did."

The memory of Zain had faded considerably. "It's not that."

"What is it, then?"

"I still don't know what we do. I don't know what a Brethren is. I don't know what the Choyan want from us."

Cleo gave him a slight smile. "I do." She folded her hands about her cup of tea. There was a bittersweet quality about her expression.

"Then tell me."

"There are new classes for that." The older woman leaned back in her chair. It creaked in response to her weight. "It's not my place. But I don't like to see a good boy troubled. I did it, you know." She looked away for a second, remembering. Her glance came back. "It was the best thing that ever happened to me."

"But what *was* it?"

"It's a spiritual thing. The Choyan come to us to be renewed. They choose companions and we share their lives, for a time. They become as children and we guide them until they are refreshed. The bonding is as close as any marriage, and more rewarding." Cleo looked up from his face to someone else standing at the rear of the kitchen. She smiled broadly. "Ah," she said. "I wondered when you would come asking questions, as well."

Rand turned in his chair and saw the Choya standing there, the *tezar* in his uniform, the one who'd saved his life once. He felt caught in the other's amber-eyed gaze. Emotions flecked the amber with liquid gold, holding him, but he found he did not want to be released.

"It's a telemedical function," Bryad said smoothly. "But it takes time. We ask our candidates to live on the upper campus, observing already bonded pairs, and learning about the humankind psychology."

Nedar's presence dominated the office. Bryad felt the force of his personality like a hammer. "I haven't time," the pilot said. "I'll meet your conditions, but you must meet mine."

"They act as filters. If you rush the process, you will be faced with returning to us sooner for a second treatment . . . and possibly a third."

Nedar gave him a piercing look. "What does it matter, as long as it works?"

"Finding suitable Brethren is difficult. We must be . . . cautious."

"Opportunity belongs to those who seize it," Nedar said, looking at the various documents studding the office wall. "You came to me. I think perhaps you need me as badly as I need you.

Bryad cleared his throat. His voices sounded weakened, obscured. "I have nothing to hide."

"Oh, but I think you do." Nedar approached the desk and leaned on it, his knuckles going white. "I think I know what you're trying to bring back out of the ashes, Reeve Bryad. And you need fresh genes to do so, to solidify the lineage and broaden it."

Bryad felt his eyes widen. He kept his face still, however, as the pilot reared mysteries he had thought hidden.

"The House of Flame was thought destroyed," Nedar continued. "But don't forget that we Skies experimented on our own. And we know that the Earthans gathered up what Flames they could to bolster their own weak line. They hid their specimens quite successfully from the rest of the Houses. They bred well and truly, outcrossing with their own blood. The revolt and destruction of the House-holding of Tregarth within the Earthans was a subject of speculation and scandal for centuries. But within my own Householding, there were some who claimed to know the truth. It was said the Earthans of Tregarth were too successful in their experimentations. That 'commons, God-blind' they'd been working with revolted and set off on their own. Did they, Reeve Bryad? Or were they Flames, resurrected, and did they come to the stars to be free? Is this a College or a House, Reeve Bryad? And how much of the truth dare you tell me?"

Bryad got up, but he said only, "I offer you life, Nedar. *Bahdur.* I admit nothing of your speculations. Don't think I'm ignorant of your politics. You want the throne of Cho as much as we want new blood."

Nedar smiled slowly. "Then perhaps we shall come to an understanding. But we must do it quickly. I haven't much time," he repeated.

Slowly, Bryad answered, "I have three students who might suit your purposes. They're all strong candidates, although we've not trained them completely. Sit down, and we'll discuss our options. You may not have time, but what we do requires caution, else the humankind die or worse in the process. The bonding process infuses your *bahdur* into them, where they purify it by processes unknown to themselves, and return it to us, renewed and whole. They're not a psychic race, although they have a superstitious tradition of such abilities. The infusion of our talent is a strain many cannot bear. We chemically blind and restrain them during the purification period, so they cannot be aware or use the power we've given them. As they are dependent on you in this time, you are dependent on them. You must understand that. Your souls will be locked together. You must care for them as sensory deprivation sets in. It sounds a cruel process and, in many ways, it is. We've found over the years, however, that *bahdur* can be overwhelming without these precautions. Even with them . . . occasionally a *tezar* must be bonded with several candidates to find one who is compatible and capable of holding the *bahdur.*"

Nedar quirked an eyebrow. "They're unaware of the potential they hold?"

"Completely."

"Good. I'm ready when you are."

Chapter 27

Gracet stared at the Choya on her threshold. Interrupted from an afternoon of reviewing evaluations, her hair was mussed and her face drawn in irritation which lightened as she saw who the interloper was.

"Palaton," she said, and opened her door wider. "I was hoping you'd come to a decision." She let him in.

His voices died finally, and she was able to talk. She sprawled on the lounge in her outer lobby. "Often, there is a natural affinity between Choyan and their companions. We've not had an instance in decades, however, where Brethren were chosen before we'd attempted to match them up. However, I can see that this affinity has a great deal to do with your decision." She curled her legs under her. "I think I can persuade the Reeve to allow the partnership. If it brings you into our fold." She did not mention the expendability of the humankind. She'd already assessed Palaton as one who would not accept that inevitability. In fact, awareness of the difficulties of bonding might drive him from the program altogether. And she wanted him too much. She saw too much in him to let him go.

"Then you'll intercede for me with Bryad."

"Certainly. He'll be pleased as well." She hesitated. "There is the matter of renunciation. . . ."

"I'm aware of it." Palaton's voices had gone stiff. She nodded, not wishing to push him further.

She reached for her comline keyboard. "Bryad, I have *tezar* Palaton here in my office . . . he's ready to make a commitment."

The Reeve's voices came back, sounding drained but fulfilled. "Gracet, that will have to be delayed. *Tezar* Nedar has come in with an urgent request. We'll be bonding him

to a Brethren as soon as you can have Bevan, Randall, and
Alexa sent to the upper campus as possible candidates."

"What? This is unheard of. Even with preparation,
Bryad—"

"No arguments. I want them summoned and in the
Bonding Hall."

Gracet leaned back. She felt the color draining from
her face.

Palaton said quickly, "I know Nedar. I'm going with
you."

She turned her gray eyes to him. "How ruthless is he?"

Palaton did not answer.

The Bonding Hall stood at the cliffside of the upper campus. Its structure was ornate and imposing, the agate blue
bands in its stone wall akin to the colors of Chaos, as the
pink glow of sunset streaked it. The flying arch of its threshold stretched high over their heads as Gracet took Palaton
in. The interior could encompass a far greater audience
than the seven who awaited them, four Choyan and three
subdued humankind in blues.

Nedar's expression opened as he saw Palaton. "I should
have known," he said. "So Chaos spit you back."

"The experience," answered Palaton dryly, "is not one I
recommend." He looked beyond, searching, found Rand
standing a little to the left of the other two. The boy's
presence comforted him. The humankind looked up, his
face strained, the turquoise eyes shadowed by fatigue.

Of the other two, the young man had his arm around
the young woman in a loose embrace as protective as it
was sexual. She seemed unaware of the gesture, her attention on Nedar.

Palaton recognized Dr. Ligo, the waddling Choya who'd
nursed him, as the physician moved among the three humankind, innoculating them for some purpose. The girl
winced as the air needle punctured her arm briefly. Unshed
tears sparkled in her eyes.

Behind him, Gracet said, "What we do here tonight may
undo all we've worked for."

Nedar answered defiantly, "Or it may propel you into
exactly the position you wish for yourselves." His voices
rumbled arrogantly.

The Choya'i declined to answer. She stepped to the Reeve's side and merely set a restraining hand on the back of his wrist. Bryad shook it off. From her expression, Palaton could tell she was not used to being repulsed.

Bryad moved forward, Dr. Ligo at his flank. "Randall, Bevan, Alexa. You have been named and have come forward. You merit this, but I must also make you aware that this is because of necessity. The role of Brethren demands courage and sacrifice. We have a *tezar* who needs help and only one of your abilities can help. This is what you were chosen for, and what we've trained you for. Are you ready?"

Of the three, Rand said nothing, Alexa murmured a faint, "Yes," and Bevan said defiantly, "That depends."

Nedar's attention went to the girl. He stared intently at her. Palaton could feel his aura flare.

"The role of Brethren," Bryad continued, "involves the bonding of Choyan and humankind. We are alien to one another, yet we can help one another. To be bonded to a Choya is a potent experience. To withstand it, we have found it beneficial to dampen your own sensory abilities. We've already begun chemical blocking in your systems to accomplish this. Don't be afraid. The condition is temporary."

"What do you mean?" Bevan demanded. He dropped his arm from Alexa, rose on the balls of his feet, tense, ready.

Dr. Ligo said, "You will be blinded and deafened, to defeat the sensory overload of bonding."

The girl gave a tiny squeak. Rand moved closer to her in reassurance.

Bryad turned to Nedar. "You've had copies of their profiles. Have you made a choice?"

Palaton knew who it would be before the pilot spoke. Nedar would go for compliance, pliability. He would rape the soul of anything bonded with him and like most rapists wanted fire and yet ultimate victory.

"I'll take the female," Nedar said.

Alexa sank to her knees as the Choya reached for her. Bevan pushed his way between them. He glared defiantly into the pilot's face. "Take me," he said. "I can handle anything you give me.

Nedar hesitated. "Can you now?" he said softly, menace underlying his lower tone.

"Yes." Bevan threw his head back.

"The bonding procedure," Ligo said, "is a layer by layer process. You won't be instantly connected any more than you will be instantly blinded."

Nedar turned to look at the doctor. "Then," he surmised, "choices can be changed."

"At the outset, yes."

Bryad added, "And I recommend circumspection. Our procedures have been developed for the safety and care of all. Defy us, and we will ask you to leave the College."

Nedar and the Reeve traded looks. Nedar did not appear intimidated.

The Choya smiled at Bevan. "Then I will take your challenge."

Bevan took a step toward Dr. Ligo. "I'm ready."

Lights in the Bonding Hall dimmed. Bevan had gone down in a hypnotic state, and his limp body now lay draped on the sculpted couch which was at the center of the stage. He breathed evenly. One hand trailed to the floor, the other crossed over his chest. Alexa stood by fearfully, an unwilling witness. Palaton watched Rand closely. What happened here tonight would influence what would happen between them, what had already begun to happen. The ceremony aroused some suspicion in Palaton. He suspected that Daman and Cleo had not been subject to much of this, that most of it had been built up over the intervening years. How much was ritual and how much was real . . . and what was necessary to preserve the integrity of the bonding?

How would it be to strip away the barriers inbred in him and share his soul and his *bahdur* with another, let alone an alien being?

Palaton stirred as Nedar was brought to his knees beside the couch. Bryad led him into the meditation exercises. Palaton had to distract his attention to avoid going down into the same maelstrom of mental preparation.

Nedar lay his hands across the boy's forehead. Palaton's attention shot back, drawn by what he felt was happening. He could see the other Choyan, Gracet, Ligo, Bryad, and the unnamed watcher, were not *tezars*. They had some awareness of what happened, but not a total understanding. Not the same awareness he did. He could feel Nedar seep into the other's mind, locking in, and then, like the backdraft of a wildfire, flaming into his mind.

Bevan jerked awake out of his trance. His mouth opened in a scream of agony. Gracet jumped to her feet even as Palaton surged forward.

"Stop him!"

Ligo paused, mouth gaping. "What are you doing, Nedar?"

The pilot bore down ruthlessly, heedless of the boy's convulsing body. Aurafire blazed around them. It surrounded them like fire setting alight a funeral pyre. Bevan began to flail at the Choya with his fists, screaming hatred and defiance as the pilot raped his soul. *Bahdur* flared.

Palaton tore at Nedar's shoulders. The other was stronger than he, had not been ill, and shrugged him away. Palaton came back, determined. He pried Nedar away from Bevan, gripped him by the shoulders, and yelled for assistance.

The boy ripped himself out of Nedar's grip. Something flashed in his hand. He screamed a last time in hatred and lunged. He stabbed twice, deep, into Nedar's chest. The Choya echoed Bevan's agonized pain and then fell forward, lifeless, in Palaton's hands.

Bevan froze. The knife slipped from his fist. He threw Alexa a look, then Rand. He turned and bolted from the hall as all the others remained motionless, immobilized by shock.

Galvanized, Rand went after him. Palaton lowered Nedar to the floor. His aura was fading. His *bahdur*, gone. Infused into the renegade boy who ran from his deed.

"God-in-all," said Gracet. "What have we allowed to be done?"

Rand raced after the sound of fleeing footsteps. He drew nearer in the darkness, his mind pounding with the memory of lost Zain. Don't let me lose Bevan, he pleaded. Don't let me lose Bevan.

He called into the night. The runner paused, slowed, then sped up again. Rand turned a corner and saw a portion of the upper campus he recognized, the massive squat building of the crematorium. He knew which way Bevan would go. He angled across the grounds, pressing, breath gasping, but now he was rested, acclimated. As fleet as Bevan was, Rand was more determined.

They burst one after another into the corridor which led to the servo exit. He could see Bevan now ahead of him, a dark ghost in the tunnel. A peculiar halo seemed to outline his form, silhouetting him. As the door to the outside swung open and Bevan prepared to slip away, Rand sprang through the air and tackled him. Together they went rolling into the night.

"Don't touch me!" Bevan screamed into his face. They wrestled hand to hand.

"Bev," Rand gasped. "Come back!"

Bevan abruptly lay still under him. He took great, hulking sobs of breath. He shook with exertion. "I killed a *tezar*," he got out. "What kind of a future do you think I have?"

"I don't know . . . I don't know. But they saw what he was doing to you. . . ."

"It's what they do to all of us. Don't you see? We saw the crematorium, the asylum. We're used and tossed away. No one misses us. No one ever comes back, Rand. No one ever comes back."

Rand's thoughts swam. "Cleo did," he said finally.

"Only one you can name. One against all the others." Bevan kicked out from under him and sat up, chest still heaving to breathe. Rand was breathing hard, too.

Bevan made a fist and raised it in the air. Sparks shot upward, sparks with heat and light and fury. Rand shrank lest one touch him. They looked hot enough to burn. They showered sizzling to the ground.

Bevan looked at Rand. "I'm running. Don't try to stop me again." He got to his feet. He stood a moment, knees shaking, as if waiting for Rand to protest.

Rand got up. His mind was filled with mistrust, his dreams split by a radius of doubt about what the Choyan intended, and what they achieved. "Go on," he said. His voice choked.

Sudden light illuminated the massive fortress wall above.

Bevan fled into the night before Rand could say or do anything else.

Chapter 28

GNask stood before the general council of the security hall of the Compact. He bowed in formal greeting. "It grieves me, fellow ambassadors and members, to do what I must do today. But I have incontrovertible evidence which must be introduced. I have had brought to my attention a plot against the Terran world which involves subjugation and interference of the deepest kind instigated by Cho."

He paused as gasps and reaction drowned out his speech for a moment. He then added, "I ask that my evidence be reviewed and that the wrongdoers be brought to justice. Exploitation of a Class Zed planet is a most despicable action and cannot be left unpunished. In the interest of equity, I will also request the president pro tem of the Compact resign his position in favor of a disinterested party." GNask bowed in irony to the recently elected Choya who currently wielded the power of the office of president.

The Choyan ambassadors, their Ivrian allies, and others surged to their feet in protest. Havoc roared through the general council. He caught a bemused glance from John Taylor Thomas. The Choya Firendan pointed at him and guards swept the Abdrelik from the speaker's podium and followed him outside. He said to his secretary as they moved through the shouting throng, "We've got the coordinates we needed. I want a move on that hidden base. Find me a renegade *tezar* who will fly us in. Evidence or not, I want to level that base before anyone else realizes what the evidence points to and gets there."

The secretary nodded wisely. He left his ambassador's side, making an exit corridor with his own bulk, his *tursh* sitting up in excited style above his left ear. GNask watched him go, a grin revealing his tusks. He had finally found a chink in the Choyan armor. If only to protect themselves, a *tezar* would step forward to pilot him in, to betray and destroy a splinter group whose actions jeopardized the whole of Cho. He had driven a wedge between Choyan factions that might well shatter the whole planet.

He had no details of the Choyan operation but he had a location where the children of Earth were being taken. For what purpose, he still had no inkling. Alexa had not been able to communicate with him that fully. But when they went in to destroy the location, he hoped to pull her out.

The downfall had begun.

Panshinea sat at the *lindar* keyboard, his fingers searching out idle melodies as Gathon told him what news had just been sent in. The emperor did not pause, though his face creased heavily.

"Where," he mused, "is my hero in exile now? Who in Cho will stand beside the Great Wheel descendant as it brings down the House of Star?"

Rindalan stood, the Prelate reedy with age to the point of gauntness, his massive crown fully revealed by the advanced thinning of his hair, and his face no less grim than it ever was. "Get command of yourself, Panshinea. What could the Abdreliks be referring to?"

Gathon said, "We know there must be a splinter group colonized elsewhere. We've had hints of it for decades."

"Cho does not colonize!" Panshinea said. His fingers danced, jerked, upon the keyboard. "I sent my hero for a cure. Ten long years he's been gone. . . ."

Rindalan looked across to Gathon. "He's hopeless in these moods. Do what you must."

The disapproving Choya gave a half bow and left. Rindy stayed by the *lindar,* saying, "You know Palaton's dead."

"If he's dead, so is all my hope." Panshinea stopped playing abruptly and rested his hands upon the mantleboard. "Vihtirne is supporting Nedar to supplant me. Do you think we can face such a challenge, dear Rindy, you and I alone?"

"Not in this state."

"No, neither do I. If I vacillate, the best I can hope to gain is time while the Skies decide whether to wait for me

to die on my own . . . or to wrest the throne by force.
What good it will do either of us to play for time, I cannot
know. But it seems to me to be the only thing we can do."
With a sigh, Panshinea dropped his hands down upon the
keyboard again, searching out a melancholy tune.

The Prelate stood in silence, a thoughtful expression
upon his aged face. He had not known the emperor still
had it in him. Perhaps there was hope yet.

The Reeve summoned their shuttle *tezar* to his offices.
Staden was a Choya of limited *bahdur* even after all their
efforts to renew him. He had retired from Chaos piloting
to run the shuttle for them from the Arizar port. He appeared in Bryad's office promptly, his mane disheveled at
this early hour.

"I want his body off-planet. Take it up until I can tell you
where to dispose of it. Maybe Chaos. I don't know yet."

The aged Choya stared at the blanket-covered body of
Nedar.

Bryad turned about as Staden shouldered it, wrapped in
the blanket, and prepared to carry it out. "Tell no one of
what you do. *No one.*"

"I understand, Reeve," Staden answered, even though
the expression on his blunt face plainly said he did not.
Bryad watched him go.

He did not understand his own actions, but he did not
want the ashes of a *tezar* mixed with the remains of the
humankind at the crematorium. It was dishonorable and
Bryad felt estranged enough from his people.

They had found the one humankind and brought him
back. He waited now in solitary for them to decide his
disposition. Gracet, as usual, had had her own opinion on
it. The other provosts were more pliable to his will.
"Think," she had said, "what you destroy with Palaton if
you destroy the boy."

Now that they had lost Nedar, Palaton's contribution had
more import. But there were always other *tezars*, there
would always be burn-out, there would also be other candidates whose vulnerability led them to this world. Bryad did
not feel kindly toward Palaton. He keyed Gracet. "Let's
take a look at the boy again.

They walked to the cell together, Gracet saying little.

She wore her hair down, clipped at the nape of her strong neck. Palaton rose as they approached. He had been holding vigil outside Rand's solitary confinement. Of the girl, there had been no sight. Cleo reported she'd returned to her dorm and stayed there. The girl would have to be moved, lest she contaminate the other students. Bryad made a note to have that handled.

Palaton stopped Bryad before he entered. "Has Bevan been located yet?"

"No." There was a distinct possibility the Zarites could be aiding the humankind, but the Reeve did not tell Palaton that. The growing current of unrest was one Palaton might sway in his favor, and Bryad had no desire to have his efforts further undermined by trouble. The control they had exerted over the Zarite civilization's growth and expansion had been a careful one, and necessary, if the two groups were to coexist. The colonizing Householdings across the continent would have to be mobilized. The humankind had to be found and hunted down at all costs. Zarite interference was a complication they could do without.

"Send Rand after him."

Bryad measured the *tezar*. "I have resources. The humankind will be found and dealt with."

"There are consequences here," Palaton responded. "There are consequences which neither of us can predict. Send the one to bring back the other. Then justice can be served."

"Bevan is afoot in the wilderness. If he has any destination in mind, it must be to get to the port, to flee. If my guards can't find him, there's a good chance Arizar itself will kill him."

"He has *bahdur*. If he can control it, or worse, if he can't, he can affect the whole countryside. Rand told me some of Bevan's background. He comes from a city teeming with crime and poverty and he knows his way around. He has resources neither you nor I can guess at." Palaton added, "we seem to be adept at underestimating the humankind."

"And how do you propose to have one boy catch another?"

Palaton paused. Then he answered, "Because he has my *bahdur* as well. Because he's asked to do it. Because he's our only hope if you wish to keep the College intact. I don't know the full extent of what you do here, or where you come from, or what destiny you have proposed. But neither am I vulnerable enough to accept any crumb you hand me unwittingly. As Nedar died, he burned a single thought into my mind. 'Is this a College or a House?' It's a question worth remembering. Do you wish me to seek an answer?''

"No," said Bryad quickly, then blanched because he had answered too hastily. Palaton smiled.

The Reeve drew himself up with dignity. "Do what you must," he said then. "You hazard the bonding." He spoke to Gracet. "Deal with them." He left.

Gracet's mouth fell into a sad line. "You've risked much," she remarked. "In this stage of bonding, his life is tied closely to yours."

"I know that." Palaton put a hand to the locked door, pointedly waiting for her to open it. "I have no choice."

He had enough God-sense left in him to see the boy's aura blaze as he entered the small storage room where they'd confined him. Rand looked up, face a pale moon in the dimness, and then smiled. As Rand stood, Palaton weakened visibly and the boy caught him, awkwardly lowering the much taller Choya onto a crate.

Rand kept his embrace about Palaton for moments longer than necessary. Gracet looked away, pretending not to see. Palaton craved the touch. It was not a physical thing, it was beyond that. When Rand let go, Palaton reached up and combed his hair away from his turquoise eyes.

"They're asking you to go after Bevan."

"I know."

He would, of course, now that he burned with Palaton's power. And he knew that was what infused him, knew when all the Brethren from all the years before had never known what it was they carried.

"This College, misguided as it is, could be a vital step in curing the disease that kills us all."

Rand nodded again. "I'll help," he whispered. "For you and for Bevan. Just . . . don't let me fail this time. Help me hold on."

They entwined fingers. Falaton felt a surge of courage and determination, as well as of fear. He squeezed back tightly. "I'll be here. And I've got you."

*   *   *

Bevan's numbed feet went out from under him. He fell with an "Oof," rolling down a scarp of dirt and gravel. His skin came off in patches as he slid to a landing and then lay panting. He could barely see. His head throbbed. He fought to stay awake, alive, moving. He'd run all night.

As he lay, the sharply blue sky of Arizar canopied him, and he focused on it. He wouldn't be safe until he got off-planet. Once off-planet, he could go anywhere. He had the power. It tingled in his veins. It pounded in his eardrums, slinked through his heart chambers, rasped in his lungs.

He knew it.

No wonder the Choyan had resorted to blinding and deafening them, cutting off as many senses as they dared, confusing the poor Brethren who carried and purified this burden. He'd never imagined such a power existed, let alone that it could be transferred. It was the power Rand had thirsted for, and now he had it.

And they'd kill him for it. That he knew as well.

Bevan forced himself to sit up, ribs aching, skin raw where his slide had torn it. The world tilted and then righted itself.

He had to find sanctuary before the drugs they'd given him had done their job. He had to survive!

As Bevan's emotion flared out, the brush he sat in caught fire spontaneously, roaring up. He leapt out of the bracken, swatting at it with a cry of astonishment. The flames licked out as he kicked dirt over them.

Had he done that? Bevan closed his eyes wearily, chest pounding with the jolting excitement, now calming. He remembered the sparks flowing from his hands in the night.

He could have. He had no way of knowing. And if he had, could he do it again, on purpose? He pointed a finger. Nothing happened. Bevan grinned raggedly. "So much for burning bushes." His voice sounded hoarse on the morning air. He stumbled into motion heading in the direction of the sun.

Sometime in the heat of the day, he fell face forward on the dirt and gravel bank of a small brook, inches from the water he craved. He reached a hand out and dunked it, drawing his fingers back to his mouth and sucking the coolness from them desperately, too tired to crawl any closer.

He did that for long moments, dunk and suck, dunk and suck. Then, finally, he heaved himself up and crept close enough to put his face into the water and drink. Different yet similar enough, it flowed lifesaving goodness down his throat.

With a sigh, Bevan curled up on the bank to sleep.

He woke to the sound of curious voices. Furred, sleek forms stood over him as he rubbed his eyes and propped himself up on an elbow. Curious Zarites surrounded him. Their ears went back, then came forward slowly as he greeted them in Trade. He held out a bloody and skinned hand, then passed out entirely.

Palaton showed Rand the hand brakes on the jet sled. He had brought up the runners, to fit the humankind's shorter leg length, but the boy still seemed too small to be riding the powerful machine. He leaned over. They touched foreheads. "You remember how to ride it."

A shared memory, Palaton riding into the wind, taking the bridges of Sorrow at breakneck speed, defying the rain and gravity. A fleeting glimpse of the alien race trapped to their deaths in the crystal. . . . "I remember," said Rand shakily.

The boy was not yet used to their communion. He understood. Neither was he. He was weak in a way he did not understand, as though his heartbeat were only an echo of Rand's. It was more than the loss of his power. A single thought passed through their minds: *He only knew he was alone no longer.*

Chapter 29

Staden had seen a lot of happenings at the College over the years, but he had never seen one of his people die. He carried the body out as Bryad bade him, loaded it in the ground shuttle, and made the journey to port. The Zarite crew watched him curiously, obsequiously, with their furred and whiskered faces, as he moved the body to the transport and waited for them to load the berthing cradle.

One of the Zarites patted him on the leg. "Where are you taking the master?"

Where, indeed? Bryad had not sent him word. He wondered idly if there would be a reward for taking him home. Staden had been away from home all these years.

"I don't know," he growled in answer. "Just do your job."

The creature ears pinked. "Yes." He ducked his sharp muzzle face and turned away.

Staden oversaw the crew's work for a few moments, then boarded his ship. He had set the still form down in the main passenger fuselage and the knowledge that it was there prickled the spiked salt and pepper hairs about his horn crown. He had spread a light tarp over it, but a hand remained free of both blanket and tarp, the cuff of its uniform bearing the braided insignia of Blue Ridge. Staden himself had come from the Commons. He'd always thought Blue Ridge produced the best.

The Zarite crew signaled that they'd finished. He strapped in and took the ship up, found an inconspicuous orbit, put the vessel on automatic, and opened communications to await Bryad's signal. He read a bit, played the computer simulated gameboard a while, practiced his reed flute. Time grated by with the thought of the dead body in his passenger lounge.

Staden had never been very talented. His abilities, both

as a Housed Choya and as a *tezar,* had been strictly limited. But his *bahdur* prickled with the presence of the other in the transport.

He got up and walked out uneasily. The form seemed still as death. Blood had begun to stain the tarp deep crimson, marking the wounds.

Even dead, a *tezar* carried some residual power until the power was consecrated and given to the God-in-all. Or so the Prelates said. The power resting in them had been given and would be taken back. But, and Staden quivered with the thought, what would it matter to the God-in-all if a little had been drained off for the needy?

He knew it could be done. He understood the transfer through bonding. The mystery of what the humankind did to purify corrupted power was another matter. But, as far as he knew, dormant *bahdur* lay in front of him with no one to claim its remains but he and God-in-all. And surely God-in-all had enough.

Staden approached the form. It took all his nerve and the hairs on his arm stood up edgily. But the wish to go home once again and the inability to make the chaos journey to do it spurred him. He lifted the corner of the tarp. He put his hand out to the dead Choya's forehead and opened himself.

The dead one's hand shot up to his throat and closed, tight as steel cables. The eyes burst open, alive and angry.

"Get me," the dead Choya rasped, "something to staunch the bleeding. And then you had better pray I let you live to serve me longer."

Bevan woke in a nest. His arms and legs had been folded gently to accommodate its size. The soft coverlets and herbs scenting it wafted about him gently as he straightened his legs, letting them hang over the edge, and gingerly stretched, every muscle bruised and cramped.

He looked about a small cottage, mud-brick and straw, a pleasant home employing some minor solar technology, including a hot plate, but other items hanging on the walls he either did not recognize or they were primitive at best. He yawned and the noise sounded like an alarm.

Instantly the room was filled with wide-eyed whisker-quivering bodies.

They fed him only after taking him to see the battered jet sled they intended to give him. It had been repaired with homemade wire and cog pins, and he only wondered what the circuit chips looked like, but it had started when he turned it over, and it would make the journey.

And it was his gift. So, as he sat hunched on a stool too short for him and ate the vegetable stew and unrecognizable patties, he thanked the Zarites for their help.

The elder, his jaws graying, nodded in turn. "We help when we can. The star masters have been good to us—but we know they take as well as give."

Bevan paused, spoon in hand. "What do you mean?"

The elder pointed to his daughter who busied herself in the kitchen corner. "She married despite their recommendation. When the time came, they came and took her kits before they could be born. That happens here. The masters are wise, yes—but her kits were healthy. I saw the bodies. Why then did they force her to give them up? Why, then, was the marriage unwise?"

He had no idea. The Choyan forced abortions on the native population? It sounded as if they were manipulating the gene pool. But to what purpose? The Zarites seemed a willing and ingenuous people.

Perhaps too willing. Bevan's glance flickered over the technology they had quickly picked up and incorporated. He did not know how long the Choyans had been on Arizar . . . but he did know it was difficult for two equal races to split a planet. Much easier for a worker/slave relationship. The colonial history of his own country had been checkered. Bevan hid his thoughts behind a chunk of dark bread.

Then he said, "Perhaps the masters are worried you grow too fast, learn too quickly. The land can be poisoned, the air poisoned, by cities which grow too fast."

The elder nodded wisely. "This we know. The masters are counseling us in these ways."

Bevan relaxed. Perhaps there was nothing sinister about the Choyan Households here, after all. He smiled. "Perhaps," he said, "the kits would have become ill later. I'm sure they'll let her have a family. She is young and healthy."

"Perhaps." The elder sounded dubious, both about Bevan's answer and the future possibility. He patted the table with clawed fingers. "You're being hunted. It's best that you leave soon."

That caught him by surprise and he choked, spitting, and then mopping it up hastily. "What do you mean?"

"Another student from the College. Tall, pale, light eyes. His jet sled is better," the Zarite answered matter-of-factly.

Rand. Still on his heels. But why?

Bevan stood, feeling a darkness grow inside. Why would Rand seek to stop him? What had the College promised him to bring Bevan back? The thought of betrayal took his appetite away. He would have to find a way to deal with his former friend.

They brought him a new jumpsuit, blues, faded and patched, but clean and whole. He dressed quickly, making the adjustments to zippers and straps. Then they ganged outside to watch him take their jet sled. They pressed a map and woven sacks with food into his hands.

Bevan paused on the sled. Technology, even this battered, had to be worth something to the family. "Can I leave it if I get to the port—can I leave it somewhere where you can pick it up?"

"Our family will take care of it for us."

"Yes, but which family?"

The elder tilted his head. "All of Arizar is our family," he said solemnly. "No one will steal what you put into their care."

Bevan shrugged. He could not comprehend a theftless society. The jet sled came alive when he asked it to, and vibrated between his legs. The young Zarites scattered, paws over their ears, faces trembling.

He left in a cloud of dust and vapor, their shouts of farewell drowned out by the roar of the machinery.

Distance did not dim the link between Rand and Palaton. Palaton rested in Gracet's quarters and tried to deal with the backlash of sensory information, the overlay of Randall's perception of the world flooding him. To avoid sending the same sort of confusing images outward, he sat, a cold cloth binding his eyes, sounds dimmed, not moving, just being. Inside his mind, timber and brush roared past as the jet sled sped and skidded down treacherous logging roads as Randall searched for Bevan. The search pattern took tedious, looping turns since the other had been on foot, but little sign had been found of him.

Palaton mused. Gracet entered quietly. He lifted his compress. Her expression voiced the question. "No sign of him yet," Palaton answered.

"Bryad will call the Household guards out. He'll have no choice. The humankind can't be allowed to reach port, to get off world, with *bahdur*. . . ."

"I understand the calamity." Palaton paused. "Nothing of this sort has ever happened before?"

"No. Usually the tragedy befalls the students. Sudden death, occasionally insanity. We've had Choyan die, too, but never has one been killed." Gracet took up a chair and sat, rubbing her arms as though chilled. "The process still takes a great deal of experimentation. Its worth is best measured by the alternative."

Palaton opened his mind to disagree, but then sight and sound and taste and touch flooded him.

Rand paused the jet sled on an overlook. The cliff point hung over the foothill, where the terrain would eventually smooth out before it roughened again. He thirsted. Dust hung at the back of his throat. Sweat soaked his torso and he could smell himself. He pulled the water bottle off the sled frame and aimed a cool squirt down his throat.

Then he saw it. And smelled it, too, faintly. Smoke on the air, a thin gray trailing. Death in the forest. His vision went suddenly spotty and then dark and Rand panicked, dropping the water bottle. He clutched his hand over his eyes.

After a blurred moment, his vision came back. The spilled water pooled at his feet as he bent to retrieve the water bottle. The smoke trail still rode the air as he blinked to see it.

It might be Bevan. It might be Zarite loggers or beekeepers. Rand brought the power back up and headed toward the trail. Riding the sled was like riding a cycle and he leaned into it, taking the curves at breakneck speed. Bevan could be hurt, even dying, in the mountainside wilderness. Branches grabbed and tore at his cheeks as he bent over the handles. The jet sled hit a hump of dirt and he sailed out in space before it hit, hovers complaining, and rose again with an angry whine. Something in him pulled for caution. It felt foreign and he realized it must be Palaton. Rand smiled grimly.

He reached a clearing where black-edged grass still smoldered and hung in the air. He looked about and then saw Bevan ducking into a growth of shadow ferns, the canopy of trees dense and green about them. He could never take the jet sled in there or it would foul. He killed the engine to dismount.

"Bevan! Wait."

The other stilled, stalled, blurred in motion. Rand halted in confusion. Then, from the corner of his eye, he saw another Bevan, in furious motion, diving at him.

The impact of the hit knocked him away from the jet sled and into the tall grass. The breath left his body with a whoop. Bevan bore him to earth and sat astride him, fists in the air.

Rand managed to gasp for a choking word. Why—"

Hatred darkened the other's expression. "Judas!" He swung at Rand's face. The blow hit his cheekbone with an astonishing pain. Skin split and swelled almost instantly. He fought back out of instinct.

The two wrestled in the grass, their blues trampling what the wildfire hadn't burned. The smell of seared foliage stained his senses. Rand managed to get on top a second and hold Bevan's fists back.

"I came to help you!"

"Then let me go!"

Rand took a shaky breath. "They'll never let you go this way."

Bevan freed a hand and aimed it at his face, Rand met it in midair and as their hands met, sparks clashed. *Bahdur* against *bahdur*. Bevan groaned, saying, "You let them do it to you. You believed them!"

Bevan's cheeks puffed out. His dark eyes blazed. "You can believe their lies." He heaved, throwing Rand aside. He kicked, hard, the point of his boot thudding home just below the rib cage. Rand curled in pain.

He forced himself to his knees as a jet sled started up. It was not his machine, that lay where he'd left it. He got to his legs, quivering, bent double in agony.

The machine sounded behind him. Rand turned and saw Bevan aiming at him. He stumbled and the sled clipped him as he passed.

There was no remorse on Bevan's face, Rand thought, as it sent him sprawling into darkness.

Hurt, agony, misery, betrayal, fear, bewilderment. . . . Palaton lay in pain as well. But his was faint, pulsing, an echo of his Brethren's. He reached out, along the connection, and urged Rand to get up.

The boy refused, curled about the core of his misery, mourning the death of friendship.

Get up.

Rand sat up shakily. Blood covered his wrist. He looked at it, unseeing. The image shot through Palaton's vision as clearly as if he'd stood over the humankind.

Stop your bleeding.

Wearily, Rand tore off the tattered cuff and wrapped it back around the gash in his forearm as a pressure bandage. The bandage provided some comfort for the throbbing pain. He felt sick to his stomach. Every breath brought a sharp stab. It helped as he got to his feet.

Go after him.

Rand bent over. His blues were torn at the knee, the skin scraped sharply and already showing purple bruising, but the injury seemed no worse. He vomited and then stood, dry retching, and staggered back against the jet sled when he was done.

The movement seemed to help. He wiped his hair from his forehead and eyes. He didn't want to go after Bevan.

You must help him.

Rand uttered a humorless laugh. He leaned against the jet sled for dear life, too weak to mount.

Palaton pressed along their linkage. *Rand, Brethren, the fire . . . he did not start it on purpose. He has* bahdur *he cannot control. Do you understand? It will destroy him. It could well destroy Arizar.*

The thought sickened him. But his guts were dry and he could do nothing more. "All right," he said aloud. "All right." He got on the machine and started it up. He needed no map. Bevan shed aura and he could read it, its sickly green hue hanging in the pure air like a poison.

It must be a poison. Look what it had already done to his friend.

The jet sled plunged out of the clearing.

Chapter 30

Gracet brought him food after dark. She knelt beside him. "What's happening?"

"It's too dark for the jet sleds to be used safely. Bevan has succumbed to fever and is sleeping. Rand, too, I think. The *bahdur* uses humankind badly."

Provost Gracet smiled ruefully. "Does it use us any better?"

He looked at her. "I would like to think so." She was a stern, not a beautiful Choya'i. He felt no attraction to her, but he admired her temperament under pressure.

"You should call him home so you can proceed with the bonding."

Palaton made a noise. "I should think we're bonded enough."

"No . . . I mean, you need to know how to seal yourselves away . . . how to keep from draining each other completely. How to protect yourselves. Bonding to a Brethren is a step by step procedure. You and Rand have given yourselves to each other naturally. Now you need to learn how to stop giving."

He sipped wearily at the cooling *bren*. "There will be time enough for that later. For now . . . the boy is hurting. Soul shock. Rand must find him."

"I know," she said. She left him in the company of her many books and her paintings of Cho, the paint crackled with age, but the vision still as pure as when the artist had painted it.

Rand slept badly. He ached and his face burned with heat, and he'd little water left after spilling most of it. The ground dug into his back and bugs crawled and bit with annoying regularity. Finally he fell into near unconsciousness and in that black inescapable sleep, he found dreams.

Palaton had been half-dozing. He jerked awake. "God-in-all." He grabbed for the arm of the chair to steady himself, his mind flooded with images being sent him by Rand—with no earthly idea of how Rand dreamed what he did.

Panshinea, shuttling down to the surface of Sorrow, gaunt Rindalan in tow. An emperor under siege, coming to protect the position of his representative at the Halls of the Compact. Enemies in position, awaiting him. The Abdrelik mission in triumph. Cho in turmoil without an emperor, without an heir. The House of Sky poised to attack the House of Star.

And Sorrow with its crystal rivers and streams beckoned to Panshinea. The emperor paused at the memorial in front of the Halls, and wept. So also did crusty Rindalan. And, like a plea to God-in-all, his name echoed from the lips of the emperor.

Palaton knew the Halls well, knew the emperor well—and knew that Rand did not.

Yet what he saw was not his memory being bounced back at him.

Foresight. The boy had to be blatantly precoging all that he dreamed.

Even Palaton had not had those talents, beyond a whisper of foreboding. What floodgates had they opened by fusing a humankind with a Choya?

If the premonitions were true, Panshinea walked into havoc created to bring him down, Palaton's name on his lips.

Palaton stood up. His body swayed unexpectedly and he righted himself. He found Gracet's bedroom and woke her, half-dragging her from the bed.

"I need a starship and a pilot."

Her face was creased with sleep, but all she said was, "We have an upper campus full of them. And there must be a ship or two in port."

Later, when she realized the import of what he planned, she protested. "This will be the death of you, and the boy, too."

"It can't be."

She shook her head. "I can't tell you what it will do to traverse Chaos in your condition. The *bahdur*, your soulstrings—you're already frail. And Rand needs whatever support you can give him."

His voices husked in answer. "I must be in two places at once. I've no choice in this. My world and my Brethren both call me."

Gracet had no further argument. She clasped his hand tightly, saying only, "The College has much to ask forgiveness for. If you cannot come back . . . remember us well."

Fatherless, lineage obscure, he had never known the depth of his potential. But now the feeling lay about him like a pall. He was heading into his destiny, whatever it might be. Palaton answered her handclasp before turning to the *tezar* waiting for him. "From Blue Ridge?" he asked, as the Choya wore a plain flight suit.

The Choya grinned back. "Salt Towers."

Palaton murmured. "Well, someone has to be." He mounted the two-seat shuttle and waved the pilot on.

GNask watched the raiding flight take off from base. The dark velvet of space delineated their silvery forms well, he thought. He mopped the corner of his mouth from habit, catching up a string of drool. The Choyan would never know what hit them. And there would be ruins enough to document his claims, ruins and skeletal fragments, and perhaps, if they could be persuaded, evidence from the mouths of survivors. The Choyan would never again be the respected, prominent race they had been.

And he, GNask, would make sure of it.

He would have to break ties with the man, of course, but that would be a welcome break. The constant whining, pitying litany of the human had become annoying. *Help me, help us* . . . the man could not possibly know the disgust and contempt in which GNask held him. The humankind came from a species which plundered its world and soiled its waters almost beyond redemption. Humankind deserved to be wiped from the face of their Earth.

He sharpened the focus on his view screen so as not to miss the sight of his fleet going into Chaos.

*   *   *

Rand woke, heart pounding. He leapt to his feet in the moonlight of the twin silvery disks hanging low overhead and he let out a cry of abandonment.

Then his answer, thin, faraway, but there. *I'm here.*

"Don't leave me," panted Rand. He put a hand to the rough bark of a tree to steady himself.

Palaton only answered, like a faint whisper within, *I'm here.*

Rand could not pull him back, he could only accept. But as shadows clouded his vision and his hearing dimmed, he knew a keening fear . . . Would it be enough? He was not alone . . . but would it be enough?

Alexa woke, restless, rousing to see the pale wine-colored sky of near-dawn. Dreams of muddy water and heavy bodies sliding through them to kill disgusting things in the silt, then swallowing them down raw haunted her.

She went to the toilet, put a finger down her throat and vomited. Nothing came up but thin, yellow bile. If she had eaten, there were no vestiges of it in her system. But she knew she hadn't. She never had, no matter how much she tried to vomit it up. It was just dreams.

She put her face against the cool tile of the wall. She was evil and knew it. Her mind reveled in thoughts she could never dare reveal to anyone, least of all someone who might love her. She lifted her face and looked in the silvered pane of plastic which served as a mirror.

Human on the outside, but a disgusting, maggot-ridden evil inside. No matter who loved her. No matter who curled up with her in the night. She had sought innocence from Rand, whose earnestness shone like a beacon through any darkness, and when that failed, understanding from Bevan who like herself often stood poised on the brink of good and evil. But no soft murmurings, no gentle stirrings of passion, no heated ruttings could save her.

She needed to go home. She needed to find that other half of herself, to be one thing or the other. Alexa put out a trembling hand as she left the toilet, found her blues, dragged them off the peg, and began to dress. An urgency rode her. She needed to be whole, whole and away from there.

Letting the twilight of early dawn and its still heavy shadows hide her, she left the dorm.

She was outside the gated wall, beside the broken slabs of granite, when the raiders came screaming in, their silvery skins red-hot as they hit the atmosphere and rained destruction upon the College. She ran for high ground, away, as far away as she could get from the screams and the fire.

Her limbs trembled with the horror of the raid and with the eagerness for the rescue she knew was coming. She flung her arms up into the sky and prayed for wholeness, for oneness with the Abdrelik awaiting her, and she remained that way until the sky hook plucked her up.

As soon as the dark thinned enough, Rand got back on the jet sled. He ate as he rode, one-handed, steering through broken terrain that showed some traces of the Zarites' efforts to tame it. The port of Arizar glowed on the horizon, shedding the light of civilization like a homing beacon. He didn't know if Bevan had also risen early although he could trace the aura hanging like a fog in the morning dew. He also didn't know what he would do when he reached Bevan again without Palaton to aid him. Would Bevan come with him? Or would they destroy each other?

Such thoughts seemed impossible, but even as he tossed the last of his breakfast to the dirt and wiped his hand on his trouser leg, the sky opened up and began to rain death.

He slewed the jet sled off the road, but kept going as he looked overhead. He thought of the campus guards Bryad had threatened to use, but knew the look of starships when he saw them, even fleetingly, red-silver splinters against the morning sky. Someone or something else had brought tragedy to Arizar.

His heart in his throat, he also realized that their main target had been behind him, in the mountains. His eyes clouded as he mourned Alexa and Cleo, Gracet and his fellow students, the funny Zarite gardener, and all the others who had had no warning.

Thank God, Palaton had gone.

The screams of the raider ships passed overhead again. Rand leaned over the frame of the jet sled and asked the engine for more power, his shadow racing the shadows of impossibly quick ships above.

*   *   *

Summer embraced the Hall of the Compact. Fruit trees laden with both flowers and their ripening burden hung over the walkways. The oppression of threatening thundershowers lingered in the air. Rindalan made a wheezing noise and Panshinea halted in his tracks.

"Are you with me, old Choya?" the emperor whispered.

"I am . . ." Rindalan returned. "But you must walk a little slower."

"I walk to my death," Panshinea answered lightly. "How else would you have me go? Would you drag me?" He turned and waited.

Every inch the Star, his hair red-gold in the summer light, his clothes of the richest thread, cut to mold to his still elegant figure, his horn crown undulled by age, the emperor paused for the shambling figure of the Prelate. He held out his arm.

"Are you prepared, Rindy?"

The Prelate shook his head. "I think not. This is a foolish thing. You cannot supplant your representative with yourself. You lay yourself open to Ronin assassination, humiliation, Abdrelik manipulation—"

"They'll not replace us as head of the general council," Panshinea interrupted, repeating his earlier vow. "Not unless it's over my dead body."

"Such a thing," wheezed Rindalan, "might be just what GNask hoped to set in motion."

Panshinea clucked. "You have little faith. As long as a single spark of *bahdur* burns in me, I shall hold the enemy at the gate."

Despite the emperor's support, Rindalan still shuffled with the effort to keep up. "Only remember, Panshinea, that our power is our secret, and you must not reveal yourself before the Compact."

Panshinea looked down. He said nothing in answer, but there was a blaze in his forest green eyes. The Prelate had no inkling whether it was determination—or insanity flaming within. The council doors opened to admit them.

GNask shifted impatiently. In the hours before the council had admitted no less than the emperor and High Prelate of Cho, he had called in favors and kept them at bay. No word had come on the efforts of the raiders he'd sent out.

He could stall no longer. When the secretary called to order the question of the day, he bowed graciously, giving way, and the emperor and his fellow Choya were let in.

He listened as Panshinea reclaimed the office which the emperors of Cho normally held only figuratively, through nominated ambassadors. He watched the Choya closely, knowing that the being could be brilliant and charismatic as well as wildly erratic. If Panshinea stayed steady, he would hold the voters with him. If GNask could send him veering off target, he would be removed just as his representative had been removed.

He had only one objection he could make without censure. As the vote came to him, all but nominal in allowing Panshinea to take the office, he raised an objection.

The emperor stood on the central dais. He turned and raised an eyebrow in inquiry. "What does the ambassador of Abdreli have an objection to?"

"Not to your good person, Panshinea," GNask answered smoothly. He disliked Trade, it did not have the nuances of his own language, but he was forced to use it and made do with it as best as he could. "The only objection I have is for the welfare and the stability of the government you leave behind. The emperor, as I recall, has no heir. . . ."

The prime directive of the Compact was stability. Any world left unstable, or allowed to continue in an unstable direction which might affect other worlds, other races, other civilizations, was either cut off—or assimilated by races which could give it stability. Even Cho was held to the criteria. Panshinea's mobile, handsome face froze.

"As I understand it," GNask said, moving to the edge of his diplomatic dais, "there is some discussion about your health and the ascendancy of another House to power. While your internal politics are none of my affair, there is the question of stability. *Tezars* are our lifeline, the support of each and every space-going member. Your responsibilities are immense."

"Our responsibilities—" Panshinea choked to silence. The gaunt Choya with him tugged on his sleeve and said something, his words lost to GNask through white sound muffling.

GNask waited, certain that he had precipitated events in one way or another. The emperor had no heirs—he had rivals in the Houses of Sky and Earth, but that ascendancy to the throne might well cost the Choyan a civil war. And no candidate had surged forward from the House of Star, a House plunging into descendancy.

Panshinea shrugged off his adviser. Agitation clear in his posture, he strode forward and opened his mouth to speak.

The council doors opened. Another Choya entered, the natural light from the backdrop of Sorrow outlining him against the artificial, dimmer lights of the inner halls. But GNask knew him, knew him from his bearing and his voices as they rang forth. The Abdrelik clashed his tusks in frustration.

"I am the emperor's designated heir. I'm prepared to take his place either here at the Halls or at home, wherever I am most needed."

Palaton strode to the base of the dais, looked up at his emperor, and extended his hand.

Murmurs ran through the assembly. Panshinea took the hand and helped the other up to stand beside him. "The heir of the House of Star," Panshinea said. "You know him as the *tezar* who saved four hundred when Chaos swallowed him up, sacrificing himself. He found his way out of the patterns. No *tezarian* drive has ever burned as brightly. He honors me by accepting as heir."

Rindy put a shaking hand on his arm. The eyes of the old Prelate misted as he said, "Where have you been? You put out distress signals—we knew you thought the medics lost—we could not locate you to tell you the truth—"

"The truth is what you make it," Palaton answered. Panshinea had sent him out into the Chaos of the unknown, into uncertainty and failure, hoping perhaps to temper him, and hoping as well that Palaton would fight to find his way back. This was not his father, and he was not the emperor's son, but they were Choyan, and for destiny and the future of their planet, they would accept each other.

Panshinea smiled broadly. "Vihtirne is going to be very disturbed. We've a hard fight ahead of us."

Palaton said dryly, "I've never known you to be afraid of knocking heads."

There was a lull as Rand brought the jet sled into the outer city rim of the Arizar port. Zarites scrambled through streets broken by cluster bomb fire, their furred hides streaked with blood and soot, their voices high with terror.

He dropped the vehicle, searching for Bevan's aura, which had grown wispy thin and threatened to disappear completely. He rubbed a hand over his eyes, trying to clear his vision and knowing it would do him no good. Alarms began to wail again. Raiders screamed close.

He was running to a concrete bunker when the world exploded and he felt himself thrown into the air.

"Rand. Rand."

Cold hands upon his brow. He woke from an odd dream of Palaton, speeding his way home, like a comet streaking through the sky, and looked into Bevan's face. Rubble piled around them. The other was battered and dirty, and blood splattered the front of his blues.

Rand hurt everywhere and he lay in the hands of a person who had become his enemy. He licked chapped lips. "Don't run."

"I have to." As an attack began again, Bevan glanced overhead, even though they were either underground or buried. "But I can't . . . I can't leave you here like this."

"I'm dying."

"I think so." The softly accented words were almost obscured by Bevan's emotion. "But you didn't let go of me. You never let go of me."

"No. I—I couldn't." The ground shook. Cement slabs around them trembled. Dust sifted down on them. "Come back with me. They need our help and . . ." Rand sucked in his breath sharply at a pain arcing through him. Bevan answered the pain by stroking his forehead again. A warm drop splashed down upon his cheek and slid away. "The power is different with every Choya. Come back and they'll teach you. Palaton will show you—" Palaton was so far away, so faint. Rand fought to stay awake.

"I can't!" Bevan bit his lip. "You know where I come from, my friend. I smile to survive, not because I have happiness in my heart. I don't have trust inside of me. All I have is doubt and fear. It grows, like a cancer. There's nothing that can cut it away."

"Friendship can. Love." Rand reached up and grasped

the other's hand tightly. "It cuts across anything . . . against time or space . . . we have the power."

And between their clasped hands a light grew.

It grew in intensity from the green and amber of their auras until the darkness of the rubble filled with it. Then it shrank into a ball and dove, straight at Rand's chest.

He gasped as it penetrated. The pain radiated everywhere, incredible, unbearable. His flesh shone translucently. Bevan echoed his pain and fear, their hands squeezed together.

It went out. The shelter went black and even Bevan's face could not be seen. A tremendous BOOM! sounded nearby and a cement slab went sliding again, opening up the ceiling of their meager hiding place. The Arizar sky, streaked with soot and flame and smoke, shone in.

Rand let go of Bevan and sat up. The agony had gone.

Bevan paled. He brushed his thick, dark hair from his dark eyes. He looked at his hand.

"What did we do?"

Exposed, they whispered. But the wonder in their voices shouted.

Together, they had healed. *Power untold.*

Rand sobered suddenly. He got to his feet and pulled Bevan up. "Get out of here," he said. "Do what you have to."

Bevan ran to the edge of the shelter. He looked back. "My friend?"

"You're right. They'll hunt you to get their power back—and maybe worse, because they don't even know what you can do with it. But I won't ever let go of you, understand?"

Bevan smiled. "I understand." He turned and raced from view.

Rand dropped suddenly to his knees. He was not as well as he'd hoped he was. He curled to his side and wondered if he would live until Palaton found him.

Palaton had his *tezar* bring the ship in despite the damage. Raiders had cracked the port like an eggshell. He already knew there were survivors at the campus, that they had fought off infantry as Households across the continent came to their aid, but massive destruction had been wrought. Abdrelik, he thought. It was their style, although the ships had not been marked. But none of that was his concern. He held the weak thread of Rand's life pulsating in his mind as it spun out, and he was out of the ship before the loading ramp was even fully lowered, casting along that lifeline.

Even then it took him hours. The aura drawing him grew so weak it was a bare glimmer among the smoke and ashes. He stalked along broken streets, listening to the wail of weeping Zarites and the grunts of work parties searching the houses and factories for the living. He reeled it in, his own essence, searching for it, praying for life.

The trail ended at the city's edge. Palaton paused uncertainly among the broken towers of concrete. He wept at the sudden realization that he was alone, powerless, but the loss of his *bahdur* was as nothing to the emptiness of losing Rand. His voices broke with sorrow.

A husking whisper penetrated his grief. *"I'm here."*

Palaton dropped to his knees in the rubble and began to dig. The cement tore at his hands, pilot's hands, the tools of his trade, until the blood ran freely.

He was rewarded by the sight of a pale, alien face smiling at him from the wreckage. Palaton drew him out gingerly, and then cradled him. This was his strength. His compass to his destiny. The child he could pull safe and alive out of the crystal of disaster.

Palaton put back his head and shouted for joy.

PATH OF
FIRE

Chapter 1

A high cold wind off the plateau region of Arizar carried with it the scent of catastrophe, of fire and ash, mixing jarringly with the freshness of pine and evergreen. A haze of smoke lay against the peaks, encroaching on the crystalline, piercing clarity of the mountains. The human named Rand watched from the observation deck of the cruiser and thought that when it snowed, which would be soon, the weather would catch the darkness and the flakes would drift down in smoky colors in mourning for the deaths they blanketed.

Choyan, humans, and Zarites alike had perished here. The window he pressed close to breathed in the chill and the odors as well as the sight. There was no glass from home that would do this. Like glass, but unlike, it was as alien as the landscape in front of him. He put a hand against it, feeling the cold. But it was the sight which iced him over with fear. He could have been here, he *should* have been here, and though he'd nearly died elsewhere, these ashes were meant to have been his grave, too.

He watched the two tall Choyan walk the perimeter of the burn scars, hunched slightly into the wind, their clothing and cloaks unfurled. He owed his life to the vigorous Choya, the leader of the small committee currently scattered across the blasted mesa examining the ruins. Yet he was linked by more than a life debt. He shared a soul with the being, a sharing he did not understand any more than he understood the manufacture of the alien glass which separated them.

He and Palaton were separate, yet one. Without being out there, he was with the Choyan. They would be talking quietly, their dual voices blending into a quartet, their double-elbowed arms pointing out and reaching to gather in evidence with a suppleness of movement he could never attain. Even sitting still, watching, Rand felt like a stick figurine lacking in richness and depth. Or a thirsty man kneeling beside a river of glass, unable to drink. *Give me whatever it is you have, share it with me, let me pilot the stars the way you do. . . .*

He blinked as the elder Choya stumbled a bit over a bomb gouged ridge in the dirt. His outer robe flapped about him, wings of a scavenger, picking out the pieces of truth fallen here and there on the burned ground. The taller, more vibrant Choya steadied him without even seeming to. Palaton, the heir to the throne of Cho, pilot of Chaos, at once alien and the very core of Rand's being. His future. His curse.

The Zarites, small, furry, supple aliens, tended to gallop after the long-legged Choyan, scattering aimlessly from time to time yet bobbing and weaving in answer to the questions being put to them, herding the Choyan without seeming to. They had met the contingent at the spaceport, bombed out though it had been, a bureaucracy ready at hand to greet the Choyan and to show them through the ruins. Like hamsters, they were, and their ears blushed and flattened, antennae to their emotions much as whiskers and tail were on a cat. They had been escorted here, via cruiser, but Palaton and Rand had both been here before—this was where their souls had fused—and they recognized the Zarites' mild deceptions even as the committee seemed to be anxiously helping and guiding them.

Rand watched as Palaton came to a stop, his bare, maned head turned into the wind as if scenting something. The thick tresses of his hair curled back from his scallop-edged horn crown. He had no ears sculpted from his fine-boned face, but he heard exceedingly well. The horn crown acted as a sounding board conductor. And there were other senses Rand guessed, as well, that he himself was lacking.

As if knowing Rand thought of him, and thinking of Rand in turn, Palaton looked back at the cruiser. His large, expressive eyes were unseeable at this distance, but Rand smiled slightly anyway. He slumped back against the window seat, wishing he were outside, treading the burned ground. He might find some sign they missed, some hope that Alexa and the others had survived, had lived to flee the raking fire and bombs which had destroyed the campus.

There had been people here, and buildings, and lovers. . . .
He had not been there when the attack came. He could
only imagine the screams and reaction. The buildings which
had teemed with life, fellow humans hoping to be compan-
ioned to the tall Choyan who had an unknowable destiny
and need for them, now crumbled into dust, foundations
little more than brittle lines in char and mud. Slag pooled
here and there where the metal infrastructure had boiled
away to nearly nothing. Rand closed his eyes against the
pain of his thoughts. He had given away his life, his past,
all his heritage to come to Arizar and learn from the
Choyan, only to lose it all. The Choyan here had been
renegades and they had been struck down by enemies from
other stars. None of them had expected this, none of them,
not Bevan or Alexa. . . .

Alexa, her short curly hair bouncing about her face, running into the night, her arms raised in supplication to the
sky. . . . Emblazoned against his eyes even when closed, he
saw her thus. Why, he did not know, only that the vision
resonated within him, and he decided that that was what
must have happened.

She must have heard the incoming. Must have gone to
see what it was. Must have been among the first to flashfire
into ash. She had never slept soundly or well. Private nightmares she kept shuttered within her would bring her gasping awake during the nights he had shared with her. Had
she seen this coming? Had it perhaps saved her? If it had,
where had she gone? He could not bring himself to imagine further.

He had not been there, had been off chasing a fugitive
from the campus . . . his darker self, his friend, his rival,
Bevan . . . and they'd both nearly perished in the attack
on the main port of Arizar, but Palaton had come to rescue
Rand, had pulled him out of the rubble, had kept the life
kindled in him.

Like mystic twins, they shared not one flesh split asunder,
but one soul, torn between them, mirroring sameness and
differences. . . . Rand shuddered and caught himself. He
put the heel of his hand to his temple. *I am not lost. I was
found. He found me. I am not lost!*

His body ached dully. He had a partial cast on one arm
and a support which ran from his right hip to his right foot.

Not a cast exactly, but as confining as one. And his fair skin was turning purple, dark green, and blue at intervals. It even hurt to breathe.

It hurt far more to remember.

He twisted his face again to the window, taking solace in watching the two Choyan stride across the damaged earth. He imagined green shoots winging upward in their footsteps.

As if he might have sensed the young man's observation of them, Rindalan paused in mid-step and put his long-fingered hand on Palaton's sleeve. His voices were reedy with age, the cords of his gaunt Choyan neck standing out as his dual voices vibrated.

"You'll send him back, of course." His robes flared about his tall, wiry frame. His large eyes glistened with the sting of the cold wind.

"I can't." Palaton halted in deference to the elder.

"What do you mean, you can't?"

Palaton turned his hand palm up and swept a gesture over the attack-scarred terrain. "He survived this. He and the other humankinds may well have been the cause of it. I don't dare send him back until we know the truth of it." He paused, waiting to see if Rindalan could pick the lies out of the meager truth in his statement.

Rindalan frowned. "You can't keep him. It would be in violation of Compact agreements. His world barely has a classification with us. No pet could be worth the risk."

"He's no pet." Palaton's lower voice took on an edge and Rindalan rocked back a bit on his heels, hearing the menace.

The High Priest of the House of Star blinked away his reaction. He hummed a bit before saying, "What, then, do you intend to do with him?"

"Bring him back to Cho with us."

"What?" The wind swirled around, snatching away the word, but Palaton heard it well enough, keenly enough, in the startlement mirrored in Rindy's eyes and the alarmed curve of his mouth.

"I can't let him go, elder." Palaton bent close, so that he could be heard well enough in the face of the approaching storm. Behind him, he could hear the Zarites scurrying about, chattering in alarm. The elements would come beating at all of them soon enough. "The Abdreliks did not attack a mere humankind colony here, nor were they attempting to decimate our furry little friends who are now so anxiously awaiting our withdrawal. Rindalan, there were Householdings here."

Rindy did not voice his surprise this time, but his brows shot up. "This is true? We had Brethren here?"

Palaton gave a nod.

"Does Panshinea know?"

"I doubt it, although he might suspect. I haven't reported it to the emperor yet."

Conflicting emotions raced across the elder's face, like clouds raced across the plateau horizon facing them. Palaton looked away for a moment, took in the leading edge of the storm, mentally calculating, like any pilot, how much time they had before it would be difficult to fly, though it wasn't his task to fly the cruiser that rested across the grounds from them. His attention came back to Rindalan.

Choyan did not colonize. It had been decided amongst them generations ago to keep their psychic powers, pure and untainted by the sort of genetic adaptation any race went through when transplanted. It made their existence more difficult, more tenuous, for they must constantly heal the damage they did to their planet, constantly balance their finite resources, constantly struggle to be as they were and as they would be.

Palaton knew a sense of relief in telling that much of the truth to Rindalan. As he viewed the carnage, his feelings had bored into him, leaving a gaping hole that nothing, for the moment, could fill. Without his *bahdur,* his genetically inherited telepathic powers, he was helpless. He could no longer master Chaos to pilot, he could not find and fulfill his own destiny—but worse, much worse—he could not save his own people and his own world from the fate which had swiped at Arizar. Those who had attacked here would attack Cho, once convinced that they had grown strong enough and the Choyan weak enough.

Palaton swore that he would somehow find the means to avenge the work done here, and the means to protect his world, and the means to restore his power so that he could fulfill his vows. Whatever it took, he would do it. By the

God-in-all whom he might never be able to see again without the *bahdur* which illuminated His presence, no enemy would touch Cho without destroying Palaton first.

He fought to rein back his emotions, which Rindy would be able to read sooner or later, shocked or not. As much as he trusted the elderly prelate, Palaton knew he was alone in this. Entirely, utterly, alone. Without his *bahdur,* his own people would be as quick to bring him down as his enemies would be. He must learn to be still and silent and patient. He bent his head over the other's hand and waited for him to speak.

That there had been renegades here could have been a shock great enough to stop the old Choya's heart in his chest. It did not, though Palaton could feel a trembling in the hand resting on his sleeve.

"What Houses?"

Only three great Houses of political power and *bahdur* had survived the turbulent course of Choyan history: Star, Sky, and Earth. The Householdings of each had their own influence and agendas, and then there were those Choyan without any *bahdur* at all, or barely enough to measure, those Choyan blind to the aura of any living thing, so oblivious that they were called Godless among their own people. But which of the Houses had sent Choyan here, Palaton did not know for sure, though he suspected. He did not tell Rindy of his suspicions.

"That, I don't know. And the evidence is gone. Obliterated." Palaton turned around, drawing away from Rindy. "That boy is all I have. He might be able to tell me." He wondered that the priest could not see through him, could not see that the *bahdur* which had once blazed as brightly in him as any sun was gone, dark, blackened out . . . now housed in the boy, like a tiny flame succored against the night. All that made Palaton what he was now sheltered inside another being who no more knew what he held than a stone would. No, he could not send the boy away. Not until he could make himself whole again. But he would not confide in Rindy. The High Priest's fortune was too entangled with that of Panshinea, who had made Palaton his heir, but he knew the erratic emperor did not intend for the throne to come to him. It was only to hold the Compact at bay, until Panshinea's own power at home had been consolidated.

Rindy moved. It might have been a shrug, it might have

been a jerk of protest. He said, "No good can come of this."

"I don't see as I have any choice. Do you?" Had he been empowered, he might have seen the aura brighten about the priest as Rindalan tried to *discern* the consequences of their action.

"My destiny is nearly finished, but yours lies far ahead of you . . . out of my sight . . . tangled by the choices you must make. This is one, Palaton. You make it too hastily."

"Haste has nothing to do with it. The boy was part of the colony here, all but bought or stolen for purposes I can only guess at. He has answers if I can find the right questions. I can't let him go. The Abdreliks are waiting for just such an opening."

Rindalan shook his head. "He will change all of us. Perhaps even the face of Cho."

"You *discern* that?"

"No." Rindy's voices quaked. "But I feel it in my aching bones, like the wind which bites at us now. You cannot do this, Palaton."

"I have no choice," he repeated.

Alexa moved a hand languidly through the slurry water which surrounded her. The chamber muffled all noise so that all she could hear was the water's movement, its trickle against the sides of the chamber, the dim hum of the pump and filter. A huge being slouched opposite her, submerged beneath the turgid surface, shadowing the pool. GNask had been in the mud pond first and red clay particles sloughed off him, floating to the pool's rim and then disappearing as the circulation pump sucked the water clean.

She did not have the Abdrelik's affinity for mud, though she enjoyed basking in the spa. She watched as the alien paddled onto a ledge and his head broke water. His grace underwater transformed into a massive body, poised, a hunter's, eyes always seeking for the furtive movement of prey, thick, amphibious skin with its sluglike symbiont moving across his broad cranium, his jowls drooping upon his chest, saliva-moist.

She thought, *I look at him and see myself, truer than any mirror.*

She caught GNask watching her and dropped her gaze.

She was hungry. She wondered if they would share flesh
together and the thought made the corners of her own
mouth grow moist. *She was predator because* he *was predator and had imprinted her in his image.* The grotesque,
bulky amphibian was more her father than Ambassador
John Taylor Thomas, her real father, was.

But GNask was not pleased, in general, with her, with
the raid on Arizar, with recent events on Sorrow where his
efforts to gain more power in the Compact had been
thwarted. Her visit to his chambers might only be another
debriefing and she might be sent away as she had come in,
hungry, dark appetite unfulfilled.

Alexa fought to control her trembling as the warm water
bathing her began to ripple away from her, concentric lines
spreading. She would look like prey herself if she did not
stop her tremors. She clamped her jaw tightly as GNask
heaved more of his bulk out of the pond. Water streamed
down his purple-green hide.

"Alexa," GNask rumbled, acknowledging her presence.

"Master."

"You have done well."

She put out an arm, slim, well-formed for a human, and let it
float upon the water, hand curled in entreaty. "I failed you. I
neither know what the Choyan did nor where they fled."

"Out of your failure has come a certain triumph. Arizar
is cleansed of them." GNask rolled an eye at her. A tiny,
pearlesque drop of saliva hung from the corner of his lip
where his tusk curled it slightly open. "We take what victo-
ries we can."

The hand she held open in entreaty she pulled back into
a fist. "We'd have had more if that fool Bevan hadn't
bolted. I had no choice but to call you in early."

"Every victory, however slight, is a worthy one." GNask
chopped his teeth together, both savoring the results of the
Arizar mission and frustrated by what had not come to
pass. "The cost may not be too much to bear."

"It is for me!" Alexa's voice burst from her and then
she sank back, in the water, appalled by the sound of it.

GNask curled his lips back further. He looked pleased.
"Ready to fight again? So soon?"

"Your enemies are my enemies."

He bobbed in the water. "Perhaps." The symbiont slurp-

ing its way across his skull put out two tiny stalk eyes,
swiveled a bit, peering at her, she thought, and she shuddered at its look. Then it proceeded to feed again, vacuum-
ing the Abdrelik's skin for fungus and microbes. "Don't be
deceived," GNask said, his voice thrumming in his chest,
vibrating the very water. "I like defeat no better than you
do." His eyelids lowered, hooding the predator's expression. "I have, perhaps, had the wrong Choya as my target.
Palaton may be even more dangerous than Panshinea."

"Palaton was at Arizar." Her voice was barely audible
across the stilling pond.

"Was he?" The hooded eyelids lowered more, until they
were a glaring slit. "And we missed him. How fortunate.
A *tezar*'s uncanny instincts. Panshinea should have been a
pilot. He would have been undefeatable if he had been.
You're sure of this?"

"Is it common for a Choya to call himself by another's
name?"

"Not generally, no. That's a form of deception not com-
monly adopted by our friends." GNask scratched a jowl
thoughtfully as his eyes reopened. "And we're no closer to
obtaining the mechanics of the *tezarian* drive. I close my
fist," and GNask did so, holding his hand out of the pool,
water streaming from between his fingers. "And the
Choyan escape like this. But their choke-hold on the rest
of us is not so ineffectual. They know what they condemn
us to, yet they continue strangling us to death!"

Alexa flinched as the big amphibian's voice boomed. The
furtive movement drew his attention instantly, rapt and
keen. She held very still, fighting the instinct to vault from
the pool and run. She knew his baser thoughts as if they
were her own, and knew he weighed her usefulness against
the delights of consuming her. She must always be certain
that she was very, very useful to the Abdrelik in his
presence.

GNask opened his fist and looked at his empty hand. "I
want to grasp knowledge. I want the drive. The law among
the stars must be the same as the law upon the earths: the
strong survive. What there is for the taking, is taken. There
are worlds out there, star lanes, which only the Choyan
know of. They guard their secrets jealously. I will rip those
secrets from them if it's the last thing I do."

Chapter 2

Broken concrete and smoking skies. . . . Bevan woke with
a start from his dreams of hurt and burning to look into a
sharp muzzled face, with rounded transparent ear flaps, not
unlike a rat from the streets of his youth. But this being
standing over Bevan watched him with a not unkindly stare.

The Zarite reached out and put a soft-furred paw on
the human's shoulder. He helped bolster him into a sitting
position. The world of hurt which had enveloped Bevan in
his dreams jarred him now. The alien blinked in empathy.

"Better?"

Bevan's lips ached and chapped skin sloughed from them
as he pulled them apart to sculpt a word. He put a finger
to them instead and the Zarite peeled his finger away gently to push a clay cup into his hand.

"Drink. You are hot."

Hot? Hot. Bevan drank, wetting his sore lips and cooling
his parched throat. Not hot. Fevered. But the Zarites might
not understand. He could only guess at their physiology
and thought they might do the same of him. He put the
mug down.

He tried speech again. "How long?" The sounds scraped
along a throat clogged with smoke and soot, made raw by
fever and dreams . . . dreams which cloaked him even when
awake. He tried to blink them away.

"Five days since we found you."

Five days since he'd left Rand to die amid the shards of
the spaceport. Five days since his own clumsy effort to take
flight had brought him crashing down and his rescuers had
pulled him from the crushed and flaming ship. He was sore,
but nothing seemed broken. He'd inhaled fumes which still
made his lungs ache. Yet this he would survive, for Bevan
had been a survivor for as long as he could remember,

from the mean streets of Sao Paulo to the Catholic orphanage which had taken him in, to this planet and the ragged future it had offered him. This disaster, too, he would survive.

It was the thing which raged inside him that he truly feared, the thing which he could not control or comprehend.

It was this thing—fused into him by the arrogant Choyan pilot Nedar, this thing which must be Nedar's soul itself—for which Bevan had killed.

It now exacted its own toll, this soulfire which consumed him like a kind of Choyan revenge for Nedar's death. To save Alexa and himself, he had murdered and run, but there was nowhere he could hide from the burning inside. And when Rand had come after him to help, his response had been to try to destroy Rand as well. There was no help for him now. The soulfire inside him devoured all that had been human, leaving him empty and evil.

The Zarite refilled his cup. "You must stay quiet. The Choyan are here, come back to look at the burning grounds."

Bevan looked up sharply. "What? Which Choyan?"

"I do not have their names. I only know they are up on the plateau."

At the College. Or what was left of it. What did they seek there? Did they look for him, still?

"Do they know . . . do you know . . . who attacked?"

"Enemies." The Zarite's ears went flat, then came up again as he answered impassively. "It does not matter. When the Choyan leave, the enemies will leave."

Bevan chewed on that answer as the Zarite crept away, leaving him alone. Sunlight slanted through a patched roof, dappling him with shadow. He had thought . . . feared . . . that the attack had been directed at him, in anger over Nedar's death, revenge being exacted on an entire world because of something he had done. That guilt, at least, he did not have. It had not been his sin which had brought fire down upon Arizar. If not his, then whose? The Choyan were a powerful people. Only the Abdreliks and Ronins went up against them. Which of them had dared an attack?

His lips went dry again. Bevan dropped a hand down to the mug, found it filled again and waiting, and lifted it to his lips. He drank it down, thinking it a futile effort to quench the fire inside.

His eyes blinked shut for longer and longer. He began to drift. He wondered for what the Choyan searched. He fell asleep musing on broken promises.

Plummer ducked out of the broken arch doorway. A slab of concrete lay askew, hiding the building's front. It looked as demolished as any of those on the spaceport outskirts. Miffer awaited him, squatting patiently on slat-sided hindquarters.

"He sleeps again?"

"Yes. But he's very hot."

Miffer straightened, looked out over the devastated cityscape, to the far mountains. A storm front angled across that horizon. It would take a few days to reach them. They would get only a tailing of rain, not the sleet and hailstones and thunderstorms the mountains would reap. Still, the shelter they were in would be put to the test. "Keep plenty of water near him. I'll try to buy some herbs tonight." The Zarite scrubbed a hand down over his pointed face. "I hope he is worth the trouble."

"The salvage crews have already paid me a consulting fee. It does us no good to scavenge if we do not know what we have."

Miffer made a scoffing noise. "What makes you think the outlander will know any more than we do?"

Plummer's voice dropped to a sharp hiss. "He's one of them. His hands have always been filled with machinery. He will know!"

"Then you do well to keep him alive . . . and awake." Miffer seemed nonplussed in the face of Plummer's frustration. "Or the consulting fees will be returned—out of your hide!"

Plummer wiped his hands down along his flanks and then on his apron. "I know," he said, a little mournfully. "I know."

A skimmer passed the next block over, its wake sending up swirls of dust and ash. The two Zarites wrinkled their faces and coughed in the disagreeable wake. Inside, the fevered human's voice rose in the murmur of nightmares struggling to be told, to be exorcised, to be understood.

Neither Zarite paid any attention to the voice or the words, as if knowing they had not the capacity or the experience to understand what troubled the human.

In the foothills below the mountains at a second site, hail had fallen, littering the ground with white stones. Rindy looked cold as he tottered after Palaton, but he asked no quarter as they walked the foundation outlines of what had once been a prosperous Householding. Palaton stopped and the elder knew it was no mistake that the other's tall body buffered the wind and weather for him. He pulled up at Palaton's elbow.

"Nothing left."

"No." Palaton's voices were pitched low, for his hearing alone.

"The Abdreliks were thorough."

Palaton's thick mane of hair bannered in the wind. "From the preliminary scouting reports, there are no Householdings left. Rindy, the Abdreliks didn't have the time to be this thorough, not the time or the firepower. This is self-destruction."

The elder lifted his chin. He considered the implication of the *tezar*'s words. "To prevent discovery?"

"Undoubtedly. And I doubt we'll find many Choyan bones within this debris. Which leads me to ask, not only where they went—but how they got there."

To cross the void, to flee this world and seek another, meant mastering FTL. It meant that the renegades had either developed pilots among themselves, or had access to pilots. That there were *tezars* who would take contracts not sanctioned by their flight schools or their emperor or even by the Compact on Sorrow, just as there had been *tezars* who had taken on the contracts of flying Abdrelik warships into Arizar, with no qualms of conscience over attacking their own.

The old Choya took a deep, shuddering breath. "I am sorry to see this," he said, and his voices trembled with emotion. "There is nothing we can do here."

"No. And the front is moving in stubbornly. You're cold, the boy is hurt . . . and there is nothing more we can find out or do here." Palaton swiveled on a bootheel. His foot ground into the mud and ashes and melting hailstones. "I think the Zarites will be relieved to see us go."

Rindy hugged his robe around his bony shoulders. "The Households here have not done well by them. I can see clear signs of genetic manipulation and repression. They're a clever people. If brethren of ours hadn't interfered here, who knows what kind of world we might tread now. Panshinea won't react well to this, Palaton."

"And you think I will?" Palaton frowned slightly, looking down at his companion.

"I know you will. I suggest," and Rindy put a knobbed finger to his lips. "Compromise."

But he signaled silence. Palaton looked away and drew in a fleeting breath of surprise. "I'll do whatever I can," he answered. He put his arm out. "It's slippery here. Let's head back to the cruiser."

Rindalan accepted the support. "It's treacherous everywhere," he remarked.

From space, Arizar looked unremarkable. It was a blue water world under a G5 star, eminently suitable for life in the Choyan style. Its scars were all but invisible to the naked eye and even those that showed under technological scrutiny were nothing that a year or two wouldn't heal. It had two small moons that barely qualified as satellites, but they paced one another and created sufficient screening for the starship which hid behind them. They did not screen the interstellar activity around Arizar.

One who watched his panel intently now saw the signs of a cruiser leaving the spaceport, picking up escape velocity, then leveling off as it attained deep space. He knew the ship, knew its markings, thought he knew who might be piloting it. He sucked his breath in, raggedly, as though through a grievous injury, and held it briefly, then exhaled. The exhalation made him cough and the chunky, stunned-looking Choya sitting in the pilot's seat next to the observer made a jerky movement with his arm as though startled.

The observer's attention flickered only for a second, then fixed back on the cruiser.

"Palaton," breathed the observer. Another tearing breath and exhalation. "Not yet. I don't have you yet . . . but I will. I'll have back everything you stole from me, and all you hold as well."

He grabbed at the stolid Choya. "See them, Staden?

There goes the heir to the throne on Cho. I worked for it—*I* wanted it. He fought me from the very beginning . . . I should have killed him at Blue Ridge when we were cadets, when I had a chance . . . he flew better than I, even then. Everything, better than I. I fought wars and won them, but he . . . he won causes! He could even pull victory out of defeat. What chance did I have against that?"

The quiet Choya did not answer. His flesh had paled to a grayish tone, his cheekbones had sunk into a cadaverous expression as though all his vital juices had been sucked from him.

But Nedar neither noticed nor cared. He shook the Choya, a hard jerk demanding attention. "I wept when the emperor sent for him . . . then wept again when Panshinea sent him away to protect him from the corruption of the throne and sent for me. It did not matter that I would be besmirched by the emperor's actions. No. Palaton was all. I was nothing. *He* was spoken of as the hero in exile. What was I? A *tezar,* no more and often less. He took my life from me . . . not the blade that wounded me. It is no wonder they all thought me dead and consigned me to your gentle care, to take me home for burial. I might still need you for that, Staden."

Spent, eyes burning with his intent, Nedar leaned back into the console seat, and pressed his hand over the healing wound in his flank. His voices dropped to a whisper. "They took my *bahdur* from me and left me only this, my hatred, to fire me. Will it be enough, do you think, to destroy Palaton?"

Nedar took another deep breath, harsh and grave sounding. He put his head back against the molded rest, ebony mane falling from his proud horn crown. He had seen the Abdreliks withdraw from their pounding of the planet. His canniness as a combat pilot had kept them in hiding, as it did even now. And he had seen the Choyan destroy their Householdings and flee in the wake of the strafing, flee across Chaos to the unknown, though he had had enough *bahdur* stolen from the unresponsive Choya next to him to remember the glimmer of their passage.

These things Palaton did not know. These things, and others, Nedar would find a way to work against him. For now, he needed allies. His patroness Vihtirne would strip away his pretenses all too easily. She could not be trusted until he knew his strengths. There were others he could turn to, he thought.

"Take me home, Staden. But not to rest. Not yet. Not until Palaton is destroyed." He gave in to the urge to breathe only shallowly, and to let his eyelids shutter down over his eyes, but his face did not relax, even as sleep claimed him. It remained contorted in hatred.

Chapter 3

Ambassador John Taylor Thomas strode along Compact grounds, disdaining the ground transport at hand, stretching his legs after a day in close quarters. It was a discipline of his, to walk when he could easily be carried, a discipline which kept him fit and still at the edge of his prime. A rain tinged wind pushed at his thinning hair, reminding him that not all things stayed the same, no matter how hard he worked to maintain such a situation.

Heads turned as he passed, making note of who walked and where, and that he wore a bodyshield and thus was not nearly as vulnerable as he looked. The shielding blurred the shadow which rose and fell at his footsteps. It would not hold against a full-scale attack, but for the subtlety of assassination, it might well save his life again. It had already done so once, though not recently.

Thomas threw his head back and looked at the sky, stippled with gray-white clouds, moving too fast now to scatter showers on the Compact city, and he breathed in the fresh air. Whatever Sorrow had been in its past, its makers had either been too wise to destroy their world, or they had been gone so long now that the world had righted itself. He envied them their wisdom.

His step slowed as he neared the crystallized stream which edged the compound sector he traversed. There was natural water throughout the city, brooks and ponds and lakes, and by the sheer cliffs which bordered the edge of the horizon, there would be veils of water falling from incredible heights, pounding into mountain tarns. But the crystallized streams and lakes of the city were not natural, and it was no longer water which filled them. A quartzlike material lined them, for they had been made into a tomb.

Thomas paused at the stream's edge. Most of those who

lived in the Halls of Compact quickly grew used to the sight. He never had and he knew of only one or two who had ever admitted to him that they, too, had been deeply affected. One of them had been a Choyan he wished he could have trusted.

The embankment widened slightly, and under the spreading arms of a copse of gold-flecked trees, Thomas found a bench and sat. Though it had not quite been sculpted for a human body, it met his needs without too much discomfort. The overlook was intentional—here the crystal stream began to widen into the lake and bridge structure leading into the central grounds, and here the dead could be seen most distinctly.

Like a fly caught in amber resin for all eternity, the alien dead had been caught in crystal. Their faces, he thought, looked both startled and amazed. Mothers gathered young to their bodies. Young lovers embraced each other as if their youth could have staved off the impending death.

No one knew what had been wrought here—what enemy had come upon and imprisoned an entire race—or how it had been done, for the alchemy to change water into quartz was impossible, yet the evidence lay before him. What a world to lose, these people who had kept it so carefully and yet lost themselves to another enemy, unknown, unnamed.

Sorrow had been chanced upon and had been deemed an omen. *This could be your path and your death,* it seemed to say, if you do not turn your road aside. And so the quarreling aliens who found it left it inviolate and founded a treaty organization upon its lands. The bodies in quartz had been left intact, though xenobiologists and archaeologists had been probing the phenomenon for centuries without much success.

There was a movement behind John Taylor Thomas, one that he heard and felt and smelled, and he knew his appointment had arrived, but he sat very still. It never did to show fear to your enemies.

"It still gives you pause, does it, Ambassador?"

"Indeed it does, Ambassador," he replied to GNask, and then turned slightly upon the bench.

The Abdrelik had lowered himself to the foot of one of the trees. The bulk of his face wrinkled. "You may dim your bodyshield, Thomas. I think there is that which bonds us."

Cursing to himself for offending the Abdrelik, Thomas thumbed down the bodyshield to a neglible level. His time with the ambassador would be short. He decided not to fence with the alien. "Where is she?"

"Quartered. She does well, considering we plucked her out of a holocaust."

Thomas watched the piglike eyes of the other. "Injured?"

"Of course not. Your daughter is a most remarkable . . . specimen. Intelligence and common sense and the wit to know when to use either."

He felt somewhat mollified. Alexa, safe. As safe as she could be after they had imprinted her. As sane as she could be . . . after. "You have what you wanted, then."

"Not quite." GNask sucked in a prodigious amount of air. GNask was an amphibious creature and the realization of how formidable he could be underwater struck Thomas. "Our friends did not like our probing. They destroyed themselves and most of the evidence we need to make our case. However . . . I think we can cause the Choyan some trouble."

"We agreed on more than trouble. We agreed to prove a tampering charge, tampering with a Class Zed status."

GNask put the back of a beefy hand to the corner of his mouth and mopped it slightly. "We agreed that if the Choyan were tampering, they should not be allowed to get away with it. Panshinea is a brilliant being, ambassador. I'll not present a case before him without all the evidence I can get. And when I get it, you'll get your daughter back."

"A visit, then?"

Something flickered through GNask's muddy eyes. "If she wishes it," he said. He levered himself to his feet. "We'll be in contact, Thomas. And do not worry. She does well with us."

With that, the Abdrelik turned and left, hiking over the knolls and onto the grassy flat leading to outer pathways and compounds.

Thomas stood to watch him go. He closed his eyes to ease his pain. It was not as if she'd died on Arizar, though he knew the daughter he loved so much had died years and years ago when the Abdrelik had first integrated his symbiont into her body. He opened his eyes and found his hand clenched, nails biting into his palms.

GNask did not know that he had had biochemists working on finding a neural stripper to rid Alexa of that imprint should she ever be returned to him. The work was long and tedious, but the last word he had had from home had been hopeful. Very, very hopeful.

"We are not as backwater as you think," Thomas muttered. A leaf dropped from the branches overhead and struck him. He looked up, then thumbed his bodyshield back on full. He was among enemies on a planet set aside for peace. He would never forget either.

Rand stayed at the observation window, despite the mellow warnings on deck that it would be closed soon for shielding. His legs and hip ached a little, a tiny, fierce, burning ache that told him both that he'd been injured and that he was healing. He watched the world which had promised him everything and given him nothing grow smaller, framed by the window.

He did not hear Palaton enter but suddenly was aware that his presence was dwarfed on deck. He turned his head and voiced his thoughts.

"There's nothing left."

"No. Very little."

The twin voices of the Choya underlined one another. He could hear strength and sorrow in both tones, the differences so subtle he wondered how he could hear it. Rand stirred, coming about. "I should have been there."

Palaton looked at him. Lines furrowed in the brow emphasized by an unruly forelock of hair and the proud, scallop-edged horn crown. "And should we have salvaged nothing from Arizar? No hope, no understanding?"

"I'm not—" Rand stopped, waved a hand as words failed him.

"No," said Palaton. "Perhaps you're not. But you *will be* and that is what counts here."

You will be. Potential. The promise unfulfilled. That was what the Choya saw in him, rescued him for. That was what the Choyan saw everywhere they looked. The potential. The realization of a tiny portion of the alien's thought process stilled Rand for a moment.

What must it feel like to look at something and see not only the accumulation of that moment, but the possibility that stretched beyond it? What if they were wrong? How could they know they must be right? They must have the confidence of the ages behind them. He pondered the feeling of certainty, what it must be like to be born with it. No wonder the Choyan headed the Compact of alien races. No wonder they were the pilots, the masters of Chaos. The only wonder in him was that Palaton had chosen to look at him and *see*.

Palaton sat in a fluid bending motion. He put out a hand and cupped Rand's shoulder, then dropped it. The gesture passed so quickly he might almost have imagined it. The Choyan were not given to casual physical closeness. Rand looked at the alien, with the sculpted bone crown that cupped and released masses of hair tumbling down the back of Palaton's large head. Had they butted heads like elk and moose in the primeval days of their race's youth? Had the crowns grown to protect the mighty brains within their skulls˙ And had the instinct to keep an arm's length away remained anyway? He would never know, he thought. If he did not know about himself, his own race, he could never even hope to know the alien mind.

He contradicted himself as he saw a fleeting shadow cross the other's gold-flecked eyes. Doubt and worry pooled within.

"You didn't tell Rindalan," he said, tripping a little over the elder Choya's name.

Palaton leaned back in his chair with a sigh. "No. How could I? We Choyan are all woven together, different strands of a single being, the God-in-all. He would not understand the bond between us."

Rand added softly, "He would not understand that I carry your *bahdur*."

"No." Palaton's face tensed as if he gathered himself. "No one would. I had thought perhaps Rindy might, but since I cannot know his mind . . . it's better not to risk it. Rand, this is very important. You must understand that I cannot do, will not be allowed to do, what I have to if this bond between us becomes known."

Rand lowered his head slightly. "I think I know."

"Do you?" Palaton looked away, out the observation window, where only black velvet could meet his gaze. "It is not for myself I ask. It is for Cho."

Rand did not respond for a moment, thinking of home, where one man might imagine he could make a difference, but probably could not, though, God knew, thousands had tried throughout history. But to be an emperor of a world . . . his thoughts as well as his vision blurred. His eyesight, he brushed a hand across his face, knowing that temporary blindness would set in from drugs given him by the College before his flight and its destruction. The drugs had been meant to artificially bind him to a dependence on the companionship of the alien sitting next to him. It needn't have been done. Perhaps the Choyan had no real concept of friendship that they would resort to such means. He only knew that the onset of blindness was slowly creeping in, he would have to endure it, and then it would fade. He was thankful he had not received a full dosage of the drugs. His burden would be lessened.

But mental clarity was another matter. He seemed to be thinking in two minds, one of his own and the other . . . he knew nothing of except that it seemed to shadow him, to contradict and baffle every word and image within his own. The voice was his and yet not his . . . he exhaled deeply and it caught Palaton's attention.

"You're weary." The Choya stood. "I wouldn't do this now if I had time to do it later . . . but you need to know how to protect yourself, how to shield what you carry for me." Palaton composed his face. "They'll not only destroy me, but you, if we're found out."

Rand thought dryly that he was just getting used to being a target himself, but the idea of losing Palaton jiggled an odd feeling inside of him, something akin to panic. He felt it bounce around, creating a hollowness. He didn't like it. "Tell me what to do," he said. He didn't pretend to understand why what Palaton was telling him to do would work; he listened and attempted it on his own. In the long run, it was like muffling the sound of his own heartbeat, the electric flow of his own thoughts. It was easier to do than he'd thought when Palaton had explained the method to him and when done right, offered relief. The battle of the two beings within him would at least quiet, if not fade altogether.

Rand paused. He looked up at Palaton. "Okay. When do I do this?"

"All the time," said the pilot. "Don't worry, it becomes second nature."

It would have to quickly. It tired him, and Rand sagged in spite of himself.

Palaton caught him. "You should be secured in your cabin anyway." The FTL alarm underscored his words.

"No." Rand's longing leapt into his inner voice, the voice he knew the best, the one which drove him to do what he did. "Let me see Chaos with you."

The Choya tilted his head slightly, looking down at the human. Palaton wore no facial jewelry as many Choyan did, the links in fiber-fine wiring customarily buried under the first, delicate, translucent layer of skin. His expression looked oddly naked. "No," he refused Rand.

There was no word for "please" in the Trade they spoke. The equivalent was "think again" or "reconsider" as if a bargain must be struck. The word coming to his lips angered him and Rand would not say it. This was not a deal being struck between the two of them. This was a plea. It was not right he would not be allowed to utter it. He dropped the shield he had just so painstakingly erected.

The second voice, the shadow in his mind, gave him a word. He said it and Palaton flinched as if stuck. His lips parted and he paused, then his voices rumbled. "You risk your sanity. Only *tezars* can safely do what you ask of me. Reality twists. . . ."

"I know what I face. I don't want safety. I want to pilot!" Rand struggled to his feet, despite the castings and the pain that shocked through him with the effort. "I want to go where you go, to see what you've seen. I gave up my home to gain the right to do this."

A wry smile twisted Palaton's lips. "You want to see what you *think* I've seen. And no one of my people would have promised to make a pilot out of you, no matter how renegade they were. You don't have what it takes and that is not a consideration of your hopes and desires, it is a fact of your genetic makeup, something you cannot change."

"And how am I to know the experience, how are any of us to know it, if you won't give us the opportunity? No one else is allowed to do what you do."

"Because no one else can."

"The *tezarian* drive comes in a little black box. I've seen it. I see pilots carry it from ship to ship. It's a *machine*. Teach me to use it."

Palaton put a hand up to the height of his brow, where the horn crown merged, as if he might rub an ache there. He lowered his hand before finishing the gesture. "I cannot."

"I'm asking you to give me the chance to earn the right."

"It is not a right!"

His voices cut through Rand. He felt himself recoiling a little, hurt. "You're telling me that pilots are born that way. Did you know you were one before you could walk?"

Palaton's lips twisted again, slightly. "Not quite that soon, but soon. Pilots are born, not made. Like diamonds. The edges are cut, polished, surfaces faceted . . . but the gemstone begins and ends a diamond. The soulfire drive," and Palaton hesitated, then finished, "the soulfire drive can only be used by one born to be a *tezar*."

"It's not right," Rand protested. "What if one of you bleeds to be a pilot—"

"What is not possible is not possible."

"You know," and Rand fought to keep his footing, every bone in him aching, but nothing aching so much as the heart pounding in his chest. "My planet isn't considered much by Compact terms. We deserve it, I suppose, for the mess we've made. But anyone can become just about anything if he works for it. There are universes out there which . . ." Rand's voice nearly failed him, but he found it again, "are new and fresh. Which can give something back to my world, if you let them. If we're allowed to get there. We have things of value we can trade. *We* are of value."

"I'm sorry. I wish I could explain it more fully to you. Piloting is just not possible to one not born to be a *tezar*. It's nothing I have any control over. It doesn't matter what world you come from. This is a Choyan matter, and even within my own race, there are many who cannot be what they wish."

Rand swallowed back a harsh response. Yet he could not cave in, could not surrender. The desire which had brought him across immeasurable distances would not let him deny it. Instead, he repeated that soft word of Choyan which had come to him out of the nowhere, the shadow. "*Desanda*. At least let me watch. For a moment. Let me see what Chaos is like."

Briefly, Palaton shuttered his eyes. Then he put out a steadying hand. "There is another who pilots this ship. We shall see if Rufeen allows it. If she does, then we'll both have a look."

Rufeen pursed thick lips in disapproval. Her heavy Earthan body filled the cabin bulkhead. "If any but you asked it of me, Palaton."

"Then you must respond to me as you must respond to anyone else. You're in command of this cruiser."

Her gray eyes considered the boy leaning against the starship corridor, just out of hearing range. "I'm a *tezar,* as you are," she said to Palaton. "I've seen everything. But what you ask—" she shuddered. "This is sacrilege."

"It's a request, nothing more."

"Our secrets. . . ."

"Will remain unrevealed to him," Palaton said, and hoped he did not lie. "Do you think a Class Zed citizen can determine what the most brilliant minds among the Ronins and the Abdreliks have not for centuries?"

She blinked. "And yet," she answered, "we do not invite them into our cockpits either."

Palaton did not flinch. "He left his home," he said. "He was promised the stars by those who could not give them. He doesn't understand fully why he can never have them, why only we can master the patterns. His heart was broken by deceit, and only you and I can begin the mending by showing him what is possible and what is not, so he can gather his life and get on with it." It was more than he intended telling her, but he found a trust in the squatty Earthan standing before him, who like him had all but forsaken her House and Householding for the position of *tezar*.

Rufeen's pearl gray eyes widened a little. "Who did this to him?" she asked.

"I'm not sure yet," Palaton answered. "But they were Choyan."

Her thick lips tightened as the implication sank in. And Rufeen made a decision. "Come in," she said, giving way and raising her voices. "And secure yourselves. We're on the edge of attaining FTL now."

She did not need to tell Palaton that. He could feel it as

though it carried an aura all its own. And the boy behind him, God-blind though he should be but was not because of what he sheltered inside of him, ought to be able to feel it as well. Palaton stepped through the bulkhead opening and reached back to assist Rand.

He helped Rand settle, feeling the awkwardness of the boy in his hands, casts and all, and enfolding the webbing about him. Then he took the chair next to Rufeen. "I thank you."

She gave him a sidelong look. "You are what you are," she said flatly. "It does little good for you to ask me to disregard it." She splayed a hand over the black box instrument board, in addition to the major panel of the cruiser. "On my mark. . . . *Now.*"

Rand gasped as the cruiser shuddered, piercing an invisible barrier of sorts, and before him the view went from the black velvet of normal space littered by diamond fragments of stars, to a soup of colors, stirred by an unseen hand. The skin of the cabin melted away and he found himself hanging in the weblike chair like a piece of meat about to be dropped into a stew pot. Sweat popped out on his forehead and his heart thumped in sudden panic.

The shell of the cruiser was gone. Where it went, he had no idea, but he rode through space unprotected, unsheltered. As Chaos swirled about him, he knew he would be devoured whole.

He tried to swallow. It did not help that the hands he gripped with appeared to be melting away, flesh from the bones, like wax. He looked at the back of Palaton's head and reminded himself he'd asked for this.

Palaton did not sense the boy's discomfiture. He had little opportunity to think of anyone but himself, for this was the first time in his life he had tried to confront Chaos without *bahdur*. He did not like the sensation. The turmoil, the colors muted by the absence of free-flowing light, yet created anyway, only to slowly bleed away to darkness, the wash and frenzy of a sea of havoc wrenched at him. He tried to anchor himself against the tide of confusion and panic threatening to rise.

"Tezar." Rufeen's gentle voices were laden with concern. "Is anything wrong?"

Admit to another pilot that he had lost his soul? Never. Palaton held himself still against the tide of havoc. "Nothing, Rufeen."

What could she suspect? Every *tezar* saw in his/her own way the various patterns of Chaos. Some saw a blinding confusion of pathways to take, for others there was often only one pathway with clearly delineated landmarks, or patterns, to sight. And for those unfortunate in the same manner he was now, there was only turmoil. But she could not read his soul now, she would be too entangled with guiding them safely through. As to that . . . he'd tested himself against old Rindy. Scoured of *bahdur,* he still had his inner defenses against invasion by others. A casual search would not batter those walls down. She could not press even if she wanted to.

And he would fight to the death before he would allow any further trespass.

But Earthans were the salt of Cho. It was in their genes to balance the forces they saw around them. She would not be of the House of Earth if she did not sense his tenseness and want to soothe it.

"*Tezar.* I know it must be difficult to let another pilot you. Would you care to take over?"

She had him caught now. He could scarcely refuse her gracious offer without revealing himself. He read her face as she looked to him briefly. No diabolical scheme narrowed her eyes, or etched her expression—yet she'd snared him as skillfully as any seductress.

Palaton opened his mouth to refuse, when Rand made a strangling noise from the security web behind them. Palaton reacted instinctively as he would for a Choyan child, leaving his chair despite the reality which melted around him as he did so. For a dizzying moment he considered an abyss under his booted feet, an abyss which fell through the depths of the universe.

Rufeen muttered to herself as she manipulated the control board. He needed no special talent to see she had become suddenly disturbed. Her movements caught his attention, distracting him from Rand.

She looked up. "The patterns are shifting."

"I would never interfere, *tezar,* I give you my word."

"*Somebody* is." Rufeen shook her head and sucked in

an exasperated breath. "There it goes again. My patterns keep slipping away. I've never seen patterns like this."

"Can you bring us back in line?"

"I think so. Old Rindy must be dreaming."

Palaton started a little at her statement, but, yes, the elder prelate had more *bahdur* than almost any two Choyan put together, although he hadn't tested out to have all the talents needed to be a pilot. Could he, in a deep sleep, be reaching out to interfere? Palaton unclipped his shoulder strap. "I'll see to him."

Rufeen's chin jerked in disagreement. "I might need you here!"

"He has to be stopped." Palaton could not tell her he had no aid for her.

She bit down on her lip, then nodded. "All right. It's a short trip. I'll burn all I can."

If he could have seen it, her aura would have appeared to flare with the effort as she turned all her energy to regaining her control of Chaos. The cruiser trembled slightly and then bore to the starboard as it answered her command at the helm.

Rand answered as well, a thin wail of pain.

He caught himself as Rand thrashed in his webbing and tore lose, bolting to his feet with a cry. His turquoise eyes went wide with panic. From a pale face came an expression of such loss that Palaton's own heart quailed.

Rand put a hand out and reached for him. Their fingers touched briefly and Palaton tasted an agonizing moment of *bahdur* which was no longer his to claim . . . and an alien wash of fear and abandonment.

Then the boy toppled to the deck as if dead.

Chapter 4

Palaton's heart dropped and he pitched after the boy.

Rufeen spared a glance over her shoulder. "What is it?"

Palaton had gone to one knee so quickly the joint numbed from hitting the floor as he knelt by Rand's side and put a hand out to turn the face toward him. Under the humankind's closed and pale eyelids, the eyeballs moved skittishly. His breath shallowed. Palaton found small comfort in that. "He's unconscious. It's a Chaos fugue."

"My apologies. If I could have kept the helm answering to me alone . . . will he be all right?"

"I'm not that familiar with his physiology, but I think so. He's been through too much."

Rufeen made a low sound of understanding. Palaton brought the boy up in his arms, awkward because of the healing supports. "I'll take him back."

The pilot nodded, saying only, "I have it under hand now, *tezar*. Thank you for your assistance."

Palaton accepted her gratitude mutely, intent only on taking Rand to the passenger lounge where he could make the boy comfortable. There were drugs available for the condition of acute disorientation, but he did not want to administer them until the boy was conscious. Any adverse reaction might not be apparent if Rand were already disabled.

No one occupied the lounge. Rindalan, as was his privilege, had a private cabin. Palaton wondered if the old Choya did indeed dream, perhaps of piloting, in his sleep, and if he had interfered with Rufeen. Palaton could not remember if there had been any inkling of the talent to be a *tezar* in the prelate's background. It was equally likely Rufeen fought with her own burnout of power, the dread that happened to then all, a fire that burned steadily and brightly until it began guttering and then—snuffed out, as quickly, as suddenly, as if it had never been.

He had always feared that. To reach for a light and find darkness. Now that he had darkness, it was not so terrible. The disease and neuropathy which accompanied burnout did not have a firm hold on him yet. The slow and agonizing death which the disease incurred was still decades away for him.

And if what the College Choyans had told him was true, then once his purified *bahdur* could be retrieved from Rand, he could begin again. No disease, no emptiness. His power bright and clean, like a purified torch which had once burned dark and smutty.

A miracle.

If it were true.

And if it were not, then how had they existed on Arizar, a colony of Householdings, renegades from Cho, an entire foothold of Choyan where his brethren had never been before? They had discovered the bonding between humankind and Choyan *tezars*. It was they who found that humans could be a receptacle, a filter, for *bahdur*. They thought they could offer this miracle.

And he, desperate for a future, had not refused. If he had foreseen, he would not have taken it, unlike Nedar who grasped it no matter what the catastrophe . . . even the death and destruction at Arizar, even that price he had been willing to pay. And his rival had paid the price with his own life.

Palaton would have joined him if it could have saved the others. He would not have paid that price. Even this emptiness was not worth the toll exacted on Arizar and the jeopardy placed on all Cho.

And here he was, bringing more jeopardy home to them. A charge of tampering would not be treated lightly. While he wrestled with the dissatisfaction at home, Panshinea would face the critics of the Compact.

There was a pattern in Chaos known as the Tangled Web. Most pilots saw it, though its actual placement and appearance might vary somewhat. They all avoided it like the plague. It was trouble, death, and destruction. Moameb had once told him that he had seen a Devourer in the midst of the Web, like a greedy spider, waiting to consume the unwary who got caught.

He wondered if his actions had brought them all into the course of the Tangled Web. He placed his palm gently over Rand's forehead, found it damp and cool, and removed his hand. He told himself again that he'd had no choice. That the Great Wheel turned without his help. That events on Cho unfolded without his plotting.

That assuaged only the tiniest layer of guilt.

He could always have turned his back on Panshinea. He could have accepted the beginning of his loss of *bahdur*. He could have refused to look into the eyes of a humankind and begin a bonding he had little understanding of.

But he had not.

Now he must endure whatever faced them and do what he could to right the inevitable wrongs which would befall. His mother had been an artist: a weaver, and an embroiderer. He thought of the hangings he'd seen in his youth, and of those gracing the walls of the imperial gallery in Charolon. Particularly in embroidery, the intricacy was made a stitch at a time, error as well as triumph, sometimes stippled with drops of the artist's own blood. Now, he realized the parallel of his mother's work to the fabric of one's life. Sometimes there had to be a little blood, a little struggle, for it to remain a worthwhile project.

But, as he bent over the still figure of the unconscious human, he vowed that any further blood spilled would be his own. He would not sacrifice the innocent in the tapestry of his future.

The thrum of the cruiser in its flight had nearly lulled Palaton to sleep when Rand stirred and his eyelids fluttered. The gentle awakening gave Palaton hope—those deranged by Chaos unreality often woke with twitches and convulsions as their minds fought with their bodies. He roused himself, stifling a yawn, as Rand's eyes opened. The humankind blinked rapidly several times.

Then, softly, "Palaton?"

"It is I."

Rand grabbed his arm. "I almost had it," he said. "Almost had it . . ." Weakened, his grasp loosened and the boy subsided.

"Had what?"

"I . . . don't know."

"Dreams," Palaton offered. "If you have them."

Rand's eyes rolled a bit in their sockets, then the boy focused on him again. "Oh," said the boy softly. "We have them." He licked his lips. "So that's what I miss every time I take the drugs."

"That, and more. I can't expose you further."

Rand's head turned slightly to see if the observation screens were open. They were not. He shifted his weight upon the couch and let out a tiny groan. "Everything hurts."

"You hit the floor rather hard."

"Mmmm." Rand's face twisted.

"Was it worth it?" Curiosity piqued Palaton. Had Rand seen with his borrowed *bahdur*? Such a thing was unthinkable, but he had to ask.

A strange expression shuttered Rand's face. "I'm not sure . . . I'll let you know," the boy said.

Unsatisfied, Palaton stood. "I'll get the meds."

"No."

Halfway across the lounge to the standard meds cabinet on the far wall, Palaton twisted in midstep. "What?"

"I'm all right now."

"You could lapse again at any moment. I cannot predict your next reaction. You could lose everything, Rand, all touch with reality and yourself. I won't allow the possibility."

The boy did not respond immediately. There was a vibration in the decking beneath Palaton's boots. Through senses other than the paranormal, he became aware that Rufeen was taking the cruiser through a series of shifts and maneuvers. The pilot's activities were also setting up rapid changes in the perceptual fields of those not manipulating Chaos or those who were not capable of it. The ripple effect would be hitting them momentarily. He did not want Rand to suffer. Palaton abruptly continued his journey, took down the meds case, and brought it to Rand.

He forcefed the meds while the boy's attention seemed distracted and though Rand almost choked on one of the caplets, he swallowed quickly and made a bitter face. It gained his attention. "Don't take no for an answer."

"I do not," answered Palaton solemnly, "intend to." He waited until Rand closed his eyes and slipped into a light sleep. Then he took up a watchful position in a nearby chair and fought the effects of Chaos upon himself. Taking a deep breath, he slipped into the calming meditation he'd learned as a raw cadet at Blue Ridge, where his true life as a Choyan and a *tezar* had begun. His grandfather's Householding had only been a temporary nest, a crib, a beginning. Blue Ridge was where his heart belonged.

He leaned his neck into the molded headrest, finding respite from the weight of his horn crown as he did so, and let himself go. He dreamed, remembering his days on Cho as a simple pilot when a *tezar* had garnered more cheers from the masses than even an emperor.

Rufeen's low-pitched voices woke him. "Heir Palaton, are you available?"

There was sand in his eyes, and his throat hurt as if he had been trying to talk in his sleep. He sat up and keyed open the interlink between the lounge and the com. With an eye to Rand, who still seemed to rest quietly, he answered, "I'm here."

"I have just requested berthing assignment. Palaton . . . there is an awkwardness. Cho will not give us clearance to land."

Awkwardness was an understatement. "What?"

"Heir Palaton. . . ."

Heir. Not *tezar*, but heir. Panshinea's heir. The heir to all the chaos which reigned at home in the wake of Panshinea's brilliant but often erratic rule and now the emperor's sudden departure to the Halls of the Compact. Was he being refused as Panshinea's heir? Was Cho already being torn into pieces by factions readying to take the throne?

"Have you been given a cause?"

Rufeen sounded abject. "My apologies. I may have precipitated this. I sent ahead for medical facilities to be readied for the humankind. Palaton, the Congress has refused to allow an alien to set foot on Cho."

He had hoped to bring Rand in quietly, anonymously, as the emperor's privilege, under his cloak. But now Rufeen's solicitousness had tipped his hand. Palaton took a deep breath, thinking.

Changing air pressure disturbed the lounge, as the far bulkhead opened, and Rindy struggled in. His robes were rumpled as if he'd not only slept, but fought in them. His gaunt frame looked more frail than ever as the prelate joined Palaton and sat in the chair opposite. He asked mildly, "Trouble?"

Before answering, Palaton put a hand out and keyed the interlink com to privacy mute their conversation from Rufeen. "It appears we won't be allowed to land."

"Really?" An eyebrow arched, sending off an avalanche of wrinkles down the elder's brow. "I'd like to see how you're going to deal with this." And he folded his hands across his tiny paunch and watched Palaton with an air of dry amusement. It was the prelate's equivalent of saying "I told you so."

In this situation as well, Palaton did not intend to take no for an answer. However, he had a feeling that the berthing refusal included an armed response.

"Rufeen, have they put any teeth into their bite?"

"We'll be shot down. Shields are up everywhere. There is an offer to put a hospital barge into orbit, so the humankind can be treated. That's all the communication we've had so far."

Her response reinforced what Palaton surmised. He was not being rejected. Only the boy. He should have anticipated the response. The Choyan had never allowed mass exposure to their private lives, where their abilities might be deciphered and revealed. They had adopted an isolationist policy centuries ago . . . and they would not abandon it now for him. What few aliens had ever set foot on Cho had done so only under acute insistence from the Compact.

Rand quaked under his hand. The humankind he'd sworn to protect, even as the manling protected his power, was in jeopardy. He didn't have the time to play politics.

Rindy grew impatient. "What are you going to do?"

"Make Congress change its mind."

"And how do you propose to do that? We're talking about representatives from four hundred and eighty-three counties, not to mention the fallow lands. Levying that kind of political weight could take months, if not years, even if Panshinea were solid in his throne."

It was a disadvantage of the Cho system of government, which was broken down into smaller, autonomous counties rather than large blocks of nations or continents. Rallying support could take a great deal of effort. Political Houses and players were deft at what they did. On the other hand, resource management was far more efficient on a smaller scale. Palaton stood up.

"Oh, I don't intend to play their game. I think I may have to appeal to a higher court."

"Higher court?" Rindy questioned. "What are you thinking of, my son?"

"Dreams."

"What?"

Palaton took the mute off the interlink line. Rufeen responded a little frostily after having been given dead air for so long. "Palaton?"

"I want you to set up a general broadcast."

"I can do that, but it won't be effective until we've de-celled into space norm. And when we do that, Palaton, we'll be within range of strike missiles. They can blow us off the air, literally, if they wish."

Palaton said gently, "I'm aware of that, *tezar*." Before she could apologize yet again, he said, "Let me know when you've gained orbit and made the setup."

Rindy plucked at a thread on his hemline. "What is it you're doing?"

He considered his elder. Rindy's wide, blue-hued eyes regarded him steadily. Palaton answered, "I'm going to appeal to the masses, Prelate. To the Godless, the Houseless. I'm going to ask for a general strike, if need be, to bring us down. I intend to trade shamelessly on my reputation as a *tezar*."

"That's unheard of! Palaton, you're playing with forces you've no inkling of. Even Panshinea would never consider such a move!"

"Have I a choice?"

The elder grew quiet. He looked at the sleeping humankind's face. "Once again, I think not. But I beg you to reconsider. You will be enfranchising their voice, the voice of the masses. You will be giving them the unsaid promise that you will listen to them in the future, that you will owe them. Such promises, spoken or not, may be very difficult to keep. The God-blind do not have those rights."

"And if I tell the Congress of my intentions, will they yield to me, do you think?"

Rindalan considered the question. His thin chestnut fringe of hair lay wispily along his bold scallop-edged crown. He scratched his fingers through his hair as if stirring up concepts. Then he shook his head. "I don't think so. They're a stubborn lot."

"Then I have to go to the commons. And, having made that decision, I think perhaps it's best the Congress not know of it. Surprise will be part of the effect. Rindy, I can't not bring Rand down with me. You know that."

"I know that you seem to think that." The prelate sighed. He put his hands on his knees, bony knees which stuck up through the fabric of his overrobe. "Desperate times provoke desperate measures, it has often been said. But are you this desperate?"

"The Abdreliks and the Ronins must not get hold of either Rand or me. Only Cho can protect us.

"But can you protect yourself from Cho?" Rindy paused. "The God-blind do not have the privileges we do for the simple reason that they cannot see as we do. Our attitudes and our laws protect them and our world from their careless actions. Be sure you're not opening the door to mob rule."

"Are you accusing me of being God-blind?"

"No. Just . . . hasty." Rindy looked away a moment, as decel alarms sounded. He pressed himself back in the contour chair as though awaiting a nasty but necessary exploit. "I cannot condone this."

But he could have taken steps to stop it, and was not going to. The elder Choya closed his pale eyes against the glare of the lounge.

As the cruiser bucked into normal space, Rufeen informed him that the broadcast link had been made and waited for him. He took a moment to compose what he would say. Then he opened the comlink and began to speak.

Rindy opened his pale blue eyes and considered him as he did so. The stare was steady and quiet, the prelate's thoughts hidden away. Rand awoke to the sound of Palaton's voices and he lay quietly on the couch, listening.

Palaton finished, then closed the com link. "What's done is done," he said. "I hope it's been done well."

Rindy said ironically, "You seem to have inherited Panshinea's love for that humankind, Shakespeare, as well as his throne."

"Do you think it will work?"

"I have no doubt it will," Rindy answered him. "But I have every doubt of its wisdom."

Chapter 5

"He dares a lot."

"He dares everything," the listening Choya responded, without turning to look at the speaker, the gold in his eyes glistening with the intensity of his response.

The speaker sat with a rustle of fabric. He took off his robe of office and folded it across his lap. The room they occupied was hidden deep within the city, hidden from official eyes and official laws and even the official religion of Cho. His name was Chirek and the robe he arranged into folds would be his death sentence if he was found wearing it. The religion of the God-blind had been crushed centuries ago by a concerted effort of the Houses of Earth, Sky, and Star—one of the few things they agreed upon, Chirek thought with irony—and had retreated to a hidden, furtive profile. The request of the *tezar* they listened to might well force the Hidden Ways back into the open, and into conflict again. Yet, as a priest and a leader of the commons, Chirek could not refuse to listen. He had sworn upon taking up his duties that he would wait for that Choya who would someday come—a Being of Change—and make all ways open to the God-blind . . . restore that which had been inexplicably taken from them . . . and all would be equal upon the face of their world. He spoke softly.

"What do you think of this Choya, Malahki?"

The luminary of Danbe reluctantly turned from a broadcast he had already listened to a multitude of times that day and faced his priest. "I know him," replied Malahki. "Panshinea tried to break him over the Relocation but instead sent him into self-imposed exile. The *tezar* is honest."

"Scrupulously so?"

"Genuinely so. He does not need to take care of every word, every action, because the honesty is deeply ingrained in him. And because he doesn't take care, he stumbles. I won't pretend to you that he is not a flawed hero. And because he doesn't dissemble well, I wouldn't want to confide in him."

Danbe was now a fallow land, in a county which existed in name only on the rolls of Congress, and Malahki's position as head of that county had been reduced to nothingness, though his role among the commons remained intense and powerful. Chirek stood, and found the hidden spring on his bookcase. A tiny cabinet opened. He put away the vestiges of his religious self and shut the cabinet. "But would you trust him?"

"Yes."

"He seeks to use us."

"They all do," Malahki answered dryly. He sat back in his chair and draped a burly leg over the tabletop in front of him. "He does so without guile. And, even so, isn't this part of what we wait for? We *will* be recognized if you back us. I can bring what forces I can, but only you, Priest Chirek, can order us out in numbers."

"The Housed are not stupid. If we crowd the streets in response to Palaton's plea, we may well be exposing ourselves."

Malahki interrupted with a shrug, as if to say that Chirek told him nothing new, which the priest realized as well. He went on to say, "We can do little until the Change comes among us, giving us equality."

The Choya lifted a finger. "I cannot wait for a deliverer who may not come in my lifetime. This may be political and not religious, but who's to say we can't accomplish some of the same ends? Whether he knows it or not, Palaton has offered us power, and the means to show that we do have influence upon the Householdings. We have a voice upon Cho. It's time to shout with it."

Chirek stood in his library, surrounded by ancient things, maintained with a love and duty to their value, but he valued the lives of his followers no less, and so he hesitated. "There are others I need to consult with."

Malahki recognized his cue and rose from the chair. He knew that the priesthood structure within the Hidden Ways was as obscure as the religion itself, and that although he knew Chirek well, he had met few of the others in the priestly hierarchy. "We haven't much time," reminded the luminary.

"I understand," replied Chirek. "But I wished to speak with you first."

"I have the honor of knowing you respect my opinion."

"That . . . and of giving you the burden of leading our people should we decide to answer Palaton's request. You'll be exposed. I'm trusting that your reactionary background will keep the Housed from looking further and deeper and seeing us."

Malahki smiled widely. "I'm even more honored."

"Good. You'll be taking a lot of abuse if we take action."

"I wouldn't have it any other way." Malahki paused on the bottom step of the stairwell which led into this secret room. "Let me just say this: when the Being of Change comes, none of us know whether the Change will begin outside or within us. Not knowing . . . can we refuse to answer Palaton? Can we turn aside any glimmer of metamorphosis, no matter how obscure or unexpected?"

A shadow of a smile passed across Chirek's face. "You ask, already certain of what we must answer. But what you forget, Malahki, is that there are other ways for us to answer Palaton without doing exactly what he requests of us. I understand what you wish us to do. I question its wisdom, as I questioned you about Palaton's character. Try and be a little patient. I'll have an answer for you shortly, although it may not be the one you want."

Malahki crossed half the distance up the stairwell in a single bound, before looking back and saying, "Don't think me sacrilegious for saying I'll pray you side with me."

Chirek laughed. "You, praying? You've already made it clear you will act with or without me."

"Yes, but it'll be easier with you."

"Only on the surface."

The gold in Malahki's eyes gleamed. "I cannot ask for more." He disappeared through the stairwell's hidden panels and there was a sudden silence in his wake.

Chirek stood by the desk and pondered his course.

Vihtirne of Sky, a proud, still handsome Choya'i, was livid. She paced the marble floor of the Householding's audience room, listening to the reports of the havoc in

Charolon, where commons flooded the streets. "How dare he?"

Her lieutenant sat at the wallscreen, tuning in various stations through the satellite broadcasting systems. His fingertips played over the keyboard idly, the two of them having heard most of the broadcasts earlier. He kept the sound muted. His thick ebony hair was clipped pelt short in the new style affected by the Skies, but the woman behind him still dressed in the old elegance of the naturally arrogant Householders. Her mane had been multitiered and coiffed, cascading down her ramrod stiff back, and her dress of emerald green swept the flooring as her bootheels, edged in metal, clicked impatiently.

"He has to be stopped."

Asten replied, "You forced his hand. What did you expect?"

"I?" Vihtirne paused in her pacing, turned, and raised an arched brow. Her facial jewelry, only the thinnest tracing of platinum and gold, accented the flush of her cheeks. "You value my influence with the Congress too highly. If I could stem this tide, I could take the throne."

Her lieutenant put his head back, taking his eyes off the wallscreens for the merest instant, and looked at her. She held his stare.

Then, relenting, "Perhaps you're right." She walked to Asten's side. "Still, it remains true, I can do nothing further in all of this without Nedar." Her brilliant, sapphire gaze swept over the wallscreens. "That should be Nedar's name they call. Although . . ." and her eyes narrowed. "Bringing in the Godless may seal Palaton's fate. They're uncontrollable. Palaton is a hero, but it remains to be seen whether he's a statesman of any kind. The emperor will not be pleased. Palaton may find his support eroded."

"Any statesman would pale in your shadow," Asten said. Another broadcast caught his attention and he focused the screens on it. He stopped as her hand dropped to his shoulder and gripped it with the strength of an iron claw. His lips thinned and whitened with the effort not to call out. The scene of the commons flooding the city of Charolon bled from his vision with the agony as her nails dug deep.

"Don't mock me," Vihtirne warned.

"I do not!"

"False flattery is much the same." She lifted her hand. "You are young and handsome, Asten, and I have yet to know if that is the limit to your talents. But there is no time for games. We have to find Nedar."

"He's not responded to any of the messages you had me put out. Wherever he is, he's keeping his own counsel." The lieutenant made an effort not to shrug away the pain of her touch. She had no sympathy for the weak. He had worked too hard to gain this position and her trust to lose it now. "Shall I rebroadcast?"

"Do whatever you have to to find him." Vihtirne frowned. "What's happening in Charolon?"

Asten took a cautious breath, sizing up the data coming in from the various broadcasts. "They've just given berthing permission."

"It did not take them long to capitulate, did it?" She watched the screen avidly, her lips half-parted. "After all these years, they've grown soft. I want to see what they do when I reclaim the water recycling patent." She laughed softly. "We all drink water, don't we, Asten?"

Her lieutenant did not answer. He was busy bringing up the message records to do as she had requested. But the short, fine hairs at the back of his neck rose. She laughed as she stroked the back of her hand against them.

A continent away, braced against the northern lands of Isaya, a Householding of Earth came to a halt, its members leaving the winter grasslands and their herding, taking conveyances and cruisers in response to a summoning. They scraped their feet free of grass and earth and dung before crossing the threshold, heads bowed, for the doors of Kilgalya were now the greatest of the doors in the House of Earth, and had been ever since the wounding of Tregarth decades ago.

If they had questions as they entered, they stilled themselves, for monitors had been set up in the great hall and they could see the streets of Charolon filling with commons in answer to a plea the communicators took delight in rebroadcasting again and again.

Old Devon stood awaiting them at the summit of the great hall. Years had bent his strong Earthan frame. His horn crown had thinned to brittleness and even curled somewhat with age. His hair shone shock-white, and his dark eyes blazed.

"This is what a House Descendant gives us to rule us." Old though he looked, Devon's voices boomed throughout the great hall and his assemblage. "They, and the Skies, choose to forget that the Wheel turns for them. We are the heirs of the Wheel. It is our House which awaits the fall of Panshinea." Devon paused then, for the swell of noise from the Choyan listening to him made speaking impossible for a moment. After the shouts died down, and the only noise in the hall was once again those muted tones from the monitors, the old Choya raised his chin, and his ebon gaze swept across the faces of his listeners. "We have our own heir, and we will not stop until he sits in place of Palaton. The *tezar* tells us that bringing a humankind here is a matter of world security. Do you accept this?"

Cries of "No!" boomed out before the question was even finished. Devon nodded in satisfaction. "If you do not, then I will not. Go to your Households. Do what is necessary to bring the Wheel into alignment. For too many centuries we who have striven for balance have been overlooked and ill-used. We will not bend our backs so that others can step up to the throne over our bodies again. There is only one restriction I put upon you: do not sully the reputation of the House's heir. Ariat must remain blameless of any action you take." The old Choya took in a great sucking breath, as though what he had said, sparing as it was, had taken all the energy out of him. He waved a hand, dismissing them. "Go and do what you have to do."

Beyond the obsidian gloss of the landing field, at the edge of sand and dirt, where the great domed berthing cradles lay, a tide of Choyan could be seen pushing against the invisible barrier which held them back. Palaton stood, leaving his seat on the passenger ferry, and looked over the crowd. The beat of their voices could be heard even at this distance.

Rindy arranged his robes over his knees. "I'll take the boy in with me," he offered. "You must meet the crowd you summoned."

"I have to. I'm looking at riot now. It would take very little to loose them—" Palaton sat down. He felt stunned.

He had done nothing to earn such devotion, such a following, and he felt helpless in its grip. Though he had hoped for a massive strike, he did not know his words would fill the streets of the capital with commons from all over the world.

The Prelate looked at him. "You knew and yet you didn't know."

"I don't think anyone could know about something like this." Palaton twisted his neck slightly to watch the horizon as the hover ferry droned its way across the field.

"This is not a criticism of you, my son, and yet you should hear it: Panshinea would have known. Vihtirne and many others would have. Perhaps they could not have commanded it, but they would have known, would have expected this."

Palaton came around until he could meet Rindy's stare. "Is this for me . . . or for the *tezar* who may well be Panshinea's permanent heir?"

"Does it matter?"

"Yes."

"Then you must find the answer out yourself, because I can't tell you that." Rindalan nodded. "Only they have that answer." He paused as the humankind groaned and began to move on his litter. "It's best you don't expose him to this. If he's seen as your weakness. . . ."

"Thank you, Rindy." Palaton leaned forward, elbows on his folded legs as the boy awoke and looked around, a bit bewildered.

"We're dirtside," he said.

Rand croaked a sound, then swallowed and began again, "Already?"

Rindy chuckled. "You slept a good bit of the trip," he said.

The boy's face twisted. "I feel like I slept inside a chalk quarry." He sat up and swung his feet over the side of the litter. The ferry shuddered under his movement. Those quick, turquoise eyes turned to the windows and took in the sight.

It was a hot summer's day outside Charolon. The bright cerulean sky held not a wisp of cloud to mar it and the towers of the city speared the horizon beyond the spaceport berthing cradles. The green of the early spring still covered the greenbelts which crossed the city's girth, though the air was hot and dry. Birds arrowed across the outbuildings, their shadows dappling the ground below like dots of much needed rain.

Rindy took a deep breath as if feeling the boy's awe at what he saw made Rindy himself experience it anew. The boy broadcast, not with power, but with the expression on his unetched face and in his luminous eyes. Only humankind had eyes like the Choyan. Perhaps this explained some of Palaton's natural empathy toward the humankind. The priest reached forward and patted the boy's knee. "You'll be with me," he said. "Palaton has supporters to greet."

Rand looked at him quickly. The wide, guileless eyes sized him up before Rand turned back to the window, saying flatly, "All right."

Rindy said ruefully, "I'm glad to have won your approval."

Palaton looked to them both, and stayed silent.

Just inside the security outbuilding that shut the commons away from their arrival, he could see the contingent of palace security waiting to meet them. A Choya'i stood to the fore, tall, her bronzed hair clipped back from her horn crown, her stature formidable, her uniform severe, and, like a brilliant gem in a simple setting, her beauty shone through. Jorana, come to see him home. Palaton wondered if he dared assume anything else about her presence.

As the hover ferry settled onto its pad, its hum fading, the gullwing side doors opened. Jorana stood in their frame and he could see her gray-blue eyes, always more gray than blue, widen a bit.

She beckoned attendants forward, the cabinet badge on her right shoulder winking with the movement. The Choyan who snapped to her soundless order did so with pale faces, for how often was it that a cabinet member came personally to direct security forces?

They wheeled out a chair for Rand, who collapsed into it a bit more quickly than he had expected. Rindy, in his stately, aged way of moving, emerged after the humankind and Palaton followed. He ducked under the archway of the hovers door frame and then straightened to find Jorana looking at him.

"It is good to see you, *tezar*, after thinking you lost." Her voices were deceptively formal, their tone an invisible barrier as effective as the sonic one which guarded these buildings.

"And good to see you, too." He did not bother to hide his own emotion at their reunion. The look of wonder which lit her face for a brief second was his reward.

Jorana dropped a shoulder and turned about to look down on the humankind. Her face ran through a gamut of expressions, from distaste to curiosity. "And this," she remarked, "is our problem?"

"None other."

"He doesn't look so worrisome to me. They looked smaller on the broadcasts from Sorrow." She leaned slightly away from the litter, body language at odds with the casual tone of her voices. "I will be curious to know why you've brought him and just why he is so valuable to our world security."

Rand's gaze flickered up at the Choya'i.

She examined him so intently, and without speech, that he reached into himself and shielded himself as Palaton had taught him, fearing that those cold gray-blue eyes must surely be spearing right through the truth of him. "I'm sorry."

"Really?" she said finally, her Trade accented with irony. "Then perhaps we should have left you to the Abdreliks and the Ronins."

"I'm not that sorry," Rand muttered. "Just for the trouble I've caused."

The corner of Jorana's mouth twitched. "If not you, then someone would have. We Choyan do not lead calm lives." Her gray-blue eyes lifted up, took Palaton's measure. "Though perhaps some of us are more prone to trouble than others. What more have you planned?"

Rindalan offered. "I'm taking the humankind with me. Palaton will stay behind to greet his supporters. May I suggest, O learned one, that you leave the bulk of the guard with him?"

Jorana gave the Prelate a long stare from under her eyelashes as if deciphering the other's motives. Then she nodded briskly. "That would seem to be best. They're all yours, Palaton."

"And their mood?"

"Who can say of the God-blind?" But a darkness passed through her eyes, and she did not elaborate. "As for the Housed . . . you've made enemies you cannot afford to have." Jorana touched his forearm, briefly. "It's not too late to turn the tide. Go back. Take your charge to a Compact base. Return to a position of neutrality."

Palaton shook his head once. "What's done is done."

"Do you think so?" Jorana looked him over. Her gaze lingered, more intimate than her touch on his arm. "I would persuade you differently."

"I don't want persuasion. I need support."

"Then I'm here also," she answered. She cleared her throat and added briskly, "The communicators are broadcasting from the general lobby. Once outside, my forces will be needed to move you bodily to the conveyance. Don't let the press rattle you . . . keep moving past them to the conveyance. Then let the commons parade you to the capitol building. They've gone hungry a long, long time . . . it will take a while for them to feed on this."

And she would know well, this remarkable Choya'i who herself had just come out of the Godblind, the Houseless, the commons. He nodded. "All right. I'll meet you later." He touched Rand on the shoulder. "You'll be fine."

The boy's head jerked in answer to his own. Palaton left them, guards bracing him, and made his way to the general lobby, where he could see the communicators and imagemen waiting for him. There was a swell of sound as physical as any tide rushing to meet him as he stepped through. For a moment, he gloried in it.

Rand could see little of the city through the phalanx that remained between him and the shielded windows of the conveyance. What he did see surprised him. Charolon looked old, a fortress city, surrounded by high-rises and courtyard buildings, not unlike major cities on Earth. The technology he had expected, if it was there, stayed hidden. He leaned back with a sigh.

The elder Choya's gaze settled on him. "What is it?

"Nothing. Just that I—well, I expected something different. Something more."

"More?"

"You're so much older. . . ."

Understanding dawned across Rindalan's face. "Ah. You expected floating towers, slide walks . . . miracles of technology?"

"Yes."

The Choya folded his hands across one knee. "The simpler way is better. Less pollution. We build with wood and stone, for example, because wood is a renewable resource, and stone can be reshaped many times. The buildings here," and he unwove a hand and beckoned, "are made of vegetable fiber, then reinforced. They will break down after five decades or so, and then be replaced."

"Vegetable fiber?"

"Genetically enhanced and ribbed. Giant gourds, if you will, cut to size and glued into place."

"You grow your buildings?"

"Put that way, I suppose I would have to say yes."

Rand craned his neck to look again. "And who lives there?"

"This section of Charolon is inhabited mainly by the masses whom Palaton called upon to strike." Rindy moved uncomfortably as the conveyance swayed over an awkward bit of road. "More correctly termed, the God-blind."

"Because they can't sense God."

The Prelate dropped his chin affirmatively. "Succinctly put, yes. All those of us who are Housed can see the God-in-all. But there is a lesser strain of Choyan who cannot. Of necessity, they remain lesser. Their blindness can, and has in the past, caused our world great difficulty." Rindy gave him a piercing look. "Just as you've done to your world."

Rand pondered what Palaton had already told him, coupling it with what Rindy said now. How would his world be, indeed, if those who had been so unheeding could have seen the presence of God in everything they'd fouled? He looked at the tenements they passed. "Do you let them live among you, anyway?"

"Homes are not Houses," the Choya answered, and the emphasis put out by his dual voices left the distinct impression on Rand that Houses were lineages, like royalty.

"What if you're born into a House, and you can't see, or you lose the seeing. Are you driven out?" Behind his question lurked the worry of how much he would have to protect Palaton.

"No. Sometimes it skips a generation. And among the Godless, there are also born those who can see the God-in-all. We have testing every few years to determine the ability. But there are enormous power struggles on Cho among the Householdings. Into one is driven out intentionally, but quite a few fall from power."

Rand looked at him speculatively. "Can you see God in me?"

"Most assuredly. All living things, or things once alive, hold the God-in-all. Some more vibrantly than others. I would hardly be a priest if I could not see God."

Rand put out his hand and stared at it. Rindy laughed and the boy flushed, then put his hand back down at his side.

"Is it daunting?"

Rand chewed a bit on his lower lip before answering. "I'm not sure," he said slowly. "I wondered if you could also see . . . evil."

"The anti-God Ummmm. Evil is easier to detect by action than by sight. But then, evil has always been more difficult to deal with than good."

"A universal truth." Rand put his head back on the conformed seat. The headrest intended for Choyan heads and necks stretched above him.

"One of many that binds us together. The Compact is composed of more similarities than differences."

Rand's gaze flickered back to him. "I think," he said, "that you would like to think so." He lapsed into silence and Rindy would have liked to let him keep it, for the manling looked weary, but he could not.

"We separated you and Palaton," he said, "out of necessity. He would never allow what we must insist on next."

Turquoise eyes watched him. Rindy patted his robe over his knees, arranging the fabric as he arranged his words. "Cho does not accept alien visitors lightly. We have had fewer than a handful over the last several centuries."

A squat black building rose on the horizon. A barrier along its perimeters gave it grounds undisturbed by the commons who had been rampant along the streets. Its ebony windows reflected back the Choyan sky. Rand saw it framing Rindy's head, intense and disquieting. He realized they were heading toward it.

"I had no choice about being here," Rand said. He felt his voice thin with apprehension. He tried to still the tide rising in his chest.

"And, unfortunately, the heir gave us no choice about accepting you. But that does not mean that we cannot take precautions."

Gates opened with a deathly quiet. The conveyance passed within. Guards who had been pacing the vehicle now spread out and took up stances within the barrier, as though bracing it. As they drew close to the building, Rand could see Choyan issuing from a side door, and they wore protective clothing similar to deep space suits, or like the garb firemen wore when facing environmental disasters. Rindy leaned from his seat.

"I will stay with you," the Prelate said.

As a friend? Or as someone who had decided to learn all that could be wrung from him? Rand swallowed questions that he knew would get no answers and concentrated on the shielding Palaton had taught him. He had no doubt he would need it desperately.

Chapter 6

Hat turned away from the wallscreen, snapping off the communicators' comments with a great deal of satisfaction as the room went both dark and silent at the same time. Like kites, he thought, they would circle above Palaton until nothing was left but bones. Or about Charolon until nothing was left of it but black powdered stones. They were gossip mongers, little better.

And what more was he than a nursemaid, the Earthan added, as he heaved to his feet. This wing of Blue Ridge was empty, quiet and anticipatory. It had been scrubbed within a layer of its original tiling by the cadets who'd abandoned it half a year ago, in waiting for the next class. They would be here as soon as Palaton, as Emperor's Heir, passed on the results of the various Choosings from around their world. In all the time Hat had been at Blue Ridge, first as a cadet, then as a *tezar,* and now as master, no one but Panshinea had ever judged the results of the Choosings. He wondered if there would be a discernible difference this time. How odd that a classmate would be judging them.

Not that he had ever been a *tezar* the equal of Palaton or Nedar. No. Modesty was not a part of Hat's makeup. He was practical, solidly rooted like the earth and stone of his House. Having left that Householding for Blue Ridge, he had never looked back. He doubted that he even heard from his family for anything less than a major death. He'd given them all up for the life of a *tezar,* and then when he'd been asked to give that up for the cadets, he'd been happy to do so. He was happier here as a master and teacher and, yes, nursemaid, than he'd ever been as a *tezar,* a conqueror of Chaos. Moameb, the old master, had read him well and when asked to take over the elderly Choya's position, leaving space had not been a sacrifice for him.

And so it made it ironic that he, who had never particularly cherished his *bahdur* and all its uses in defining Chaos and piloting FTL drive, he would never lose his *bahdur* as a *tezar* would, burning it out, suffering the atrophy and death of the nerve pathways that conducted those psychic powers until there was no power and there was only aching, agonizing illness and death awaiting. The fate of a *tezar* would ever be his, as it had been thought to have been Palaton's.

He had never thought Palaton gone, lost in *bahdur* burnout, though his disappearance had never ceased to be grist for the mill of the communicators. In truth, the weeks and turnings of Palaton's travail had passed to Hathord like all time passed, measured by the growth of the classes of cadets at Blue Ridge. If he had worried about Palaton, perhaps he might have joined in the speculation, but he had not. No Choya or Choya'i he had ever known had burned as brightly as Palaton. Therefore, it was impossible for him to imagine the void without him. Palaton would not simply flicker out. He would smolder for decades before his brilliance was lost. Hat just knew it would be that way.

As for Nedar, the war pilot would undoubtedly go down in flames as well, but in action, not in solitude waiting for inevitable disease and death. Hat just knew that would be the way as well.

Although he had not heard from Palaton in years, Nedar came back to Blue Ridge from time to time. He had, like Palaton, rooms in the graduate quarters. His quarters were kept locked and unoccupied until the arrogant Choya returned to throw them open. When he possessed the rooms (Nedar never occupied a space, he *possessed* the place with all the vibrancy that was possible), the cadets would come to see him, a Choya of incomparable ability, a legend in his own time as Palaton had also become. To Hat's pleasure and surprise, his old classmate welcomed the cadets. He regaled them with tales of Chaos and listened patiently to their questions.

The only thing he would not discuss with them was *bahdur*. It was considered a breach of etiquette anyway and few ever tried, though it was always on their minds, like sex. How did it feel when it burned bright and how did it feel when one began to lose it, to grasp for it, to have it fail you. . . . How does it feel?

Those questions Nedar would brush aside with a steely, dark glance and simply leave hanging in the air. Usually the cadet who asked would fall prey to embarrassment and leave, not to return that evening or perhaps during the entire term of Nedar's stay. Even the brash knew when they had overstepped Nedar's bounds.

That look of rancor had never been turned toward Hat nor did he ever fear that it would. He and Nedar were friends, though how such a thing had been fated, he could never be sure. He had come to Blue Ridge only because he had the talent to do so and because the resulting contracts would be invaluable to his family. Nedar had come because the Salt Towers refused him and, despite his arrogance, he had an inborn need to pilot that was as necessary to him as breathing. Hat had seen that in him right away.

He'd also been friends with Palaton, but Palaton had many acquaintances. He was not given to the dark moods which singled Nedar out, but he felt those of the other Choya keenly.

As Hat rambled through the empty corridors, he thought of those early days before the friendship had begun. The fear of flying clenched a bit in his stomach. He could fly, but he did not want to. No. Nursing the cadets here, sharing in their joy and fears, that made him much happier. Flying used to tear the very insides from him and he could tell no one of it.

Then that dark day when one of the cadets had died early, far earlier in training than any cadet had ever died at Blue Ridge, brought his fears colliding with the future. It had been a horrible, horrible accident. Death was always waiting in the shadows at any of the pilot schools—they eventually flew blind, relying on nothing more than the wings of their thrust glider and their *bahdur,* the beginning of the final tests—for those who would become *tezars*. Months of mathematics and physics would follow once wings had been won to make a pilot of universes, but here at Blue Ridge, one first had to learn to fly the uncertain winds of Cho. When the sensory deprivation began, there was always a death or two. That had been expected.

This had not. And in a way Hat had never learned, Nedar had somehow been a part of it. No one knew of it but Hat and Moameb, the elder *tezar* who then ran Blue

Ridge with the aid of his staff. Hat had been sent as a
runner to fetch Nedar to tell him that he had been found
faultless. No one else would ever know Nedar had even
been under a cloud of suspicion.

So Hat had come upon Nedar in his rooms, silent, brood-
ing, drinking, and the stink of fear shrouded him. He sat
in his swivel study chair, his booted feet propped up, a glass
in his hand. That a Choya such as Nedar could be afraid
had struck Hat speechless and he'd just stood on the threshold of the other's rooms.

Nedar had eventually looked at him. "What have you
come to tell me?" he'd demanded.

But in his voices, Hat heard that which could be pitied.
Nedar *feared*.

"If I fail here," Hat said, "I can never go home. I fear
that every day."

Nedar dropped his feet to the floor. He let a pause hang
in the air before answering, "What has that to do with me?"

And then Hat had given him the news that the investigation had been concluded and he had been found blameless.

From that day forward, something else, unspoken, had
passed between them. It remained to this day and so, when
a voice, low and guttural, issued out of the shadows, Hat
turned to it unafraid. He had been more than half-
expecting it.

"Nedar! You've come home."

Hat banked the fire in his study. He watched the flames'
reflection upon the etched planes in his friend's face. Nedar
had always been handsome. Now his face was sharp-edged,
almost painful to look at, his eyes smoldering and sunken
within it. The *tezar* nursed the drink in his hand, barely
sipping at the amber liquid now and then as if only to
moisten his voices.

The tale he'd been told astounded him: renegades, a hidden colony, the luring of *tezars* to their Householdings in
order to maintain a legacy of starflight. Destruction and
torture . . . Hat sat back in wonder.

"No one has said anything of this," he voiced. "We had
never heard of Arizar before the Abdreliks accused us before the Compact. And there has never been any mention
of colonization."

"And there won't be, publicly. They were scoured from Arizar, Hat, burned to ashes too difficult to sift. There was no evidence left for the Compact. I wish I could say I was sorry, but the renegades were merciless in their own purposes. They intended me to die," finished Nedar. "My body was given over to be disposed of. But I was not dead! My *bahdur* stayed kindled within me, an ember that I drew on, until I gained enough strength to fight back and free myself."

The gauntness, the hunger in the eyes, now Hat understood them. "Nedar, I—"

"No. Listen to me. If I stay, I'll bring that danger to you. Palaton has returned as well . . . and I don't yet know, if he is an enemy or if they used him as badly as they used me. But I do know this—" And Nedar's intensity burned him more hotly than the hearthfire they sat near. "He was there. He was alive when I was taken for dead. I cannot trust him until I know the truth."

"Nor I," blurted Hat without thinking. He bit his lip as silence followed. "How did you land? We were shielded against—" he stopped. Against Palaton.

Nedar smiled. The warmth did not reach his eyes. "I came down in his wake as soon as the ports opened. Not far from here, actually. I knew I wanted to come home to Blue Ridge. You know it's the only true home I have."

"And you may stay as long as you wish. You know that, Brethren."

"As long as it doesn't threaten you or the cadets. But no one, Hat, can know I'm here. Not even my House or Householding. I will not unwittingly bring danger on any of you."

Hat had been on the edge of his chair. He sat back a little now. "You can't think that Palaton was part of it."

"I don't know what I think of our friend." Nedar took a shallow drink. "A hero can be duped as easily as a fool, if he's blind enough. Panshinea has strings on him, or thinks he does, if our emperor has made him heir. We both know our emperor has no intention of relinquishing the throne as long as he's alive. But if I know Palaton, he thinks he can break those strings, or at least resist the dance when the emperor begins to tug on them. Who knows what lured him to Arizar."

"I understand."

"Do you?" Nedar murmured. "This will be difficult for you, Hat, if my enemies come tracing me.

"Blue Ridge takes care of its *tezars.* To protect and serve, even our own. It's about time." Hat stood. "You can stay here until after hours. I'll have dinner sent in."

Nedar saluted him with his nearly full glass. "Thank you." He leaned back in his chair and half-closed his eyes, watching the fire.

Hat shut the door gently so as not to disturb him.

They did not want to touch him. He saw that in their faces, even through the protective face masks, as they reached for him and took him away from Rindy. Rand let out a word of protest, but the elder Choya looked sternly at him as if to say that he carried the honor of humankind and Palaton with him, and Rand bit his lip as he read the other's expression. Within the black box, he was led to a gridded room. They stripped him, even of the braces and bandages, laid him down on a grille and, after examining his eyes, gave him a pair of ocher-colored lenses to wear. Then they passed him through a series of light waves, standing behind a barrier as though he might carry the deadliest of plagues.

Rand lay on the grille and tried to think of other things. Despite the light which battered him and hurt his eyes even through the protective glasses, the room was chill and he shivered as he suffered the sterilizing. They spoke about him as if he couldn't be listening, but they spoke Trade instead of Choyan and he could not help but hear.

"What do we have on these things?"

"There's a lot from the Quinonans' data base. They did a fair amount of field lab work before they were stopped by the Compact for tampering. Want me to bring it up?"

"Do that. Let me take a look at him."

There was a pause, during which the female technician, at least he thought it was a female, he couldn't tell behind the suits, snickered, saying, "Well, we know he's mammalian and has external sexual genitalia—which, I would say, is fairly cold sensitive."

He felt his body heat with a flush that must run from head to toe. There were a few more scraps of sentences as they worked on their data base information. He overheard, "He can't be too contaminated. This is Bay station bandaging. They would have done some decon work."

"Save that. Get it over to sterilization and we'll rewrap when we're done. No sense in wasting new material on him."

No, there was no sense wasting anything on him at all. Rand turned his head as a light bar passed over him, blasting him with its brilliance. He narrowed his eyes to a slit. He was being watched from behind a barrier.

They saw him move.

"Lie still!" Aside, "We'll have to run that scan again. I want him strapped down if necessary."

Rand licked lips gone suddenly dry. He forced himself to stay in his current position, even though the leg they had unbraced ached horribly and he could feel a twitch in his thigh muscle.

It must have shown on the scan, for one of the Choyan asked sharply, "What's that?"

"Muscle spasm, in all probability. Yes. That's one of the limbs we took braces from."

"Note that, for rehabilitation. It doesn't seem to cause him much pain."

Rand thought of asking the Choya if he wished to trade places. The light bar basted him again and he managed to stay still as it passed. There was a long moment and then the head technician said, "That's done. We'll need a physical exam. Any volunteers?"

The female spoke with a shudder in her voices. "Not me."

The second tech said, "Cavity searches, orifice registration, the full works?"

"We need it on record."

A sigh. Then, "I might as well as long as I'm suited up."

Rand watched uncertainly as one of the tall, suited figures separated itself from the other two behind the barrier and strode toward him. The Choya pulled a recessed drawer from under the gridded table and Rand heard a rattle of instruments.

He bolted upright. Pain lightninged up his leg and into his hip and he spasmed in agony. The Choya's gloved hand shot out and pinned him in place. "If you insist on partaking of our hospitality," the masked face told him, eyes hard as gems, "you will have to suffer some of the disadvantages as well. We won't have plague or pestilence brought in, deliberately or accidentally."

Rand gasped as he fought to bring both his pain and fear under control. "Just what . . . do you think I am?"

"As to that, I'm not sure. I'll have a better idea when I've read the Quinonans' field report. You're a Class Zed. That's borderline enough for me." The suited Choya laid him back down and leaned over. "It's pleasanter if you relax."

They were no gentler with him when the sterilized bandages and braces were brought back in. The Choya who'd been working on him stepped back with a grimace, that could be easily read behind the faceplate. "I've done enough dirty duty. Trista, you get in here and rebandage him."

Rand lay sore and bruised, draped weakly across the gridded table. The Choya had treated him no better than a piece of meat. The bandaging was a relief only in that the operation seemed to be a preliminary to letting him dress and get out of there.

The female technician worked brutally efficiently on him, retractioning leg, arm, and shoulder and wrapping him as quickly as she could. The first had returned to the work desk behind the barrier. Her supervisor called to her, "Hair, skin, and urine samples. All other bodily fluids."

Trista made a noise between her teeth. Rand lifted his head. She clubbed it back down with the palm of her gloved hand to his forehead. "Stay down," she ordered briskly.

He felt the scrape of a scalpel across his inner thigh, bringing the skin up raw and tender. "I can give you," he began, but the Choya'i interrupted briskly, "I'll take what I need," and she proceeded to do so with a catheter.

He gritted his teeth on both the anger and the hurt rising in him. When she'd finished, she leaned over. Her eyes were a strange yellow. "I'll have your clothes brought in."

"How about a little vivisection?" he spat out.

Her eyes shadowed darker. "Don't worry. We'd do it if it was called for. I haven't taken an alien apart and put it back together in a long time." Her head snapped out of his line of vision as she stepped back. "Wait here."

Rand hadn't the ability to leave, much as he wished to. He lay still, listening to the other techs argue about the reliability of Quinonan reports.

"This can't be right."

"What can't?"

"Even taking that he's got single pan brain capacity, look at this."

There was a Choyan laugh, dry and short. "According to this info, Kirlon stonework has more esper readings than humankind. I can't believe it."

"Nothing more sophisticated than occasional resonance sensitivity? Are you sure?"

"This is Compact data, confirming the Quinonans'."

"No wonder the Abdreliks are drooling. These guys fail in the Compact and GNask is looking at a big stew pot for dinner."

Rand's stomach clenched. They thought of him as no more intelligent than fodder. What use did Palaton have for him, then? What did the *tezar* see in him that these other Choyan did not? And where was Rindy in all of this?

After long moments, the female tech entered the room, his clothing draped over a metal extension.

She dropped his clothes on the end of the exam table, saying, "Dress yourself."

She did not ask if he needed help, nor did he ask for any. He had to lean upon the table heavily to stay upright, but he finished the task he began.

Rindy appeared beside the barrier. "Doctors, are you quite finished?"

The tallest of the suited technicians turned to the Prelate, "I'd like to run some general IQ tests and a few esper exams."

Rindy looked at him consideringly. Then he shook his head. "We have full Compact data available on that score. It would be useless and time-consuming. I think I must insist you remand him back into my custody if you're quite finished with the decon sweep."

The tall Choya with the gem-hard eyes said dryly, "If we'd been any more thorough, he'd be dead," and turned away.

Rand did not doubt him. He sagged onto the arm Rindy held out for him. The elder Choya looked down at him.

"There are some trials in life," Rindalan stated, "which are unavoidable."

Rand could not answer him. He concentrated only on putting one foot in front of the other. From behind his shielded *bahdur,* he could feel them as they watched him leave. Hatred and contempt. He wondered what humankind had done to earn it, or if the Choyan thought of all aliens in the same light.

Chapter 7

"Who on the Blasted Plains authorized him to be treated like that?"

Palaton's angered tones brought Rand's sagging eyes open wide for a moment as a pair of imperial guards lowered him to the couch of the quarters selected for him. Rindy had already bowed a Choyan courtesy and left them in the corridor. Only Jorana stood to take the brunt of Palaton's outrage.

She stood with purpose, gray-blue eyes watching as the guards saluted her and left. As they passed beyond her range of vision, she turned smartly to Palaton and said calmly, "I did."

"You did? *You did!* And what did you succeed in proving? This is my ward. I gave my word to protect him—"

"From your own people, as well?" interrupted Jorana mildly. She pushed a clump of bronze hair from her brow which had escaped from its hair clip.

Palaton's ire transmuted into a few Choyan phrases which Rand had never heard, did not understand, and had no doubt it would be useful to know someday. The Choya'i's face pinked under the onslaught, but she did not step back. She waited until Palaton finished, then said, "I could get no one to guard him willingly elsewise. You bring him out of Chaos into turmoil—would you have him be a target and unprotected simply because our guards are xenophobic and I could not control or convince them otherwise? This way, at least, I have a number of Choyan I can count on."

Palaton took a deep breath. "*I* will guard him."

Jorana looked from Palaton to Rand, who lay awkwardly where he'd been placed, his braced leg sticking out in front of him, his arm and shoulder almost at right angles to his rib cage. "And you've done an admirable job of it, so far."

His jawline worked as though he chewed on words but could not quite spit them out. Jorana waited with a half-smile curving her lips, then stepped back as though she deemed the duel finished. "We have business to discuss, heir to the throne."

Palaton crossed the room and arranged Rand more comfortably, then drew a light quilt over him. "Will you be all right?"

Rand nodded wearily. He murmured, "They hate me."

"No. They fear you."

"And there's a difference, isn't there?"

"Among civilized people, yes." Palaton adjusted a pillow under his head. "Or so we hope."

"I'm not going anywhere," the boy said. "For a while." Rand put his head back on the crown-rest pillow and closed his eyes.

Palaton took the signal to leave and joined Jorana. Without a word, she led him from the palace wing and back downstairs.

Palaton followed silently to the room he'd come to know as Panshinea's library, with the hidden entrance from the outside atrium, and a fireplace that usually blazed brightly in the emperor's presence, rain or shine, but now was empty. Jorana's emotion filled the room instead. He did not have to have his *bahdur* to feel it himself.

"You shouldn't have brought him here," Jorana said, and her voices vibrated on both the levels of anger and concern. "Nor called on factions you can neither control nor predict the actions of. Do you have any idea what you've done?"

"I couldn't not have brought him here," replied Palaton evenly, though he did not look at her when he said it. "He's a pawn, without the defenses to protect himself. He has answers to questions we have yet to ask and because he holds those answers, he is a danger both to himself and to us."

"To *you*," Jorana corrected.

His eyes came up then, to her face, and he saw the storm cloud of emotions running across it. He did not have to empathize to be rocked by the force of her expression. "To Cho," he repeated firmly.

She took a step closer. "You jeopardize all we've worked for. I kept you alive for this."

"To be Panshinea's puppet?"

"No! To be his *heir*. And you are. It was his vanity to think he had all the time in the world to consolidate his throne and his line . . . a vanity that exemplifies why the House of Star suffers."

Palaton blinked. He said blandly, "Even for you, you speak frankly here. I would not put it past Panshinea to have his own palace thoroughly recorded."

Jorana half-spun away from him. "I know where I trespass—unlike you."

Indeed, she knew exactly what she did within the palace grounds. If she felt free to talk within this room, then so could he. There was meager solace to be found in this conversation. "So you think I trespass?"

"You presume."

"Jorana, I didn't have any choice."

"And what," she leveled at him, "will you do with him?"

"Keep him safe. Hope he's happy. Give him the future that was stripped away from him."

"There is no future here for him. Consider what you've done, Palaton, very carefully. We are still at a stage where it can be undone."

He did not answer her charge or take the hope she offered him.

"Make no mistake about what Panshinea has offered you . . . he's not going to give you the throne. You're his heir only so long as he needs you. But he does need you."

Palaton watched her. He answered, "And make no mistake about why I presented myself as his heir . . . Cho needed the stability. I'm not opportunist. I think you know that of me."

"I know that you're a *tezar* first and a politician last. Calling on the God-blind. . . . For all his faults, our emperor is a brilliant politician. He juggles as well as anyone I know. Even he wouldn't have dared as much. Malahki has taken up residency on the steps of Charolon to await audience." Jorana sucked in her breath. "Panshinea won't leave you even the crumbs of yourself."

And what would she think of him if she knew he did not even have the *bahdur* to defend himself? He wondered how she could look at him now and not see the weakness of his aura. Did she see only what she expected to see? He wanted to tell her what had happened to him on Arizar, how he'd been offered hope and help, and now was stripped of his very essence, of all that made him a Choya and a *tezar* and held only a thin thread that he might reclaim it. Would she then accept the boy and help him? Softly, he asked, "And what would you leave of me?"

"It's not what I would leave of you . . . it's all that I would give you. I may be newly risen, I may be out of the ranks of the Godless, but my *bahdur* shines as brightly as any of the Housed. We could build what Panshinea cannot."

He felt her embarrassment and shame, begging for a liaison he had already refused her years ago. He ached to tell her of his emptiness, to see if she could fill him, and knew he didn't have the right. He shook his head. "I'm in no position to offer anyone a future. The resolution of the humankind's future and Cho's trust are my priorities now. Are you willing to wait, knowing that even then I may not offer you what you wish? I can't ask you to tangle your fortunes with mine."

As gentle as it was, it was still a refusal. Jorana sat then, a movement that translated as near collapse. "Rindy came back with you. Did he approve?"

"No. He put one of his tablets under his tongue and gave me a sour look while I tried to explain it to him."

She put her chin up. "You speak with humor, but you can't mean it."

He spread his hands. "I won't change my mind. I *can't* change my mind. If there is humor, it's that of acceptance. The boy is from a Class Zed planet. To let him go now, with the little he knows and understands, will bring a tampering charge against Cho. Not against me. Against *Cho*. There are those in the Compact who would love to prove such a case."

"We're strong enough to do without the Compact."

She left him speechless for a second as his own jaw dropped. Jorana did not blink as they stared at one another. Then Palaton caught himself. "Perhaps," he agreed. "But I don't think the Compact is strong enough to do without us."

"And must we Choyan carry the burden of the ills of all races?"

"If necessary." He spread his hands flat upon the empty desktop between them. "The people sealed within Sorrow faced an enemy we know nothing about—and who may return. As good as we are at making war among ourselves, there are none of us who could manage such a death for an entire race of people. Would you have any of us, Ronins, Abdreliks, Ivrians, Gormans, any of the others, face that enemy alone?"

The defiance bled from Jorana's finely planed face, dissolving into sadness. "You're noble."

"No. I just recognize the burden inherent."

"I disagree with you." Jorana thrust herself out of the chair, standing over him once more. "We've been staring into the frozen waters of Sorrow for generations. Most of us don't even see the faces staring back. But you do. No matter what I say, you'll do what you think you have to do, even if it destroys you."

"I'd like to think it won't go that far. But, yes. I'll do what I have to do."

"It's too bad Panshinea doesn't have this room recorded." Her glance flitted around the study. She strode to the exit. "He could learn from you."

"Jorana."

She paused at the doorway. "What?"

"Do I have your support in this?"

She shook her head, mane cascading to her shoulders. "No. Not for the boy. But I'll do whatever I can for you. You're my burden, I guess."

She left quickly, the door shutting soundly at her heels. Palaton waited a long moment, then realized he had been holding his breath, and let it go.

He sat down at Panshinea's desk. It had been cleaned of any of the emperor's business, and a fine layer of dust overlaid it. He whisked the dust away with the side of his hand as if he could dismiss his own fears that quickly.

Everything that Jorana had said had merit. He could deny none of it. He wondered what she might have said had she known the entire truth. How much of her foresight stemmed from power, and how much from shrewdness? It scarcely mattered if it helped him navigate the chaos of Panshinea's reign. He sat poised on the brink of calling her back and confessing. There was something inside of him that would not let him do it.

The door opened hesitantly. Gathon, the only Sky to hold power under Panshinea, looked in.

"Ah," he said, "here you are, Palaton. My greetings are tardy."

Gathon was of that breed of Choya who aged well. He held enough flesh to keep his facial features from growing gaunt, but he did not grow huge the way an Earthan might. Yellow-white streaked his Sky black hair, more white than Palaton remembered, but after all, they had not seen one another in years upon years. The dark, pebble brown eyes still watched with a penetrating gaze, and the minister held himself well. He did not yet feel the weight of his horn crown upon a feeble neck. Weight he might feel from his many responsibilities as Minister of Resource, but he looked as if he had held up well. He put a hand up as if to ward off some of Palaton's examination. "We need to talk, if you're not too tired from the journey."

Palaton shoved his chair back a little from the desk. "All right."

Gathon came in and sat down opposite him. He folded his hands in his lap, at ease, almost with the serenity of a Prelate. Perhaps he had found a measure of religious peace in dealing with the land's well-being, Palaton thought. "What can I do for you?"

Palaton tilted his head. "Serve me as well as you've served Cho and Panshinea."

The minister smiled tightly. Like Palaton, he did not wear facial jewelry under the translucent panes of his facial skin. Age etched his expression sharply for a fleeting moment.

"I do not necessarily serve both Cho and Panshinea in the same breath," Gathon said. "Or in the same task. Much as you serve as a *tezar* and as you may serve as an heir. I am not for you, Palaton, but neither am I against you. I will help inasmuch as I can. That having been said, I would like to give you my first recommendation."

Palaton held his tongue. Gathon waited a polite interval before continuing, "It's in both our best interests to get Malahki out of Charolon."

Palaton remembered only too well the luminary of Danbe and the incident which had forced Panshinea to drive Palaton away from Cho for so many years. He was somewhat surprised that the God-blind reactionary was still alive. This could be a difficult consequence of his actions. The revolt and Relocation of Danbe had been a bloody one. Malahki would not be an easy Choya to dismiss. "And do you think Malahki will listen to me?"

"You summoned him. I expect you will have some influence on whether he returns to his county or stays and goes underground yet again."

Palaton took a deep breath. It was time to pay the price of his support. "Done. First thing tomorrow morning. Soon enough?"

Gathon looked at him from deep, dark pools of brown. "It shall have to be."

"Anything else?"

The Minister of Resource looked at his folded hands. "What of the humankind?"

"What of him?"

"Does he have . . . full run of the palace?"

"He's not an animal, Gathon."

The Choya looked up. "Of course not. But neither is an alien a usual guest within these or any walls on Cho. What can I expect?"

"Expect nothing. He's here under my protection for a short time."

"Tampering charges from the Compact cannot be taken lightly."

"One guest does not constitute tampering with an entire people!"

Gathon stood up slowly, gathering himself. "I would hope not. He'll need protection. I'll arrange it with Jorana's staff." He paused. "You are not needed here, Palaton. Your emperor left a well-oiled machinery of rule in place."

"I gathered that. I don't seek to usurp that rule."

"Then, knowing that, and knowing that you are not asking what Cho can do for you, you might ask yourself what you intend to do for Cho."

"What can I do?" Palaton spread his hands.

"Panshinea chose to stay on Sorrow. He chose to leave you behind, here. What are you that he is not? You are that rare Choya who has been able to step beyond the Houses and the God-blind. You are a *tezar*. We have not had a *tezar* as an heir in several centuries. Know yourself,

and perhaps you will understand the needs of Cho as well."
He bowed and left, back ramrod stiff as he strode through
the doorway of his emperor's library.

Palaton watched him go. It was no accident Gathon had
accosted him in the only sanctuary in the palace where
Panshinea had no "ears."

Unsettled, he sat very still for a few moments, his head
bowed in deep thought. He had to believe, he told himself,
that it was also no accident he had been made heir to the
throne of Cho. Whether by Panshinea's design, or his own,
or by the God-in-all, he was meant to be where he was
now. He *had* to believe that. And, believing, he must then
explore the future of his involvement. Palaton clenched a
fist. Did Gathon challenge him—or did Gathon sentence
him to no future at all?

Chapter 8

Bevan struggled to open his eyes. It would do little good to use them, he knew. The drugs that the College had given him to prepare him for becoming a Brethren lay over his sight like a dark storm cloud. The cloud he had become used to, steeled himself for it—it was the unexpected rainbows which accompanied it which he could not bear to see.

He passed his hand over them. Lying on his back, there was little to see beyond the ceiling of the hut the Zarites called home. But he could hear the whispering voices of his hosts, moving about him in shadows, living as quietly and surreptitiously as they could with a stranger in their midst. He lifted his head and the prism dance of colors began. Every organic object in the room haloed with an aura of light. He squinted his eyes against the brightness. The Zarites paraded before him in a profusion of auras. Bevan closed one eye to dim his vision. Nothing could he see clearly or sharply . . . but everything pulsated with color.

He tried concentrating on the nearest blob of serene blue. From out of its haze and vague outline, the Zarite Thena, who'd been nursing him, emerged. She leaned over him and helped him sit upright.

In her soft drawl of Trade, she asked, "How are you feeling?"

"Better." He gulped down a wave of disorientation as her face dissolved into brilliant dots of color and then coalesced into facial features again. He blinked and for the barest whisper of time, he saw normalcy about him. Then the storm clouds boiled up again, and the balls of prism color began to bounce about again. He felt Thena push a clay mug into his hand. He knew thirst and drank greedily whatever drink it was she gave him. He would kill for *bren*,

he thought, or coffee. Yes, coffee like that which could
be bought from the street vendors and corner cafés of
Sao Paulo, once his home, coffee rich and dark and
steaming. . . .

The residue of liquid in the mug began to spit and boil
and hissed into steam. He dropped the mug with a shout as
it grew red hot in his hand and then exploded into shards.

Thena immediately grabbed up his hand and wrapped it
with a cooling cloth. She made a tsking sound through her
rodentlike teeth.

"What happened?"

His Zarite nurse lapsed into crooning sounds as she
soothed the compress about his hand. He looked to the dirt
flooring and saw the clay shards around his feet. Color
oozed from them as if it were blood, crimson, alive, ebb-
ing life.

"I did that."

"I think so, yes," Thena said. "Even in your sleep,
things . . . shatter. Break. Catch fire."

"It's bleeding. . . ."

The Zarite's translucent round ears pricked forward in
puzzlement. "It was just a mug. How could it bleed?"

"Can't you see it?"

Thena said patiently, "See what?" She patted his hand.

How could she not see it? Bevan blinked away watering tears and stared at the broken object. The red haze
oozed away, soaking into the dirt floor, as Thena grabbed
a whisk and dustpan and efficiently cleaned up the remains. He put his free hand back to the nestlike bed to
steady himself.

His uniform from the College hung upon his body. He'd
always been slender, now it seemed to him he must be
nothing more than skin and bones. He could hear his
breath rattle through his lungs, his blood *swishing* its ways
through the canals of his body, the beat and tempo of his
heart, and even the air drumming upon his ears. It was as
if life had suddenly become too much to bear, too loud,
too harsh, too strident in its demands upon him.

He narrowed his eyes to focus on Thena, trying to drive
away the aura obscuring her Zarite features as she came
back to him. He saw the worry, a cloud of its own, pressed
upon her expression.

"You are sick," the nursemaid said, "with a poison we cannot drive out of you."

The poison of Nedar's soul or whatever the Choya had driven into him was what rattled through him. He doubted if the Zarites had a cure for that. "I'm getting better," Bevan told her and heard his deep and raspy voice as if it belonged to a stranger.

She shook her head. "The disturbances are getting worse. And . . . there are strangers come to Arizar, searching."

"For me?" All thought him dead. Even Rand, in all probability.

"For whatever they can find. The Choyan came, and left, after looking at the ashes of their Brethren. They tell us nothing. . . . They are masters. They owe us nothing. They came and lived among us and we used them as much as they used us. Now . . ." her glance slid away, then came back to meet his. "Some of us are glad they are gone and some of us are afraid. Will we remember wisely what they have taught us? We don't know. But we do not want them back!" She led him to the table and chair. A Zarite kit scooted from under the table in an explosion of peach and white fur and cloth. A door banged in its wake as Thena sat him down.

"What about the others? What others? Spaceships, probes . . . ?"

Her ears moved. "Danger, I'm told. Much danger comes with the others."

He could see her fear billowing in the aura about her as well as hear it in her voice. He did not doubt it for a second, though his ability to see it surprised him. "What are you going to do?"

"We're not sure. We may have to move you again."

This was the third Zarite household he'd been in. The first he scarcely remembered. The second was little more than a blur.

"Tell me about the others." Concentrating on Thena seemed to help clear the cobwebs. It would be important to know who was coming after him.

Her lips flattened about her teeth. "They come in darkness. The ships are brought down on the outlying lands. And they kill those whom they question."

No probes or drones, then. Someone was using FTL to

access the planet. *Tezars* on contract were forced to remain
neutral over their objectives, until the contracts had expired
or were breached. The others could be Abdreliks. Or
maybe Ronin. Without the Choyan here to protect the Zarites, they would become fair prey. Or . . . perhaps it was
his presence which drew the seekers. Perhaps if he went
off-world . . . the Compact would sooner or later step in,
as well. Arizar might become like Earth, classified Zed, on
probation, worthy of joining the Compact of those who flew
the stars.

Except these worthy people did not fly the stars. The
technology they had, they had cunningly stolen and adapted
from those Choyan who'd mastered the planet. Difficult, if
not impossible, to tell how they ranked in developmental
technology. The Compact might adopt a neutral stance, not
protective and refusing interference. Who, then, would protect them?

"I can't stay here."

"You're not a master. Where would you go?"

"Where I came from." Bevan stared at a bowl of food
as Thena pushed it in front of him, followed by a new mug
of cooling drink. The Zarite *tsked* at him again. He began
to eat mechanically, the taste of the food overwhelmed by
the sea of colors it swam in, some of them downright unap-
petizing looking. After as many bites as he could stomach,
he said, "When do you want to move me?"

"Tonight. Soon it will be dark."

He nodded. Thena hesitated, then put a hand gently on
his head. It felt like a benediction. "I will miss you," she
said. "You were as helpless as one of my kits when they
brought you. I think you will conquer this poison."

He wished he had the confidence she exuded. She stood
over him until he cleaned the bowl. Light had gone from
bright to waning before he stood and she helped him to
the outside latrines. Once outside, the sharp outline of
mountains to the east of the small village of Zarites cut off
the setting sun abruptly, and darkness fell like a scythe
across the area.

As he fumbled to zip zippers and buckle buckles, Thena
made a hissing sound through tight lips. Her back to him
out of his sense of modesty, she was looking away, through
the gray and black shadows of outlying huts.

He sensed the tension in the sound. "What is it?"

"I . . . do not know." Zarites were not nocturnal, but her night sight had to be better than his, which was as haunted as his day sight.

He left the latrines and joined her. He could sense not only her worry, but a sharp inquisitiveness coming their way, a curiosity clawed and dangerous, crawling steadily after him. He felt the search prickle his skin.

"Get inside with the kits," he said.

Thena hesitated. "And you—"

"It may be the others come to move me. Don't worry."

Another sharp intake of breath. Then his nursemaid made up her mind and left him, to protect her own.

Bevan stood alone. He did not believe it was a Zarite searching for him through the early night. He remained motionless for another moment and felt the menace waft over him and slide away uncertainly, then touch him fleetingly again. He lifted his empty hands and looked at them in the dimness, deciding what he could do when the enemy came to meet him. How could he protect himself when it was all he could do to stand? All he could reliably do would be to keep moving and provide less of a target. He had to lead the hunter away from those who had helped him. He lurched away from Thena's hut.

He heard a Zarite shout and then a squeal. Red flares burst skyward from the far side of the huts. Bevan stumbled and went to one knee in the damp grass. His breath came short and quick. Winded, so soon. Only a few steps and he was done for. Where and how had he hoped to run?

Something passed him in the night, a shrub away. Leaves whispered sibilantly against its going. He smelled a musky scent, not unpleasant, but . . . strange. The difference tingled through him, pinging off alarms in every sense he had of danger. Then, nothing. The hunter had passed him by.

And then the sound stopped. Whatever it was now stood beyond him, but not so far away that a good lunge would miss him. Bevan fought to catch his breath. His panting must be heard . . . surely. The drumming of his heart. The telltale growl of his stomach as it digested food it had not wanted in the first place.

As he crouched, waiting, still and quiet, his sight adjusted until the twilight was only a gray mass and he could see almost as well as in the daylight, though the insistent colors had gone. And if he could see. . . .

Bevan moved imperceptibly in the gloom. His ankle protested the change of weight as he moved from one crouch to another. Grass dampened the cloth covering his knee. He looked up and saw in silhouette the creature stalking him.

Slender and willowy, with a mane of sharp, quill-like objects draped about its neck and shoulders.

Ronin, he thought. It could be none other. The Ronins carried a deadly poison in their quills. It was against Compact law for a Ronin to go off-planet without being de-quilled or at least detoxined.

Bevan stretched his lips in a humorless smile. Why was he positive that a single touch of one of those quills would be fatal? Why not? What use to send a Ronin after him without all the weapons available at its disposal. Laws that could be made could be broken. The creature moved like an assassin, coming after its target through darkness and deception. Its intentions had to be equally as deadly.

A click of teeth. The Ronin moved as if alerted by his very thoughts. The face in profile disappeared as it turned to seek him out. The quilled headdress rose in readiness.

"Come out," it said, in heavily accented Trade.

Oh, no. No, he wouldn't do that. Bevan stayed quiet and watched the creature pivot about, searching. It sensed him, but it did not know exactly where he was. Could it be that Bevan's night sight was better than the Ronin's? He might yet have some advantage.

Bevan went to his stomach and crawled a length away. The Ronin swung about, still looking in the wrong direction.

"A trade," it said. "The lives of those who looked after you for that of your own."

A pledge already broken before given, from what Thena had told Bevan. He dropped his face to the dewing grass and tried to think. The poison within him welled up as if fueled by fear and adrenaline and he battled with it, panic beginning to spew up inside, rattling at his bones and beating at his clenched teeth to be let out. He fought to breathe silently. Inside his skull, the blood pounded crimson. He could not die here!

Bevan leapt to his feet. The Ronin spun about sharply, quills shaking.

"I have you," it said in triumph.

Bevan's world burst loose. His vision went from grays and blacks to crimson. He went white-hot. He burned so hotly he did not know how his skin could contain or withstand the heat. He could feel himself hurtling at the creature, but his feet stayed rooted to the ground.

With a shrill scream, the Ronin assassin burst into flame. The conflagration raged, lighting up the night, engulfing the creature. It had no chance to run or drop . . . nothing. One split second and it was a raging torch.

The stench of burned flesh and plastics filled the air. Bevan toppled to his side at its scent and coughed, as smoke billowed up and around. The Ronin stayed upright, fated to burn like a candle.

The pyrotechnics brought the Zarites creeping out of their huts. Thena pillowed Bevan's head in her aproned lap as their voices shrilled through the air, counting their own dead.

The Ronin had been busy. Five had been struck throughout the village. Four were dead outright, one, lying in drool and foam, arched in convulsions, as it died a slower death, quill poisoned.

Thena smoothed his hair away from his forehead. Light flickered over them from the blaze of the enemy who burned like torch. "You cannot stay with us," she said. "We must find a way to get off off-planet."

Bevan hardly heard her. He watched the creature burn. He had done that. He knew it. But how?

Chapter 9

Morning came hot and clear over Charolon. Palaton rose with the sun, probing his memories, his mind seeking for that which he could no longer intuit. He settled for a steaming hot cup of *bren,* eggs, and fried bread, a pilot's breakfast. Gathon had left a stack of messages for him, out of courtesy. As Palaton looked through them, he saw they'd all been handled even before he arose.

The only matter which had not been handled was that of the God-blind, huddled by the thousands upon the streets and steps leading to the palace. Huddled and waiting for him to meet with Malahki, their chosen delegate.

With his throat still warm from the *bren,* Palaton went out the front door of the palace and descended the half-dozen steps which separated the emperor's domain from the former luminary of Danbe. Malahki had been sitting. Roused from a game of triblow by the jostling and sudden attention of the press communicators, he looked up and then got to his feet.

Palaton remembered a fiery orator from a God-blind river valley community who had stubbornly refused to relocate his people despite the recommendation of the Resource Board and the direct command of his emperor. The massive Choya who faced him now had changed little. The lustrous ebony mane had not grayed, though perhaps it had thinned. The elaborate horn crown, as forceful as Rindalan's, had still not been shaved to the more delicate form currently in fashion, and the brown eyes heavily flecked with gold still bored into him, seeking and lively.

They grasped hands. Calluses from the frequent playing of a hand *lindar* rubbed Palaton's fingers. He smiled at the memory of drinking dandelion colored wine with Malahki and listening to the luminary strum and pluck a lifetime of music from the *lindar*.

So long ago and yet like yesterday. He thanked the God-in-all for saving Malahki's life in what had become the bloodiest forcible Relocation in recent Choyan history. Letting Malahki's spark go out would have been a criminal shame.

A shadow flickered behind Malahki's intent stare as he dropped the handshake. "Do you remember," he said, "the throngs of children who came out to greet you when you brought the emperor to Danbe?"

Palaton nodded. "I could not forget."

Malahki turned and waved a hand over the crowds behind them and across the square and beyond view. "They are here again today," he stated simply and dropped his hand.

A roar from the commons. It shook and echoed among the pillars of the massive stairs leading to where they stood. The recording gear of the communicators immediately swung into position to catch the noise. Palaton found himself startled as well as moved. He could not say anything until the roar died down for, even as close as they stood, Malahki would not have heard it.

While they waited for silence, Palaton thought of Rindalan's and Jorana's warnings. He looked over the crowds. Thousands filled every standing space he could see. He feared for their safety and wondered at the devotion they held for Malahki, for it was obvious he had brought them here.

When the noise abated, he said to the Choya, "Will they let us speak, do you think?"

"We have been waiting for this opportunity." The gold in Malahki's eyes sparked a little.

"Then come with me. I know a garden behind these walls where we can sit and talk." He held a palace pass in his hand. Its buttons gave a warding against the various sonic barriers that fenced and secured the palace from intruders. He waited until Malahki took the pass and fastened it to the front of his light summer jacket, then Palaton turned and felt Malahki following.

The roar of the crowd and the shouts of the nearby communicators crashed like waves upon the shore as he had guards secure the front doors behind them. Inside the muted walls of the palace, ancient fortress that it was, little could be heard but a faint baffling. Malahki stood stiffly until Palaton dismissed the guards and said, "This way."

The intricacies of the imperial palace had been designed to be mazelike, but Palaton knew the garden well. He did not take Malahki there through the library where he had talked with Jorana and Gathon the day before, but through the farthest wing of the palace and then through a garden gate. There, the morning was still shadowed, dew lay heavily on the grass, and the beautiful eyes of sunrise were just opening their rainbow colors to the first rays dipping over the rooftop.

They sat on stone benches which had been used so often through the centuries that they had been grooved by the sitters. The benches faced opposite one another, close enough for quiet, intimate speech.

"You must send them home," Palaton said. "Charolon can't take care of them on the streets."

Malahki's mouth twisted. "She could, but she won't. We are the commons, the God-blind, the *Godless*. We had no voice, but you gave us one. For that, Palaton, we would all stay here and die of neglect."

Palaton shook his head. "I haven't given you anything. You took it by sheer numbers, made them pay heed by the very force of you. But if you stay, if the Congress begins to fear that force, there will be more blood in the streets than was shed beside the River Danbe. You know that, Malahki. You knew that when you answered my plea."

"We won't leave."

"You have to. I have no power. I am nothing more than a pawn to take up a place in Panshinea's absence."

Malahki sat back on the stone bench. He threw his arms up on the carved back. He dwarfed it with his bulk and his energy. "I wondered if you knew what you were doing when you asked for our help."

Palaton answered wryly, "I'll admit that I did not anticipate the response."

"Your honesty is refreshing." Malahki's eyes narrowed. "But that won't keep me from taking advantage of you. We're here. Acknowledge us, acknowledge our voice, or we will never leave, even if all that is left is our blood staining the gray rock of Charolon."

"You wouldn't do that."

"I wouldn't have to. The city guard would do it for me. What do I care if I die martyred if it makes you Housed, you high and mighty, *look* at us once in a while."

Palaton knew a moment of despair. Malahki did not care for his own life, he could see that written in the Choyan frame dominating the bench opposite him. The other had an agenda and Palaton realized he could not turn him aside.

"Delay," he said, "in whatever it is you plan to do. You must."

"I think we've been put off long enough. We've waited centuries upon centuries. We are more than slaves, yet less than you. How can you preach patience?"

"Because I haven't any choice! All of us are on the brink of change which could well be catastrophic. I'm here to try to stem the tide but a moment . . . just long enough for us to be prepared, to survive what is coming."

Malahki hesitated. Uncertainty dimmed the brightness of his eyes. "Disaster will make Brethren of us all."

"A disaster like that would leave us open to all the sharks of the Compact. You know that, you have to know it."

"I know that we brought home a *tezar* the Congress wanted to keep in exile, despite the appointment of the emperor. We did that . . . and it won't take them long to realize that as well. And if we can do that, we can help to put our next emperor on the throne."

His threat hung in the air between them. Palaton said, "I cannot hear treason like that."

"Hear, no. Feel . . . possibly. It's been a long time since a *tezar* was made emperor."

Palaton looked away. "Malahki, don't sign your death warrant with me as your witness. I won't take any responsibility for this."

"But you must! You're the one who awakened us to the possibilities. God knows, I've tried . . . but it was your plea which caught their conscience, which motivated them to do what they could, however small it seemed at the time. I have told them it takes many grains of sand to form a beach—but it was you who gathered them here. Why let them go? Why let them fall from your grasp?"

"Because I will not take up that responsibility! Malahki—"

and Palaton got to his feet, unable to contain himself. "I *cannot.*"

"A Housed Choya with a conscience." Malahki's stare raked him over. "I never thought to see it. I will preach patience. I will ask them to leave. But I will not force them, not will I give them empty promises. That will be your responsibility. Fulfill them or fail them, Palaton. You're on your own." He lumbered to his feet as well. He gave a crooked smile. "I'll follow the garden wall out."

He had to duck his head to pass below the arch. Sunlight flooded the garden abruptly after him, as though he, like the high walls of the palace, had been blocking it from entering.

Palaton stood frozen, trying to contain the emotions which had risen in him. What would he do if the God-blind did not disperse? How could he bear the brunt of another bloody massacre, an event which Malahki seemed to relish, if only for the martyrdom?

There was only one other to whom he could appeal . . . one who held sway over both those who could see God and those who could not though the church's position had always been to stay neutral. But Rindy would listen to him, that he knew. Palaton found himself standing with clenched hands. He forced them open at his sides, and looked about the garden. The eyes of sunrise, in all their myriad colors, looked back at him. For a moment, he wondered what Choyan hand had first planted the flowers, in what long ago century. That brief thought gave him comfort. They had survived. One only needed garden walls thick enough.

Beyond the gate, the white and gray stone of the ancient fortress looked like chalk cliffs in an old and forgotten canyon, hemming him in as he traversed it. Silent, too, was this portion of the palace, far from the intrigue and hubbub of the front steps. Malahki sensed the movement in the shadow on the far side of the wall before he saw it in the corner of his eye. Nonetheless, he came to a halt, weight balanced, ready for a fight if need be. He calmed at the sight of the graceful Jorana moving into full view.

"I wondered," said the luminary of Danbe, "if I would see you here."

"I did not dare disappoint you," answered Jorana. She

held her chin high, defiantly, and her full bronze hair was severely cuffed back from her face. She wore her uniform and cabinet badge and there was wariness in her voices as well as her eyes. "What do you want from me?"

"I," said Malahki teasingly. "I dare command a Housed and a cabinet member?"

She whirled on her heel to leave. He put a hand out. "Wait, Choya'i! Temper, temper."

Jorana's mouth tightened before she relaxed it to say, "I have duties."

"Yes. Yes, you do." Malahki's voices throbbed with double meaning. "Have you forgotten your roots so soon? Was it really so long ago that you were one of the commons, hoping to pass your test and become Housed?"

"Not long enough." Jorana stayed, tense, her body poised for flight like that of a bird balancing on a wiry branch.

"I would expect not. I have not come to criticize your progress, Jori, only to remind you that you have not long to attain your goals. Palaton's bloodlines are an excellent cross for you—and, more than ever, he can use the political strength your position can give him. You will suit him well. Have you tried to convince him of that?"

"He's been in exile."

The corner of Malahki's mouth twitched. "That," he answered, "I know."

Jorana's chin dropped a little. "He sees me. He knows I am here."

"There is no better time than now . . . Palaton is getting a baptism of fire while Panshinea stays out of range. You can help him consolidate his position. And you can console him through his difficulties as well." Malahki's voices dropped slightly. "I wish I had such consolations offered to me."

She trembled. Her eyes flashed as she looked up. "I did not crawl out of the commons so you could pimp for me!"

"And I have never suggested such a thing. Cho is faltering. She needs the powerful leadership of a Choya and a Choya'i. I would like to see that Choya'i be you." Malahki's gold-flecked eyes grew stern. "Your care was in my hands. I raised you well. Talent or not, you would still be one of us had I not done what I did for you."

Jorana said numbly, "I haven't forgotten. You took an orphan from the river and gave me life. You sent me to Niniot to be educated. You made sure I was sponsored for the Choosing. Don't you ever suggest to me that I've forgotten." Her eyes grew suddenly moist. "Oh, God, Malahki—I love him. If he asked me to die for him, I would."

"Ask him to give you a future."

Jorana looked away. She brushed a tear from her face. "I asked him once, a long time ago. He refused me. I cannot ask him again, not yet."

"Then, if he won't give you a future, you must take it from him. Take a child from him and leave. We'll shelter you. You have every potential. You might bear the child we're seeking, the Bringer of Change."

"No." She shook her head. "No, don't ask me to do that."

Malahki put out his hand and caught her wrist. His grip imprisoned her as she rocked back on her heels and pulled to break away. "There are drugs. . . ."

"No. I won't do that to him."

"Send word to me, and I'll have them smuggled to you."

"No!" Her eyes brimmed and tears dropped from them like a summer shower. She went limp in Malahki's grasp.

"Send to me when you're ready," the luminary repeated. "We'll be waiting." He let go of her abruptly and left, moving into the garden passage, his dark mane of hair the only streak of shadow in the lightening garden.

Jorana put her hand to her lips and tried to stop them from quaking. "God," she said under her wavery breath. "If only the river had taken me."

Chapter 10

rrRusk stood impatiently, waiting for GNask and his human shadow to appear in the audience room. The ambassador had acquiesced to speak with him, but the fleet commander knew that forcing the issue with his superior would cause him many difficulties later. GNask had ambitions and if rrRusk could plan his strategies correctly, he would ride the tail of that comet. He had no more ambition than that. Let GNask bear the brunt of government. Abdreliks preyed on each other as well as on lesser kinds of life. rrRusk knew well the tendencies of his own people. He found pride in it. They were all fit. They did not mate for sentimental reasons. They had few weaknesses.

What they did not have to continue conquering worlds was the *tezarian* drive, that black box of wonder devised by the Choyan. A simple feat of engineering and navigation kept the Abdreliks from their desire, and all the decades of trying to decipher the drive and its workings had failed. The box was simple enough. It augmented standard instrumentation panels whenever used. It was how the Choyan used it, rrRusk had become convinced, that made the difference.

He stomped a heavy foot in impatience. His skin itched. He'd given up his symbiont to go into space and the various antifungal creams were never as efficient at purging his skin as the constantly feeding symbiont had been. His flesh crawled now in this artificial atmosphere and chafed under the tight spots in his uniform, at the neck, armpits, waist, and knees. He fought the impulse to scratch maddeningly.

The far door opened and GNask's impressive yet graceful bulk entered. rrRusk came to immediate attention. The ambassador had not given up his *tursh*. His symbiont rode the side of GNask's fleshy neck, at rest, its small stalklike eyes tucked in. The *tursh* was as much an antenna to GNask's emotions as the ambassador's booming voice.

rrRusk relaxed just a fraction. He caught sight of the humankind wandering behind GNask, small, fragile, a delicate morsel, and felt his jowls begin to grow moist at the thought. She gave him a look as she put her chin up, her dark curls bouncing away from her pale face, and in that look was a kind of amusement. Did she sense his hunger? And if she did, why did that amuse instead of frighten her? Disconcerted, rrRusk almost did not catch the ambassador's first words.

". . . commendations on the job done at Arizar."

"I accept your remarks on behalf of my fleet," rrRusk got out. He paused. "My pilots refused to do more than they had contracted for. They agreed to disrupt an unauthorized colony. They balked at capture."

GNask showed his primary tusks. "That explains the small failure of your expedition. Can it be, do you think, worked out?"

"Perhaps. There was much anger among the pilots. Choyan do not condone colonization, particularly of their own. The *tezars* keep to themselves, but I sensed their rage." rrRusk watched the girl dart from one side to the other side behind GNask. She captured his eye quickly, with her preylike actions, and he had to force his attention back to his superior.

GNask noted his distraction. He turned his massive head and barked a single word at the girl. With a laugh, she drifted to a stop at his heel. The ambassador turned back to rrRusk.

"Convince your pilots that it is not only in our interests, but in their best interests, to continue to track down these renegades. Their actions have cast aspersions on the actions of all Choyan. If the Compact were to set forth tampering charges, it would weigh heavily on them. Those who still refuse to honor their general pilot contract can be switched to other needs. But there will be those, rrRusk, that you and I can sway. There are Households on Cho in financial disarray. *Tezars* are becoming rare in many families. They need money. I can meet those needs, once you ferret them out."

"Loyalty has its price."

GNask looked him full in the eyes. "Always," he said solemnly. "And its rewards." The humankind behind him peered out again, coal dark eyes smoldering in her pale face. But there was nothing furtive in her movements this time. The eyes were hard, assessing rrRusk until he felt a momentary discomfort. The emotion provoked a strange reaction within him, he who had rarely backed down in his own water. He changed his estimation of the small being. What a huntress this one must be among her own kind! He almost did not hear GNask's next words.

The ambassador stated, "Until tampering charges are proved or disproved against the Choyan, Panshinea has given up his position on the security council. That means, rrRusk, that you and I will have opportunities that we have never before been afforded."

rrRusk made a tiny move, signifying his pleasure at being held in the other's confidence. "It would be well to take advantage."

"We will." GNask's heavy brow furrowed deeper. "It would be a shame, would it not, if Cho's own internal situation disintegrated to the point where Compact security forces had to intervene?"

rrRusk again felt surprise. "I will be ready," he pledged, "to move once you feel such a situation has arisen."

"I thought you might. Choose your *tezars* accordingly. There will be no second chances." GNask turned his back to the commander and rrRusk knew he had been dismissed.

He left, with the feeling of the humankind's dark eyes boring into him, taking an alien measure he could not understand, and it bothered him. He was not used to meeting his match among inferior races. She had done nothing overtly to challenge him and yet . . . his opinion of her had been inexplicably changed, remolded.

He wondered if GNask knew what he had in the humankind, if she'd ever turned the full brunt of her eyes upon the Abdrelik who thought he had mastered her. He noted his thoughts for future advantage.

Rindalan wearily finished translating the code of the transmission from Sorrow. Panshinea's fury burned its way through every word, and the Prelate sat back, every knob in his spine aching with fatigue. The chair's headrest helped

bear the weight of his horn crown. He thought again of
having it shaved down—God-in-all knew it was the style
these days—but he'd been born with its munificent burden
and he was loath to change now, even though he felt too
fragile and brittle to bear its full weight.

Shaving his crown down would not lessen the burdens
Cho and Panshinea had placed upon him, and that, Rindy
thought with a sigh, was his real problem. He rubbed his
eyes. Coupled with the emperor's rage at Palaton's actions
among the Godless was a buried appeal to come back to
Sorrow, to aid Panshinea in his effort to consolidate the
Choyan hold upon the Compact.

"Those days are nearly done," Rindy murmured to himself. "Pan, old friend, you will have to admit it soon. The
tezars will have to share their ways. We need new blood.
We are thinning, dying out, and there are no Choyan coming forth to replace us. Well . . . perhaps to replace you.
Yes. There seems to be no shortage of potential emperors."

Rindy reached out and took hold of his mug of *bren*. It
had cooled considerably while he had decoded his message.
The elder sighed again. He detested cold *bren*, yet he was
loath to get up from his chair to find the warming plate
and reheat it.

"Cold comfort, then," Rindalan said and saluted the message board in front of him. His stylus rolled off the keypad
on the arm of the chair and came to a crooked stop on the
side table. The elder considered the stylus before returning
to his mug. He would have to summon Qativar in the morning. He could trust no other to aid Palaton in his place. As
much as he disliked travel, he would answer Panshinea's
plea and go to him.

Rindy thought of the days when he had ministered to
flocks of Choyan, young and old, and those memories were
fond ones. Now he had but one or two in his ministry . . .
but those, he told himself, affected the welfare and future
of all. Was he or was he not derelict in his duties?

He was old. Shortly God-in-all would judge him for his
decisions. That time would come soon enough.

In the meanwhile, he could only follow the course he'd
set for himself.

Rindy put his empty mug down, and his eyes closed in
sleep before his fingers uncurled from the cup.

*   *   *

Bevan dreamed of Sao Paulo, but he woke to the fresh, clean, and bitter cold air of Arizar, blinking in confusion at the difference between his dreams and waking reality. Sao Paulo, warm, humid, teeming with the smells of the poor who overwhelmed its streets. Arizar, almost virgin, cast in winter coldness, air not yet fouled by hundreds of millions burning fuel to cook, to produce technology, to incinerate garbage.

He blinked again, and the confusion of time and place left him. Gooseflesh rippled his café au lait arms. The blue sleeves of the College uniform had torn away, exposing him to the frigid air. Around him, he could hear the chatter of the Zarites, punctuated by soft squeaks and coos. They carried him litter-bound and he bounced from time to time as they skirted rocky terrain. He sat up carefully and peered over the litter's edge.

"I can walk," he announced in Trade.

The Zarites looked up at him, the bearers showing their teeth in their effort to keep the litter steady. Bevan felt like some potentate being born through the streets of Baghdad.

The Zarite who seemed to be in charge of his procession, a soot-colored male with pale yellow eyes, looked at him from his position to the fore. He wielded a walking stick with great effectiveness, but now the instrument paused in midair, as if in thought itself.

Then the male shook his head. "No," he said flatly. The walking stick descended and the brisk pace continued.

"Well, then, how about breakfast? The sun's up and we've been at this since mid-evening."

The walking stick hung in air again. It came down with a thump. "All right," said the Zarite. "Food and water."

Bevan held on as the litter descended to the ground and he could clamber out. Pouches and bundles were opened up and passed around by the time he could join the circle of nine who escorted him.

Thena's cooking was abundant and good. Though his companions mostly spoke Trade to accommodate him, he had gathered enough Zaritian to understand some of the side comments made. He garnered the impression that food was his bearers' wages and they thought themselves well paid by his nursemaid's efforts.

Bevan curled his legs under him and appreciated the flakey-crusted vegetable casserole himself, cold though it was. As tiny chips of crust cascaded upon his lap, he brushed them off reluctantly, tempted to wet a fingertip and capture every morsel. The Zarite sitting next to him pushed a second hunk of casserole into his hands, as if sensing his appetite.

Bevan half-finished it before he spoke. "What's the plan for when we reach the port?"

The head male glanced his way, pale eyes steady. "What kind of plan should we need?" he asked, nibbling at a crisp green fruit to punctuate his response.

"As bombed out and damaged as the port is, they're not going to let us take a ship." Bevan spoke slowly, so his meaning could not be mistaken.

"All things among us are one," the male said enigmatically. "There will be no difficulty. The only difficulty lies within yourself."

Bevan had been raised within the solid walls of the Catholic church. This sort of reform Zen type of philosophy did not leave him with a comfortable feeling. "Look, we're talking a cruiser, a pilot, and fuel."

The male peeled back his lips, showing his rodent incisors. "The ship will be available. Fuel is sufficient. I am told the underground tanks suffered no damage. As for pilot . . . that is your concern."

"Where am I going to find a Choya with the *tezarian* drive?"

The circle of Zarites stared at him as if he had announced himself to be God and spoken in tongues. The leader shuttered his eyes a moment, hiding his thoughts away, then looked back at Bevan.

"You must pilot. There is no need for other."

Bevan sputtered. Fine flakes of crust swirled out like a snow cloud. "Maybe you don't have a need for a driver, but I like to get where I'm going."

The Zarite tossed the core of his eaten fruit away, stood, and dusted his hands. "Then that is your concern," he said. He retrieved his walking stick. Breakfast appeared to be over.

Bevan sat there frozen by amazement, not sure he liked the division of chores. Sure, getting a cruiser seemed like the harder part, but finding a pilot rated a close second. A paw tugged on his elbow, and he got to his feet reluctantly.

Double vision set in abruptly, prisms flashing across the faces of the Zarites around him. Bevan swayed in sudden disorientation. They pushed him over the rim of the litter and into its bed. With a bark from the leader, the bearers hefted their burden and set off at a jog.

Bevan clung to consciousness. One thing at a time, he told himself. Something would work out. Perhaps he should adopt the Zarite philosophy which appeared to be that all things were available to those patient enough to wait for them.

But his Catholic orphanage background had ground another belief into him, that of trial and retribution, of sin and redemption, guilt and confession, a great wheel of action and consequences. Whatever happened to him now was redemption for the heinous sin he had committed. He knew that. The hell he had earned he now carried with him.

Chapter 11

"Congress has requested your presence after today's session."

"Me?" Palaton asked, and one of his eyebrows climbed slightly.

"You and the humankind," Jorana answered.

"Ah. They want a look at him." Palaton pushed aside his readouts of the *tezar* contracts, initiations, and fatalities over the last decade. This conversation sounded as though it might take most of his attention. He leaned back in Panshinea's chair. This, more than the fragrant carved wood chair in the palace throne room, was the center of Cho's rule, he realized as he did so.

The monitor framed Jorana's visage. The image was one of the few vanities he'd ever seen about her, and he wondered why she would tune the monitor's framing in that way. But she was Choya'i, and their ways were sometimes even more baffling than those of the aliens he'd met in his career. "Gathon suggests that they wish a formal presentation of you as heir."

Palaton could feel a sudden frown. "That is an imperial ceremony, not a Congressional introduction. Impossible to do without Panshinea and probably illegal, as well."

Jorana pouted her lips ever so briefly. "Argue the subject with Gathon, then. I'm only the messenger. By the way, I've been able to find a round-the-clock guard for Rand, someone who will stay with him dawn to dusk and be on call after that."

"Who?"

"His name is Traskar. He's a former *tezar*. He's not normally on duty here in Charolon, he's agreed to come in from Niniot."

That the Choya had been a pilot meant that he would

be free of the xenophobia Palaton feared. But he disliked having a Choya around who'd been burned out, and was perhaps ill or unstable. He had no recollection of the name. "Where's he from and why is he grounded?"

Jorana grinned at Palaton's question. "He schooled at Salt Towers. He lost both arms and a leg in a bombing raid about forty years ago."

"I see." Prosthetic replacement was fairly sophisticated among the Choyan, but Traskar's wounds had been so extensive that he would have been hampered and retirement would have been recommended. Flight training at Salt Towers meant that, at one time, Traskar had been among the aristocracy of his House. His own loyalty to Blue Ridge chafed a bit at that, but if Jorana recommended him, she must have reasons. Palaton knew he should trust Jorana's judgment and that his questions reflected that he did not. "He sounds like a good prospect," he said.

"I thought so."

Palaton had had no time for Rand other than to check on him briefly in the morning, and the manling had not been awake then. "Will you brief Rand on the appointment? I haven't had time to check on him."

Jorana nodded. "He's doing fine. It's difficult to watch him. He's so awkward. The splints don't help, of course, but he's so spindly and all at angles."

"They're not a graceful race. It's all in the eyes," returned Palaton.

"Not only the eyes, but the hands have been busy. So far he's discovered the passive heating and cooling system, the recessed wall lighting, the entertainment console, the automatic *bren* brewer, and the all-hours Congressional broadcast. Not to mention the bath masseuse. He's as curious as a *chiarat*," the Choya'i commented. "And I did not know humankind had a hankering for *bren*."

"This one does. You'll let him know when to be ready?"

"I will." Jorana ended her call and the monitor's soft edges lingered after her image faded to dark slowly.

Palaton found himself staring at the darkened surface, considering what the Congress really wanted of him. They would want a look at Rand, perhaps, to see a humankind in person. The various delegates would be no more sophisticated than the counties they represented. Palaton hesitated

to expose Rand to scrutiny, but he knew that to refuse
Congress at this juncture would be even more unwise. He
had defied them enough, now it was time to ease into the
position Panshinea had occupied.

The emperor of Cho was not only a leader, he was a
judge. He would settle disputes which could not be settled
by other means and he would judge those settlements
which had been made to discern the fairness. He was the
final appeal on all decisions and sentences, and he was the
final recourse on policy concerning the natural resources of
the planet they all worked so hard to maintain. They did a
balancing act and although colonization might relieve some
of that necessity, the adaptation effect on genetic selection
had always posed new problems, and Cho had decided long
ago not to colonize.

For all matters which would pass before him, he was
nothing if Cho could not trust him. And it would not trust
him if he was revealed. How could he think to stand before
the five hundred plus members of Congress and pass their
examination? No matter how well he dissembled, there
would be someone who would know he was an empty shell.
He had to have Rand at his side. But he did not know if
it would be enough. Palaton bowed his head in deeper
thought.

Rand looked in amazement at the vest Jorana held up
for him. "What is that? It looks like an armored jacket."

"It's your batteries." The Choya'i helped him shrug into
it and pulled it into alignment so she could fasten it. The
buttons appeared to be magnetic. The seam closed without
warning and with very little notice of where the opening
lay. Rand patted it. The garment was heavy enough, but
flexible.

He had been waiting all day for something to happen,
anxiety gnawing inside him, looking for Palaton or Rindy
for company, left to himself and to the wonders of the
apartment which faded quickly after initial inspection.
Water here was not more unlimited than it had been at
home and the energy systems were remarkably similar, yet
the Choyans had thousands of years of technological civilization beyond Earth's meager time line. Where were the
real wonders? Now that Jorana and Palaton were here, they

had precious little time to answer questions as they prepared him to appear before Congress.

Palaton eyed the vest. "It fits well enough."

"What does it run?"

"Bodyshield." Jorana's voices were muffled as she stepped behind him and tugged and pulled. Then a shimmery effect enveloped him. "I had this cut down from a child's suit . . . if I can just get it to fit . . . there! It's up."

Rand looked at the two of them through it. "What can it stop?"

"Most lightweight projectiles, bodily assault, light and sonic waves. It won't stop the projectiles, but it'll disperse most of the energy and keep the damage to a minimum."

The shimmer disappeared. Rand slapped a hand on his flank. "I think this thing can do the job without the shield."

Palaton laughed. Jorana looked at him. "You're wearing one, too," she said.

"It'll ruin the lines of my uniform!" Palaton stood resplendent in the colors of Blue Ridge, his chest lined with chevrons and badges of service.

"Think what an enforcer could do to those lines," she retorted, holding out a Choya-sized vest.

Palaton looked wryly at Rand and then, with a shrug, stepped to her and shed his summer jacket. "At least let me wear it underneath."

"That will buffer the activation." Warning underscored her tone.

"I'll take that chance," Palaton answered dryly. "I'm willing to risk that any Congressman can shoot that well."

The Choya'i looked up as her fingers briskly strapped the vest into place. She tugged and pulled strongly enough so Palaton gasped in spite of himself and she made a face at Rand behind Palaton's shoulder as if she had done it on purpose.

Rand watched the two of them, sensing a bonding that neither wished to acknowledge, yet that existed between them as concretely as a chain. A tang of homesickness went through him as he remembered the way his own parents had reacted to each other with almost the same familiarity.

"What's the matter," Jorana asked. "Got pilot's ribs?"

Palaton looked at Rand. He said, with a great deal of

dignity, "Pilot's ribs are an affliction reserved for those who crash-land. My craft usually comes down intact."

"Providing, of course, you ever get it off the ground." Jorana slapped the vest into position, was rewarded by an "oof" from Palaton, and stepped back. "Put your jacket on and see if you can trigger the shield quickly enough."

Palaton shrugged into his jacket and the shimmer appeared almost immediately. To the look of faint surprise on Jorana's face, he responded smugly, "Pilot's reactions."

She conceded with a shrug of eyebrows. She checked her chronographer. "It's time."

"What about Rindy?"

"He's waiting for a transmission from Panshinea and, I suspect, he's more tired than he's willing to admit. He said facing Congress was a bit more than he could handle right now," answered Jorana.

Palaton ran his palm over the last seam on his uniform. "I know how he feels." He looked at Rand who answered with a salute.

"What's that?"

Rand explained it. "Ah," said Palaton. "Quaint gesture. I suggest you keep it to yourself. It's not far from a street slang which commons use and it is not considered flattering."

Rand felt himself blush as Jorana laughed behind him, and pushed him toward the door.

The retired *tezar* guard came to his heels alertly. Traskar was tall, though not next to Palaton, who was the tallest Choya Rand had yet seen. The older pilot's face had been lined by sun, the filaments of his facial jewelry in onyx and gold disappearing into heavy wrinkles. Rand could not tell where Choya left off and artificial limb began, but there was a stiffness to his movement that most Choya did not have, except for aged Rindalan. His gray-streaked brown hair was plaited back into a thick and lustrous ponytail. He wore the imperial colors of red and crimson, but his chest was devoid of service badges, except for an insignia which he had proudly told Rand delineated the Salt Towers flight school.

"Conveyance?" asked Traskar in crisp accents.

"No," Jorana told him. "They're to take the Emperor's Walk. They're less expected that way."

The guard checked his timepiece. "In that case, we had better hurry. We have somewhat limited mobility." And the wrinkles deepened on his face as if it hurt him to admit a loss of agility.

Rand had only met with Traskar briefly, for the guard stayed outside the quarters, but he felt as if he should not let the other suffer. Traskar was one of the few Choya he'd met who would look him in the eye. "I'm sorry," he apologized, taking the blame, "but with these splints I can only move so fast."

The Choya stared down. He had green eyes with a multitude of brown flecks in them, as if nature could not decide whether to gift him with one color or the other. "We will slow for you," the guard said solemnly. He held the door open to let them pass.

It was an underground slidewalk. The summer heat had settled within the passageway and though jets of air attempted to cool them in spits and spurts, Rand felt his forehead dampen as they gained the entranceway. Jorana had left and it was just the three of them.

Traskar suggested, "Bodyshields."

Palaton scratched his chin thoughtfully. "It'll be hotter."

"But safer," the guard returned. He had the holster open on a hand weapon the Choya called an enforcer, and Rand thought privately that it looked like it could do a great deal of damage, shield or no. "*Tezar*," the guard continued, "you are also the heir now."

Palaton sighed as if disliking to be reminded, and a shimmer surrounded him. Rand found the button Jorana had guided his fingers to before and activated his own. What breeze there had been instantly ceased.

Palaton ducked his head under the lip of the tunnel entrance and Rand saw, with surprise, that he'd had to do so. Traskar also bent his head somewhat as he escorted Rand inward.

The walk was not functioning. Palaton approached a panel inset in the wall. Trade as well as what Rand presumed to be Choyan was inscribed on the instruments. The automatic mode seemed to be malfunctioning, for the panel had gone to manual. Palaton manipulated the panel, but the walkway stayed within its roadway, still and motionless.

Palaton's lips pursed for a moment, then he looked at Traskar. "The solars are down. There's a power drain."

"Fans against the summer heat," the other responded.

"No doubt. We shall have to walk it, indeed."

"Ambush?" suggested Rand.

The two Choyan looked at him. Sorrow rather than wariness rode their expressions, but Palaton smoothed his face out quickly. "No," the pilot said. "Other problems. There are always power outages at midsummer."

"Can't you bring it back to automatic?" Rand asked.

"No," Palaton said shortly. "That's not possible anymore." Palaton led the way down, leaving Rand to wonder if solar energy were the backup manual power source, what could possibly have been the automatic power origin.

The walkway tunnel blossomed into a tremendous underground mall, which was silent and empty. There were no shops here, but the entire palace could have been swallowed up easily. He saw stations for water and latrines and wondered if this had been intended, at one time, to be an evacuation shelter of some kind, perhaps for imperial staff from one end and Congressional staff from the other. It had been light outside, and within, small globes lit as they approached and faded to a minimum of illumination as they passed. A bronze railing loomed in the foreground. Rand slowed as he saw that it fenced an immense series of craters.

He paused at the nearest rail. "My God," he said, leaning over and looking. A star cruiser could have been berthed in the crater. "What happened?"

"This," Traskar explained, "is a war memorial."

Rand whistled softly. "Who won?"

"We did," Palaton answered dryly. "Else we'd be up to our asses in Abdreliks by now."

"The Droolers did this?" The craters must be pre-Compact history then. Centuries old.

Traskar agreed. "Aye, and more." The guard slapped a wide palmed hand down on the railing next to Rand. "Took out the Congressional halls that time. Never again."

"Or so we hope." Palaton stepped away from the railing and strode on again. He paused to adjust his step to Rand's shorter and hindered stride.

Beyond the craters, as globes came to life, Rand could

see the infrastructure of an incredible building . . . towers and spiraling walks in midair, hallways and courtyards, machines which lay sparkling and half-destroyed in the golden gloom. Overhead trams hung from arches which spanned the building. He spotted what he thought were robotics in disarray, technology he had not seen on Cho in any form.

All of it lay beyond the railing, consigned as a memorial, dusted by the ages even sheltered here, underground.

It took them a great deal of walking to pass the wreckage. Rand watched it. He wondered how the Abdreliks could have attacked with a Choyan pilot guiding them.

He must have voiced his wonderment aloud, for Palaton answered. "They didn't. We all had FTL navigation then. We spanned our own heavens, each of us, without knowing there were other races who could do the same. The Abdreliks had poor success with their navigators. The Ivrians range closest to us in reliability, but only on short FTL runs, bordering on known space. Our first contacts were brief, abrupt, and hostile. The Abdreliks, particularly, are . . . were . . . an avaricious race. They took a great deal of discouragement and might never have come to terms if it had not been for the discovery of Sorrow."

Traskar said, with a growl in his lower tone, "That war gave us the mastery, though."

Palaton looked back over his shoulder. "That it did," he said slowly. "We were forced to the limit and discovered just what we could do with Chaos. After that, after the Compact was settled, the others saw how easily we could travel vast FTL distances without navigational worry and began to contract for us to pilot them as well. The Ivrians continue to work on their drives, but ours is unquestionably superior because of its accuracy." He looked over Rand at Traskar, as if willing the guard to say something else, but the guard grew silent.

The walkway began to slope upward. Rand felt it in his knees, particularly the one forced to remain straight by the splinting, and in his lungs. Palaton and Traskar adjusted their speed for him once again. He grew heated inside the bodyshielding. His shirt would be soaked with sweat by the time they reached their destination.

An intricate piece of sculpture edged the slidewalk. Rand paused both to look at it and catch his breath. "What is it?"

Palaton eyed it. "A light fountain."

The wiry tracings remained dark, however, despite their approach. Rand put a hand out and touched it. It was almost ethereal in its beauty and he wondered what it must look like dancing with light, even to his dimmed vision. "It's incredible."

"One of five throughout Charolon," the pilot said. "Sculpted by Cleota the Fair. No one can bring them to light any more."

"They're broken."

"No," Palaton answered slowly. "We seem to lack the ability to activate them."

Rand looked at him quickly. "I don't understand."

A darkness flickered through the other's eyes. "Neither do we. Come on. The Congressional session will be ending soon. We don't want to keep them waiting."

The guard drew Rand away to follow in Palaton's footsteps. Rand turned back once, to look at the faint, gleaming outline of the war memorial as the vast shadows in the underground cavern threatened to swallow it forever. Whoever had built that building, the walkway, the fountain . . . was something more than the Choyan who lived here now. Was this why the Choyan rarely allowed visitors dirtside? Was theirs a civilization faltering and growing dim itself? Did they secret themselves away to hide behind a reputation built centuries ago which they could no longer uphold?

Palaton looked back and their gazes caught. The Choya's fair face darkened with a humanlike flush as if he had, for the briefest moment, an inkling of what Rand thought. Then he blinked, breaking the contact, and turned away, to lead Rand out of the passageway and into the still light summer's eve.

Chapter 12

As they moved through lengthening shadows, it became perceptibly cooler inside the shielding. Rand wiped his brow on his sleeve, hoping new sweat would not immediately drench him. The streets were nearly empty. Conveyances sat idling, resting on the pillows of air on which they rode, floating eerily above the street lanes. He eyed the nearest one. Technology humans did not quite have yet for long-term, maintenance-free operation, but it was not so far from their reach. Another generation and they would have it, efficient and well-tooled.

Questions had him grinding his teeth with the effort to keep silent, but he did not let them go. He instinctively felt Palaton would not answer, even if he could. The Choyan quickened their pace and he stumbled after, bones aching and muscles trembling. He determined to keep up, caught himself, and fell into step. As they did not wish to reveal their weaknesses, neither did he.

The winged building which replaced the wreckage he had passed underground had neither the beauty nor the size of the first. There were no soaring walkways for interconnection, no trams balanced upon gossamer cables, no windows facing in impossible directions. He did not know how old it was because it had the outer appearance of age, but he knew that part of that had to be facade. Stone and marble and tile gleamed dully as the sun, still hot, sank lower on the horizon.

He saw figures separate themselves from the shadowy columns and approach cautiously.

"Broadcasters," said Palaton, and there was a sneer in his voices.

Traskar stepped ahead of Rand. "They won't come much closer," he said.

Rand looked for the camera gear. There appeared to be none. "How do they—" and his question cut off. He saw now what appeared, like a third eye, in the center of their broad brows. If it was a camera, it was so thin and flat it could be worn like a headdress. They wore vests like the ones which powered his bodyshield and he wondered if they powered the broadcast signals. Would they be relayed to a nearby station, amplified and then rebroadcast or taped? Or had they the ability to broadcast directly to any receiver tuned to them?

They did not draw close, but Rand felt their camera eyes upon him acutely as the three of them passed and began climbing the shallow steps to the front of the Congressional hall. He had his *bahdur* cloaked, yet it fed him the emotions of distrust and fear and resentment coming from the watchers.

Palaton paused till Rand drew even with him. Casually, yet protectively, he let an arm drop over Rand's shoulders, and the bodyshields merged into one large shimmer. "Steady," he murmured.

Rand nodded.

They passed under a flying arch and over a threshold which, momentarily, canceled out their bodyshields. A mechanical Choyan voice intoned, "Expected and admitted."

He had felt nothing and looked about for the sensors. Nothing met his inspection. Traskar had fallen in behind them and his heels struck the marble flooring with a military staccato. Their bodyshields had resumed the moment they crossed into the lobby. Palaton said softly, "Take your shield off. Jorana may be right concerning security, but this is diplomacy."

Rand did as bid. In the bright light of the lobby, his vision grew less accurate, and the shimmering protection had worsened it. He did not miss the shield as it evaporated. Palaton dropped his arm from his shoulder and took his shield down as well. "If you have to bring it up," he warned, "split seconds count."

"If I have to bring it up," Rand answered, "I'll be diving for the floor first."

Palaton didn't respond, but Traskar let out a gravelly laugh.

He could feel their eyes upon him, these representatives

of the Choyan counties. His stomach knotted and his pulse quickened. Now that he looked upon them, the Housed elite of Cho, he could see the difference between these Choyan and those who had thronged the streets on the broadcasts he'd watched in the solitude of his room. The horn crowns were defined and elegant, not coarse and brutish. The clothes were cut in styles he did not know, except that the fabrics were rich and lustrous in colors he could not name, which blended into one another and then raced away like droplets of water along a waxed surface, separating again. He realized that these were among the aristocracy, even among their own, and their gazes were sharp and considering of him as he passed.

These were those chosen to know what was best for the planet and its people because they had the inner sight, and the ambition, and the destiny.

And, from the emotions filtering through to him, the conceit, the greed, and the shrewdness. Rand blinked as he fought to contain the power Palaton had given him. He resisted the impulse to shield himself again. It would not work against these probing thoughts.

Palaton slapped a palm against a richly burled door. It opened to him, and its twin by its side, revealing a vast gallery. At its center clustered podiums. The aisles were wide enough to drive a car down. The ceiling domed far overhead, and he could see the tracing of the setting sun through it.

Traskar said, "I'll be on standby here, sir."

Palaton nodded, a bit absently, Rand thought. He touched Rand's shoulder again. There was a definite warmth as they connected and Rand knew a panicky moment when it seemed as if all that filled him went flooding to his shoulder, to drain into that touch, to abandon him, to flee. He felt as though he were dying, and his knees began to buckle.

Palaton's power, seeking return. He had fought it instinctively, but now he wondered if he might have been able to let it go, to pierce that curtain which separated them. Too late, for the tide surging in him returned to normal, and the moment passed. Rand looked up. Had Palaton felt it?

The Choya did not look at him, but kept his attention on the audience which was rising to their feet as they en-

tered the aisle leading to the center podiums. Rand felt the
intensity of his purpose.

Though not all seats were filled with Choyan, they
weren't necessarily empty. Here and there thin, transparent
screens stood in place. Rand's head turned as he went by.

Palaton slowed. "Broadcast screens," he said. "For those
who wish a proxy presence. The screens are not necessary
to transmit an image, but are a courtesy for those of us
on the floor. Sometimes it's difficult telling the transmitted
images from real presences."

One screen activated as they drew even with it, and Rand
found himself looking into a three-dimensional projection
of an older Choya'i, her silvery hair combed back from a
brow so delicately adorned with crown that it was almost
nonexistent. Real or projection, her eyes drilled into him,
and he felt the force of her will all the way through him.
Yet, through her seemingly solid body, the screen could be
faintly seen.

There was a momentary gap, as she received the transmission that he returned her look. The Choya'i nodded
almost imperceptibly. Rand felt Palaton's hand on his
splint, drawing him onward.

"Don't take time to make either friends or enemies,"
Palaton said under his breath.

A rising tide of noise followed them, gaining strength as
they came to the podiums in the center of the hall. The
floors were sloped downward, so that they stood in an am-
phitheater, which offered an equally good view from everywhere, except perhaps where they stood, a position where
someone was always at their backs. He could feel sudden,
steely tension in Palaton's lean body as they reached
their objective.

The empty seats filled. The inactive screens came alive.
Only in a few, rare spots, could Rand see true emptiness.
When the hall filled, the voices stilled. A massive Choya
stood, his shock of white hair in such disarray that it was
nearly impossible to tell if he were horned or not.

"Welcome to the heir," he said. His voices boomed, bass
drums in double, and Rand winced slightly at the sound.

"Welcome to the heir," the audience rejoined. Palaton
bowed slightly.

"Thank you for bringing me home," he answered, as if

there had never been any trouble at all coming back, as if this multitude of five hundred or so had been responsible for working a miracle.

Palaton never raised his voices, but Rand could hear the faint echo as they were broadcast to the far edges of the hall. He felt awe and quenched it by thinking, *Hold on. The Greeks knew how to do this.*

As if by recalling this, his mind descended into a maelstrom of questions. Who had been their Egyptians, their Greeks? Who had birthed their civilization? What secrets had they left behind them, besides light fountains, which these modern-day descendants no longer knew?

Palaton reached out and touched Rand again, catching up his free wrist. "May I present to you, noble assemblage, the humankind I have taken under my protection. He is known to me as Rand."

Rand felt a heat inside him, as though every pore had been invaded, and the concentration went to the core of him and burned there, telling him of the penetrations. The *bahdur* inside him coiled as though it might strike, and he worked on the control Palaton had taught him.

Palaton looked on him mildly, and there was pride in that look, Rand recognized with surprise. He swallowed back the turmoil inside of him.

The white-haired Choya sat abruptly. "Him I do not choose to greet."

Palaton's fingers tightened about Rand's arm. Rand knew that dizzying, sinking feeling of *bahdur* about to abandon him again, and realized that some of it must indeed be escaping to Palaton—he felt it, too, and that was why the pilot kept taking hold of him, as though he could sip bits of it back, like taking drafts of a steaming cup of *bren*. With the realization, he felt some of Palaton's shock as well as his tension.

"I apologize to the Congress," Palaton said, straightening, but not loosing Rand. "I cannot tell you of the particulars of the guardianship, only that this manling is under my protection, and that his safety is vital also to the safety of Cho. Compact or not, we have enemies we have held at bay for centuries, and we have done so because we are both smart and prudent."

The majority of those within the hall had seated them-

selves. A wiry old Choya'i, with a permanently humped
shoulder remained on her feet long enough to shout, "I am
not one to accuse a *tezar* of hastiness, but the decision you
made alone was one for all of us to consider."

As she sat down, Rand saw a projection screen at her
back, and realized she was not what she seemed, though it
made her objection no less vehement or immediate. Cries
of agreement followed her presentation.

Palaton did not wait for the cries to cease before he
bellowed, "There are times in a crisis when there is no
place for democracy. This was such a time."

The shock-haired Choya snorted loud enough to be
heard at the podiums. "Prove it," he said.

Palaton bored a look at him. "I am a *tezar*," he threw
back, "and not accustomed to having my judgment
questioned."

"You are the heir, and you had damned well better get
used to it," called back another Choya, one of flaming red
hair, and bold, twisted horn. He wore black and silver and
had not, Rand remembered, gotten to his feet at all when
they entered.

Palaton turned slightly toward him to retort, "I am the
heir, not by reason of birth, but because I am a *tezar,* and
I saw a duty, and I fulfilled it."

"Then I might have been heir as well," responded the
redhead.

"So you might," said Palaton, "if you had had the courage to do it, and Panshinea had accepted you."

Color to match his mane rose in the other's face, but his
lips clamped shut and he did not answer again. A murmur
had arisen at Palaton's words, and then died out again.

"I took the Emperor's Walk today," said Palaton into
the quiet. "I saw dust and disarray. I wondered how long
it had been since most of you had seen the ruins and remembered what it means to us."

The old Choya'i said, "Don't chastise us, Palaton. We
also serve who stay here and sift laws through our hands
and weigh the meager resources of a dwindling planet. You
travel the stars. We traverse the narrow roads of possibilities dictated by what is left of Cho." She rubbed her
humped shoulder as if it pained her. Her image wavered a
bit as though her movement disrupted the broadcast.

"Our people," responded Palaton, "are still our greatest resource, and I suggest to you that a goodly portion of them are overlooked by you."

His words dropped like a bomb and Choyan exploded to their feet. In spite of himself, Rand took a step backward as voices rose in volume. He saw Traskar straighten and come down the aisle a step or two as if anticipating trouble.

The shouts drowned out one another until they died down again, and Rand was left with only a partial coherent sentence, ". . . they cannot know what is good for them . . ." before all had grown still again.

Palaton said, "I have not done for them what you will not."

There was a grumble of mollification, as though the Congress had been somewhat appeased, though not entirely convinced.

"Send them home," came a call from behind them. Palaton swung about to place it.

"I have asked," he returned. "I will ask again."

The shock-haired Choya stood. "We have voted, Palaton," and his words fell like chimed notes in the silence. "For censureship. You have been asked here today to receive this verdict. Your acceptance as heir remains unverified until such time as we can come to agreement. I will add, for my own sake, and the sake of my Householding and county, that it is hoped you will be candid with us as soon as it is possible as to the purpose of your guardianship. We are Choyan. But even though we are who we are, it is not necessary that we carry the burdens of a thousand thousand worlds who do not choose to rise above themselves."

Palaton dropped Rand's wrist. It had gone numb and prickly at the same time. Rand felt a shock as though he'd been slapped.

"What does he mean," he whispered to the pilot.

"He means," answered Palaton grimly, "we're on our own."

Chapter 13

Rand dreamed of a love spooned close to his body, curled about him, caressing him and whispering in his ear. The night kept his eyes closed, he could not see who welcomed his body with such passion and intimacy, but he knew the touch. Alexa, who'd been lost on Arizar, the first and only lover of his memory.

He dreamed he opened his eyes and saw her looking at him, her pale face, framed by short, curly dark hair which gleamed blue-black in the darkness. He said, "Why are you here?" because toward the end of their days at the College, she'd turned from him to Bevan and the two of them had locked him out of their intimacies and he had never understood why.

"Because," whispered his dream Alexa, "you're alive and Bevan is not."

His voice stuck in his throat. Her lips moved over the curve of his neck and the words tumbled out, following her, "But you're dead, too."

"No," Alexa told him. "No more than you. I'm alone. You're alone." And she moved her hand about him, stroking him lightly.

Even in his sleep he began to rouse and his senses blurred dream with reality. The black, white, and gray of night became shot through with a golden fire. The haze swirled around him, curtaining him away from her eyes, settling about him like a shroud, separating the two of them from their lovemaking.

"No!" he protested, trying to shrug off the curtain blanketing him. Alexa withdrew further until she stood by the side of the bed, her slender form pale in the shadows.

"Find me," she whispered. "Please."

"Alexa!"

"Where?"

"Look for me." She held out a hand in entreaty, child-like, despite the lushness of her womanly form. "Please."

He tried to call out again, but his voice strangled in his throat. Her form shimmered and disappeared in a golden torch which dwindled even as it burned.

Rand bolted up in the Choyan bed, breathing hard, his voice stuck in his paralyzed throat, his effort to call out harsh in his own ears. He blinked several times. His body had responded to the memory of the lovemaking. Rigid and aching, he swung his feet over the side of the bed, unable to return to resting.

As he swallowed down his emotions, his eyes adjusted to the room, but the golden fire he'd seen seemed shot through everything, a pixie dust coating which lingered everywhere he looked. The blindness creeping in on him made it difficult to distinguish light from dark, but now, if he concentrated, the golden fire settled on the outlines of the furniture and various objects in the room, delineating them. He could see, yet could not.

His arm and leg itched abominably. They had ridden a conveyance back from the Congressional Halls, but he'd gone to bed aching and sore. Now the braces irritated him to the point where he felt he could no longer stand their constraints. He shrugged off the arm brace tentatively, flexing his limb. The soreness had all but abated. He worked his wrist and his fingers gingerly.

He bent down and unfastened the leg brace, fumbling for the straps and catches with only his fairy dust vision to aid him. His leg held him as he stood, wavering, then more solid upon his feet. His bones told him they would ache when it grew cold and damp, ache like an old man's rheumatism, but now they were healing, young and green, and he felt as though he had been freed.

Alexa had not been here. His mind knew it even if his body did not, and his body's enthusiasm gradually waned as he made his way about the Choyan quarters. But how real the dream had been. His throat caught at the sensations still draining from him, the pain of losing her yet again.

Had he thought of her because he was alone, abandoned to Palaton's guardianship by a planet which did not care for either him or his people's struggle?

He found a chair and sat in it abruptly, his legs buckling from under him, not from lack of strength but from the shock of everything. Alexa had fed emotionally from both himself and Bevan, but in the end she had abandoned him, too. He had never understood her explanation. "You're not dark enough," she'd said and left him. And, although he was fair while Bevan had had a South American's skin, he knew she hadn't been talking about color.

She had often dreamed violently, startling awake in the night, with a half-scream or a smothered snarl, tangled in the bedsheets as though she had wrestled to gain consciousness. Their lovemaking had always been best when she'd come to his dorm room, shared his bed, cuddled with him until drowsiness threatened to claim them both, and then left, for there would be no rest if they slept together.

Going to Bevan had not changed that in Alexa. Bevan had told him. What demons did she fight in her sleep, what demons had she hoped to meet in Bevan's own darkness to match her own, and why had he, Rand, not been good enough to help her? Why would she call for him now . . . and did he hear her spirit, her memory, or had she somehow survived the holocaust on Arizar?

Rand sat, trembling as the summer night grew cold and damp with morning fog, and wondered. When the sky outside his window began to lighten, he felt a need not to be alone, got up and dressed, and trespassed the rooms which had been given to him for other boundaries.

Palaton heard the whisper of a trespass at his doorway. He turned his head, saw the figure which had broached the security system, and smiled despite his first worry. "You've had a long day," he said, "if you're just heading to bed."

"And you," answered Jorana. She stripped off her coat of office and the belt of arms she wore. The enforcer made a dull thud as it hit the floor where she dropped it. She came to his side, leaning upon him, her scent dusky. "Should I leave?"

"No. I don't think so." He pushed himself back in his chair, and reached for her, drawing her into his lap. "I thought you were angry with me."

"Always," she answered. She stroked a forelock of his hair back from his brow. The caress of her fingers tangling in his hair sent a pleasant wave through him. "You're a *tezar,* and I know that, I know you'll always be leaving me. But that doesn't keep me from worrying when you'll be back."

He listened to the slow beat of her heart for a moment before answering. "Before we start this again," he said, "let's talk about expectations."

"I have none."

He tilted his head back, eyeing her. "None?"

She traced the quizzical expression on his face lightly. "No. I can't ask that of you, can I, as long as you're entangled with Panshinea? And if I did, your answer would not do justice to either of us. You're not free."

"And you? Are you free?"

Her frown passed quickly, marring the smoothness of her forehead for only a second, yet he saw the tracings of deeper lines there, of the subtle aging of a Choya'i. "I know myself," she said, ducking over him and kissing him at the base of his crown. "There's freedom in that."

He could not answer that, for the echoes of her accusation went far deeper than she knew. What would she say to his bastard birth, forbidden by the Housed, his ignorance of his father and the genetic capabilities passed down to him? What would any Housed Choya say? For that, and the *bahdur* stripped away from him, made him less than the commons who ranged the streets of Charolon. He would be as nothing in her eyes. Would she still love him then?

He closed his eyes and let the touch of her hands take away the fear which had begun to pulse like blood through his body.

Rand came to a halt in the vast maze of hallways. He knew which way he wished to go, which direction it was that pulled at him, but the strangeness of the night and the corridor stopped him. He put his hands to his eyes. A wave of need threatened to overwhelm him, then it receded and left him staggered, his back to the wall, his skin awash with the tingle of the emotion as it ebbed away.

His heart pounded for a beat or two, then steadied. It was as though he had two bodies, two hearts, two skins— and nothing separated them. Then he would be torn apart, but even before that, he could barely stand it, because that

which was himself and that which was the other was alien
and yet not. It was as though what he was becoming could
not live within his human skin.

Rand put his chin upon his chest and concentrated. It
had to live there. It was his trust. He'd promised to keep
it until there could be found a way of returning it and if it
changed him somehow, then that was the price to be paid.
He waited, withdrawn, until the emotion bled away entirely
and he knew he could continue. The emptiness which drew
him remained, and he knew only that he had to answer it,
though he had no hope of filling it.

He took a step out from the wall into the corridor and
came to a halt, throwing his head back, stopping in fear,
for a Choya stood there, had been standing there, for
how long?

He did not see the Choya well, his sight dimmed and
startlement muting the fairy dust illumination. He swallowed hard, for it appeared a weapon filled the left hand
of the Choya.

But the lines of the being relaxed somewhat, in shadow
silhouette. "The humankind, I trust?"

"Yes."

"You should not wander. Jorana's troops are nothing if
not effective. Imperial protection may be the only safety
for you . . . but even they will shoot in the dark."

"I didn't mean. . . ."

The Choya cut him off, disinterested in hearing excuses.
He leaned forward slightly and Rand was struck by a pair
of pale blue eyes, intense, driving all notion of his face
from his mind. "Do you know where you are?"

"No. But I know where I'm going."

The pale blue eyes receded into shadow again. "Com-
mendable for any intelligent being. Then I shall not bar
your way."

Rand thought to stride on, but a hard hand gripped his
shoulder. "You are a stranger in Charolon. Don't walk in
the night any longer than you have to. There are those of
us who do not welcome strangers, and those of us who
would find you easy prey."

A cold bolt followed the words, a bolt stabbing through
Rand with the intensity of an attack and he stifled a gasp
of alarm and tried to center himself. This was like the scru-

tiny he'd faced before hundreds that last evening and yet different. Ruthless. It did not care about what damage lay in its wake, or if it was perceived as intense or a casual brush. Rand licked his lips and concentrated on repelling it, sending it aside gently. A thought flashed across Rand's mind, a thought with a voice so unlike any he had ever felt before that he knew instinctively it was not his, had not come from within, but perhaps from this towering Choya. *He has a mind of stone,* and the thought had a kind of cold satisfaction.

And the attack ended as abruptly as it had begun.

Rand swallowed and said only, "Thank you for the advice."

The hand loosed him and let him go on his way. He fought the impulse to turn back and see if he was followed, by glance or otherwise, but Rand couldn't find the courage to do so. There was a weakness in his newly healed limbs and he had to find Palaton or collapse in the hallway.

Palaton woke, his bed still a nest of linen that smelled sweetly of Jorana. They had made, but not consummated, their lovemaking, and he woke with an ache and hunger for her sharpened by her visitation. As his eyes cleared, he saw the awkwardly planed figure standing silently across the room in a corner, watching him.

Palaton thrust himself out from the covers. He cursed first in Choyan, then found Trade coming to him. "How did you get in here?"

"Does it matter?" Rand asked softly.

"Of course it matters." With dignity, Palaton gathered a sheet about his waist. "There's enough security on these quarters to kill a battalion of assassins."

"I simply walked through."

"Walked through?" Palaton's gaze narrowed. "And where are your splints?"

"They bothered me. I took them off." Rand's voice sounded thin, tired, and troubled. "And, yes, I just walked through."

Palaton approached the doorway to his apartment quarters. The alarm system indicator showed it to be fully armed. He hesitated to tempt the system, the sonics barrier was set for severe incapacitation. He would not want to be caught in the barrier himself. He looked back toward Rand who had pulled up a large upholstered chair beside the fireplace and sat down.

"Did you feel anything?"

"My ears buzzed a little."

"That was all?" Palaton's voices rose a little, incredulously.

The young man shrugged, a movement that would have been elegant in a Choya but looked disjointed in a humankind.

"Remind me to make a note that humankind hearing systems are not as . . . vulnerable . . . as our to certain sonic ranges."

Rand's face twisted. "I'm not sure that would have helped."

Palaton paused, halfway across the room, his mind on business, but a note in the other's tone catching his attention. He crossed the room and took the chair opposite Rand. "Why are you here?"

"I needed to not be alone. And . . . I sensed you, also, not wanting to be left alone."

"And so you found me. How?"

That shrug again, so awkward that it made Palaton's skin crawl to see it. "I just did."

The wings and hallways of the palace were immense and intricate, though Rand had been placed not too far from the apartments given to the heir. Palaton shook his head. He groped for a rational explanation. "Between us, there is power. You know that."

"I followed it, then." Rand looked toward the large, curtained windows, where sheer panels let a translucent dawning through. "Maybe that's how I got through the security system."

Using his *bahdur*? Palaton did not like the thought. He chose his next words carefully. "Did you draw on me?"

"No, I . . . I just answered a call. I knew I had to be here. I knew that I, or you, couldn't be alone."

Palaton sat silent for a moment. "But how did you know that?"

"I don't know." Rand's turquoise gaze considered him. "I don't know where I end and you begin. I don't know if I'm me or you. I had this dream, you see, from my own memories and it was abruptly jolted away, and I was bothered by it. So I sat up in my room for half the night and then I knew that what I dreamed was from myself, but it was also from you." He paused, and looked toward the bedding. "Did you have a companion who left too early?"

"And if I did," Palaton said wryly, "I would hardly make it known."

"I'm not asking if you failed. I just want to know if . . . I don't know." Rand buried his face in his hands and his next words came out muffled. "I don't know if I'm me or if I'm you."

There was no precedent to know what *bahdur* did when infused into another, particularly an alien another. The thought that Rand might be using, squandering, his reserve of *bahdur* haunted Palaton, but he did not want Rand panicking. He had felt the flow between them on that Congressional podium, the gifting of his power, a spark, even if only for a moment. Palaton felt for the first time in days that there was hope of becoming whole again. "There is nothing to separate you from yourself," he said. "You carry my essence, like a flame carries heat, but unlike a flame or that heat, it won't consume you."

Rand's face lifted. His expression hardened. "Think not? Do you know what I dreamed yesterday?"

"No," Palaton answered quietly.

"I dreamed of flying. Not in a starliner. I dreamed that I was set off from the mountaintops, thrust leaping into the air, in something like, oh, a glider, and I rode the winds. There was golden fire under the wings and rippling over the landscape, and I could read the thermals from the shape of the sparks, how they flowed. I stayed aloft forever. I never wanted to land. But that wasn't me flying, that had to have been you. Even my dreams aren't my own . . ." he paused. Rand raised a hand to his face. "I'm nearly blind today. The neural blockers have set in. I don't know how long it will last. But . . . I'm not blind. Everywhere I look, fire outlines it. I can see because you burn, you all burn, everything in this room burns, and because it does, I can see it."

Palaton held his breath a moment. The boy saw through *bahdur*. He was no longer a passive receptacle. But how could Rand be using it? Compact data scored humankind extremely low on all esper testing, despite their personal mythology. Did his *bahdur,* cleansed by Rand, burn so brightly it now spilled out? And if so, how could he hide what was occurring from his peers? He faced an alien who had been God-blind and now was not. But what should he tell him? What could he tell him? He did not see with human eyes. He did not know what Rand saw. "Perhaps it's a side effect. You may not be able to rely on it."

"There's nothing here I can rely on except you and maybe old Rindy. It's little enough. It keeps the shadows separated. If I look away, everything fades. If I lose this," and Rand turned away from him, to the cool and empty fireplace, "I'll be imprisoned inside myself. You won't even need Traskar to follow me around. I think I'm frightened. That's why I didn't want to be left alone."

"I won't let that happen to you."

They stared at one another. Rand asked, his voice carrying a fine, thin edge of despair, "How can you stop it?"

The humankind needed all the truth Palaton dared to let go. "I don't know . . . yet. But what you can see is partly augmented by my *bahdur.*"

"By your power?"

"Yes."

Rand reached out with one fingertip, outlined the edge of the elegantly carved side table which leaned against the side of his chair. "The edges sparkle, like fool's gold or as if fairy dust touched, pale yellow, tiny pricks of light."

"Everything?"

The manling nodded.

Palaton had never seen like that. The auras he could read had come mostly from emotion, from other Choyan, though if he concentrated, he could detect faint auras from the organic, living and once alive, things about him. When he'd had his power. Now, he saw only the bleak, colored surfaces of whatever he gazed upon. "I have never seen like that," he said, "but that means little. We're all of us unique in our powers."

"And private." Rand's mouth twisted. He rubbed his arm.

"Do you hurt?"

"I ache a little."

Palaton got to his feet, glad for an action he could undertake. He opened the comline to the apartment. "Staff, I need a physician in my rooms as soon as possible. Tell them to bring ID. I've left my security armed."

Rand had closed his eyes. Slate colored bruises underscored them. Palaton crossed to the chair and put a hand on the other's shoulder. The skin, the bones underneath the loose cloth of the shirt, felt not so alien as he'd once expected. "Are my dreams so terrible?"

"No." There was faint movement of his eyes under his blue-veined lids, as if he was recalling everything. "They gave me what I want." Rand's right hand clenched. "If only I can keep it."

Palaton could feel the sudden tension in his body. This humankind, this foreigner to Cho and its people, had the drive to be a *tezar,* but it was not his to claim. It was Palaton's *bahdur* giving him the forbidden, Palaton's soul and essence, and was he going to be destined to watch it burn through Rand and be lost forever to either of them?

Palaton had to retrieve his power, whatever the cost, before it destroyed both of them. He pulled his hand away, lest the other sense his thoughts and conflict. Before he found it necessary to fill an awkward silence, the threshold filled with a Choya'i, as close as any Choya could be to being fat, her massive body pausing long enough for her to pass her security badge through the laser reader, allowing her access to the rooms. Her silvered hair cascaded down her back from a horn crown so small as to be almost nonexistent, a mere ridge upon her brow.

The physician carried a bag in her wake and pulled up. Her face twisted, and her facial jewelry swirled in its opalescent colors, the random patterns accentuating her expression. "Perhaps," she said wryly, "you should have called a vet. I have no practical experience in treating non-Choyan."

The snide remark, coming from an Earthan whose genetic drive to find balance and serenity was usually deeply ingrained, threw Palaton off-guard. Rand sat up higher in the chair, opening his eyes, pain mirrored in them.

The physician set her bag down on the small side table. "I do, however, have access to your records of treatment from the bay station and in decon, and broken bones, stress fractures in your case, seem somewhat universal." She eyed

Rand with gray eyes muddied by flecks of brown. "Took your braces off, did you?"

"Yes," Rand said faintly. "I itched."

"As well you should." The Choya'i took print-outs and resonance imaging copies from her bag and looked them over. She touched corresponding areas on the boy's limbs. "Here and here."

"Yes."

She deftly rolled back his sleeve and opened the trousers at the inseam. "You still have considerable bruising at the sites where we suspected stress splints. I'll prescribe a mild painkiller to keep you quiet for another few days and I would like to remind you," the physician lifted her head, looking down a prominent nose, "the absence of pain does not mean that your healing is completed. Palaton," and the physician looked fully at him. "He'll need nutritional and herbal supplements as well, to strength the bone."

"And the braces?"

"He should do well enough now with them off, as long as he stays quiet. That's about all I can do for you." She paused, and bent his arm back and forth several times. "Does this hamper you?"

Rand looked puzzled. "No. Why?"

"One elbow," she said briskly. "Looks strange. I thought it might be handicapping." She snapped her case shut and stood up. "He heals quickly. The trauma should be fine in a few more days." At the threshold, she paused long enough to add, "I'll have your prescription sent up." She left, the impact of her presence vibrating in her wake.

Rand commented, "I'm healing very quickly. Perhaps your *bahdur* has something to do with it."

"No," Palaton countered quickly. He caught himself as Rand stared. "I mean, that *bahdur* does not heal."

"It doesn't? No mind over matter?"

"Not in that sense."

"Never?" Rand frowned in puzzlement. "Are you sure?"

"I am positive," Palaton said sternly. "Never in the history of my people has there been the ability to heal in such a way."

"Oh." Rand leaned his head back in the chair. "I don't think I'll need a painkiller. Just sleep." His voice grew fainter and trailed off. The faint lines in his face relaxed and his mouth slackened. Palaton realized the boy had gone to sleep.

He stood over him for a while, listening to the rhythm of the humankind's breathing. He found himself in the guardian posture, sentry over the young, when he looked up and saw a reflection of himself from across the room. Palaton did not move for a moment, meeting the stare of his image.

"What else," he murmured, "can I do?"

Chapter 14

"Rindalan," commented the predominant Choya as he preened, "is an old fool who has asked me to continue the indulgences he committed with Panshinea and extend them to the *tezar* chosen as heir. I refuse to be a party any longer. With Congress against them, I would be stupid to do as he asks." The rooms glittered with accumulated wealth and art, different from the ancient stone walls of the palace, these newly plastered partitions, hung with heavy tapestries of great antiquity. The blazing noonday sun streaked the room with bright light and deep shadow. The speaker stood proudly, short of height for a son of the House of Star, but wiry and big-horned, his strawberry blond mane clipped close in an unsuccessful attempt to tame its curls. His large eyes blazed sapphire blue, piercing and cold.

His companion answered from a shadowed table, virtually impossible to be seen, but for the glittering of his eyes. "I'm glad to hear one of our Prelates has his senses about him, Qativar."

"I can do nothing else. Rindy has left me nothing but the dregs of his power, which he clings to like a lifeline. He should have retired long ago and left Panshinea to his own devices, to rise and fall like the Descendant on the Wheel that he is." Qativar's eyebrows rose elegantly. "Surely I can't be the only one who has seen this." He pulled on the seam of his summer jacket, having forsaken the more traditional robes of a priest. His movement might have seemed vain to those who did not know him, but to those who did, the plucking was not vanity, but pragmatism. He was undoubtedly straightening the hilt of a wrist dagger or checking the wiring of a hidden stunner. His wiry muscles moved under the sleek jacket, giving the impression of

strength and bulk equal to that of a much taller Choya.
Qativar was as formidable as his movements hinted.

"You know you aren't, or our unseemly alliance would
never have come about." The speaking Choya rested his
hands upon the small conversation table. One fingertip
traced the rich, curving burl of the wood's grain. "Have
you told Rindalan you intend to break from him?"

Qativar paused. He looked at his companion apprais-
ingly. "That would be foolish, don't you think? The longer
I stay in his confidence, the better I can work against him.
He leaves for Sorrow soon enough, anyway."

"We are of a mind, then."

"Did you ever doubt it?"

"Doubt never entered my thoughts." The other Choya
stood, cloaked by shadow, moving back closer still to the
corner as if the stone wall itself would absorb his exit.
"Word is that Vihtirne of Sky is trying to retrieve her water
recycling patent."

Qativar gave a last pluck. His head tilted in consideration
of this information. "The counties could be in turmoil if
she brought that pressure to bear. But can she do it?"

"I don't know yet. The legalities of the original forfeiture
are obscure. Centuries have passed. Her heirship to the
patent isn't contested . . . it seem probable that the courts
may not have any recourse. She is a foe to be reckoned
with, Qativar, whether or not she accomplishes her desire."

"Not without Nedar. She has no one to put forth for the
throne without him, and he's nowhere to be found."

"He could be on contract."

Qativar scratched his temple. "If he is, Blue Ridge will
know where he is. Check the flight school for records when
you have a chance. And mind your step. I want no traces
coming back to us. When we move, we will be so swift
neither Panshinea nor Palaton will ever see us coming."

"To that end." The other moved, shadows shifted, and
the room emptied.

Qativar listened keenly. The air in the room changed
pressure, ever so subtly, the slightly musky fragrance of
another Choya's body drifted away, and he knew his co-
conspirator had left. His fingertip brushed the collar of his
jacket. "And as for you, Asten, my friend," he said under
his breath, "Vihtirne of Sky will take you out for me, when

she discovers you sniffing at the heels of her beloved Nedar. I have valued your support over the years, but you weary me." The Choya sniffed a little, put his shoulders back, and left the rooms of his apartment.

Rindalan gave a snuffling laugh. "He walks like a child," the old Choya said. "But you find pride where you will, like a newborn's parent."

Rand laughed as Palaton made an indignant noise. His dark hair ruffled in the slight summer breeze reaching the broad veranda. "It's better than limping along stiff from here to here." He took a deep breath and sat down. The view from the veranda overlooked the palace's massive gardens, floral and produce. "The air smells different. I don't know what it is or how to describe it."

"Words may never come to you." Palaton abandoned his posture of indignity. His gaze followed that of the humankind's. "I have been on many worlds, and their differences amaze and astound me, and yet the subtleties of their variations are not always easy to grasp." He took a deep breath. "I'll leave you two. Gathon has set up briefings for me, and there is still the matter of the God-blind to settle."

"What do you intend to do with Malahki?"

"What can I do? I've talked with him once. He expects something from me I cannot deliver. The streets have to be cleared. The commons have to return home. It's clear Congress will not back me nor will they suffer a continuing strike. I have to get the situation settled soon." Palaton took his hands off the veranda railing, preparing to depart, when Rindy raised a hand in entreaty.

"One or two minutes more, to meet Qativar. You promised me."

"I'll do what I can, but for a useless figurehead, they're keeping me busy." Palaton turned, as footsteps echoed behind them, and the short, vigorous figure of Qativar pushed past the draperies and into the open air.

Palaton met appraising blue eyes with a shocking coldness to them. Then Qativar turned to Rindy, grabbed him up in a hug that seemed to rattle the elderly Choya's bones. Rindy gasped with good humor and breathlessness.

"Qativar, enough, I'm too old for this."

Delight spread across the young priest's face as he released Rindalan and resumed facing them. "It's been too long, Rindy. I don't agree with what you've asked me to do. Cho needs you too much at home." His gaze came to rest on Rand. "Is this the humankind who caused so much trouble?"

"It is," answered Palaton evenly.

"He hardly looks like a danger." Qativar extended his hand. "I believe you favor an open-palmed shake, do you not?"

"I do." Rand took the other's hand carefully and they completed a familiar, yet alien handshake.

The young priest leaned back against the veranda railing. "Rindy has told me he intends to brave the vicissitudes of politics on Sorrow, to aid Panshinea however he may. I might quarrel with that, but he is my superior and I would surely lose. What I don't argue with is that you're going to need my skills to keep your balance here in Charolon."

"First we have to find a balance," said Palaton wryly.

"Indeed." Qativar smiled anew. "So I'm pleased to bring news which even Rindy hasn't heard yet."

The gaunt Choya turned, his thin hair ruffled by the fine breeze, his horn crown seeming to prickle at the sound of Qativar's voices. "What is it?"

"The Council of Prelates has asked for a cleansing. I know Palaton has little time to give for the ritual, but I've been able to sway them to let us use the Earthan temple here at Sethu, rather than forcing us to travel cross-country. Once cleansed, and backed by the Prelates, Congress can't continue to hold a grudge against you."

"A cleansing?" burst out Rindalan in surprise, while Palaton said, "Now that's a two-headed *drath*."

"*Drath?*"

The Choya looked to Rand. "Serpent, I believe the word is in Trade. A double-edged blessing." He took a chair and drummed his fingers upon the arm. "Can't this be sidestepped?"

"It probably could be, but it shouldn't," Qativar answered. "Heir Palaton, this gives the Houses the opportunity to know your power burns bright and clean, despite the lapse you suffered last year, and that the heir to the throne is a vigorous and healthy Choya. We need to know that, to feel confidence in you, to accept you as a leader in

Panshinea's place. Knowing your health, the Congress cannot continue to second-guess the decisions you're making. Once you have that acceptance, you can begin to find the balance you need. Rindy," and those brilliant cerulean eyes searched out the older Choya. "Don't you agree?"

Rindy shifted inside his robes, appearing spindly within the voluminous cloth. "I'm not sure. I'm still stunned." He lifted his eyes. "There could be an advantage, I think, more than just proving yourself."

"And what might that be?"

"A subtle reminder to the Godless of what you are and they are not."

Palaton kept his face impassive. "I would have to leave Rand behind."

"Regardless, you would anyway. He has his convalescence and he's still in danger on Choyan streets." Rindy crossed his legs and covered one bony kneecap with a flap of his robe.

Palaton could not protest. He could not reveal his weakness to these two. Rand had turned his face to look down on the gardens as if afraid the new Prelate might be able to read his expression. Palaton hesitated a moment or two longer. A ritual cleansing for a *tezar* was little more than walking through the ceremonies anyway. It could not restore his *bahdur*, though that had been the intent centuries ago.

It could, however, reveal the fatal emptiness within him.

Exposed now or later. Palaton saw Rindy watching him intently. Later, he thought. Where there was life, there was hope. "All right," he said. "I'll tell Gathon to make the arrangements. When shall we do it?"

"It had better be soon," Rindy said. "I can stay with the boy if it is."

"I'll be all right," Rand protested gently, but no one paid attention to his soft voice.

"Good," said Qativar. "I'll work with the Council."

Palaton stood. "Make the arrangements," he said, his voices vibrating strongly. "But Rand stays with me."

Shock issued from Rindy, who had obviously thought the matter closed. "Palaton, this is a sacred cleansing. We have Traskar to attend him in your absence."

"I am Rand's guardian. There are forces both on Cho

and in the universes who will tear him apart, given the opportunity. I've no intention of giving it to them." He met Qativar's cold stare evenly. "Do whatever has to be done."

The Prelate dropped his chin and bowed his head. "Heir Palaton."

"You can't leave me like this," Bevan said, grabbing at the arm of the Zarite buckling him into a webbing.

"We've brought you this far. It is for you to take yourself further," the creature told him.

"This is a life pod!"

"Inside a cruiser. We've a launch programmed. You'll be picked up, no doubt, somewhere outside the boundaries of our normal space."

"You can't know that." Bevan fought panic, both at his inability to see the world as it really was, and at the complacence of the Zarite.

"Master, we can't do anything else for you. Without a pilot, we cannot take you off-planet. This launch will take you out and release the raft before the plane self-destructs. This will carry you beyond the range of any attackers waiting for such action. Then, the life raft will bear you within tracking range of Compact rescuers. What more can we do?"

Bevan looked about at the confining capsule. "I'll die in here," he said, and felt his throat drawing tight.

"You'll get off-planet. This is all we can accomplish." The creature paused. "I'm sorry, Master Bevan. I can't promise you anything more."

Bevan felt the webbing draw tight about his chest and arms, as he was slung up in midair, so as to baffle the acceleration experienced from a planet berthing cradle rather than that of a launching from, say, a bay station. He fought the instinct to loosen the webbing, to ground himself, to get free.

The Zarite ran a soft-furred hand over the console. "We've checked. You have adequate drinking and food supplies for three weeks. Surely in that time, someone will have heard your signal and picked you up. The capsule is designed for survival."

Bevan closed his eyes tightly. When he opened them, the

view was without aura and darkness. He met the light green eyes of the alien facing him. "I accept your aid," he said and swallowed tightly. "It's all we both can do."

The Zarite nodded. His whiskers fluffed a little. "Would that it were more," the native said.

A thrumming vibrated through the metal and plastics surrounding them. His round, transparent ears flicked up and then back.

"We're readying for launch," the Zarite said. "I cannot stay."

"Nor can I," answered Bevan with bitter humor. He put a hand through the safety webbing. "Thank you and all your brethren for me."

He felt rather than saw the soft yet strong grasp of the creature in response. The Zarite left and the bulkhead of the life pod closed with a firm and solid thud. Bevan shook in his harnessing. He was not the best of travelers. Coming to Arizar, it had been Rand's steady and sure temperament which had calmed him . . . that and Alexa's flirtatious attention. It seemed forever and a day ago that they had been students smuggled away to a mysterious future at an alien school. Now he had no one.

He looked about the capsule interior. His vision sank into its prismatic miasma and he let out a virulent Portuguese curse, then smiled. Father Lombardi would have beaten him for that one, as tolerant as the orphanage padre had been in his time. But the man had had limits.

"What about you, Bev, old boy?" he murmured through drying lips. "What are your limits?"

His heart thumped as he sensed the movement of the berthing cradle into launch position. The capsule was set up to gyro, to stay always at a certain center of gravity regardless of the ship's movement. That, at least, gave him some comfort. He would not spend half of his brief voyage hanging upside down, though once in space, there could be no upside down.

The ship began to tremble, its thrust building. Bevan swallowed tightly. He closed his eyes, unwilling to watch through his peculiar vision.

Behind his eyelids, a bonfire built, flames burning orange red, then turning blue, and then white. When the bonfire burst across his inner eye, blazing through eye tissue and dreams, the ship launched and Bevan sank deep into his safety harnessing, his face contorting with the force of the thrust skyward. He put a hand out through his webbing as if to grab for one last piece of dirt just before he blacked out.

Chapter 15

The emperor of Cho filled the screen, his still presence even more commanding than if he had paced or gestured. He was dressed less flamboyantly for the Halls of Compact than he would be for home, Palaton thought, but he was a true son of the House of Star regardless. His light complexion balanced off the thin artistry of his gold and white-gold jewelry tracings. His eyes of pale jade which deepened to rims of forest green fixed on his watcher as if he could divine, even across subspace and through the monitor, Palaton's thoughts.

If they could have stood side by side, Panshinea would have been a little shorter and heavier. His face sagged with lines at the corner of his eyes and mouth, and his neck had begun to show his age as well. He favored the dramatic, as seen in his lavish hair of reds and yellows, graying at the temple, and the red and gold echoing of his uniform. He was no blood relation to Palaton, except by the weakest of associations through their House, nor did Palaton think that this man might be his unnamed father. He knew better, and so did Panshinea. What bound them now was thicker than the cord of parentage.

Palaton kept his silence, waiting for his emperor to speak.

When Panshinea did, the transmission thinned his voices down to a single tenor. "Perhaps," he said, "it is well the streets are full of God-blind. If not . . . the Housed might have sent their guards in, and we would have war on our hands instead of anarchy."

"You think the censureship that serious."

"It could be. I think more serious is that Devon of the Householding of Kilgalya has named Ariat the heir for the House of Earth. If we are in Descendant, as seems more surely true every day, then the Earthans have a legitimate claim to the throne. They will leave their coveted neutrality for it, I think."

Palaton had not heard of that. It was to be suspected that Panshinea's information would precede his . . . but he wondered why Gathon or Jorana had not chosen to inform him. Was the information speculation only, and Panshinea, in his usual brilliant, intuitive way, formulating his strategy as if what was speculated upon must be? "Have you *fore-seen* this?"

"God, no. Common sense will tell you what the Earthans will do when they come out of their corner." Panshinea shifted before the monitor then. He had been sitting, now he stood.

"What about the flight schools?"

"What about them?"

"I have just authorized completion for three of the smallest classes ever graduated since the plague of Fangborn's century."

Panshinea's eyes narrowed. "Again?"

"Last year's was this small as well?"

"Yes." The emperor turned slightly, lifting a shoulder, and he stood as if knowing that full view of his face was blocked by the movement. "I thought it a fluke."

"We're not advancing candidates out from the Choosing among the Godless. More and more God-blind communities are not participating."

Panshinea moved again, a furtive motion not meant to be seen. "You've been busy."

"You left me little to govern but this and civil unrest from the Houses." Palaton did not let the emperor continue to hide from him. He asked for a different camera range and got it, revealing the emperor's face. He pressed for an answer. "If candidates are not forthcoming from the Choosing, what are the God-blind doing with them? Could Malahki be building a House of his own? And if he is, how long have you known about it?"

Panshinea tilted his head. His green eyes gazed directly into the monitor. "Intelligence doesn't indicate that Malahki is making such a move. The commons are not producing the candidates they used to. Neither are the Houses. Despite all our efforts, the talent appears to continue breeding out. Why else do you think I wanted a *tezar* for my heir?"

A multitude of reasons flooded into Palaton's mind: chief among them knowledge that Panshinea could siphon off *bahdur* to augment his own fading capabilities as he burned out. As if his swiftly flitting thoughts could be seen, Panshinea laughed.

"I asked for a hero. Now we have one. What will you do?"

Palaton reached up to the monitor switch, ready to end transmission and the audience. After a moment's pause, he said, "I'll let you know when I decide."

"Do that," his emperor replied. "In the meantime, work the Houses against one another if you can. They all have their weak spots. Ask Rindy for counsel. And probe deeply through whatever course of action Gathon suggests. I sometimes feel he has his own agenda."

The screen went dark.

Palaton continued to sit there. He had heard of screen-dark transmissions, in which the subject unknowingly continued to remain on-call, revealing that which was candid and damning. He had nothing damning to reveal to Panshinea, but he would not put it past his emperor to have such a feature on the monitor screen.

He sat back at the desk, the reports from the various flight schools in front of him. He had already signed and released what he needed to. But they drew his attention, as if trying to communicate with him.

If he'd had his *bahdur,* the mystery might be revealed. Now he sat with naked eye and felt frustration roiling through him. There had been no apparent shortage of renegade *tezars* to evacuate Arizar when needed, he thought bitterly.

Palaton straightened in the chair. He ran a finger over the flight school charts. The listing here included only the results for the new cadets. He keyed open the interlink to Gathon's offices. The minister himself answered.

"Gathon here."

"Palaton. I want an analysis of *tezars* we've lost over the past twenty years or so."

"Dead?"

"No . . . lost."

"A solemn subject. The Patterns of Chaos have claimed some of our best."

"I know," answered Palaton. Even those who could master Chaos did not always keep it under control. There were maelstroms of random space which could not be navigated, like the Tangled Web, or other even more treacherous areas which they all learned to avoid. Then there were those, like Nedar, who had died off-planet and been sent home. His body, as far as Palaton could determine through discreet inquiries, had never arrived. Likely the ship sent out from Arizar had been taken out by the raiders on their way in. But there were others, legendary pilots of ability, who had simply disappeared. *Or had they?* "Have it transmitted to me as soon as you can compile it." He closed the com. He had suspected it on Arizar, and then forgotten it thanks to the strain of the last several weeks. But if the House of Flame were rebuilding itself at the expense of all Cho, it would strike first at the *tezars,* draining them away.

And it meant also, if they were quietly taking candidates out of the Houseless as well as winning over fatigued pilots ready to chance all for rejuvenation, that they already had a strong arm here on Cho.

The only way Palaton could begin to trace them was by the ashes they'd left in their wake, a trail of destruction which showed the path they had taken, but not what lay before them, which would affect all Cho. That he would have to discover for himself.

He wondered about the sudden rise of Qativar and what might await him in the temple at Sethu. Should he go, knowing the ritual would do nothing for him, and that he might trip a trap cunningly laid for him? Should he endanger Rand?

It occurred to him that he had put Rand's safety before his own duty to Cho. It was a bittersweet knowledge. There were loyalties that sometimes conflicted between a Choya and his House and world . . . *tezar* to *tezar,* for example. Thinking of that, Palaton tired of waiting for Gathon to transmit the material he'd asked for, reached for the interlink and called Blue Ridge.

"Blue Ridge. Hathord here."

Palaton found himself grinning broadly at the image of

Hat on his monitor, square, stolid, old Hat, his thick Earthan shoulders more than equal to the weight of running a flight school. "Hat!"

The Choya's eyes widened like plates. "Palaton! Your highness," and he dropped his chin in obeisance.

"Forget it, Hat. I've seen you bare-butt naked and you've seen me hanging by my chin strap, dangling at wit's end off a cliff. If I'm the heir, it's only because Panshinea found a use for me and I was foolish enough to volunteer."

The Earthan met his stare again. "Nonetheless," Hat said, "there are formalities. Congratulations."

Hat's hands were out of sight, but Palaton retained a mental image of him juggling, always juggling, a typical Earthan seeking for the balances of the various natures on Cho. "Thank you," he answered.

"And welcome home." Hat turned, looking offscreen, though he said nothing. There might have been someone else there, but even though Palaton asked for an adjusted camera range, nothing showed.

"Thank you. I sent your graduation list back, through Gathon."

"Good. The cadets are anxious." Hat's expression shone for a moment, through the wariness. Palaton was sorry to see it settle back into place as the Earthan asked him, "What can I do for you?"

"I'm looking for a memorial list. All the *tezars* who've been lost."

Hat's glance flickered down, then up again. "I haven't had time to keep one. Moameb did, but the data would be old. Of course, the information has been sent in to Charolon, I just don't keep it separate here."

Hat knew, as did Palaton, that the names of those comrades ought to be able to be recited by heart. Palaton had been away, on contract and out of touch, but Hathord had not. He was lying to Palaton.

"I suppose you saw the censureship broadcast yesterday. I'm in trouble again."

"But for all the right reasons, as usual," Hat said impassively.

"There are greater loyalties than to one's House," Palaton told him. He would not say it more directly than that, for if he had to, no such loyalty existed between him and Hat anymore.

Hat's dark eyes met his uneasily. "I'm sorry I cannot help you."

The comradeship and bond between them had been denied. Palaton nodded, saying, "I understand," though he did not, and then he said farewell. He darkened the monitor without waiting for Hat to answer.

Nedar came out of the blind corner of the study where the monitor could not perceive him. "What was he about, do you think?"

"I think," Hat said bitterly, "that he was trying to see if your body had come back."

"Ah! Do you know I had forgotten I was supposed to be dead?" The pilot laughed as he flung himself into Hat's favorite chair. "Palaton's troubles have almost made me forget mine."

Hat lowered himself to a second chair, one not built for his sturdy body. It could not take his mass and he was reduced to perching on it. "If he knew you were here," Hat said, "he would tear Blue Ridge apart to get at you."

"And he would expect you to tell on me?" Nedar arched an eyebrow. He fingered his glass of wine. "But he reminds me of something I'd forgotten. We are *tezars*. That is a kinship which runs through our veins, along with our blood." He tapped the edge of the glass against his chin. "Out of the mouths of enemies come certain, undeniable truths."

"What are you talking about?" said Hat, frustration darkening his face.

"Let me think on it a little longer. I'll let you know," answered Nedar thoughtfully. He lifted his glass and dashed the wine back.

If he could not even count on the support of his comrades, then he had to go to Sethu. If cleansing would lift the onus of the judgments he'd made, then so be it. But Jorana had not reacted well when he'd told her his decision. "No."

Jorana shook her head a second time. Strain showed in the delicate tracings of her face, a slight pinching about her nose, the fragile translucency of her skin. "I can't advise this. I have no way to protect you inside the temple."

Palaton said only, "There should be no danger. Even the Earthans can't afford to be that obvious."

She put her hand to her brow as if a sudden pain had struck her there. "May I remind you that it was the House of Earth which sent an assassin against you the last time you resided inside these walls."

"I'm reminded. But there was no evidence then, or now, that the attack was aimed at me specifically. It could have been done to weaken Panshinea." And if he could only tell her, Palaton could list a fistful of other enemies who might wish to strike at him.

A faint glittering came from the depth of her eyes. "Circumstances remain the same today. If you were the target, you'll be putting yourself within their reach again. If Panshinea is the target, there is no better way to weaken him than by bringing you down now."

He sat back in his chair. "There should be a chink in your logic, but I don't think I can find it."

"I would be very poor at what I did if I let you do this."

"And I have no way of knowing if I can ever be good at what I hope to do if I don't do this. The Prelates demand it of me. I've thrown enough customs in the face of the Houses by what I've done for the God-blind. I can't afford to break with any more traditions." He shuffled a report on the desktop. "Rindy seems to agree that it should be done."

"Rindalan is too close to the God-in-all now to see the face of Cho clearly." Jorana paced a step, turned and came back. "I love the old Choya dearly, but age clouds his judgment."

"What of Qativar, his second?"

"I'm not sure of him." She paused. The late afternoon sunlight caught and fired in her bronze, tousled hair. The image of her snared him, as a lantern might a moth.

He found himself staring and broke the spell by saying, "No background on him?"

"We have background. He's come a long way in the years you spent in exile. The order is desperate for young blood and he appears to have earned their trust." And she shrugged.

Palaton found himself smiling. "We, of all people, cannot discount intuition."

She smiled back. "No, we can't."

"Still," he added reluctantly, "this is a course I have to take." Another road pre-chosen for him. He felt hemmed in. He knew he took time Jorana didn't have, but he also felt reluctant to let her go. "What would Panshinea do?"

Jorana considered his question. The thoughtfulness showed in her voices as she finally said, "Panshinea would go, hoping to extract a miracle from bare rock. And if he could not produce a genuine one, he would do whatever was necessary to provide the illusion."

"Do you want me to work miracles?"

"Getting out of there alive and cleansed would qualify." Jorana paced a step or two away, then turned. "We don't even know if going will affect the censureship."

"No, we don't. But I can't sit here any longer, Jorana. I can't sit here and say, I did what I did because I have no choice. I've got a choice now, and I'm making it. If disaster follows, I'll deal with it. But what they and you and even Panshinea forget, is that as a *tezar,* I'm a damned good war commander. I won't let my wings be clipped so easily."

She smiled a little at the emotion in his voices. "All right. You're right. I did forget you're a pilot, with all that you're heir to. I'll make arrangements." She left him. Palaton watched her go before succumbing to the doubt which he had not shown in front of her.

What was a pilot without the powers which enabled him to master Chaos? What was he now? What would he be tomorrow? Did it matter what he had been and now could not be? Jorana did not know what it was she put before him.

Qativar radiated youth as much as Rindalan radiated wisdom. He entered Rand's chambers with a spring to his step and the boy watched him cross the room, wondering if Choyan children were like acrobats and ballerinas, touching ground only long enough to gather purchase to leap into the air again. He did not know how the Choyan reckoned age . . . he was young among his race or theirs, but what of Qativar? Old enough to have gained a position second only to Rindalan in the priesthood . . . but Rand knew from what had been left unsaid in his presence that Qativar was without equal in that respect.

"Alone again?" the priest asked, though it was obvious the quarters were empty except for Rand.

"Not now," Rand answered.

"Ah." The Choya smiled. "Then perhaps you might enjoy my company?"

Rand put aside any wariness, based on Rindy's recommendation of this vigorous Choya. With a foot, he dragged a chair close. "Have a seat. I get tired of talking to myself."

"Do you? Ah." And Qativar smiled again. "You have a quick and easy mastery of Trade, although you often use the lower form." He lowered himself into the other chair.

"Thanks, I think. I learned it at my father's knee." Rand sat back in his chair.

"From your father? What connection does he have with the Compact?"

"None. He hoped to. He was a businessman."

"I see." Qativar eyed him. The brightness of his eyes, thought Rand, was something that Rindy no longer possessed. Just as age wrinkled humans, it seemed to fade Choyan. "The Compact does not deal with Class Zed worlds on a very profitable basis."

"I know. But he wanted to be ready when we changed classification. He thought we would. He thought it was just a matter of time. He's one of those," Rand explained, "who think we have a great deal to offer."

"The enthusiasm of young races," responded Qativar, as if that explained something. He reached into his summer jacket and pulled out a napkin, unwrapping two sticky buns. "Dinner is a long time past. Hungry?"

They shared the sweet bread, licked sugary crumbs off their fingers, and sighed in contentment at the same time.

Qativar left the sticky napkin draped across the side table. "Rindy asked me to keep an eye on you. I think he thought perhaps our age would be a bridge to one another. He knows Palaton is busy weaving himself into the pattern of the emperor's politics. That can't leave much time for you. You must have questions?"

"I don't know enough to ask." Rand licked his lips a satisfying last time. "I know Rindy was upset when Palaton insisted on bringing me tomorrow."

"That's understandable. Religion is a private matter, even among Choyan."

"Will I cause him trouble?"

Qativar shrugged. "Either the Earthan priests will accept you, or not. If they don't, this is only one way of smoothing Palaton's weaving. He needs to regain control over the commons. And he needs to prove his diplomatic ability among the Houses, which are squabbling louder and louder with Panshinea away. He has an advantage no other heir might have had: he's a *tezar,* and pilots are well thought of."

"But they wanted him cleansed for that."

"There's a reason." Qativar glanced down at the arm of his chair and idly traced a pattern in the fabric. "*Tezars* are often burned out by the work they do. It destroys them, slowly. If Cho is lucky, we have a *tezar* coming to the throne in the prime of his powers, virtually untouched by that burnout."

"If not . . ."

"It drives them mad," Qativar answered. "As evidenced by Panshinea's erratic behavior. The emperor is too far gone now to realize that he can no longer rule. It will be a struggle to replace him, peacefully or otherwise."

"Mad?" repeated Rand carefully. The other did not seem to notice his care.

"Eventual insanity is a hazard of dealing with Chaos. If we are lucky, a *tezar* has a long and fruitful life before coming to that conclusion."

He had never known. He knew that Qativar had settled a confidence on him, something those born off the planet of Cho were normally never told. *Palaton, facing insanity, as well as dishonor.* Rand felt the thought settle in him like a forewarning of doom. "And if Palaton can't pass the ceremony?"

Qativar met his look steadily. "He must. We need him on Panshinea's throne. If he's turned away . . . we might still save him."

"How?"

"A Congress of evaluation." Qativar stood up briskly. "But we'll cross that impasse when we come to it. Your presence is not a crux tomorrow, humankind. Palaton will succeed or fail on his own merits." The Prelate towered over him. "And that's the way it should be, should it not?"

Rand owed Palaton his life, and there seemed to be no

way to give it back. He thought of asking Qativar for help, and hesitated. He only knew he was a stranger here. He didn't know if he was among friends or enemies. Instead, he agreed with the priest and then let him out of the apartments, both grateful for and disturbed by the company Qativar had brought. Sleep took a long time coming.

Rand was not sure if he were sleeping, dreaming, or remembering when Palaton gently shook him. He had a vague sensation of tumbling in darkness when his focus sharpened and he looked into the alien face leaning over him.

Palaton said, "It's time."

Rand had a thought that he must remember this, that when he lost his sight altogether, he must retain the vision of looking into the proud, strange face of the other, the large expressive eyes, the awesome impact of the earless head sculpted into a massive bone crown that cupped masses of hair. Someday he would be returned and he would be in exile, and memory would be all that he had of this tethering with Palaton. He sat up. The room sorted itself into the various shades of gray dusted with illumination he had begun to grow used to. He stood up.

"We're leaving?"

"Almost immediately. Are you ready?"

"What are we going to face?"

Palaton turned to the bank of windows. "I don't know yet myself. Every religious ceremony is dependent upon the recipient. There are seven steps of cleansing . . . the priests may not allow me to continue when they discover you with me."

"It's that serious?"

Palaton nodded.

There had been nothing in the random images of Palaton's life which occasionally flashed through him to let Rand know what they were facing. He took a step, favoring his sore leg. "Leave me behind then. I can wait another day or two to get out."

"It's not a matter of that. I need you with me."

Rand thought of what Qativar had told him. "They'll be testing your powers?"

"No . . . but the absence of them may become quite visible. I've never gone through this before . . . empty."

Palaton's voices were so bereft that grief clutched at Rand's throat, stopping his reply. He clenched a fist. "I'd give them back," he got out, and stopped yet again.

"I know. And if I had the ability, I'd take them back, so long as it didn't harm you."

Rand leaned back against a chair for strength. "What if I were dead," he asked suddenly.

"Then all hope would leave."

"Are you so sure?"

"I am not willing to find out." Palaton put his hand out and brought Rand back to his feet. "There are Gods on your world, are there not? Then why are you so afraid to meet One?"

" 'Because' strikes me as the only answer I have," Rand said.

Palaton began to laugh as he escorted the other to the apartment doors. He paused long enough to pick up a light, Choyan summer jacket from the back of a door hook and to disarm the security system.

As far away as home seemed, nothing had prepared him for Cho. A leaden summer sky hung close over the city, waiting for the crack of lightning and the drum of thunder to loosen its tears. The street smelled of baking dirt and tar. Birds darted here and there after bugs which he could only catch glimpses of before they were snatched eagerly out of midair. He saw a small, scruffy looking animal race away from the tires of the conveyance, but it had gone before he could point it out to Palaton and ask what it had been.

Age hung as close over the city as the threatening storm. It curtained every major building, oppressive and dark. He saw walls so solid nothing might bring them down. Palaton caught the object of his interest.

"We build," the Choya said wryly, "for longevity."

"Nothing new?"

"Not in this sector. We build new for the commons. They're hardest on our resources. We have Housesteadings going back thousands of years."

"And where is yours?"

"I haven't one, now. My grandfather lost it to debts."

"What happened to it? It must still be there, right?"

"It's still there, but it's not available to any of my family. Someone took it over. Probably another Star, but possibly a Sky. Skies love to see another House fail. If you want to know what I call home, it's Blue Ridge."

"Blue Ridge?" Rand savored the name. He knew it from the overflow from Palaton. Cadets and barracks and steaming *bren* on deathly cold mornings, the wind screaming down off a blue mountain plateau, *thara* trees in bloom . . . yes, it had the feel of home to it. It reminded Rand most nearly of the New Mexico mountains where he'd spent part of his youth. Never mind that he'd never actually seen a frail, fernlike *thara* tree outside of his mind.

"Both the Householding of Volan and Blue Ridge are half a planet away," murmured Palaton.

"But not lost."

The other looked at him silently and Rand wondered if his stolen memories had left the other barren, if he had taken that away as well. His lips parted for a reply when the sight of a dark cloud of flitting, squealing shapes swooped over the dome of the conveyance, their passage rattling the windows.

Their wings thundered against the sullen air. He could see piercing beaks and bright quick eyes, watching him, watching them, as the flock passed over, wheeled in midair and turned into the climbing sun.

Rand turned his astonishment aside to see Palaton smiling. "Nightchasers," he said. "Noisy and spectacular. There must be a rookery close by. Perhaps in one of the parks." He settled back into his chair and closed his eyes, inviting no further comment and leaving Rand to soak in the sights of the fortress city.

The technology he'd expected was not to be seen though he knew it had to be there, layered underneath. When the clouds occasionally parted, what sky could be seen was a brilliant cerulean. If fires burned, they must burn cleanly. He watched out the side windows avidly, trying to catch sight of what this city took for granted.

The city sights had thinned considerably when Palaton roused from his meditation and opened his eyes. Rand was appreciating the wildflowers that dotted the empty lots and ran along the roadside, their faces mosaicking the countryside.

"What interests you?" asked Palaton, leaning forward.

"The flowers."

The other looked. "Daybrights," he named them. "They grow wild, like the weeds. By midday they will have faded, their blossoms as brittle as straw by nightfall, and their crumbled heads on the ground by midnight. But tomorrow morning, the new buds will be ready to open."

"They're strong."

"Strong?" Palaton's eyebrows arched. "They barely last a day."

"The bloom might, but the plant is everywhere. Think of the roots it must have. You don't irrigate out here . . . it catches water when it can. But still it grows. I bet if you stopped maintaining the roadway, it could push it aside, crumble it to pieces."

Palaton looked past him in silence for a moment, then said, "There are ways to measure strength. I was not aware of this one."

A hangar loomed along the roadway. Rand could see a skimcraft being readied, crew walking up and down the runway to fuel it and clear the area.

He glanced at Palaton. "You piloting?"

The other's skin darkened to a rosy hue. "Not this time," he answered. "And we haven't far to go."

Rufeen waited for them, her uniformed figure partially obscured by the squat tail fin of the skimcraft. It hadn't been built for speed, but for comfort. The Choya'i smiled broadly as she caught sight of them.

"Well, manling. You look a good deal healthier than when I saw you last."

"And you look . . . more uniformed."

Rufeen looked down. "Indeed, I do. This is what's expected of an imperial pilot. I think the colors suit me. Choya, shall we be seated? I'm told that commoners have found out we have flight plans and there is a demonstration march en route. We need to grab some sky."

Palaton muffled a sound, following Rufeen as she ducked her head and entered the skimcraft. Rand wasn't entirely sure what kind of sound it was that Palaton choked back, but the Choya's reaction had been interesting.

*   *   *

They followed the sun. It was still bright noon when they landed, and another conveyance awaited them. They had outrun the storm and the city. Here was country that was almost entirely barren, a near-desert ecology, open space running as far as the eye could see. There were no day-brights edging the runways, but Palaton took the time to point out the shrubbery laden with a starshaped yellow flower. "Tinley," he said.

Rufeen gave them an amused glance. "Starting with the birds and the bees, Palaton?" she asked.

"The boy has an interest."

"The boy has a thirst," she corrected mildly. She looked to Rand. "Take the throttle for me on the way back?"

"What?"

The Choya'i shrugged. "Piloting a skimcraft takes little skill. Want to try it?"

"Yes."

She ignored Palaton's hard look. "I'll expect you then," she said. "Don't let the Earthans make a convert of you."

Rand met her teasing glance. "They wouldn't try," he said, fairly sure of his welcome from what Palaton had said earlier.

"Perhaps. There is that about you which does not feel alien. Who knows what an Earthan would try?"

Rand watched her turn her mocking stare aside and grow quiet. He looked at Palaton. "Are they so different?"

"Yes, and no. There are three major branches of Choyan: Earth, Sky, and Star. We're Stars. The Earthans are less technological, more empathetic with nature. Their skills run to agriculture and animal management. They're also used to being a buffer between the Stars and Skies. They're always searching for the equilibrium of things. Making an alien a religious acolyte might appeal to that search and balance. I don't recommend you do it, however."

It took Rand a bare second to realize that Palaton teased him a little, as well. "Rufeen," he asked, "what about letting me try a landing, too?"

Palaton's head snapped back to study him while Rand kept his face bland and Rufeen burst out in laughter. It took a moment for the tension to fade from Palaton's jaw-line, and he gave a tiny nod of concession to the human. Rufeen put a hand to Rand's wrist.

"Look, there," she said. "Over the next rise."

Rises gave way to foothills and foothills to cobalt mountains, shadowing even the sun in their vastness, growing not distant but formidably close, and before them he saw the building.

It had been a mountain once, before being sculpted down and tunneled through to become a temple. Rand saw it rise on the horizon, intricate, commanding, graven in blue and white stone. The sheer beauty of it stung his eyes as the conveyance pulled closer.

Spires pierced the skyline, and the foundation straddled the earth solidly. Archways and gateways offered a maze of an entrance. The windows were open to the elements and a faint wind whistled through their shutterless hollows. It would be as tall as a New York skyscraper and as vast as a city block when they reached it. Rand looked at it and realized that anywhere else he would ever journey, this temple would remain forever in his memory as one of the wonders of civilization. As they drew nearer, he marveled at the stonework.

He had never seen rock or marble like it. It reminded him of the only time he'd ever seen the Atlantic Ocean, stormy blue laced with gray and creamy foam. As he looked at the temple, it seemed to him that the very sky above, clear and far from the storm which had threatened Charolon—and even the white diamond of the stars in it— was being drained away, funneled down into this temple, and forced to root in the earth.

He found his breath. "Do they know what they did?" he asked of no one in particular.

"Yes," responded Palaton's low, rich voices. "We believe they did, as ancient as it is. They tied the sky to the earth and even the stars did not escape them."

As Rand dropped his gaze, he saw the robed Choyan pushing out to meet them. The conveyance huffed to a halt and settled on the valley floor.

Palaton ducked his head and got out. He reached back for Rand, saying, "One battle at a time, the war will be won."

Rand felt his heart thump in response. How difficult would it be to fight a people who could see God?

Chapter 16

Qativar threaded his way across the darkened bar, pausing now and then to cast a harsh glare at any Choya who dared to lift a hand to him, his face bleak and scowling in the dim lamplight. He saw his quarry on the diagonal and his scowl deepened. He joined the bulky, broad-shouldered Choya, his voices lowered and pitched so only the two of them could hear what was said.

"I told you I never wished to meet with you in public."

"Public?" Malahki pitched his voices in a like manner, difficult for him, and the gold in his eyes sparkled like ore in a deep, dark mine. "The scum of the earth drink in here. If any were sober enough to see you, I doubt they'd know or remember you."

"I did not," Qativar answered as he seated himself in the booth, "get where I am trusting to chance."

"Nor I." Malahki put a hand out and pinned the other's wrist to the tabletop. Underneath the transparent top, a child's game of illuminating patterns was inlaid. Most of those patterns could no longer be lit by the dwindling psionic power of their race . . . but one or two of them now flickered briefly under the onslaught of Malahki's barely contained rage.

Qativar let himself be held for a fraction of a second, then he twisted his wrist free of the hold. Malahki's empty hand fell to its back, palm upward, fingers still grasping, and Malahki left it in that position.

"Have you what I asked for?"

"I have," answered Qativar evenly.

"Then give it here." Malahki twitched his fingers.

"I might ask what you intend to do with it first. *Ruhl* is difficult to procure."

"Not by you it seems, and I might ask the same of you."

Qativar slipped his hand inside his summer jacket and produced a minute vial, liquid gleaming inside. "I doubt if my uses for it are the same as yours." He pressed the object into Malahki's callused palm.

Malahki's hand sprang shut like a trap. He pulled the object to him and secreted it inside his waistband. "An aphrodisiac has but one or two qualities."

"*Ruhl* is powerful enough to make any of the Housed lose their minds for a cycle or two." Qativar was rewarded by surprise in the other's face.

"Not unless used in nearly toxic quantities."

Qativar shrugged. "You have your weapons, I have mine. Either way, the commons will be free some day."

Malahki rocked back in his chair, feigning nonchalance. "You and Chirek have your ways. Both of you think I know nothing of either . . ."

"We're on the same side by chance," Qativar interrupted, his blue eyes hard and cold in the corner's dim light.

"But with the same end in mind."

"I do not speak for Chirek. He goes among the commons, ministering to them. I go among the Housed, lying to and cheating my enemies. I think my method may prove to be the more valuable."

Malahki stood. He patted his waistband to reassure himself the vial was still there. "Regardless. Thank you, Qa—"

The priest stopped him with a slice of his hand through the air. Malahki halted with his head up, for a moment looking for all the world like a wild animal caught in a sudden, blinding beam of light. He blinked once or twice and then pursed his lips.

"I stand corrected," he said with irony. He gave a half-bow and left.

His order of wine came to the table and Qativar sat looking at its golden hue. After a moment, certain that no one followed after, the Prelate raised the glass to his own lips and drank.

Ruhl muddied the senses. It would so disturb the *bahdur* of a Choya that it was like an extreme intoxicant. Impregnation among the Choyan was a choice of both sexes, and both must cooperate, to be fertile. But *ruhl* changed the rules of that choice ever so slightly. Qativar wondered whom Malahki intended to drug, and why. It would be interesting to know.

As for himself, he had an entirely different use for *ruhl*. In his laboratory experiments, he had almost standardized the dosage, to thin out that threshold between intoxication and toxicity. He had succeeded in reducing *bahdur* to a minimal level . . . a level every Choya, even a commons, could achieve. If he could make it permanent or even stretch the effect to a considerable amount of time, say twenty cycles, he could homogenize his people. Genetic superiority which was kept closed by the Housed would be no more.

And if *bahdur* could be reduced by drug dosages, then it stood to reason it could also be enhanced, under controlled circumstances . . . anyone could then become a *tezar* . . . drink the right drug at the correct dosage and any Choya could master Chaos.

And he would have the key to doing so.

There would be no more burnout . . . and no more Houses trading on inherited superiority. There would be a world of commons, with access to excellence if and when it suited the common good. The Choya who would be emperor, then, would be the Choya who had brought this profound change to their world.

Oh, he and Chirek were on the same side, all right, but Qativar sincerely doubted if they had the same motives. Chirek believed that the Being of Change who would someday move among them might be a Choya who would bring the barriers of the Houses down, allowing intermarriage and commingling of the powers which had kept them so separated. Qativar also doubted that one individual would have the power to so collapse the Houses. That would be a matter for revolution, and revolution would destabilize the planet enough that the Abdreliks, the Ronins, perhaps even the Ivrians and Nortons would come swooping in like scavengers to pick them apart.

Besides, though rare and seldom acknowledged, there were Housed who strayed and sired offspring with the Godblind. It was this constant interflow which kept power springing up among the commons, sometimes even input strong enough to make a child talented enough for a Choosing. But no Being of Change had come among them yet, no one Choya powerful enough to turn the class structure of Cho inside out. Not yet. Unlike Chirek, Qativar had no desire to wait for a miracle of birth. He trusted to scientific progress for his hopes. He had thousands of commons willing to volunteer, in exchange for the future. It mattered not to him whom he might sacrifice in attaining his goal.

He put down his empty wine glass, concentrated on dimming the light in the bar even more, then left.

Rufeen took a look at the committee of Prelates gathering on the pink and beige sands, with communicators orbiting their ranks like scavengers, and said only, "I'm staying with the ship." She rocked back on her heels, with a stubborn twist to her lips.

Palaton answered mildly, "As a *tezar* should."

She looked at Rand, crossed one eye in mocking solemnity, and disappeared back into the cockpit of the ship.

Her levity had struck through the shell of nervousness beginning to wrap around Rand. He gave a quavering laugh. Palaton looked down at him.

"Ready?"

"I don't know yet."

"Remember to shield your mind. Remember who and what we're among. Those who join the priesthood are among the most sensitive of the Choya. They will be able to divine what you are."

"And what you're not," Rand answered.

A look not unlike fear passed quickly over Palaton's features. He nodded then. "That is a possibility. I'll face it if I have to." He took a deep breath. "Sethu is ancient, even among my people. *Bahdur* is probably ingrained in its very rocks." He looked down the ramp. "They're waiting."

A Choya'i stood to the fore. She was Earthan, of course, her mane braided back where the sun put chestnut streaks in the sable tresses. She did not have Jorana's sleekly elegant form, but she did carry beauty and power only partially hidden under blue robes so dark they appeared to be black at first glance. Her eyes of purest brown took a steady, even measure of Rand even as the priests gathered behind her shifted nervously and would not meet his curious gaze. They were all dark-maned and dark-eyed, similar to the Skies although the Skies generally had light colored eyes and even darker hair. But the Earthans had not the slim, tall lines of the Skies whom Rand had met; they were a solid people, like the rocks and dirt of their world. Earth, Sky, and Star, Rand realized, all had distinctive body characteristics and coloring, while the commons were a muddied pool of all and none.

The Choya'i extended a hand to Palaton. "I am High Priest Tela," she said, her voices an incredibly beautiful soprano, one an echo of the other. To hear her made Rand shiver. What a singer she could have been.

He put out his own hand for the Choyan touch of welcome. The High Priest looked at him and hesitated just a moment before touching upward palms with him.

It was not fear he felt or saw, but a lightning moment of distaste. "Thank you," he said, "for welcoming me."

There was no reaction on Tela's broad face. She either did not hear the irony in his voice or did not condescend to react to it, although Palaton flicked a quick look at him. Tela dropped her hands and folded them. Rand watched her, wondering if she fought an impulse to wipe them on her robes.

"Your acknowledgment of welcome is premature," she said to Palaton. "We do not know if we will accept the humankind. We have not yet decided if the sacrament will be breached."

"And I have had such poor manners as to have forced him upon you," responded Palaton. "But he is my ward, Prelate, and as such, I was loath to leave him behind."

"We have a life," Tela told him, "that does not bear off-world scrutiny."

"As I am well aware, having been off-world most of my adult life." Palaton's jawline stayed tense and Rand realized that they fought with words, as if in hand-to-hand combat.

Tela's right eyebrow arched. "And I am reminded that I, as a simple priest, have not." She looked at Rand. "We believe as we do for our own survival," she said. "The plague of Fangborn's Century, among other reasons."

"As we reach out to others, for our own survival," Rand answered.

"Yes. Your world has many problems it has not solved.

It would be well to know that some problems are never solved, that the process is an ongoing attempt, and that one can never cease."

"But some ideas are better than others," Rand came back, "and some avenues ought to be taken. We only want advice from those who have experience. We can't afford to make a wrong choice."

"Perhaps," suggested Tela mildly, "you've already done so."

"Then," Rand said, "tell me and I'll try to do better."

"Do you speak for all?"

"No. I don't have that right. But I can be a messenger."

"Interesting." Tela raised her rich, brown eyes to Palaton. "He does not retreat, does he?"

"No. Just because he needs my protection doesn't mean he's craven." Palaton put his hand on the back of Rand's neck where it appeared to rest casually, but the index and thumb pinched ever so slightly into Rand's muscles. He stood very still.

The High Priest looked back to Rand. "You're aware, are you not, that you've chosen a hero for your guardian?"

Palaton's fingers pinched slightly deeper. Rand swallowed before answering, "If honesty and integrity are heroic, yes."

"Ah! He's not aware of your exploits as a *tezar*?"

"No," said Palaton evenly. "He's not been enlightened."

The priest smiled. "Perhaps he should be." She turned on her heel. As if suddenly aware of the communicators and all those third eyes watching her closely, she put her shoulders back and held her horn-crowned head a little higher. "I am not convinced that it is necessary the manling accompany you."

"I was not aware I had to convince you," answered Palaton. "Nor do I know of any argument which I could use. Either you do, High Priest, or you do not make this allowance. If you do not, I will return to Charolon. If you do, I will return to Charolon. How important and successful the interlude, is up to you."

"Yet you came to Sethu."

"Yes. I came because I've been away from Cho for many years, and my soul hungers."

She looked back over her shoulder as if struck. Rand felt

Palaton's hand close tighter. The Prelate asked, "And does the manling also have a soul?"

Rand answered for himself. "We think we do."

"Thinking so is an important step." She turned around again. "We have much to consider, my Prelates and I." With another glance at the communicators who seemed to obey an invisible borderline of how close they could approach, she drew aside the group of priests and acolytes who had accompanied her though all had remained silent throughout the exchange.

Palaton dropped his hand from Rand's neck. He shrugged to relax his own suddenly cramped muscles.

"How successful were we?"

"I don't know," Palaton said quietly. "She and the others undoubtedly had their minds set before they came to greet us. Having made the offer to me, they could scarcely refuse the sacrament out of hand when I appeared with you." He turned his back on the group. "Sethu is isolated now. At one time, these sparse foothills were a forested country. Rivers abounded. The Earthans led a full and bountiful life here."

Rand looked toward the horizon, a high desert profile, which was difficult to imagine forested. "What happened?"

"We logged it down. But before that, we were so populous here that we even changed the weather patterns. Our technology, our very presence built up a huge thermal dome of air, changing the jet stream permanently. We lost the rain. When we lost the forests as well, with the watershed, we lost everything. We could terraform it now . . . we know how to do so, but it makes little difference. Over the thousands of years, it has adapted permanently to its climate, and though you can make the desert fertile to some extent, you can't maintain it unless you change the weather pattern again. That we cannot do without affecting other areas. So we balance. We only balance."

"No permanent solution?"

Palaton came around to face him. "The only permanent solution to life," he remarked, "is death."

Rand felt cold even in the heat of the sun. He shifted uncomfortably. "Tell me what Fangborn's Century is."

"Fangborn was an emperor. The last of the Skies. They gave us space, you know," mused Palaton. "We Stars took it from there after Fangborn, and kept it."

"He brought plague to Cho?"

"Unwittingly. With the first trade between other species. We were hard hit, and at first, our epidemiologists didn't know it was an alien infiltration. It's a convenient excuse to remain xenophobic. My people hide behind it, thinking to protect what they are." Palaton spoke softly, so as not to let his voices carry.

Tela came away from her group. She set her chin. "I cannot force my priests to work with you," she said. "But they have volunteered to accept your presence, citing that your affiliation alone with the humankind is a symptom of your need. We do not know if the . . . other . . . has a soul or not. Perhaps this would be an opportune time to observe and decide, if Cho is to be drawn into conflict with the Compact over such a species. Therefore, we have decided to take both of you in." Her eyes glittered at Rand. "Fair warning, manling. We *will* search for that soul of yours."

"Good news," muttered Rand, "you're in. Bad news . . . they intend to dissect you."

"What was that?" asked Palaton, bemused.

"Nothing. I hope."

Chapter 17

"It's blasphemous," Hat said, clearly disturbed. "The communicators only have reports, but it's said the priests took them both in, the humankind as well."

Nedar studied his boots, crossed at the ankles, as they rested on the priceless *giata* wood table in Hat's private quarters. "What could they do but rely on reporters," he countered. "Communicators aren't allowed on temple grounds. They can only get so close." The great unshriven of their society, media manipulators had centuries ago been excommunicated from the temples of every House.

"It's not that." Hat perched on the edge of a great study table. Its slab of gray marbling, and the heavy-bodied Choya's shadow in its reflection was just another dappling of its smooth surface. "He took the other with him."

"He only pulls his burial shroud closer around him," Nedar said, dropping his feet to the floor and sitting up. "It's getting late. You have cadets to chaperone. They did well today?"

"Well enough." Hat rubbed red-rimmed eyes. "Our numbers dwindle, Nedar, and there seems to be little I can do about it. To fail at becoming a *tezar* often means dying in the attempt—and yet, those who perish have *bahdur* bright enough to bring them here. If not lost to death, what might those lives do for Cho? Why should we lose them to death if they're not good enough to fly?"

"You would change the qualifications to pilot?" Nedar's voices sharpened, but the weary schoolmaster did not seem to notice his tone.

"Oh, no. No. It just seems a waste. Failure ought not to bring death. We're losing our *bahdur* generation by generation."

Sometime during Nedar's absence from Blue Ridge, Hat

had obviously been influenced by some of the radical philosophers who were part of the Choyan fringe. The pilot did not believe in such philosophies, but it was obvious that fatigue, like wine, brought Hat's melancholia bobbing to the surface. He cupped a hand about the other's shoulder. "You worry too much when you're tired."

Hat lifted his head. "The glider trials start tomorrow."

Nedar had not been paying much attention to Hat or the cadets. The information startled him. Tomorrow would bring death close, without a doubt. There were always cadets who could not fly blind. "I hadn't realized. Hat, it's for the best. We both went through it. It's our first law: nature selects for survival. A *tezar* cannot master Chaos unless he can fly blind, dependent only upon his *bahdur*. Everything happens for the best."

Hat looked at him steadily. "I wish I had your confidence."

Nedar gripped the other's beefy shoulder tighter. The brief thought that Hathord was out of flying shape, out of his prime, went through his head before other, more powerful thoughts flooded in. "You forget your House, my friend. You were born to worry and nursemaid, as well as to fly. The cadets don't know how lucky they are to have you as flightmaster. Tomorrow will take care of itself, and we *tezars* will take care of Cho, as we've always done." He released Hat. "Are the corridors empty? I have a hankering to sleep in my old quarters tonight."

"No one dares venture in that wing anyway. You know the superstition . . . they fear treading in a pilot's footsteps until they themselves have their wings. I'll have a breakfast tray left here waiting for you in the morning. We'll be at the plateau early."

Hat took far greater care than Nedar did at hiding the other's presence in the school. But that was the difference between the two of them. Hat did not know what he could do to undo a sighting if Nedar were found by one of the cadets, so he used all the caution he could to avoid the problem. Nedar had already decided upon a permanent solution if the problem arose.

"Tomorrow will take care of itself," Nedar said. He left Hat leaning upon the *giata* table, musing at the shadows about him.

It was a cold, brisk night at Blue Ridge. He pulled his jacket closer about his shoulders as the weather permeated even the enclosed corridors between the wings of the various barracks and halls. He took care to muffle his steps as he walked, not from caution, but to keep his thoughts clear, for there was a torrent of them, a flood, set off by word of Palaton.

Palaton did not hide in disgrace. No. He'd had Cleansing offered him on a silvered platter by the damnable order of priests, a hierarchy which defied even the boundaries of the Houses. To be sure, each House had its order, but they wielded power regardless of their House and Householding and well the smug bastards knew it. So why this concession to Palaton, who had brought the commons thronging into the streets and seemed unable now to disperse them? Who had brought the tainting footsteps of a Class Zed being to Choyan soil? Why?

Because Palaton was favored and he was not. Despite all that he had risked and lost for Cho, he was outcast. Burned out. Forsaken by all but Hat.

It would not be so if he had his soulfire. That possibility among all others leapt high in his frenzied mind. It would not be so if he had *bahdur*.

And despite Hat's fear of the morning, if the cadets slept lightly, they didn't do so out of worry. They would be pumped, waiting, agonizing over the first break of light, primed to do that for which they had been trained their whole young lives . . . to fly! To cast themselves into the wind and control a winged machine to keep themselves aloft. Their zest would blaze tonight. He could almost taste the sparks spilling out, fizzing along the stone corridors, bouncing like drops of water in a searing hot pan.

A gnawing hunger opened inside of him and Nedar came to a halt in the empty corridor. He rubbed a hand across his brow as if he could brush away the blurred thoughts and concentrate on the keener ones. They came in a crystalline rush. For a moment, he stood appalled, and then his old arrogance cloaked him.

Whatever morals bound him, he tossed them aside. He deserved it more, and without further rationalization, he turned abruptly and made his way to the wings where the young cadets were housed.

He made his way outside and stood in the gloaming where they could not see him, and heard them from their windows. Hat must sleep the sleep of the deaf and dead, if he thought his students safely abed. They sparred and gibed at one another and, for a moment, Nedar fondly remembered his old days.

The glow of memory sped away. As he had thought, he could taste the spillage of their power, wasteful, sparking and fountaining with no purpose or even a care to its usage. He stood, and his lips opened greedily as if he could sip the *bahdur* from the cold night air. His nostrils flared as if he could gulp it down. His heart pounded as if it, too, sensed the nearness of that which was more than life to him.

Bound in that temporary ecstasy, he thought more of what he intended to do and why he should and should not do it. He hesitated, and then shrank back against the walls as a cadet leapt out of a window with a crow of triumph.

They'd wrapped his head with a scarf, blinding his eyes, and pushed him from the high-ledged window. He landed deftly enough and, with an arch of his back, flung his hands into the air in triumph.

"I've landed!"

Fog puffed into the air with his bellow. A Choya'i leaned out above him. "See! I told you he would land heads up."

"It takes more than that to make a pilot!" Two windows down, a volley of protests and goodnatured teasing.

The blindfolded cadet tore his scarf off with a flourish. "Have I won the bet?"

"No! No!"

"What? You want me to fly higher? Very well." The student stuffed his scarf into a pocket and began to scale the building, climbing to the third floor roof.

The windows sprouted Choya, all looking and hollering at the cadet. They lay on their backs to look upward, half-in and half-out of their rooms, their warm voices issuing wisps of lace upon the midnight air. Some coaxed him down, others called for peace and quiet, and some urged him on.

Nedar watched, his own breath caught in his throat, for the cadet reminded him of himself, brash, daring, talented. He saw the Choya wrap another blindfold about his eyes.

A last jeer. "No fair levitating!"

The cadet snorted back a disdainful reply and then inched forward until his booted toes hung over the edge of the roof. He bounced a little on the balls of his feet. Then all grew still.

The night breeze teased the end of his blindfold, snapping it behind him. He poised on the brink and Nedar wondered what doubts might be running through his mind. Would his power guide him to a safe landing? Would he twist an ankle, break a leg . . . or tumble in sudden panic and fall to an unexpected death?

The Choya snapped upward and leapt outward, his arms extended, and he threw his body into a gravity-bemusing somersault. The scarf streamed behind him, a white streak against his face that cut into the dark envelope as he plunged. His body rolled and twisted slowly, seeking centering and ground. If he fell on his neck, paralysis would be the least of his worries.

He came down feet first and his knees gave to take the shock, but he stayed upright. The Choya took a deep breath and then straightened once again. Nedar saw the tremble of his hands as he threw them into the air.

The roar of approval cut off abruptly. Heads popped back into the windows in sudden silence. A lone voice called out, "Threlka! The proctor's coming through. Take the back door in."

Lights went out and the bank of windows fell into moon-scored darkness. Threlka unwound his blindfold, made a bow to the now nonexistent audience, and took a staggering step. He winced a little.

"Idiot," he said under his breath. He stuffed the blindfold back into his pocket and, hugging the wall so as not to be seen from the windows, made his way toward the back entrance, where Nedar waited.

The pilot could smell the spent *bahdur*. He could taste it. He could almost see the rippling aura about the weary cadet whose brash mood had been snuffed out so abruptly. He could hear the crackle, like summer lightning, of the power surrounding the other.

Through half-open lips, Nedar gulped down a whistling breath. The cadet heard it. He came to a stop and, eyes narrowed, peered toward the corner.

"Who's there?"

Their gazes met. Nedar, used to the dark, undoubtedly saw him better than Threlka saw Nedar. In that split second their eyes held, Nedar decided on his course and lunged. Hunger spurred him. Need closed the gap before their bodies met. The Choya shuddered in his grasp just before the cadet's neck twisted and gave with an ugly sound and the *bahdur* flowed out of him like water from a broken pitcher.

Nedar drank all that he could. It would not stay with him. It would run out of him just as it had run out of the dead cadet. He could not bond the *bahdur* to stay within him, bank its fires, use it sparingly. He did not care.

For the moment, he was full.

The deed over, he stayed in the shadows, the cadet's sagging weight in his arms. Then Nedar looked up to the roof. He took the body with him, affixed the blindfold and kicked it off. In the morning, cadets who'd drunk too much would swear that Threlka had made the jump safely, but with the body before them, with the overwhelming evidence in front of them, it would be obvious they'd been wrong. Or, perhaps, that Threlka had made a second jump, unseen.

It would not matter. The cadet would be dead.

It did not matter. Nedar moved quietly across the roof and marveled at the auras rippling in the nighttime sky. He'd forgotten how bountiful the power could be. He vowed he would never again be empty for long enough to forget.

Chapter 18

Bevan woke, for the fourth or fifth time in his recent memory, which, like the universe about him, seemed to be expanding and collapsing. He sat sullenly for a moment in the near perfect darkness of the eggshell raft, for waking was little different from being unconscious. His stomach roiled, protesting the lack of gravity as well as the need for food. He reached out blindly, found the water hose, pulled it to him, and took a sip to wet his mouth. The water tasted stagnant. He wondered how many days had passed. Three, perhaps, or four. Maybe only one, but long enough for the ship to have obtained FTL and then cast him off. He had been awake when that had happened.

Now he sat, catching glimpses of Chaos despite the shielded windows. His mind saw what his eyes had not been meant to. He could not shut out the random visions any more than he could control them. Helplessness flooded him. Never in his whole life had Bevan settled for being a victim. Not on the streets of Sao Paulo, where human life was less precious than garbage, which at least could be recycled. Not in the orphanage where his soul was one of many being harvested by the Theresites.

Illumination seared the darkness. Bevan put his hands to his head, clawlike, as if he could keep his brain from exploding. Chaos speared its way inward, frying his eyes from the inside out. He sat and rocked, moaning, his voice thin and distant until the vision fled, driven away by his frantic efforts. He dropped his shaking hands to his lap.

Impulsively, he reached out and opened the portal shield. The turmoil of Chaos boiled in front of him. His senses churned, keyed to the miasma, and he reeled back in the safety web.

But he could not turn his gaze aside, as the metal and

plastic of the life pod melted away and it felt as though he hung in the midst of all eternity. If there were a hell, this was indeed it.

But this could not be hell, for he rode the heavens, did he not, the starry firmament which ruled over earth and hell alike? Bevan writhed in his webbing, caught and dangling over an abyss of midnight and rainbow. His eyes watered at the brilliance despite the portal screening.

He cuffed tears away. He hung so long he became aware of the straps cutting into his limp form, and of the stale smell of his clothing, stiff with old sweat. There was a center to this Chaos and he had become it and, once having found a center, not all was as chaotic as he thought. He looked and saw a magenta river flow by. It curved across his vision, then plunged over a sudden cliff, dropping in a veil-spreading waterfall that boiled at its termination.

Bevan watched the river flow by again and again, to the same destination, until his mouth grew dry and he realized he'd been watching the phenomenon with his jaws agape, stunned at the sight. Fraction by fraction, he forced his head to turn, painstakingly seeking another pattern in the churning heavens.

He found a weeping willow tree, its leaves cascading to eternity like a shower of sparks from fireworks. Beyond, a cup spun alone. Then an immense butterfly swooped through.

Bevan grasped at that as if someone had thrown him a lifeline. The butterfly pattern was indicative of a random attractor . . . a planet or a sun, perhaps, for although the pattern seemed stable, it wasn't, but it was stable enough that something with an extreme gravity pulled at it and shaped it.

How had he seen such a thing? And, if seeing it were true, what did it mean to him?

Nothing. He was held in its grip, not it in his. And yet . . . Bevan clung to the hope, as he clung to his webbing, that if the butterfly held true, there was a chance of finding his way out.

He put his hand out. He touched barriers that his vision no longer illuminated for him. He was caged though he did not see the walls. His fingers played over the crude instrument panel of the life raft. There was little he could do to manipulate himself. But if there were a way. . . .

His sight abruptly failed him. He plunged into the abyss. His hearing picked up the thud as the portal shield came back into place, curtaining him away. The abrupt loss sickened him, disorienting him beyond caring, and he twirled in the webbing, sick and vomiting, his senses so distorted he could not control either them or himself. Mercifully, he lost consciousness again.

"The counties are restless," Vihtirne said. She sat by her monitor, nails tapping on the desktop. "I want a vote called."

The transmission from Charolon came in, streaked and faint. Sunspot activity, she thought, but narrowed her eyes anyway. "With Palaton gone for several days, now is the time to force the issue."

Asten was not within full focus range of the monitor. She caught only a glimpse of his three-quarter profile, and his glossy dark hair. The Choya, as was his duty, was intent on the activities within the Congress. She missed his sweet attentiveness, she thought, and tapped a nail on the mike and watched him start as the brittle sound of it reached him.

"I heard you," he said smoothly, and looked back at the camera. "I've brought some pressure to bear on Caldean. Let's see if he can withstand it. . . ."

Havoc reigned on the floor of the Choyan Congress for moments longer. Then a strong voice called out, "I question the placement of the contract."

Vihtirne listened with pleasure, her lips parting. Those strong tones belonged to Caldean, all right, and whatever Asten had done had lit a fire under the frizzy-headed statesman. He stood to the fore of the chambers.

"I have here financial statements which suggest that the Householding of Trenalle has overestimated its worth and ability to complete the aerospace contract as given. We all know that Trenalle is a venerable Householding of the Stars, but where is it written in stone that those who pilot for us must also build the cruisers? These figures tell me that the contract will be a burden for Trenalle and that the chances of the project being finished on time, on budget, are slim."

An elder Choya'i's reedy, thin voice cut through the sudden swell of sound. "Shut up and sit down, Caldean. The contract's been awarded. This discussion is moot."

All cameras, from Vihtirne's several monitors' viewing, focused on Caldean. He hunched his shoulders, bunching his body, and a stubborn look etched itself into his brow. "The contract is not placed if there is a question. And I question it, dear Sopher, and so should you."

The camera view swung to Sopher, a tiny bit of a Choya'i who looked as though all life's juices had long ago been sucked out of her and her carcass left to dry in the sun. True to the style of the last century, her horn crown had been shaved to the skull. Nothing gathered and bolstered her mane of hair, which age had thinned until little remained but singular long, silver strands. But her eyes did not know defeat. She put a hand to her throat, upping the volume on her broadcaster.

"I question the whole propriety of these proceedings. We have an heir to the throne. Why do we sit in session without him?"

"Because," and Caldean gave an exaggerated bow in the direction of his Congressional opponent, "these are urgent matters which cannot wait for the discretionary appearance of the heir. His vote is only good as a tie-breaker. This contract must be implemented as soon as possible, or Cho will lose the bid, and I'm told the Ivrians are waiting, beaks clacking, to take up the slack. I don't want to see this production go off-world any more than you do! We can produce these cruisers. But I strongly question the good judgment of handing them over to a Householding which teeters on the brink of bankruptcy. This contract will not save them, but rather will break their back. There is no wisdom in favoritism of this sort."

Sopher showed a tooth. "Financial attacks are even more insidious than moral attacks. Does Trenalle not get a chance to defend itself?"

The camera shot panned wildly as a weary Choya got to his feet. "The Householding of Trenalle," the speaker got out, "cannot dispute the facts on record. We do, however, dispute the conclusion. We need this contract. We can do the work on time." But the look on his face was one of defeat, as if knowing that the matter had already been settled.

Sopher, on her desk monitor, no doubt caught the same look. Vihtirne switched her camera selection to view the Choya'i as she pondered the Choya across the Congressional floor. Asten came on as an over-voice, "He knows he's beat and so does Sopher."

The Householding of Trenalle had always been shy of *forecasters*. They could not *see* the consequences of the contract, but could only hope. Caldean's objection, however, must have raised new doubts in a family already plagued with too much doubt.

"Now," said Vihtirne eagerly, "it remains only to place the contract." She went back to her main monitor to catch Asten's confident nod.

Sopher said, "I yield to Caldean. The contract must be placed with another facility." She consulted an electronic log. "An underwriting bid was presented by Householding Depner, of Sky. Does that meet with your approval?"

Another din of noise resolved itself in a call to vote, and when the voices had done rolling out, Vihtirne sat back in absolute triumph. Not only had the contract been snatched from the House of Star, but now it rested within the grasp of her own family of Sky, for Depner was a cousin. She had hoped for such results.

Asten murmured, lips barely moving, "I trust you are pleased."

"Beyond that, my love. The sooner your business is finished, the sooner you can come back to me."

The corner of Asten's mouth twitched and he moved his head quickly, out of camera focus, as if to avoid revealing more. The movement happened extremely rapidly, but Vihtirne noticed. May the seven steps be denied him forever, for thinking she might not. That he feared her, she knew. That he might loathe as well as love her, she had just seen revealed.

Vihtirne shut off her monitors and closed down the broadcast. She threw her mike across the room. Then, after a moment, a smile creased her face. What was such a tiny flaw in the face of such triumph, after all? And Asten dared not fail to return to her. Not yet, anyway.

She moved to thrust herself from the chair when a tiny noise echoed in the sound chamber. Vihtirne turned to face it, chin up, back stiff, not knowing if she faced a clumsy retainer or skilled assassins.

Nedar took three steps across the tiled floor. His handsome sharp-edged face showed more years than it had the last time he'd graced her with a visit, but the delineation only increased his good looks. He wore the black leather jacket of Blue Ridge and she wondered if he'd been hiding there, gathering himself and information, before answering her call. "He is too young to appreciate what he might be throwing away."

Those voices melted something hard inside of her. With Nedar, she could be all Choya'i, all curves and no edges. She had picked him to rule her, as, indeed, she had picked him to rule all Cho.

"Where have you been?" she demanded.

"On Palaton's heels, trying to catch the scraps. I wasn't fast enough with Panshinea. It seemed wise to give up the chase for a while. Palaton appears to be doing himself more damage than I could." Nedar stripped off his gloves. It appeared he had flown himself to her private airstrip on the Householding grounds. "Am I intruding?"

"Never." Vihtirne got up and closed the distance between them. Tall herself, Nedar was yet taller. She had to tilt her head back to meet his expression. "I missed you. And no one asked you to chase Palaton alone. That is what the House of Sky is for. That is what I am for."

He put his hand on the curve of her throat, caressing it, and then he rotated his hand about so his fingers rested on the back of her neck and he pulled her closer yet, so that their lips might touch. He said quietly, "I won't give the kill to anyone but you . . . when I have Palaton cornered, you will get first blood, my mistress." And he sealed that vow with a kiss which burned with his fervor and his *bahdur*.

She succumbed willingly and let him overflow her with his power. Of all the Skies, she thought, he was the most like her, twin to her in ambition and talent. He would not fail her. And as she gave in to his embrace, there was a tinge of fear which sweetened the eroticism. Nedar was more powerful than she. There was danger in this liaison. The knowledge made her blood run hotter. She had no choice but to surrender to these moments.

Chapter 19

The Prelate guiding Rand to his quarters stopped and opened a door. A sun-fresh smell flooded them. Rand put his head inside the doorway and saw a small but cheerful room. The priest pulled a flask from his belt. In Trade which Rand could barely understand, the Choya said, "Bathe. Rinse with this, for bathing." He let go of the flask hastily as if fearing their hands might touch.

Nonetheless, as the object bridged their hands, Rand caught a fleeting sense of loathing along with the fear. He gave a nod to show he understood and the Prelate took to his heels down the temple corridor.

Rand shut the door behind him. The doorway had arched overhead so high it might even dwarf Palaton's lofty height. Rand craned his neck to look up at it. Had Choyans grown smaller . . . or was this merely an architectural style? He did not remember the doorways of Charolon being so high.

The temple carried a sense of antiquity, like Charolon, but the room was also filled with objects that spoke of the kind of technology he'd missed at the imperial palace. Rand touched a light panel, and the sunlight flooding the room instantly dimmed . . . yet he was within rock. Looking about, he saw a chimney, its flue-opening actually a reflective panel. He touched the light again and the room brightened. Simple . . . if the roof were just over him. Interesting, buried in rock, just how might it be done to several hundred rooms and corridors? He dimmed the light down to an acceptable degree and left it.

His bag had preceded him. It lay on the Choyan long cot as if tossed there. He pulled out shirt and trousers, modified gear to fit his height and weight, the fabric tough yet soft to his touch. At the desk next to the cot, there were several appliances which did not respond to any attempt to operate them. Rand sat for a moment, arms on his knees, each hand filled with a recalcitrant object which did not seem to have an activation pad or switch. Yet they looked utilitarian enough. One he guessed to be a horn groomer of some sort, and the other a portable lamp which could be attached anywhere it was needed, moving the light source around the room. Yet he could not activate it as he had done the main system.

Rand tossed the appliances back on the desk. He shed his uniform and searched out the washroom. The shower was a light mist, easily adjustable by voice, though it was a bit slow to respond as if unused to Trade or his accent. He had thought himself grown fairly proficient in the language, particularly since his association with Palaton. Could it be they both spoke atrociously?

He opened the flask. A noxious smell made him jerk his head back. The waft of disinfectant nearly gagged him. Bits of stems and ground leaves flooded the liquid in his palm . . . made herbally, whatever it was. Almost reluctantly, he palmed his skin with the fluid. The misty shower foamed it up and as he washed and it foamed, the smell grew more pleasant until it was bearable. He scrubbed every inch of himself thinking that this procedure was at least easier and less humiliating than the decon he'd undergone at landing.

Scrubbed and dressed, he left his room in search of Palaton. He knew where the other had turned off, but went past the hall, for he found himself in a curvature of corridor he didn't remember. Rand retraced his steps to his room and opened the door. Yes, his worn clothes lay spread where he'd dropped them.

He'd seen no intercom. Rand closed his door and stood for a moment, thinking. There was a whisper of cloth on stone.

He turned. A tall Choya in a hooded cloak approached. The Choya paused, as though as uncertain as Rand felt.

"Prelate," Rand ventured.

The being drew close enough for Rand to see a heavily cheekboned face, eyes of gray and brown, and a wide, thick-lipped mouth stretched in an uncertain expression.

"Humankind," the Choya responded after a moment.

"Perhaps you could direct me. I'm looking for heir Palaton's rooms."

"Your guide?"

"Has not returned."

The Choya's nostrils flared as if sniffing Rand's scent. He felt the color rush to his cheeks. Was this being not going to pass him on unless certain he'd been disinfected? The Choya's face relaxed. He lifted a hand. "Follow the corridor at the third door. The door was open when you came through before. Now it is closed. You will have missed the corridor. Heir Palaton is occupying the room marked with the crescent moon and star."

"Thank you."

The Choya bowed with a rustle of cloak and hood. "It is nothing." He passed by Rand, moving with that same swift, long-legged stride of Palaton's that Rand could not keep up with.

Rand counted the doors down and found the closed corridor, as told. He entered it.

A chill hung here that he did not remember. The walls were bare, he thought he remembered friezes. His still drying hair clung damply to his skull and the back of his head, cold and stringy. He held little sense of direction since entering the temple, but his *bahdur* gilt sight seemed to be reacting oddly. It flickered as if being masked or drained as he went deeper down the corridor. At last he found the door marked with the crescent and star symbol and put his hand on the latch.

"Rand!"

Palaton called Rand's rooms and got nothing but silence. He toweled his mane off thoughtfully, wondering if the manling were still in the shower, although the water restrictions in use here scarcely made for luxurious bathing. He did not mind . . . bathing was one of the first rituals of cleansing he would face, and the underground springs here were legendary.

He did not like being separated from the humankind, but he knew he dared not make waves, at least not yet. High Priest Tela had been more cordial than he had expected, though he knew Rand walked a dangerous line between guest and prisoner. With Choyan courtesy, they waited for Rand to condemn himself. When that happened, they would act, but not before.

Yet even what the Earthan priesthood would do then, he could not predict. If this had been a Star temple, under Rindalan's influence, Rand would simply have been removed and returned to Charolon to Traskar's and Jorana's watchful care. Here, although not in the hostile territory they would have been in if they had gone to a shrine of the Skies, he had only his past history with the Earthan House to worry him.

If removing Rand would bring harmony and balance back to Cho, it might be conceivable Tela would order it. More than removal might be in order if the Earthans thought to strengthen their claim as a House Ascendant on the Wheel, whose time had come to occupy the throne.

Yet without Rand, he had no hope of completing this cleansing without being revealed. It was a calculated risk which Palaton would have taken willingly with his own life, but hesitated to do with another's, even a humankind's.

Palaton finished dressing and called again. There was still no response. He did not like the implications and, without waiting for the Prelate whose duty it was to guide them into the cleansing, he left his rooms in search of Rand.

He found the manling's rooms easily enough. As he opened the door, he could smell the herbal disinfectant's lingering aroma. He looked around and saw the room had been stripped of many of its amenities, most of them triggered psionically. *Keeping secrets*, he thought in amusement.

But Rand was not here. Palaton stepped back. He shut the door. He waited until the aroma which had flooded through the doorway had dissipated, then stepped several paces back the way he had come.

Yes. The aroma hung in the still air of the corridor. He hadn't noticed it before. The fragrance thinned as his body moved through it, dissipating the herbal scent. It took him to a closed corridor entrance.

There were symbols on the high arched doorway. Palaton saw them in alarm. If Rand had gone this way, he had blundered into part of the inner sanctum, where even Palaton hesitated to go.

He opened the corridor. Yes, sharper here, the herbal aroma. Palaton strode inward, hurrying, hoping that Rand had not gone where those not of the priesthood weren't allowed. There were chambers called the Ear of God carved deep in this part of the mountain. The corridor should have been locked and shut against any intruder. He could not begin to guess how Rand had opened, or even found, this hidden way. He removed his boots so they could not mar the hidden way, tucked them in his belt and entered hurriedly.

The corridor swallowed the sound of his running steps. It curved before him like the crescent moon of its birthing, and Palaton ran a good distance of it before he saw its end, shadowed and dim, and Rand standing there. The humankind had his hand upon a door of mysteries. Palaton recognized the sanctum with a gut-jolt of fear and cried out to stop the humankind from opening it.

"I'd like to know who directed you there," Palaton said, sitting on his cot and pulling his boots back on.

"I might recognize his eyes," Rand answered. "They were fairly distinctive. But as to the rest, his crown and such . . . no."

Palaton stamped his feet deeper into his boots before looking up solemnly. "They could have executed you if you had entered."

"Or you." Rand took advantage of Palaton's extra towels to dry his hair, which felt cold and clammy as though the corridor had been a tomb.

The pilot shook his head. "I know better. I wouldn't even have entered the corridor if I hadn't been looking for you."

"They separated us on either side on purpose."

Palaton nodded. "That is likely."

"Do you think Tela set me up?"

"I don't know. If she had, as High Priest, it's likely she's the one who would have directed you, to ensure the working of her plan."

"So someone else took advantage of an opportunity."

Palaton shrugged. "Speculation."

"They don't really want to kill me, but they wouldn't miss the chance if it came up."

"I think," Palaton said, "that you have the core of it. It would be wise to remember that next time you wander off."

Rand shuddered. He ran his fingers through his hair,

combing it into obedience. "You shouldn't have brought me here."

"I was hoping . . ." Palaton paused. "I am a religious being, Rand. I have faith in the rituals I grew up with, although they can't cure a *tezar* with neuropathy. I had hopes, if you were with me, we might accomplish that which we need to do."

Rand's turquoise eyes watched him closely. "Do you think so?"

"I hope so. This is not an area of rational thought." And Palaton gave a slight smile.

Rand thought of Qativar's soft advice. How far would Palaton go in endangering Rand simply to regain his *bahdur*, fresh and burning brightly once more? He looked at the other and for a moment, another vision blinded his eyes, that of Palaton pulling him from bombed out rubble on Arizar, saving him, embracing him in relief with the fervor of a mother for her child.

Choyan do not befriend humans, but he had thought that he and Palaton had that bond, and that he could rely on it. Now he did not know.

A soft knock on the door interrupted his hesitancy. It was the Prelate come to guide them.

The vibrations of environment-maintenance machinery hummed in his ears. The Abdrelik-comfortable air of the bay station sank into his lungs, humid and odiferous. John Taylor Thomas shrugged under the surveillance monitoring, uncomfortable and ill at ease, his stomach rebelling against the tranquilizers given him for a hasty FTL flight, and his inner ear telling him he was still not on solid ground. The Abdrelik scanning him made a smacking, growling noise in his ear and Thomas refrained from looking to see if the alien had drooled upon his shoulder. He had little else he could control here but himself and as for that, he clamped down rigidly. The Abdrelik finished his scanning and moved away with another barking grunt and began to scan the two men the ambassador had brought with him.

Something clanked within the staging bay. Thomas flinched, looked up, and heard metal groan. The artificial gravity of the satellite did little to quell his sense of being off-balance and he wondered if GNask had done this, too,

on purpose. Another clank vibrated through the metal
beams of the bay and then a portal began to blossom across
the bay from him.

Thomas felt his stomach clench. His daughter should be
with GNask. He had been promised and thus taken from
the secure neutrality of Sorrow of his own free will. He did
not think that GNask had chosen now and by this method
to end their partnership, though it was inevitable that one
day the Abdrelik would do so. The ambassador had little
illusions about the conclusion of their association, and, not
having them, hoped to avoid it. But today he'd chosen not
to avoid because he'd not seen Alexa in nearly three years
and at this moment he could not surrender to fear.

But all the same the palms of his hands grew damp and
he could not contain the tic along his jawline which deepened as two shadowy figures, one immense and the other
like a tiny, glimmering comet caught, in its orbit, approached. The Abdrelik wore only belted shorts and grip-
boots, his vast fleshed bulk like that of a hippo brought to
shore. The symbiont of the Abdrelik rested on his shoulder
as if it were a pet, stalked eyes watching Thomas inquir-
ingly.

"A happiness," said the Abdrelik, "which I promised
you." He hunkered down on his squat hindquarters and let
the comet shimmer past him, though the girl stopped of
her own accord within arm's reach of GNask.

"Alexa!"

She looked up, her pale face framed with lustrous dark
curls, her eyes deep within the planes of her expression,
their color lost to him momentarily. "Father," she answered
softly, but came no closer.

Thomas went cold. "What have you done to her?"

"I?" murmured GNask. "Nothing. Ask the Choyan when
we face them in court. If they will answer us."

Alexa brought her chin up. "Come as close as you
please, Father."

Her tone was chill, menacing and yet teasing, as if she
mocked his love and concern . . . and fear. Her eyes glittered in the shadows of her face. She held out a hand.

Thomas swallowed. He turned on one heel and snapped
his fingers. The second man in his employ came to abrupt
attention and strode forward, carrying case in his hand, and

before he reached Alexa, he already had a syringe in his fingers.

"You guaranteed her health and safety," the ambassador said as the man caught his daughter up and she let out a squeal of protest. "If you don't mind, I will prove it to myself."

GNask shrugged, an elephantine ripple proceeding down his bulk. "As you wish."

Alexa hissed with pain as the physician drew blood and skin samples. She fastened her gaze on her father and said nothing further as the physician proceeded with a cursory exam, hair, nails, scrapings and what other evidence he could take.

As the physician freed her, Alexa pulled back with a snap. "Happy, Father?"

"Not yet. But I will be." Thomas watched as the physician retreated across the bay, until the man was sandwiched between himself and the remaining man, a security enforcer. He pushed back memories of his child, his chortling toddler with a bold and lively sense of humor and adventure, shoved them down along with the gorge which had risen in his throat. The cold and capricious creature facing him bore little resemblance to the daughter he'd lost. "Are you well, Alexa?"

"Before you assaulted me? Passably. Lonely. I get very lonely among the Abdreliks." She ran her hand through her tangled curls and gave her head a little toss, actions at odds with her words.

GNask shifted his weight. She jumped a little at that and gave a slight, nervous laugh as she resettled.

"Is there anything I can bring you?"

Alexa looked at him in solemn thought. "Peanut butter," she said, finally. "I miss it. And coffee, perhaps."

"Books? Disks?"

"No. I have . . . no interests there." She looked over her shoulder as if to catch a signal from GNask, but none that Thomas could see had been given.

"I want you to come home with me."

This time GNask did move, his face rumpling up and then smoothing out, but Alexa had not turned to catch the expression. She only tilted her head again, eyes like deep coals, and said, "Someday."

GNask cleared his throat. "Our time has run out."

Unable to bear another second of the interview anyway, Thomas strode back, dropping into the brace of his escort. Alexa pitched forward and impulsively embraced him. She whispered, "Daddy," in his ear and then was gone before he could hug her back. The Abdrelik guard muscled Thomas and his two men into the outer staging area. The ambassador stumbled through as the portal clanged shut at his heels. He gathered himself and gained the boarding ramp of the cruiser waiting for him, the staging dock floor littered with fuel and power lines like webs trying to ensnare him. He made the cruiser just in time to be horribly, desperately ill.

His physician knelt by him in the narrow bathroom and passed a cold, damp cloth over his forehead, steadied his jaw, and wiped his mouth as well. "Better?"

Thomas gulped and rocked back on his heels, unable to get up from the flooring. He looked at the physician. "Did you get enough blood?"

"I think so."

Thomas squeezed his eyes shut as another wave of nausea ripped over him. "I pray to God so," he said and gritted his teeth.

"We'll know soon enough," the research physician answered with a great deal of satisfaction. He reached across the cruiser's toilet and mopped at Thomas' forehead again. "Now let's get you ready to go home."

Thomas turned and looked out the facility doorway, as if he could see through the cruiser's walls and across the docking bay, to where his daughter remained. "Not yet," he murmured. "I'll go home when my daughter does. Take me back to Sorrow."

The physician had no reply to that.

Chapter 20

"There are seven steps," Palaton said, his voices lowered to nearly inaudible, but he knew that Rand could hear him and, more importantly, that the other was listening. "Seven steps of contrition."

"I've lost count." Rand spoke as if he could not imagine the Choyan sinning, and Palaton smiled faintly in reaction to the tone of the other's voice. "How many do we have left?"

A pause came out of the darkness which enveloped the two of them inside the stone walls of the temple. Then Palaton answered, "For some, the bathing is enough. For others, nothing suffices." Palaton let out a heavy sigh. "The only cleansing I will find here will be for my diplomatic career." As to that, he expected limited success. The Earthans had shown their prejudice in quiet, subtle ways. The Prelate assigned to Palaton's cleansing spoke abominably bad Trade. Palaton had not known whether to take offense, for Trade was the second language of Cho and all generally spoke it passing well, but among the priesthood, there should be no need for use of a language not born on Cho. Therefore a priest might not have the Language mastery a merchant did. Had it been a reluctant concession of the temple-mates or had it been an oblique insult to the presence of an alien? And then there had been the intentional misdirection of Rand into sacred areas where trespass often meant death. Two quiet days had gone by since, if he could still reason time correctly and nothing further had happened overtly.

Now they sat in darkness, cleansing the sense of sight, somewhere within the labyrinth of the mountain temple, deep in the roots of the building, where building and sculpture ended and nature began. Rand had kept quiet until they were isolated here, cleansing their sight, so shut off by walls of solid stone that he'd felt free to speak.

"You must have a sense or two that I missed," Rand answered, finally, softly.

"Well, of course, there are the five of the physical body. Then there is the spiritual sense."

"That's six."

Palaton stirred uneasily on the rock which cradled him. For Rand to know of *bahdur*, to be carrying it, was enough of a betrayal of his people. To delineate the many ways in which it enriched the Housed, in which it was used in everyday life, went a step further, a step which Palaton was not willing to take. He said only, "And then there's *bahdur*."

"It's not the same?"

"No. The God-blind can sense God the way you and I can sense and detect the wind. They know the God-in-all exists because they see His works. But they cannot know Him directly."

"Yet all Choyan go through this."

"Yes."

"But how can it help the commons?"

The Choya absorbed for the barest moment how quickly Rand was taking in the world he'd come to. How quickly he'd referred to the God-blind as the commons. "Religious philosophy," answered Palaton, "abounded everywhere, but it was the Houses which organized it, and to be one of the Housed, one had to have *bahdur*. The Godless were administered to, to be kept in their place, to remind them what they lacked, to inspire them to achieve positions within Householdings if they could." *As if wishing to have* bahdur *might light its fire within their breasts,* he thought wearily to himself. *As if it might be something anyone could aspire to.*

"Why cleanse the senses?"

"Because any purification is a rebirth. You and I cannot be reborn, and neither can our worlds, but it became decided and known among our Prelates that the senses with which we perceive ourselves and our world *can* be reborn, cleansed, purified. And since most of the way we react is based upon our perception of the situation, change can be more effectively initiated if the perception is altered."

"It doesn't work for *tezars*."

"No." Palaton shifted again on the bed of rock. The sound he made was muted by the depths of the temple. "Not strictly speaking. In theory, each Choya is born with a bonfire, a soulfire, within him. It lights his soul, illuminates the way for him. When it is burned out, it is burned out. There is nothing left but ashes."

"Then how could I have helped you on Arizar?"

Palaton could sense Rand moving, sitting up, reaching for him across the cave darkness. "I don't know," he answered simply. "And those who could tell us are either destroyed or fled."

Gravel crunched underfoot. He smelled Rand before he felt his touch. The humankind crouched by the carved rock he lay on and took up Palaton's hand. The feel of the other's hand became intense . . . warm, strong, uncallused young fingers holding Palaton's fingers. He could feel the sparks of *bahdur* crossing, the boundary of mortal flesh and striking him, as if seeking to come home. He welcomed the shock.

"What is the worst thing a *tezar* can do?"

"Take a contract to attack other Choyan, I suppose."

"Has it ever been done?"

"Not before Arizar . . . and I can only think that those who piloted thought they were attacking renegades."

"Were they?"

"I don't know . . . yet. But I intend to find out."

Rand's hands seemed to cool in his. "What else?"

"Choyan who steal the *bahdur* from other Choyan."

"Steal it? Is that possible?"

"Rarely, but yes. It is a futile, horrible, parasitic crime." Palaton thought of Panshinea, who practiced it from time to time in a vain effort to keep his own power. He thought of *tezar* candidates he'd known when a cadet who fed off others only to fail themselves as well. "It is like pouring wine into a glass which cannot hold it. It will slowly drain away and it will take another death to fill it again."

"Taking *bahdur* causes death?"

"Generally. Do you see, Rand, how we took hope from Arizar? As Brethren, you seemed to be able to do what we could not do for ourselves. And we did not die relinquishing it—we only had to protect you from what you carried. The neural blockers the College developed . . .

blinded and deafened, the enormous sensory input you would have received otherwise became manageable."

"No." Palaton could sense Rand's shaking head. "Not all Brethren can carry *bahdur*. There were those who became insane on the upper campus. Bevan, Alexa, and I *saw* them. And there was a crematorium there, too."

"Then their sins are compounded. When I find them . . ."

They lapsed into silence and sat, waiting for the priest who could barely speak Trade to come and take them to the next step.

The solar of the temple was crowded with the priests and acolytes taking their late lunch. Sun streaked through the curved paned windows, striking the tables and diners below with hammers of light and heat. High Priest Tela paused in mid-step, then made a clucking noise and, tray still in hand, bypassed the solar and went instead to the eating nooks in the winter garden. She and the Prelate shuffling at her heels were the only diners there.

The Prelate, a thin, emaciated, nervous young Earthan did not sit comfortably opposite her, but perched, his face furrowed with anxiety as he began to pick at the meal he'd gathered on his tray. Tela watched him. He'd taken a buffet of every item set out for lunch and arranged it on his tray, but if he ate a tenth of what was before him, she'd be astonished.

"Kale, you waste food. Or perhaps I should say that food is wasted upon you. Either statement would be correct."

The Prelate paused, spoon trembling in his hand. His face paled. Like most of the priesthood, he shunned the facial jewelry of the Housed. To Tela, he looked like a blank canvas upon which nothing, not even life, had yet made an impression. Why, then, so much fear? So much anxiety?

Kale's lips worked before he said bitterly, "Do I have to take your insults as well? Was it not bad enough to give the heir and his foreign dirt to me?"

"You bear the burden remarkably well," Tela murmured and picked up her drink to sip it.

"More insults. I bear what I have to." He looked away from her, down at the neat mounds of food and began to pick at each, a morsel here, a morsel there. One or two he began to actually chew and then spit discreetly into his napkin.

"They seem to be courteous guests. Palaton, I would even venture to say, is among the more devoted of the *tezars* I've seen. As for the other . . . he keeps quiet and does as he's told . . . I don't think we could expect more of him."

Kale's gaze flickered up at her. "I don't know why you allowed it here."

"There is enough controversy stirring on Cho without adding to it." Tela picked up a greenfruit and crunched it. "Besides, no matter what we did, it would have caused comment. Beyond politics, Kale, our duty is to see to the spiritual well-being of our fellows." She paused to chase a bit of seed around her teeth. "How goes their progress?"

"We're nearly finished."

"So quickly? It's only been a few days."

"They cannot count time in the caverns, and I do not care to. A cleansing is not metered in daylight or night-time hours."

"Of course not." The High Priest smiled encouragingly. "You placed them last with the sightless?"

"Didn't I just say so?" Kale picked a forkful from a mound, tasted, then bolted down the helping as if starved.

"Actually, no." She picked up a slab of bread and mopped gravy with it. "Do you think Palaton gives full weight to the ceremony?"

Something stirred in the corridors behind her. She thought of Choyan leaving the solar and did not worry more. But Kale looked up, paled further, and gulped down an empty mouthful.

"What is it?" She swiveled about in her chair, to see a wing of Choyan enter, robed as acolytes, faceless within the depths of their cowls, weapons in their hands. The nearest one grabbed her shoulder with a hand of iron and the other following came forward with a scarf to muffle her cry of protest.

"It is nothing," Kale answered, as the Choya to the fore plunged his knife deep into the High Priest's breast and dropped her lifeless body to the slate flooring of the winter garden. "Not any more." He slashed a hand through the air. "You know where they are. Go. Go. I will not know further what you do!'' He sat down and began to devour every bit of food upon his tray, heedless of the body beside him. Or perhaps the murder gave him an appetite. He did not look up as the assassins left the winter garden and made a fleet-footed run toward the temple's labyrinth.

The stone drummed. He could hear its tonality in the very bones of his body, thrumming in his skull.

"What is that?"

Rand stirred. He let go of Palaton's hand and flexed stiff fingers. "What's what?"

"Noise. Quiet. Let me listen."

Rand had grown used to the startling idea that an earless people heard far better than he did. Perhaps the bone caught vibration and translated it. He listened, but heard nothing. He held his breath lest he disrupt Palaton's concentration.

"Runners," the Choya said. "Through the temple." He got to his feet and, searching through the darkness, gathered up Rand and got him on his feet. "No one runs in the temple."

"Urgent business?"

"If the business is that urgent, I don't want to be here to see what it is." He began to move, taking Rand with him. "Jorana will have my head for this, if I have one left for her to harvest!"

"What is it?"

"Death."

Rand stumbled. Palaton hoisted him up again, saying, "Use your senses."

"I'm blinded in this murk." Panic jangled his insides, but there was nowhere to go.

"No, you're not. Concentrate. You'll have to guide us both."

Rand had long since succumbed to the blackness of their voluntary tomb. He had spent half his time with his eyes closed, merely listening to the sound of his breathing and the Choya's breathing. Choyan breathed differently, a little longer, and a little further apart. Now he braced himself, with Palaton's hands hard upon his elbow.

"I need *some* light to see."

"There isn't any, not here. You're filled with the ability

to see what's beyond your eyes. Let it spill over or we'll both die here."

Rand tensed. "What if this is part of the cleansing?"

"It isn't." Palaton urged him a step forward. "We've got to get out of this chamber. When they bring light in with them, we'll be blinded. It will overwhelm us. We'll never see who struck us."

Pixie dust flowed from him as he squeezed his eyes tight and then tried to open them wide, to see, what was unseeable within the inky atmosphere. Like sugar sprinklings, tiny points of illumination dotted faint outlines of rock and boulder. Rand began to move forward, hesitantly, gaining speed as his feet proved his vision sound. He drew Palaton with him.

"Which way," he said, and his voice sounded unnaturally loud.

"Through a door, preferably." Palaton's voices, dry with irony.

Rand turned on his heel. There was a door back the way they had come. Palaton tugged on him. "Not that way," he said. "They'll be in the corridors."

"Then this way." He found another door, barely etched in the rock, a passageway confounded by the stonework itself, but his eerie vision found it and sparkled its outlines clearly to Rand.

The door would not yield to him. He ran his hands over the stonework, grit tearing at his nails and rasping the tender flesh. A nail tore to the quick and he swore at the sudden, raw pain. Then the door moved. Palaton stood with him, running his hands alongside Rand's, and it was the pilot who said, "It's balanced in the middle, not hinged to the side. It should be coming open now."

And it did, though the passageway was narrow and short. Rand put his hand up to Palaton's shoulders, saying, "You'll have to bend far over. It won't take your height."

Palaton's response, as Rand pulled him over and shoved him through, was too muffled to understand. The boy thought only that he muttered "Ancient." He waited until Palaton said clearly, "I'm through," before pushing in himself.

They shoved the thick and heavy door back into position behind them. The corridor beyond felt labeled with time and dust, like a shroud or curtain draping itself down upon them. Palaton shuddered.

"I haven't the sight to look at it," he said, "but I don't envy you."

"It doesn't look much different. This way." He put his arm about Palaton's waist, taking the other's arm and wrapping it about his shoulders, so they could walk in tandem, though it had to be uncomfortable for Palaton who had to stoop to Rand's height.

The other felt stiff in his embrace. Rand could feel the tension in the Choya's body. Palaton looked down at him. Rand saw a flicker of expression through his *bahdur* enhanced vision. There was conflict in that face. Did he not trust Rand? He unbent and leaned back down, gathering up Rand. Side by side, they fled down the tunnel.

They made good time shuffling through the fine, siltlike dust and age which layered the corridor.

No one and nothing had been through here in many a year. More than that, Rand could not clearly tell. "What if this is a dead end?"

"A possibility against a certainty? We'll take the possibility," Palaton said, his breath warm against Rand's ear. "Keep going. They have to be following. There are ways of tracking us."

They found a kind of lumbering speed and kept at it forever, until Rand's ears rang and he realized his heart raced, and the air he panted down seemed too thin and insubstantial to breathe. He staggered to a halt. Palaton let go of him and breathed heavily as well.

The Choya turned in the passageway. As Rand watched through weakening eyes, he paced a step or two forward, palms over the rock face.

"This tunnel is not hewed by craftsmen. We're in the belly of the mountain itself."

"Are we?"

"By the feel of it." Palaton straightened. "Though you can tell better than I." He rubbed his nose as if the dust tickled him. "Come my way. I can feel the air stirring. I think the passageway opens up again. Can you see?"

The flat, one-dimensional sprinkling of dust swirled into a diffuse cloud and for a moment Rand could see nothing ahead. Then he sensed that what he "saw" was open space. "Enough to think you're right. I can't see the floor well, though. It could be a pit."

Palaton strode forward, dragging his boots. He said diffidently, "Catch up when you have your breath."

Rand tried to reach out and snag him, but the other was gone, out of reach, enveloped by that swirling cloud of dark and golden sparks.

Chapter 21

Bevan woke, and knew it could be his last time waking, felt the feebleness of his heart rate and heard the shallowness of his breathing in his ears. *I'm little more than dead*, he thought, and added bitterly, *even the peace of dreaming is being taken from me*. His crusted eyes began to water, but whether they were tears or simply the effort of raw flesh to soothe itself, he did not know. He blinked but his eyes, so blistered by the sight of Chaos, took little comfort from the salty tears bathing them.

He hung in the safety webbing, his bones gone paper thin and brittle. His teeth wobbled in their sockets, so it was just as well the pod's solid food had long since run out. Better for his body, too. He was no longer strong enough to flush the excrement from the raft. He hungered though, and that was pain enough.

He reached for the sipping straw and let brackish water soothe his swollen tongue. He probed at the teeth he deemed most loose. They gave way before his examination, but stayed in their sockets though unsettled. Loss of calcium? Massive loss of mass? Bevan giggled at the thought. Perhaps his teeth were rooted solidly enough in his jaw and it was his brain which had grown loose.

Sleep still clouded his vision, for it appeared the life raft walls were solid again, between him and the warp of space they traveled. He knew better and when he was done gripping the straw with lips which felt like ground meat, and drinking water gone stale and hot, he spat the last swallow of water across the life raft. Gravityless, it splattered as it sprayed and droplets floated about. The recycled air was not humid enough, drying him out, and the spray would be absorbed soon enough.

Bevan narrowed his eyes and the solid walls faded until

he hung, suspended in black velvet, twirling like a emaciated and mummified spider in its web. He put out the hand of his mind, something he'd invented over the past many days, a projection only, he thought, and stirred the soup of Chaos. It roiled to his touch. The feel of it brought a certain satisfaction with it, rather like playing with mud as a child and squelching it through his fingers. Yet if Chaos were mud, then he could build with it, and this fabric was more elastic. He could trouble it for a while and then it would sluggishly slip back into its patterns as though it had rules and shape and conformity, which Bevan knew it could not. Nothing was as it seemed.

Yet it amused him to dip into the stew pot and stir it about. He did so again, stringing the substance like taffy not cooked long enough to hold and watched it drip and dribble off his immense imaginary hand.

The life raft shuddered. Bevan felt its jolting movement and stopped in his play. He licked his lips. The pod steadied and he hung very still in his webbing, as though his movement had rocked the tiny ship. He heard nothing, felt nothing more. Bevan laughed. He was ineffectual inside the raft, he could do nothing to alter his course nor save himself. The retros to bring them out of FTL drive would fire when the computer, if it still worked, had been set by the Zarites to do so. He could not signal for aid. In a matter of days, perhaps hours, he would no longer be able to drink or breathe, for the resources of the pod had nearly run out.

He stirred the slime of Chaos once again.

The life raft began a counter-rotation. He felt it slowly accelerate into a spin. And down, it was dropping down, he felt it in the sink of his gut. Bevan's forehead popped out in sweat, dehydrated though he was.

Yet a jolt of triumph shoved away the fear. It pierced him with revelation. The sweat dried upon his face as if it had never been, the air as thirsty as he had been.

"Son of a bitch," he murmured aloud through cracked and swollen lips. "I know their secret!" And he began to laugh at the simplicity of the revelation, never caring that the life raft was dropping like a stone down an empty elevator shaft, that his ears had begun to buzz with the heart rate of a racing engine, that his life was precariously on the line.

He reached out with his imaginary hand and *pushed*, shoving himself and the life raft into real space. The vehicle shuddered as it answered his call.

There was a moment of dead silence. Bevan clutched his webbing. The swirl of Chaos faded and the too solid walls of the raft returned, surrounding him, pinning him, down, encasing him, a death egg.

The life raft came out of the dead quiet with a cacophony of whistles, bleeps, and shrills as the tiny console erupted with signals, the pod eddying into known space, sending and receiving.

Bevan began to cry, his eyes burning to issue tears, his chest caving to breathe sobs. Now if only he were *somewhere* and someone was listening.

He could still come out of this alive. Perhaps even sane. Perhaps.

He waited, half-holding his breath, until the life pod began to jar and thud and he knew he'd been pulled into a hold. A teeth-rattling clunk made him gasp, and tears-brimmed in his eyes from the realization that he'd been found and docked.

The stale air of the pod exploded with a whoosh outward as they cracked the pod and Bevan sat, dazed and blinking.

A smooth-quilled Ronin leaned in. He looked about and saw Bevan dangling in the safety webbing. A broad grin streaked the ugly alien's face.

The irony of having come all this way only to fall into the hands of the Ronins struck Bevan and he began to laugh. But he could not stop, as his heart began to race and his head to pound with the laughter which sobbed in and out of him as if he were nothing more than a fleshly bellows.

Jorana entered security. The commons on the streets had calmed. Many of them had acquired day work permits over, the last several days and thronged only at night, clamoring impatiently for Palaton's return. Things appeared to be settling down, but the nerves in her fingers pricked at her, and her horn crown ached with worry that she had decided to assuage. "I want an update at Sethu." She narrowed her eyes to accustom herself to the slightly darker aspect of the room. Monitors of every size and shape lined the walls, viewing not only Charolon, but all of the counties. Security workers looked up, saw that she had arrived, and dipped their heads down quickly and busily.

The head of surveillance crossed the room, a plump Choya'i of the House of Star, with more gray than red-gold in her hair, and eyes of blue so dark they were violet. "I was just about to send for you." She drew Jorana toward the corner where the monitors were busily tracking the foot-hills of Sethu. "Rufeen just called in."

Jorana sucked her breath in, suddenly apprehensive. She sat down at a bank of monitors. Rufeen was not on-screen, but her voices were recognizable and confirmed as genuine by the tracking computers.

". . . attack, right shield up and holding despite damage. I seem to have driven them away for the moment." A pungent swear word which *tezars* seemed to favor flavored the transmission.

The Choya'i Melbar leaned over Jorana's shoulder to brief her. "Rufeen contacted us about eight minutes ago, early for her status transmission. The cruiser is under attack by forces from the temple."

"From the temple?" Shock underscored her words. "Military?"

"Not that we've been able to identify."

She relaxed a tiny bit. The Houses had their own military, but had not used them in personal attacks for over three hundred years. She'd hate to be in office when precedents were being set. "What's going on, then?"

"As near as we can tell, and Rufeen speculates, the attackers are simply trying to drive her away."

"Isolating Palaton."

Melbar's indigo eyes considered her and then she nodded. "So it would seem."

Rufeen's burly and flushed countenance suddenly dominated the monitors. "Melbar—ah, Jorana. I see the reinforcements have been called in."

Jorana leaned forward slightly. "We may not have much time, Rufeen. Please give me status."

"Look for yourself." The pilot moved slightly out of frame. The camera had been set to look out of the cockpit, toward the temple and the purple mountains beyond. It was bright daylight, yet a stubborn haze appeared to be occluding the view of the temple.

"What is that?" muttered Jorana in irritation.

"That is the temple at Sethu on fire. Why the bastards came out here and attacked is beyond me, unless they want to commandeer the cruiser for evacuation." The camera view, apparently cued to verbal, refocused on Rufeen.

"Where are Palaton and Rand?"

The camera view shifted again. "In there somewhere."

Jorana sat, stunned, watching purple-black smoke begin to boil out of the ancient temple. "What in God's name happened?"

"I don't—uh, oh. Company." Rufeen disappeared abruptly.

"Take me with her," Jorana snapped to Melbar. Technicians around them began to transmit computer directions to the monitoring equipment aboard the shuttle. She could see a priest, dirty and disheveled, and unarmed, talking to Rufeen at the edge of the ramp. "Get me audio."

"Trying," a technician intoned even as he played his machinery for fine-tuning. "Coming up.

Fuzzy, but audible. "Blast each and every one of you bastards into desert lint—"

"*Tezar* Rufeen. My temple is burning, my High Priest is dead. My House is split against itself—I beg your forgiveness—I came to tell you that Heir Palaton is missing and presumed dead also. There were assassins. . . ." The Choya's voices thinned off and died away.

"Did you see the body?"

"Of Tela? Regrettably, yes . . ." The Choya swayed, as thin as a reed, and the high mountain wind seemed about to snap him in two. "Of *tezar* Palaton and his companion, no."

"Then they're not dead," Rufeen snapped, "until I see their bodies piled across my boot toes."

The priest bowed. "*Tezar* Rufeen, I cannot tell you where they might be within the mountain . . . but the assassins are many."

"Bring me a body. I won't be leaving until then. I don't know if you're one of the bastards or not, so I suggest you go work on putting that fire out. I find out you're one of them and you can join the High Priest."

The emaciated Choya bowed and scurried off before Rufeen could change her mind. She came back up the landing ramp in two jumps and secured the ramp. She seemed to be aware that the monitor had followed her.

"Missing," she repeated, "presumed dead." Rufeen stared into the lens. "I'll believe Palaton is dead if and when I see it. They wouldn't be hammering away at me if they knew . . . they don't want transport available for a rescue if they flush him out. Got that, Melbar?"

Melbar intoned, "I've got that, Rufeen."

Jorana sat back in her chair, wetting lips gone sand-dry. "She's probably right." She stood up. "Gathon has to be notified. Rindalan, too. I'll take care of that."

The graying Choya'i inquired softly, "What will you tell them?"

"The only thing I know for sure. Sethu is in flames and Palaton is missing. You keep me up on surveillance. I'm sending troops out to assist."

Melbar nodded and bowed out of Jorana's way.

She stopped at the doorway face-to-face with Gathon. The Minister of Resource looked drawn and gaunt. It was apparent she would have no need to tell him of the events.

He put a hand on her forearm. "I must notify Panshinea."

She hesitated. Then she agreed. "If you must."

"Seal off surveillance. Let no one in or out of the palace."

Jorana had not thought of that. She nodded. "Rumor control."

"Essential now. Jorana, the commons on the streets will turn if they find out Palaton is missing.

"All right." She pivoted. "Melbar, seal your area. We'll release everyone as soon as the situation is settled."

A wisp of gray mane came loose and trailed across the Choya'i's forehead as she nodded in response.

Gathon's thin lips tightened. "Now I must do my duty to my emperor." He left the room ahead of Jorana.

Gathon hurried to his quarters. Anxiety tightened his chest. His undersecretary looked up curiously as he locked the door behind him, sealing the rooms for all effects and purposes. The Choya who served him was a good worker, for all that he'd come from the God-blind himself, and he sat now, impassively watching Gathon.

"Set up a subspace transmit to Sorrow. I need the emperor as soon as you can get him."

Chirek frowned. "What is it?" the undersecretary asked.

"Palaton has disappeared. There has been an assassins' attack upon Sethu. The ancient site is in flames, I'm told. We can fear the worst."

"But you have no confirmation?"

"No."

The undersecretary rolled his chair to the transmission console. "Then," he said soothingly, "there's always hope, isn't there?"

Gathon let himself slump down into a second chair. "So I've always told myself. But second chances come in precious small amounts." He rubbed his forehead wearily as his aide worked on spanning space and Chaos with the news.

Rindy visibly paled and rocked as though slapped. Jorana caught him by the fore-elbow. "Your eminence!"

"I'll . . . I'll be all right." Rindalan's hand shook as he pulled a pill vial from his pocket and fished out a caplet to put under his tongue. "Nothing is certain. Faith will play a great role in this."

He began to collapse slowly. Jorana got her shoulder under his arm and guided his spindly, yet solid-weighing form down on his chaise. Papers and books scattered as she dropped him down. He gasped once or twice and then settled. She pulled a pillow behind his shoulders. The color had begun to return to his cheeks by the time she stood.

He grasped her wrist. "They do not have him, or they would have brought the body out to Rufeen, either to display it or to transport it back here. Do you understand?"

She nodded.

"They do not have him yet!" Rindy lay back on the pillow and his eyelids fluttered.

She wanted to find comfort in the elder Prelate's words, but there was none for her. She pulled his robes about him, found him cold to the touch, and adjusted the thermostat slightly before leaving his rooms. The Earthans might not have him, but who knew about the fire?

Qativar came quietly into the room from the veranda, where his presence had been forgotten by Rindalan and unknown by Jorana. He stood at the head of the old Choya's divan and listened as Rindy dropped into fitful sleep. Then, chewing thoughtfully on his lip, he made his way out of the apartments. There were advantages to be gained from this situation. Rindy's collapse was only one of them.

Chirek waited until Gathon was immersed with Panshi-nea, discussing possibilities and weighing inevitabilities. He left the Ministry with very little notice, a commons among Housed, unimportant. His heart weighed heavily within him. Palaton had, perhaps, been the very Being of Change he had hoped to bring to his people. He had to think out his course very carefully now.

Head down, he clattered down the imperial steps and did not notice the wall of security going up behind him, Jorana directing guards and having sonic barriers raised. He had to talk with Malahki—and it seemed likely he'd find him at the hiring halls. Yes. That seemed a good place to start.

Chirek put his head up and hurried into the hot summer air, his heart beating quickly with his urgency.

Nedar stared at Vihtirne and Asten, who stood smugly at her heels. "Your source is reliable?"

Asten answered tightly, as if resenting being questioned, "My source is impeccable." The two glared at one another.

Vihtirne lifted a hand. "If the heir is gone, we must move quickly, Nedar. Cho cannot be without an heir. There will be havoc trying to fill the throne, and havoc will draw attention we don't want. Our time is near."

The pilot threw his head back, ebony hair cascading from the movement. "Don't count Palaton out. Never."

"Then what do you suggest?"

"We have our own satellites viewing Sethu, do we not?"

"The general regions only," answered Asten sulkily.

"Can we pick up the cruiser?"

Asten's eyes narrowed, and then he nodded. "I think so."

"Then do it. And let me know if it makes any movement at all." Nedar watched Asten stalk off, reluctantly leaving Vihtirne alone with him.

The beautiful Sky tilted her head to look at Nedar. "What is it you have in mind, my love?"

"The cruiser won't leave without a body or proof. We'll know nothing until it moves."

"And if Palaton is alive?"

"Then he'll board the cruiser to return to Charolon as quickly as possible to put an end to . . ." Nedar's lips curved, "speculation."

"So, if and when the cruiser takes off, we still know nothing."

"Ah. No, Vih, when the cruiser takes off, we know everything. Palaton is found, dead or alive. Until then, anything is possible."

"And if he's dead or alive . . ."

Nedar put an arm out and drew the Choya'i to him. He put his slight smile to the curve of her throat. "And then I take a fighter, and I make sure the cruiser never reaches Charolon."

Vihtirne leaned slightly out of his embrace, her eyes wide. "And the Earthans at Sethu take the blame for whatever happens."

"Does it matter as long as I give you the surety to move on the throne?" His words buzzed pleasantly against her neck as he drew her close again.

"No," said Vihtirne with a great deal of satisfaction. "No, it won't matter at all." She gave herself to the pleasure he was offering her.

Chapter 22

Alexa stared at the small, silvered hand mirror she had hammered out for herself from scrap metal she'd smuggled from the docks. The Abdreliks disliked mirrors. They saw what they wanted of themselves in water. She did not know if they thought themselves ugly. In her dark times, she might know. She might think it was because mirrors could reflect and reveal the presence of a stalker, scaring off the prey. She had originally intended on making a dagger, but lacked the ability to make it strong enough to pierce Abdrelik hide and small enough to keep it hidden, so she had finally made the hand mirror.

She pinched a curl into place and lay back on her cot. The cabin walls gave her scarcely more room than she would find in a mausoleum. The bay station thrummed with power. GNask was back. He would be here for a short time and leave again, going back and forth between here and Sorrow. They were in a high, outer orbit above Sorrow. If she turned on the monitor permitted her, its narrow range of channels would show her the planet. She might even be able to catch a glimpse of debate being televised from the main floor on a second channel, but debates did not interest her. They were waiting, both she and GNask, only the Abdrelik had some inkling of why they waited and she did not.

She suspected he was about to strike, something he could not do from Sorrow's surface, where all pretended neutrality. The bay station stayed in the sector for easy access, yet out of range of Sorrow's enforcement. But strike who and where and why, she did not know.

Unless it were Cho. That was a target she knew to be firmly ingrained in GNask's mind. Sooner or later it would be Cho.

She let her mirror drop gently to the carpeted floor. It landed with a dull thud.

These times were worse than the dark times. This was when she knew how truly alone she was, how abandoned by her race as well as by the Abdreliks, and how she had abandoned herself. These times, thank God, had gotten fewer and fewer as she descended into a dark well of hunger and predatory desire. But they did happen, though less frequently, and when they did, she despaired.

Where was Bevan, who'd loved her despite her darkness, and where was Rand, beacon to them both? Did heaven exist for any of them? Would they remember to pave a way for her . . . could she ever hope to reach them?

A tear started at the corner of her eye and ran down her warm cheek. It felt hot, and then cooled as it terminated. A second followed, and then a third, and then nothing. She had no more water to shed for herself or her friends.

She lay quietly for a moment, then looked up and saw a signal light blinking on her console. Alexa hurriedly sat up and scrubbed her face dry. She straightened her suit and stood up to leave as her cabin door received a signal to set her free.

She recognized Fleet Commander rrRusk and gave him a slight smile, nothing more, knowing it disconcerted the Abdrelik, for Droolers had little understanding of human body language. She went to GNask's side and stood quietly, waiting. His *tursh* sat on his bare shoulder. It gave a slug-like stir as she approached and two stalk eyes looked down at her. Did it recognize her, she wondered, as something it had penetrated once? Awakened, the *tursh* began to feed, slurping tiny, imperceptible fungus and bacteria off the Abdrelik's hide.

The two Abdreliks had been speaking in their own guttural language of hoots and humphs. When finished, GNask looked down at her.

"You will be pleased, I think."

As always, she wondered why he wished to please her. Was a happy spy a better spy? And if he kept her with hopes of returning her to infiltration again, why didn't he just get on with it?

Alexa masked her face to hide her thoughts and murmured, "What is it?"

"Our allies the Ronin have just presented us with some valuable cargo. It's in decon now. I'll have it ready for you in a moment. But that is only one piece of excellent news. The other is . . . we have intercepted a rather hasty, uncoded transmission. Eavesdropping, as it were."

She waited patiently.

GNask mopped the corner of his upper lip with the back of a purplish paw. "Panshinea's heir to the throne is missing."

"Which means?"

"The implications are boundless. Civil disorder, at the minimum. Chaos, perhaps." GNask looked at rrRusk and rumbled with pleasure. "What do you think?"

"I think we can be ready and then wait."

"Good."

"Ready for what?"

GNask put his beslimed paw on her wrist. "We are part of the Sorrow security council. It's our job to help when situations appear out of control. We will be ready to go to Cho on a moment's notice."

She saw only a slight flaw in that. "And where will you get your pilots?"

GNask grinned more broadly, revealing more of his tusks. "I only need one to lead the way . . . and I think I might have just what I need in decon."

rrRusk moved in response to the ambassador's gesture, pelting into a run with an odd grace for such a huge-framed being.

Alexa stood still. In her dark times, she would know and understand—perhaps even be light-years ahead of GNask in his plans. Now she felt slightly befuddled.

The bulkhead opened across the bay. She heard a high, singsong giggle amid the squeak of wheels as rrRusk grabbed a cart and pulled it their way. Whatever lay on the cartbed seemed to be in perpetual motion, kicking, rolling, and singing.

Alexa's bewilderment increased as rrRusk hauled the cart to them. GNask had been hunkered down. Now he brought his bulk upward and leaned over the cart. He looked to rrRusk. "Have you confirmed what the Ronin told us?"

"Yes, your honor. There's no doubt of it. We have tracking records on the life pod."

GNask made a smacking sound. "Good. Very good. Come here, Alexa. I think you might know our pilot. He's crossed chaos all the way from Arizar. The *tezarian* drive in the raft shows it has been activated. I do not think the journey was accidental. Come see for yourself."

Half-cast in the Abdrelik's shadow, she felt a sudden, cold reluctance to approach the cart as whatever occupied it kept up a litany of giggles and singsong. She did not move. GNask reached out and flung her against the cart's side.

"Look!"

Her heart jumped. Had she died and not known it? Had the Abdrelik dealt her a lethal blow? She took a deep breath and felt mortality coursing through her as she recognized the occupant. Alexa looked down and saw Bevan, dirty, stinking, his dark hair in strings, and his face sunken as though he had died but his breath had not yet left his body. The man rolled onto his side and looked up at her.

He let out a high, pealing laugh. His eyes went up in their sockets and he collapsed.

Her legs folded under her and she, too, collapsed, but her mind stayed clear and her eyes open. Bevan, alive.

Insane, but alive.

And how in God's name could he have navigated Chaos to get here?

"Palaton!" Rand's panicky voice echoed around him, and the vibrations of it raised dust motes which crashed into the clouds ahead of him.

"A little quiet would be prudent," the Choya admonished, unseeable, yet only a stride or two away by the sound of it.

Rand forced himself to relax. He edged forward in search of his companion, saying, "You disappeared."

"Not for long." The immense horned crown emerged, capping Palaton's oval face which followed. Oddly, the rest of his body stayed curtained. The effect was eerie and ghostly. A hand strayed forward. "Come on."

Rand passed into the cloud, feeling the mix of fresh air hitting air that had grown close and stale. He felt like he was being pelted, the hairs on his arms standing on end from a kind of buzz.

"A light and sonic field," Palaton explained. "Mild enough. I don't know how old it is. Perhaps it's lost some of its lethal intent." He let go of Rand's hand. "If they did not want us dead before, they will now. We're in trespass here, of what I don't know, but it was meant to be kept hidden."

The natural tunnel and rock formation gave way to a vast gallery, carved and polished, with solar reflective panels that brought light down from some chimney stories above, passing it back and forth until it bloomed here. This was the grandfather of the lighting system for his own room. Rand blinked a little, his enhanced vision whiting out, overlit. He could not, however, miss the vast banks of tables and shelves and equipment sitting silent, arranged by some system he could not fathom. Palaton strode forward.

"There's a natural dryness in here. Most mountains don't have that. Moisture seeps in. There may be a salt deposit from the foothills tunneling in here. This is a repository . . . and from the size and depth of it, I'd say this encompasses most of the records of the House of Earth from its very origins. We Stars have one, too, but I have no idea of its location." He pivoted. "We came in the back way, I'd say."

"Then there must be a front." Rand caught up with Palaton.

"Yes. And if they've figured out which way we went, they'll know this is where we have to end up. We can't stay, however profitable it would seem to be in the short term."

"Profitable?"

"Yes." Palaton touched a table with his fingertips, brushing it so lightly that all he did was stir the dust. "Too bad. I would never have thought of anything so audacious. All I need is here."

"All you need for what?"

Palaton gave him a measuring look. "The House of Earth," he said, "is famous for its balancing act. It's taken on the role of buffer between the Skies and Stars as far back as recorded history. That neutrality was sometimes forced on it, and sometimes assumed, and sometimes the Earthans were able to force their neutrality on us. There is information here, had I the time to ferret it out, which could break that neutrality. I could impel the Earthans to join with the throne, forming a power bloc it would be damn near impossible to break, two Houses against one."

"Then let's do it."

Palaton shook his head. "If we do, they'll be certain to be waiting for us at the end of the other passage. We'll never live to use the advantage gained."

"We can come back."

"The library will have been moved. The Earthans can't take a chance that I've found it." He lifted his chin. His nostrils flared slightly. "The fresh air comes from this direction. We should have light from here on out. Let me stay in front. You may need a shield."

He trotted down the wide aisle, reading off signs graven in the rock, detailing some of the histories stored in the vast gallery. One slowed him, in surprise, Rand thought. . . .

"What is it?"

"Look here." Palaton opened a book with covers of bronze. The paper inside had been protected with some kind of coating, shiny yet tough. He could not read the Choyan language, but the manuscript was peppered with pictographs, some modern and some akin to cave drawings. Rand moved his hand over the protective covering. "How old?"

"A million years, perhaps. Or more. Not the book, but the reproduced drawings."

"I understand." Rand watched as Palaton turned pages. "Look. It's a cleansing."

He could not mistake the tremor in the *tezar*'s fingers as he brought the huge book closer. Palaton became silent, turning to the next page.

"What is it?"

Palaton looked up, stark emotion in his eyes. "It seems," he said quietly, "that the cleansing is more than a ritual. Once, it was meant to work. It was devised because it *did* work. What have we become, that we no longer know what we are, or how to help ourselves?"

"Then it can work again. Read it."

Palaton gave a quick shake of denial, of frustration. "I don't understand," he said. "Not the words, but the intent."

"It has to be there!"

"It's not!" Palaton slammed the book shut and let it fall to the floor. Dust exploded upward, a huge cloud that made Rand's eyes water and tickled his nose. He rubbed his face vigorously.

"It's not there," Palaton repeated. "Lies, old lies, myths."

"Maybe not. Maybe not if the House of Earth thought it important enough to keep in here."

The Choya looked at him, his eyes hard. "You don't know," he said, "what it means to lose *bahdur*, never to fly again, to face the prospect of dying painfully bit by bit."

"And you don't know what it means never to have been offered any of that. Ever." Rand stood his ground.

His words were met with silence, and then Palaton retreated fractionally. "You're correct," he said. "I have no idea." He stared across the wide cavern. "Although there is knowledge enough here to teach us both. And if there is knowledge here, my own House may have something it can share with me. Come on. We need to make haste."

And Palaton began to move again, swiftly, sorting through the corridors and aisles of the warehouse as if he knew a way instinctively, letting nothing else stop him. Rand hurried to keep up. His leg began to ache, reminding him that it was not prepared for a stint like this. He rubbed his thigh as he jogged after Palaton, not daring to stop.

But it was a near-hidden alcove, in the shadows even of the lighting system, that stopped Palaton in his tracks.

"What is it?" asked Rand.

"Flames etched in the rock, in the stylized manner of a house sigil. The Fourth House."

"I thought there were only three."

Palaton advanced to the alcove, drawn there despite the urgency of their flight. "There are. Not many know there might have been a fourth House, destroyed in the dawn of our technological civilization. I was told, but I didn't know whether to believe . . . now the Earthans offer me proof. Is this the moment they hoped to erase from their future by killing me? Did they foresee this discovery?" Within the alcove now, surrounded by bookcases and cabinets, Palaton stretched over and above, to trace the sigil. "Flames out of ashes . . . my mother knew. There is a tapestry and embroidery hanging in the palace gallery . . . I'll show you one day, if I can. She was an artist. She reproduced this sigil without ever having seen it." Palaton slapped a palm down on a cabinet. He opened it and fanned through files, scanning at a speed which Rand's odd vision could not follow and there were no illustrations to interrupt the script.

Palaton slammed the cabinet shut. He swung to his left and pulled open a wooden cabinet, simple yet elegant in its lines. Inside the cabinet, drawers swung out. Palaton again began to thumb through the contents. "Listen here," he says. "A diary so old it would crumble if I touched it directly. It's been protected like the other manuscripts. 'The root which branched us all has grown dark and diseased and we must excise it, lest the branches too grow twisted and evil.' "

Rand could see a sheen overlying each page. "The House was corrupt?"

"So they thought." Palaton put the diary back. "It appears the three remaining Houses operated in concert to destroy the fourth. But what could have challenged them so?" He fumbled through other files, found another protected one and slid it out. Muttering as he read, he suddenly grew silent.

"What is it?"

Palaton looked up. "Nothing," he said, "that I can tell you." With pain etched on his face, he closed the folder. He relented, saying, "Some of the answers, though not most, and from them will spring the most agonizing questions. The Earthans are not innocent in this. There were hunts for decades, searching out and destroying whatever Flame stock could be found. The Earthans pretended to participate, but in secret they took in those they could find and interbred them in their own lines. The purest Choyan they could find they used for genetic experimentation." Palaton pushed the folder back into the drawer in disgust. "I thought we had grown beyond that."

"Maybe," offered Rand, "this is what did it."

"Perhaps." The Choya straightened. "All of this is priceless. I could not pick a single scrap of information to carry out with me." He paused. A tiny, white triangle of paper edged out from a cabinet near the side of the alcove. He went to it and opened that storage unit. A dossier had been examined, and recently.

Rand caught a stirring up his spine, a chill of fear and apprehension. He twisted abruptly. His ears thrummed. "Palaton. . . ."

"I hear them." He paused. "This is about me."

"What?"

He looked up, with a wide grin. "This is my death warrant." He ripped it cleanly out of the folder and slipped it inside his shirt. "Sometimes paper trails are eminently useful." He closed the folder briskly and slammed it back inside. "Like any good philosophy, it creates more questions than it answers. I have a name, if not a reason." His neck stretched as he looked up and his eyes gained a sharp purpose in their depths. "Can you run, do you think?"

His bones ached. His lungs burned from the faint drifting of salt in the air, but he denied himself. "I've got a second wind. Which way?"

Palaton pointed. Rand broke into a sprint and he could hear the other at his heels. The gallery drummed with their speed. They sounded, he thought, like a herd of wild horses racing across the frontier. He did not begin to gasp until they reached the sudden maw of the cavern, jettisoning them into the sunlight and the yelps of their pursuers as they were sighted. Palaton turned his head a bit without breaking stride, pointed, and altered his course. They must circle the mountain if they wanted freedom. He could not do it if he thought about it. Rand lowered his head and galloped at his heels.

Rufeen met them at the loading ramp, the cruiser ready to go. The vehicle vibrated with power beneath their feet. Rand staggered, with Palaton propelling him forward. Purple shadows fell across the landing strip.

"It's a good thing a *tezar* never leaves his ship," she said. "I've fought off two groups of unwelcome visitors. I wasn't much impressed by the reception committee, but they're throwing you one hell of a farewell."

Palaton fought for breath. "Just get us out of here . . . before they decide . . . to shoot us down."

"Strap yourselves in," she answered briskly, as she closed the portal and strode to the front.

Palaton made for a chair. He looked back to see Rand crawling determinedly across the liner floor. The boy's face was gray and pale. He helped him up.

The vehicle shot forward into taxiing motion with little preliminary. Rand collapsed into the chair and let Palaton fasten him in.

"Will you be all right?"

Rand wearily nodded, too spent to talk.

"I don't think this is a normal color for humankind."

Rand's lips worked and he got out, "Only the dead ones." He coughed.

Palaton found a cold drink and passed it to him. "If it counts for anything, your stamina impressed me.

Rand drained the container with one gulp. He paused long enough to say, "It counts," before melting into the chair.

Palaton looked out the window. "I should imagine we impressed the Earthans, too. We circled that mountain on foot, at a run, in less time than it took them to try to cut through it and cut us off." He put a hand to his chest. Paper made a crinkling sound. "I don't plan to do much more running."

"Good." Rand put the cold container to his forehead, chest still heaving.

The aircraft accelerated rapidly, making the thrust off ground and into the air. Rufeen let out a call of raw triumph.

Palaton said mildly, "I think we finally outdistanced them." He leaned back into his own chair.

Chapter 23

Dusk was nearing Charolon's skies, though it was still a few hours away, but this was summer's eve, hanging low over, the city. Chirek wove his way between drunken commons staggering along the glidewalks. The walks had been shut down for the day because the solars of the city had already been drained to meet the demand of the cooling systems and none of these Choyan had the ability to psionically power the walks.

A beggar staggered into Chirek, and steadied himself by grabbing his sleeve. Chirek straightened. He leaned a little so the stinking Choya would hear him well, and pitched his voices although he had no *bahdur* to give them command.

"Find your home and go there. Palaton has no further use for you."

The beggar struck the palm of his hand upon his crown base as surprise pierced the veil of his stupor. Chirek added. "Our God watches and weighs you. Go home before He finds you lacking for the Change."

The beggar wiped his lips hastily on the back of his hand and bowed away. "I'm sorry, sir. I . . . I'm going." He backed into the flow of the crowd, was jumbled aside, and disappeared.

Chirek looked after, wondering if what he'd said would do any good. If it did not, then the ministry of his life had been wasted. He brushed the filth and grime, but not the stench of the other, away, found his bearings, and continued on.

The hiring hall was silent. A few Choyan read the monitor displays, their gazes furrowed in concentration. He made his way through the lobby and spotted Malahki at a far table, a bottle of fine wine in front of him as if the hiring hall were a sidewalk cafe, and he enjoying a view. Chirek cleared a path to him.

Malahki's eyes widened. He kicked his chair down as Chirek sat down next to him. "This must be important."

"This is disaster."

Malahki poured a glass of the sparkling yellow wine which matched the highlights of his eyes. His knuckles were scarred over, Chirek noticed for the first time, as if Malahki had hammered out a life for himself bare-handedly. "Were you followed?"

"I came on foot. The walks are still full enough that it would have been difficult to follow me. Also, other things occupy the imperial staff."

Malahki sipped at his drink. "What is it?"

"Palaton has disappeared at Sethu."

"What?"

"His pilot reports an attack on the imperial cruiser, in an apparent attempt to drive her away. Assassins hit the temple in force. Sethu is burning. Palaton is missing, presumed dead."

"Earthans," said Malahki as if he swore, and he slumped back in his chair, stunned.

"I think they mean to take the throne. It nears their turn in the Wheel . . . they will have the right, eventually."

"Shit. Earthans couldn't cope with the Compact. Who is their heir apparent? Ariat, no doubt. A young buckling, a nothing, and he's the best they can put forward. Where's their sense?"

"That matters little. What matters is, what are we going to do?" Chirek thought he saw a tiny veil cross Malahki's eyes, as if the other prepared to hide something from him. He blinked, disbelieving what he'd seen.

Malahki answered carefully, "What can we do? The House of Earth operates without our input, just as the others do."

"Malahki, our people still fill Charolon. If they think Palaton was killed, their fury will fill the skies. He spoke for them. He gave them hope that they might at last have a voice within their own government, *bahdur* or not. By the Wheel," Chirek said and pushed back in his own chair. "Sethu won't be the only site in flames. We could have riots all over the counties."

Malahki pushed his wine glass with a blunt finger. "We can't give the Houses an excuse to bring us down in the streets. All right. I'll spread the word the strike is over. I'll begin to pull them out."

"And I'll go to the priesthood. We'll do what we can, although we can only move one or two at a time." Chirek finished his wine. He put a hand out and caught Malahki by the wrist. "You're more than a commons, luminary. You see more import in this than I do. We each have secrets from the other—you do not know my life any more than I know, yours—but don't seek to profit now. The streets will run with blood if you do."

Malahki smiled slowly. "Do all priests see so deeply?"

"I can only answer for myself."

"Then I will answer for myself. The Fourth House is trying to rise from its ashes. The Earthans hid survivors after the great scourging. What we may see happening now is the splintering, the sundering of the House of Earth, and the House of Flame being lit anew. If that is happening," and Malahki put his face closer to Chirek. "There isn't a damn thing either one of us will be able to do." He pushed to his feet. "Time is running out."

They had crossed the hiring hall when a scream rang out, its piercing wail cutting across the meager sounds of the street and the hall where they mingled. Malahki put a hand to a bulge in his vest which harbored an illegal enforcer. Chirek stepped back to give him room.

The hiring hall doors burst open. The scent and smell of smoke curled in and shouts and screams followed. A young Choya flung himself into Malahki. Malahki's fist swung and the other went down. His companions stumbled over him, still shouting, and ran off. Chirek could see Choyan running, the streets full. Store view screens exploded as they were smashed in across the street. No one stopped or paused as looters tore down the outer security wall, cracking open the warehouse behind the storefront like breaking open a melon.

"What's happening?" Chirek got out.

"We're too late," said Malahki. "It's begun."

Qativar watched the streets from his windows. The raw energy and frenzy of the rioters filled him. It carried a rush with it that only *bahdur* could approximate. The excitement and anger of the mob sounded and he could hear it all the way up to his veranda, as well as from the communicators covering the events on his monitors. He had their commentary turned low. Below him was the real thing. Like a tiny spark, he had torched the fires which raged below.

Qativar dropped a screen into place. There was a certain satisfaction to it, even if he could not personally enjoy running amok in the streets. And, in the aftermath, his men would pick up stragglers, new subjects for experimentation. He would profit on many levels if this riot continued unabated. Troops had been swallowed by the floods, inundated by sheer numbers, when their first appearances had been passive, as if hoping the sight of them alone would make the rioters desist. Violence meeting violence only begets more, or so the theory went.

But the commons saw no reason to respect or obey the troops, sweeping them up and carrying them along, disposing of the bodies downstream on another street or in an alleyway. They looted the stores in a feeding frenzy of longing to have what the Housed had, and could afford, and they could not. Greed added fuel to their anger.

Qativar might be a priest, but his Householding specialized in reconstruction and, from what he could see of Charolon tonight, there would be a great need for their services in the near future. As a consequence of their actions, he might even get government approval to test a drugging program among the commons. Yes, there were a great many possibilities.

"I can have a fighter ready," said Hat, "but I want to know why. You're asking a great deal of me.

Nedar knew that he did. To have a fighter taken from Blue Ridge, fueled, armed, and ready, without proper flight permits might cost Hat everything that he had earned in his service to the flight school. "It's necessary."

Hat's stolid presence did not flinch in the transmission. "That's not good enough. Charolon is in turmoil."

"My need has nothing to do with that."

Hat's deep brown eyes flickered. "Then what?"

"There is a traitor, Hat, whom I cannot let get away with trying to destroy Cho. That's as much as I can tell you."

"The Houses are calling for calm and a put down of the Godless."

Nedar could feel Vihtirne and Asten shift impatiently behind him. She had summoned one of her staff to assist him, and he also stood waiting, out of line of sight of the monitor. "There is a loyalty between us, old friend, which runs far deeper than the blood of the Houses. We are *tezars*! Without us, Cho has no destiny in the stars. Let the Houses destroy themselves with their foolishness. We only need each other."

"And the traitor?"

"A fellow *tezar*."

Hat flinched then. "Palaton—"

"You do not know," Nedar repeated firmly. "Can I have the fighter?"

Hat's square form appeared to compress with indecision, and then he put his shoulders back. "All right. I can have it ready in fifteen minutes."

"I'll be there," Nedar said.

"How—"

"Vihtirne has a teleporter standing by." It underscored the power backing which Nedar now had. Teleporters were extremely rare among Choyan . . . but Nedar had one as a resource. The pilot pressed. "Hat, nothing which has happened since Palaton was named heir has been accidental. *He* filled the streets with the Godless. *He* engineered this riot to prove his power. You and I both know he cannot be dead. This is a ploy to bring down Congress and strengthen him. I cannot stop him at Sethu if I cannot get to him."

"All right." Hat stepped back from the screen. "It'll be waiting for you."

"Good." Nedar ended the transmission. He turned to Vihtirne.

An odd smile played on the lips of his patroness. Asten had left, on some mission of hers, he supposed.

"And do you believe that, Nedar?"

"Believe what?"

"That the *tezars* have a greater loyalty to themselves than to their Houses?"

"If I believed that," he said, putting an arm about her waist and thrilling in the bend of her figure as he drew her close, "I would not be in your Householding now." He stilled her next question with his lips, but he could not help but wonder.

Could he build a House of *tezars*? And if such a thing could be done, how could the other Houses hope to stand against it?

Why had he never seen such a possibility before?

But Palaton's disposal remained foremost before any other plans could be made. If the Earthans had killed him first, so much the better. This time Nedar was not willing to trust to chance. "We must hurry," he whispered urgently to her. "Now is the time to strike."

Qativar entered the High Prelate's quarters gingerly. He had not been summoned, but the alarm did not stop him, for he still wore a security badge encoded to these rooms. As the badge gave him safe passage through the barrier, he did not feel the pressure. Perhaps old Rindy did not even have his security system on. Foolish, if trusting, of him.

It was not that he had no right to be here. It was that he hoped to come without foreknowledge, to surprise the old Choya, to perhaps strain the old heart even further. A subtle assassination, if necessary. Things would be a lot easier if the wily old priest were gone, his meddling nature stilled by the finality of death.

But Qativar had legitimate business to relate, news to bring, even if startlement did not do the work he hoped it would. He stepped quietly upon the wooden floor. Squares gleamed beneath his feet, polished to a high gloss by centuries of servants hand-rubbing the wood. One of the boards gave out a fine tone, a noise barely perceptible. If Rindalan were asleep, it would not wake him. If he were drowsy, it would not alarm him. If he were awake, he would now be listening for another tone, another board to speak and tell him of intruders despite the alarm system.

Qativar kept his steps firm. He did not have Rindy suspicious of him, as far as he knew, and it behooved him to keep it that way.

Another board groaned gently, almost the sound of a Choya'i responding to lovemaking. The noise brought a prickling to the nape of his neck. He shivered in spite of himself. The room opened into a hallway, which curved seductively into a sitting room. He could see the glow of a dim light awaiting him.

Rindy had been awake then, sitting up, though perhaps he drowsed now. Qativar slowed, assembling his words within his mind.

"Palaton?" Soft, thin, yet still a strong inquiry from the parlor.

The young Choya stepped into its dim light with a bow. "Your eminence. Talking to ghosts?"

"Qativar! What are you doing here at this hour?" Rindy had been seated, his feet bare and crossed upon an ottoman, loose dressing gown about his spindly figure, and he closed a book upon one finger. "Do me the kindness of hoping for Palaton's return, as I hope."

Perhaps the news itself would be sufficient to do the damage. Qativar composed his face. "I have some news, your honor, which I thought best to give you in person."

Rindy did not stir within his upholstered chair, though his face grew wary. He had heard, Qativar supposed, a lot of news within his lifetime. "What is it?"

"The commons have heard. They are rioting. The streets of Charolon are being torn apart. No one seems able to call them to heel." This last was said with satisfaction which Qativar did little to disguise. He looked toward the small, decorative stained glass of the singular window of Rindy's parlor. "If you look, you can see the flames on the horizon."

Rindy swore then, a single, despairing oath. He sat back in his chair, leaning his horn crown upon its rest, and closed his eyes wearily. "Jorana left me to rest. She must have thought it best I not know." Then he looked a second time at Qativar, and this time his eyes seemed to bore deeply. "Why do you bring me this pain?"

"It's our duty," Qativar replied evenly, but his mind raced ahead of his words. If not this shock, then perhaps another. "If they won't listen to anyone else, perhaps they'll listen to the Voice of God. I came to ask if you'll go out there with me, to help."

Rindy took his finger out of his book, dropping the object upon the floor heedlessly. He stood and gathered his evening clothing about him. "If you'll give me a moment, Qativar, I'll get ready."

Qativar bowed, the better to conceal the flash of triumph across his lips. The mob would batter them. He would be safe, but he could not guarantee Rindy's life. It didn't matter to Qativar if Rindy's death produced a martyr. Eventually the events being shaped would make martyrdom useless and forgotten, of no consequence.

It was the immediate death which mattered, the removal of a stumbling block to Qativar's plans. He kept his face averted as there came a din of noise from the other room, of Rindy dressing in haste. He did not straighten until he could wipe the look of triumph from his features and contain himself.

Chapter 24

"Nothing else explains the Choyan interest in humankind on Arizar. Nothing else would be worth breaching Class Zed restrictions on racial contact. Somehow, humankind are able to navigate Chaos as well as Choyan. They have been able to divine the *tezarian* drive." rrRusk straightened proudly at the end of his conclusion.

Bevan had crawled out of his cart and lay on the filthy dock floor, his head in Alexa's lap. She patted her, fingertips gently on his face from time to time, loathe to touch the tangled dark hair which had once been so enticing. He twitched and sang to himself, unaware of her touch though he had crawled to her for comfort.

"We have nothing which indicates that. Alexa's own experience leads us to believe the Choyan seek a spiritual encounter." GNask lifted his lip in a sneer and sucked on a tusk, loosening a bit of his last meal. He spat it out across the bay. "Ghosts do not navigate FTL space."

rrRusk's beady eyes flicked a quick glance at Alexa before he countered, "We have had Choyan at our disposal from time to time. Even intense anatomical study of both the body and the drive has not given us the information we seek."

Alexa fought to contain a shudder at the implications of the commander's words. Torture, vivisection.

"I scarcely see where this *thing*," and GNask shoved a massive foot into Bevan's side, "will help."

"He doesn't need to help if he can pilot. If he leads the way, your honor, I can follow."

Alexa looked up in sudden shock. "Cho," she said. "You won't go in to protect them. You'll be attacking." And met GNask's gloating face.

"Exactly, little hunter," he said. "Now you understand."

She could feel her skin grow hot. He had been playing with rrRusk, waiting for her to draw the conclusion he and his commander had come to. She looked back down. "He is not capable," she said finally, unwillingly.

"Perhaps not by himself. But with you at his side, I have no doubt he will succeed."

Alexa shuddered. This gross thing which groveled at her feet had once shared the most intimate acts with her. How could she touch him intimately again, body or soul? Now he repulsed her. In her dark times, he would represent a miserable, craven prey . . . darting furtively, uselessly, from her hunger.

She did not let GNask see the repulsion in her eyes. "How much time do we have?"

"Now," said rrRusk. "We must prepare to strike now. It will take us some time to attain FTL and then cross Chaos."

Bevan jerked. His head snapped back and their eyes met, hers and the young man's. He had once had beautiful, dark, soulful eyes. Now they were like sunken cesspools.

"How do you expect him to get us there," Alexa said bitterly.

Bevan's face glowed as if her voice had awakened him. A death-grin split his filthy face. "Alphabet soup," he said. "It's like stirring alphabet soup. And we go from A to Z!" He cackled, lost his breath, and doubled over, wheezing.

Alexa leaned over suddenly, hugging him to calm him down as he fought to catch his breath. She looked back over her shoulder at GNask, defiance in every word. "I can't help him like this."

"What do you need?"

If he would do this to her, then she would punish him back. "Your bath," she said. "I need to clean and comfort him."

GNask's face grew stiff. The *tursh* which now rode the crown of his brow in lopsided fashion shrank in fear. Alexa watched him decide. He would not touch the bath again until he'd had the waters drained and cleaned, a difficult proposition in deep space, she knew that. She would be depriving the Abdrelik of one of his essential pleasures.

GNask turned his back on her, growling something at rrRusk as he passed. He slammed through the bulkhead leading to the living quarters of the bay station.

rrRusk cleared his throat. "Make it so," he said, but Alexa already knew she'd gotten what she wanted.

She pushed Bevan gently out of her lap and stood. "Carry him along," she ordered the war commander and brushed past him as well.

The Abdrelik let out a snort and then did as he'd been told.

Palaton looked over Rufeen's shoulder. "I thought you said you repelled the attackers."

"That I did, but I didn't say we didn't take any damage." Rufeen glared over the panel. Scorch marks scarred its normally pristine cover, and there were both dented and melted holes. Wires and fibers hung out in confusion. "I can't send and I can't receive."

"Neither can the panel," Palaton said wryly. He kept smiling at Rufeen. "Well, there's nothing that can be done. Try whatever repair you can. The security net will catch us coming in. You'll have no trouble landing, *tezar*, and we'll be home. In the meantime, they'll just have to worry about us."

"In the meantime," Rufeen said frostily, "no one knows the whereabouts of the heir and his charge and I can't get the scores of the five-team kick-down game."

"You play?" said Palaton, momentarily distracted. He showed his teeth and tapped one of the incisors with his nail. "Had to get it capped after a game, but I made the winning goal."

Her face twisted. "I played defense," she said. She sighed. "Cho may be collapsing, but they still play kick-down."

"Naturally." He put a hand out and clasped her shoulder. "I'll be resting in the back. Let me know if you need me up front."

The pilot nodded, dropped the com panel with a *tsk* of disgust, and swiveled about in her chair.

Rand was draped limply across the passenger lounge. Palaton sat down quietly, thinking the other slept, but Rand said, "What's wrong?"

"Nothing. The ship took a little damage in the siege. We can't communicate right now."

Rand swung his feet to the floor and sat up. "Anything to eat?"

"Still hungry?"

"Yeah. I'll take anything that's wrapped in that purple paper. Forget the gray stuff."

"Carbohydrates and sugar, huh, forget the vegetable matter?"

"Is that what it's supposed to be?" Rand wrinkled his face as Palaton opened the fuselage galley and rummaged about for short rations. "You couldn't prove it by me."

Palaton found several carbo bars and tossed them over. "This should hold you for a while. We'll be home soon enough."

"If we're not, you'll hear from my stomach." Rand unwrapped a bar and devoured it. He licked sticky crumbs from his fingers.

Palaton found a seat and settled down, and watched the humankind enjoy his food. There was a joy of life to these beings that transcended age and maturity. He sensed that if a humankind ever lost that joy, he would be a sorry creature indeed. Like water that ran deep and sure, it might go underground from time to time, but it needed to bubble up to the surface, ensuring life. He allowed himself to enjoy it now, that which welled unconsciously from Rand.

He had dozed off without knowing it. He awoke with a start to Rufeen's hand on his shoulder, thinking of dusty crypts and fountains which ran from broken pitchers, asking "Do You Remember Me?" That last he had just recognized as his mother's memorial when Rufeen shook him awake.

"What is it?"

"I'm getting a partial transmission on the backup. It's very weak and fuzzy, and we can't respond." Rufeen's face was carved in solemn planes. "I think you better come up front and hear this." She looked at Rand, who had also come alert. "You, too, perhaps."

They crowded the cockpit. Rufeen amplified the transmission as much as was possible on equipment meant only for stopgap emergencies. The pilot translated into Trade and Rand heard the news as it echoed after.

" . . . barricaded the new Congressional Halls. Curfew has been set, but there are not enough troops to effectively maintain it. All citizens are requested to stay inside. . . . Firestorm has cut off efforts to save the eastern quarter. . . .

Uncontrolled looting in the merchant's quarter. . . . " Static broke up the broadcast. Palaton looked sharply at Rufeen. "What is this?"

"Riots," she answered. "Over your assassination at Sethu."

"What?"

"It's been reported. The commons erupted."

"This has to be stopped. Is this all over Charolon?"

"From what I heard," Rufeen said grimly, "It's all over Cho."

"No. I can't allow this—"

"What can you do?" asked Rand evenly. "You can't get the truth through to them."

"I'll do whatever I have to."

Rand put his shoulders back. "Then come with me." He extended his hand, palm upward, to Palaton.

Rufeen said only, "I'll keep trying. We'll make the air-strip in three hours."

Hair wet from the damp, and wiry body, which had gone scrawny in its deprivation, squeezed into one of Alexa's old suits, Bevan sat hugging himself as she tried to feed him. The smell of the cooked food made her ill and she fought off the desire to hunt, to bring down her own meat, sweet and red with juices, body temperature, fresh.

Bevan put out a hand suddenly to clutch hers. The spoon in their entwined grasp quivered.

"I know their secrets," he said. "They poisoned me for it."

"What secrets?"

Bevan looked deeply into her eyes. "I can cross Chaos," he said. "I know how they've mastered it."

"Teach me."

He shook his head and dropped his hand away from hers. "You couldn't do it. Neither could the Droolers, if I told them."

"But you could."

Bevan gave a jerky nod. He took the spoon from her fingers and began feeding himself vigorously.

Alexa sat back on her heels and watched. "What about Rand?" she asked suddenly.

Bevan paused. A bit of applesauce ran from his mouth.

He wiped it up with a fingertip, then sucked the finger clean. "I don't know. Maybe."

"The Choyan have him. He's being held on Cho."

"Vampires," said Bevan vehemently. "They'll strip his soul away."

"GNask has a grievance before the Compact. It's about all of us . . . all of us who were taken and poisoned . . . but we need Rand, too. We need to save Rand if we can."

Bevan's gaze shifted back and forth. "You weren't poisoned."

"Remember Arizar? Remember the upper campus, with its dead, and its crazies? They don't care what happens to us. We need to get Rand out of there."

Bevan dropped his spoon into his food tray.

"You loved Rand more, didn't you?" he asked with sudden lucid insight.

Alexa winced. "I loved you both. I couldn't help it. But Rand never understood what you did. . . . He never understood what it was to give up all of yourself—"

"Even the dark side," Bevan finished.

Their eyes met.

"Yes. Even that," Alexa admitted.

"If we save him, will you let the Abdreliks have him?"

A sudden fierceness gripped her. She leaned close and vowed, "No. Never."

"Promise me?"

She put a kiss on his brow, saying, "I promise." And sat back. "And what about you? Do you promise?"

Tiny golden lights seemed to illuminate his sunken eyes. "No promises. I can get you there," he said. "But it will be the death of me." He let out a trilling laugh and began to dig his fingers into his food and eat, slop running down his hands.

Alexa stood up. She faced the bulkhead viewer and signaled to be let out. The door blossomed open. rrRusk waited for her in the outer corridor.

"He's ready," she said.

"We'll be transferring to the launching cradles as soon as GNask is notified."

Alexa nodded. "Who goes with Bevan?"

"You do. You'll have a minimum crew. I have a wing of the fleet ready to follow."

The Abdreliks weren't risking anything if they could help it. But she and Bevan would be alone. There were possibilities in the situation, she thought, as she went to prepare.

Rindy clutched at Qativar's arm. The buildings rang with noise. Trash, torn from shops and streets, skirled around them. The face of Charolon had turned dirty and begrimed and morning would no doubt show an even bleaker aspect. Running Choyan swept past them, oblivious, intent upon other missions, looting, destruction, their arms full of goods and weapons and their faces etched with . . . what? Greed, joy, excitement? One of them hit Rindy hard, and spun away, scarcely turned in his frenzy. The elder Prelate clutched even harder at Qativar.

"How to catch them," Rindy said, his reedy voices hard to hear above the crowd. "How to catch them to hear us."

Qativar had begun to doubt his own safety. "They won't listen. I was wrong to bring you here."

Soot and smoke enveloped them as the shop they passed began to catch, its inside already gutted by looters, its doors hanging upon bare hinges. Qativar coughed and hurried Rindy past it. They had barely made it beyond the gaping maw when the catching fire roared and exploded outward, orange flame spewing at their backs. Rindy let out a gasp but hurried onward. Qativar looked back once, wondering what it was which fueled the fire in an empty building. Hatred, perhaps?

He found a satisfaction in the wonderment. For his works to be fulfilled, he needed that sort of fuel. He stored the memory for the future.

Rindy pulled away from him at the corner. The street swept into a circular drive. There was a greenbelt at the core of the boulevards, a strip of green which had stayed pristine, despite the destruction along the street itself. Rindy put his head down, thin hair drifting in a frizz about his crown, and loped to the park.

Qativar stepped off to follow him. He dodged a conveyance careening about the street, full of commons whooping and screaming obscenities at him. His eyes narrowed at the insults. They grinned back at him as if they might consider stopping to argue the matter. He shrugged deeper into his priestly garb and raced to catch up with Rindalan.

The old Choya had mounted a pedestal within the green-belt. The statue which had occupied it, one of Panshinea, lay crumpled on the ground, smashed to blocks of ungainly ruin. Rindalan flashed him a determined look. "I'll draw them," he said. "And then we'll do what we can. They may be God-blind, but they aren't God-*deaf*." He spread his arms, sleeves falling back upon his knobby elbows, and began to sing.

It was then Qativar realized what he dealt with, what powers, what charisma, what belief. It staggered him to hear the chanting voices of the elder Choya. It stirred his own heart, despite the machinations Qativar dreamed of, and he knew he had an enemy he must defeat if he would go farther toward fulfilling his ambitions. But all he could do now was stare upward at the Choya on the pedestal and marvel. Above the sirens and screams, the crackle of flame and the shriek of alarms, Rindalan could be heard for blocks around—more than heard—his demand was one which *must* be answered, and the Choyan clawing at shielded store fronts began to turn in their tracks and listen.

The Choyan came, as Rindalan had said they would. Soot stained their faces. Anger and disappointment flashed in their eyes. Choya'i who wore rags held the hands of their riot-dressed children tightly, wariness on their faces. Youths bucked their heads on the fringe of the crowd, the noise like loud claps emphasizing Rindalan's chanting voices.

Suddenly, the old Choya stopped. He had been looking skyward, now, his gaze blazed down to the immense crowd at his feet, crowding the greenbelt, pressing upon the circular intersection.

Qativar felt his chest hurting from the inhalation of the smoke. Two burly commons leaned on him. He put an elbow back to remind them to give him a little room. One God-blind grunted as the elbow made contact, but his gaze stayed avidly turned toward Rindalan.

Power, thought Qativar. *He's using his* bahdur *upon them*. And what a kind of *bahdur* to have. A feeling of distaste rose in his throat. No one should have the power to sway anyone subconsciously. Not for good or evil.

Rindy held out one hand, palm down, his arm quivering from age or effort. He could not hold the hand steady, though his jaw tightened from the effort. "God hears you," he said. "God sees you, though you cannot see him. God weeps that you are suffering."

Someone shouted across the silence, "Does He tell you so?"

Rindy nodded. He dropped his trembling hand by his side. "He does. And why shouldn't He? He speaks to all of us. You can hear Him, too. Above the noise, the flames, the cries of riot, you can hear Him. Listen."

Qativar watched as Choyan looked skyward, their faces going innocent, in search of miracles, in search of awe and wonderment, their eyes aglow in the summer dusk. *How could the old Choya do this?*

Yet Qativar heard it, too. He told himself it was the summer wind, heated by the fires, choked by the flames, but there was another sound, a moaning, a keening, a gentle wailing which might almost be the voice of the city itself in despair. Whoever heard it could not doubt the agony.

A Choya'i threw herself to her knees, wrapping her arms about her two children. She sobbed into their manes. "Forgive me," she cried.

Rindy put his hand out again. "Go among your neighbors," he said. "Tell them what you have heard. Have them listen. Stop what you're doing. Go home and listen. We are all one people. Listen to the despair and answer in peace."

For a moment, Qativar thought he had done it, this spindly old Choya, his priestly robes flapping in the hot wind rushing through the greenwood park. Then someone threw a rock—a chunk of the broken statue—with a cry of anger. Rindy looked toward the cry. He did not duck. The missile struck him just below the crown. Crimson fountained and the priest swayed. He looked to Qativar who opened his arms just in time to catch Rindy as he toppled from the pedestal and the crowd erupted in hatred.

Chapter 25

Rand sat down in the fuselage. He put his hands on his knees. He could feel Palaton standing nearby, fighting to contain the anger and frustration and concern that he felt. Palaton's own *bahdur* told him that as he searched for it within him. He knew that if he searched deeper, he could find more answers to the things which had puzzled him, but he did not want to ask the questions.

"You can't take the blame for this," he said, looking up at Palaton.

The pilot bowed ever so slightly to listen. "And why is that?"

"You had no way of knowing what might happen at Sethu."

Palaton sat down wearily with a sigh. "Ah, but I did. The Earthans have tried to stop me before. I knew they were behind one of the attempts. Possibly the second, as well. So Jorana and I had discussed this possibility. It was more important to force the Congress to give me a vote of trust."

"More important than your own life?"

"Yes. And more important than yours. I'm sorry, Rand."

Rand shrugged. "I've been on borrowed time since Arizar." He turned his left hand over and traced the lines in his palm with the fingers of his right hand. The left hand showed possibilities, and the lines of the right hand revealed what he had done with them. The lifeline in both hands was admirably long. He wondered why. "Take it back," he said. "Take your power back. You can't hesitate any longer."

"I would if I could."

"You can." Rand watched Palaton's face steadily. Now the other's eyes turned from him slightly. "I saw it then, I see it now. You threw the book down, but it told you what you needed to know."

"You saw nothing!"

"Our *bahdur* tells me otherwise. I saw an answer, but you rejected it."

Palaton twisted in the chair. "I was right to do so."

"We're going back to a city in chaos. From what Rufeen said, everything you've been trying to prevent just exploded."

"Not quite." Palaton put a hand to his head and rubbed the base of his crown ever so lightly, and Rand wondered if its weight bothered him. Did Choyan have headaches? It seemed they must. "If the Houses join in open warfare, then what I fear most is happening. But not yet. The commons are warring against the counties, against what they perceive as injustice. We are a civilized people. We had come far and fallen far, but we're still here."

"You won't be if the scavengers come to pick at what's left of Cho after civil war."

"Don't you think I know that! Why do you think I came forward . . . just to save Panshinea's hide?" Palaton shut his mouth abruptly. He collected himself before adding, "You know more than you should. I won't endanger you further."

"It's too late for that," Rand said softly. "I know what you are. I couldn't understand the xenophobia . . . the fear of those who met me. What was I to be feared? I could understand the disgust, but not the fear. Then, at Sethu, I started to understand. You keep off-worlders away to hide your abilities. As a *tezar*, one to one, you can shield yourself. But you can't shield an entire race . . . nor can you fully explain a society in two distinct stratas. Those who have psionics and those who don't. This isn't just a religious difference for you."

Palaton said nothing, but watched Rand steadily.

Rand's mouth had gone dry. He swallowed, knowing that what he was saying would probably cost him his life. "And the level of your psionics ability is dwindling, generation after generation. You have appliances, machinery, whole cities that can't function the way they used to because no one has the ability to trigger them now. The *tezars* are probably the most talented . . . you used it to make the

FTL drive function, which is why none of your enemies have been able to duplicate it. But at the same time, you're burning your talents out . . . out of yourselves, and out of your people."

"As for what I am . . . I guess I'm a human oil filter. I don't know. As a Brethren, I'm supposed to take this psionic power and filter it through me. Cleanse it. Refresh it and return it to you. Only I was never supposed to know just what it was I had."

"No," agreed Palaton. "None of you were."

"And because I do. I am now expendable. You can do what you have to."

"No."

"You have to, dammit! I won't be the only reason an entire planet goes down. Not for my world and not for yours!" Rand found his fists clenched and his heart pounding in his chest.

"That, too, we have in common."

"Then what are we going to do about it?"

Palaton looked at his own hands. "Whatever we can, I guess."

"Tell me what to do."

"Close your eyes and empty your mind."

Instead of emptiness, he found it filled with Chaos. He grasped for Palaton in fear like a drowning man and found nothing to catch.

Nedar heard the thunder of implosion as the teleporter sent him on his way. His head thickened and dulled with the rapid pressure change and although there was a hollow, terrifying moment when he was nothing, the next moment he could feel himself pushing out, being birthed into *someplace*. Nedar caught himself with a stagger as his boots made contact with solid ground.

He could not imagine a Cho where teleporting had been common. His stomach roiled at the abrupt method of travel and his head pounded. As his eyes cleared, he saw himself on the edge of the airstrip at Blue Ridge, the mountains sharp and clean behind the outline of a fighter plane.

Nedar smiled as Hat reacted to his sudden appearance. The other's eyes widened like a child's.

"Nedar! You're here. I . . . I've never seen that done."

Hat looked him over as if fearful something might have fallen off on the way.

Nedar reached out and took his flight jacket from Hat's arm. "Another lost skill with some usefulness to it."

Hat shook all over in denial. "I could never travel like that." Still in motion, he pointed to the plane. "It's all ready for you."

"Good." Nedar mounted the wing ladder and settled himself inside. Hat watched with a mournful look. He gave a *tezar* salute. "Wish me luck," he called down.

Sadness etched Hat's broad face beyond his years. "If it were anybody but Palaton. . . ."

"A traitor, by any name, is still a traitor."

"I know." Hat dug his toe into the ground. "Fair winds, Nedar."

Nedar snapped the canopy shut and the plane roared into life.

Qativar absorbed the shock of Rindy's fall, going to his own knees as the Prelate toppled onto him. The elder's neck snapped back with a sound like a breaking stick, and the Choya advancing on them stopped abruptly.

Rindy wore the richly colored robes of the High Priest of a House, and though they were torn and dirtied from his efforts in the streets, they were unmistakable. The commons surrounding them now absorbed the fact that the Prelate might be dead, and they might be found at fault.

Their superstitions won and with shouts of defiance and warning, they scattered. Qativar abruptly found himself alone with the old Choya in his arms.

He had gotten more than he bargained for. Why hadn't he run off and left the old fool to the whims of the crowd? He did not need to be found here with Rindalan dying in his embrace. It would do his cause absolutely no good at all if he died as well.

But it had been the other's fervor which had captured him, just as it had captured the other listeners. Qativar's face burned in shame that *bahdur* could be so perverted. He got to his feet with a grunt and resettled his hold on the other's spindly frame. He could not leave Rindy now. He had been recognized as the old priest's companion. He would have to take him back to die.

Conveyances littered the streets, stripped and burning. He began to walk back toward the palace, a whole city's quarter away, looking for a vehicle that had perhaps just been overturned and left, abandoned, rather than destroyed.

Ashes and sparks drifted through the hot summer air. He could see, over building tops, where the wind that came from fiercely hot and burning buildings swirled into maelstroms of energy, but here the air was relatively still. It settled in choking layers. Qativar found tears coursing down his face.

He walked until his feet and knees and arms went numb, then leaned against the nearest building, searching for a smooth panel to take his weight among the jagged store and security fronts torn open. The old priest stayed quiet in his arms, but he could hear the noisy sound of Rindy's labored breathing.

Qativar squinted through the thickening dusk, now lit with an orange-red glow from within, like a glowing ember inside the gray drift of ashes. Moon or stars could not be seen . . . black and white clouds funneled across the evening sky. Qativar coughed. It did no good. He spat out the taste of soot.

He turned his head. Above the dim cry of alarm and fire pumps, he could hear a drone. He turned and found himself in the service alley. The loading docks were in disarray, most of them stripped, but an idling ferry sat, its cargo long gone, its hovers still on.

It was better than walking the rest of the way. Qativar staggered toward it, arranged Rindy on the flat bed and sat next to him, punching out a new destination on the instrument panel. The ferry shuddered beneath them, then slowly rose higher and began to cruise down the alleyway.

Havoc met them in the streets before the palace. He could see that the commons had barricaded the new Congressional Halls. They were laying siege to the Congress. He rolled Rindy off the ferry and took the back glidewalk toward the palace, hoping that his movements would not gain their attention.

He stopped short of the sonic barriers surrounding the gray and black stone palace. Bizarrely, the atmosphere of the city surrounded it, camouflaging it, and the palace cum fortress could barely be seen at the edge of the summer night. Troops saw him as he sagged to the bottom steps, unable to bear Rindalan any longer. They dropped to their knees, enforcer muzzles targeting him.

Qativar found more than a sob in his chest as he cried out, "Get Jorana. This is High Priest Rindalan, and he's dying."

Chaos swallowed him. He found his heart beating in time with a pulse of light which kept surging past him. He was not the center of this universe. He hurtled through it, dropping. Rand flailed, trying to halt his descent into—what? He could not be in Chaos itself, could he?

And where was Palaton? Rand tumbled like a parachutist in free-fall, spread his arms and legs to slow the tumble. As he spun, he slowed, and he could see a golden thread trailing out behind him, a fine anchor line like that spun by a spider, and he the four-legged arachnid.

The thought gave him a sudden jolt of fear . . . but it wasn't him, it was that other who lived inside his skin, that thin skin which threatened to rip now and then, spilling the other out. It would be havoc to lose that other now, he knew, and he held tight to the sense of him. The moment he made the decision, he could feel Palaton's presence. He could not see the pilot as he could see Chaos, but he could feel him, could hear the slow steady beat of his heart, could smell the slightly musky Choyan smell. The knowledge that the other was near slowed his descent abruptly, and he hung in the balance.

As he watched the random activity boiling around him, he thought that what they measured as random might not be random at all—but the pattern so vast that only across infinity might it be measured. Who was he to calibrate the infinite across the finite? The abrupt rise and fall of fractals might be nothing more than the peaks and valleys of a heartbeat, the span of space a pause between breaths.

He had attained calm abruptly. Yet, just as sharply, that other probed at him. *Danger*. Rand squirmed a little in the base of the tangled web his fall had woven. He was secure in Chaos until that time when Palaton had achieved what he desired, or let him fall to death. But he no longer felt alarm. A warm, drowsy peace enveloped him.

Danger.

He put a hand out. A shower of golden sparks trailed from it. He bridged dead space and touched another, briefly, so unexpectedly that he jerked with the thrill of it. *Someone not Palaton.*

"They're killing you, Rand. And they're killing me, too. But I know the poison."

The sudden recognition of the South American lilt brought a choke to his throat. It was Bevan who spoke . . . his voice trapped eerily here, as though this bit of Chaos was purgatory.

"Where are your senses? We're in this together. We're coming for you, Rand, me and Alexa. We're alive, and we're coming for you."

"Bevan? *Alexa?*"

The spiderweb holding him trembled with the sound of his voice.

"Coming for you like alphabet soup. From A to Zee . . . the Choyan do it, too. Get this, my boy. We can do it better. Better and faster. We're coming in!"

Rand grabbed for the sense of something pushing past him, rushing past the web he'd strung, hurtling through Chaos as he had been only moments before, but whatever that something was, it slipped through his fingers. He had it for a shadow of an instant, long enough to know that it was Bevan and Alexa . . . and others, a dark hunger driving them. Abdreliks? He did not know what an Abdrelik felt like.

I do, said Palaton grimly in his mind.

Whatever it was rushing past him, it knifed the web strands cleanly. The anchor strings of golden light which held him safe ripped clear and he plunged downward.

Chapter 26

"We're losing him."

"No," said the physician. "He's stabilizing."

Jorana stepped away from the door of the Prelate's apartment. Rindy lay, his body shrunken and pale under the medical sheets, every fiber of the sheet which covered him monitoring a function, in a room of the apartment which Panshinea had years ago ordered made over for the aging Choya. It was a room she had hoped never to see in use. She could not imagine Rindy gone, his *bahdur* snuffed, his vigorous love of life and his people shut away.

The physician on duty, a narrow-faced, near hornless Sky, stepped away and eyed the monitors. "I like the looks of that," he said. "What we have to worry about now is blood clots in the lungs. He's taken quite a fall and a beating."

She could not stay, no matter how her heart directed her. Melbar's staff had spotted some air traffic disruption along the northern and easternmost edges of the county security net. She had to see if the traffic had been identified. And Congress was under siege, and she waited, with Gathon, to see if they asked for deadly force to be freed. Much as she thought Congress ought to be left to stew in its own juices, she would have to respond if the vote came through.

Qativar stayed just inside the doorway. He looked as if he'd been dragged through a pit of ash and smoke. "I'll stay," he said, "if I may."

Jorana hesitated. She was still uncertain of just why Rindy had left the palace, and how Qativar had found him. But Qativar was the Prelate's aide, his chosen protègè, his own heir to the throne, as it were. If Rindalan trusted him, who was she to question the point?

She was, by the very nature of her training and her position, suspicious. Still, with the medical monitors in place, Qativar could scarcely harm Rindy further. Either the elder made it—or he didn't. "All right," she said. "Let me know how he's doing."

Qativar nodded, and she left the apartments. Traskar joined her in the hall. She turned to face him and set her jaw. Traskar was one of the mistakes she had made which she had had to face every day for the last five days. He should have gone with Palaton and Rand to Sethu, and damn the protocol of a cleansing. If the High Priest had allowed an alien within the temple, she might also have allowed a guard.

"They're beginning to cordon off the imperial grounds."

The grounds were vast—so vast—and yet the numbers of the commons seemed to multiply by the hour. Done with burning and looting the other quarters of the city, they were now flocking to the palace and the new Congressional Halls. "I want lifters on the back grounds, fueled and ready to go. Make sure one of them is a med-evac. And I want every Choya with the talent to throw illusions on a roster, in my hands, in fifteen minutes."

Traskar nodded. He broke into a run.

She did not want to think they had come to burn the palace, but the reality of the situation told her it could very well be otherwise. Would Malahki sacrifice her for such a powerful movement?

She thought he would.

She broke into a trot again, heading toward the surveillance wing.

The medical techs left him alone with Rindy after a quarter hour, convinced that the Prelate finally had lapsed into a comfortable rest. The head physician took a critical look at Qativar, touched a bruise on his cheekbone which had not hurt at all before and smarted sharply when touched, and said, "Get yourself cleaned up so I know what to treat on you."

"I'm all right." He did not take his eyes off Rindy.

"Nonetheless, we've made him sterile." The Sky looked Qativar up and down. "And you're not."

The young Prelate knew when to relent. "All right," he said. "I'll use the refresher here in the apartment."

"Good. You can sit with him, if you like, but I doubt he'll wake till morning. The monitors will let us know if there's a problem." The physician brushed past him, joining his tech in the hall. They shared a low laugh and moved on.

Qativar knew they did not laugh at him, yet heat rushed to his face and he half-turned, thinking of a challenge. An unpriestly response, he told himself, and turned back to look at Rindy.

He could feel the *bahdur* from across the room. Not banked or shielded by dint of his personality, the power seemed to emanate from Rindy as it had while he had tried to reach the God-blind. Perhaps, in his coma, he still tried to reach them, to save them from themselves, those too blind to see what it was they destroyed. Qativar had served the elder these past seven years, hand and foot, as undersecretary and aide and even servant, as well as protègè, yet he had never felt the *bahdur* unleashed as it had been this night.

And the vigor of it threatened him even as it resolved him in his course. No Choya, by chance of birth, should be so gifted while millions were not. Nor should a Choya be allowed to reign by virtue of that power. Equality was the only answer and Qativar was more determined than ever to achieve it. But could he when Housed talents like Rindalan stood in his way? He, who had become a Prelate because his talents were so sparse that he'd been lucky to have even passed the tests for that, could not stand against them one by one. He patted his sleeve, testing for the tiny vial of *ruhl* he always kept with him. It was still the only hope he might have.

If Vihtirne of Sky won back her water recycling patent, the Water Resources of every county would be thrown into disarray and all the counties would become vulnerable to his schemes. He had only to keep testing his drug and wait patiently.

But what a boon it would be to his plans if Rindalan were to pass beyond now, leaving him the High Priest of the House of Star. He would have access to the House library and to the very network of power he hoped to bring down. He had only to stand and wait and let nature take its course. For it was obvious that, though Rindalan's spirit was strong, his flesh was weak. The vessel might prove too aged to contain the power within.

Rindy stirred. Despite the cradle holding his injured neck and head steady, he thrashed a bit, then subsided. Then, eyelids fluttering as if he attempted to wake, the elder whispered, "Water."

Without thinking, Qativar moved to the pitcher on the medical stand. He poured a glass and then it struck him. What chance for recovery did Rindalan have if his *bahdur* abandoned him?

Carefully, so that monitoring cameras could not catch his sleight of hand, he removed the vial from his sleeve and tipped its clear liquid into the glass. He did not carry a toxic dose—as a poison, it left residues in morbid flesh, though it passed so quickly through the system that if Rindy lived but an hour or two longer, its traces would be gone. He swirled the glass to mix its contents, then stepped to his Prelate's side.

Rindy, half-conscious, rallied enough to drain the glass. He lay back in the cradle, his horn crown immense and his thinning fringe of chestnut hair wild among its curves, the planes of his face sharp-cut. Qativar dropped the glass in the disposal and stepped back to watch the poison work.

The deep lines etched in the other's face began to smooth out as the *ruhl* intoxication soothed whatever half-conscious dreams he had. The fretfulness with which he had begun to stir left him. Satisfied, Qativar turned to go shower and change clothes, the smell of the fire still on him, smoky and pungent, when Rindy spoke.

They did not have an auditory monitor on him. What he said would be of little importance. The medical equipment surrounding him constantly evaluated his vital statistics and left his audible ramblings in privacy. Qativar paused, wondering what value a *ruhl*-induced dream might have, and he listened.

"Palaton?" Rindy moved a hand and his brows arched as if he tried to force himself to wake. His eyes fluttered open, unfocused. "Palaton, is that you?"

"Yes," answered Qativar. He stepped back toward the bed, offering a hand which Rindy gripped tightly.

"I did a foolish thing."

"Not to worry," Qativar said. "Get your rest."

Rindalan tried to move his head and failed. His unfocused eyes sought Qativar's. "I'm very tired."

"Then sleep."

"This is a sleep I fear I might not wake from. Palaton, I have something I must tell you."

Qativar debated, then squeezed the hand he held tighter. "What is it, Rindy?"

"I will not go as your mother did, without your knowing. You don't remember me . . . but I tested you when you were just a child. You were the youngest candidate I ever tested, but your grandfather insisted."

Qativar knew of Palaton's grandfather Volan, a domineering Star who had bankrupted his Householding, depending too heavily on the financial fortunes of the *tezars* his bloodline produced. Early testing would have been typical of the Choya.

Rindy paused, wet his lips, and then said, "I found out that you had no acknowledged father. Your mother refused to name your sire. Your grandfather feared the genetic lines had been soiled, but you tested well and truly. But what he did not know was that I and the Earthan priest who worked with me identified the out-cross. You come from the Fourth House, Palaton, the House destroyed. Your lineage from that House is true and clear. The Earthan priest confirmed it. We were sworn to secrecy, he and I. Your grandfather dared not touch me, but he had the Earthan priest killed later. Yet, from the attempts made on your life, the priest must have told what he knew. The lineage of a Flame is greatly feared, and with reason. You must know yourself, Palaton, and protect yourself. They will not cease until you are dead." Rindy halted, breathless.

Qativar eyed the heart monitor. It showed the beginning of an erratic beat. "I'll remember, Rindy."

"Take care, Palaton. Forgive me for keeping a secret." Rindy's eyes fluttered shut. Slowly, he released the grip he had on Qativar's hand.

Qativar stood a moment longer, but the old Choya had merely lapsed into sleep. He watched the heart monitor. It stayed erratic.

He smiled. By the time he'd showered and changed, the deed should be done.

Pondering what rewards he might reap from the unexpected confession, Qativar left the room.

"Palaton, don't leave me!" Rand screamed as he plummeted, heart drumming, breath tearing his lungs as it seared outward. He would never stop falling, not even after death, he knew and he clawed in desperation.

He could feel that other leaving him, pulled out by the pressure of the fall. It was as if his insides were being ripped out, through his screaming mouth, the pores of his skin, his eyes, golden sparks pouring outward, the very substance that kept him alive.

He had to let it go, he knew that. But he could not help himself. He shoveled his hands through it, trying to hold on, trying to stop the inevitable. His heart beat faster and faster, deafening him, swelling in his chest, causing incredible pain.

He clutched his chest. He could feel his heart bursting, the pulse in his eardrums booming. He was dying, and he knew it.

And then the golden fire leaving him arched through space, bridging from him to another, and he saw the other, a proudly horned figure, and they were connected, intimately, through the umbilical of power. What flowed from him, flowed into the other. Palaton looked at him and fear carved his face.

"No," he said and pushed back.

Rand lost consciousness of even Chaos.

Palaton went to his knees. A bitter sob tore through him. He choked a second one back and took the boy in his arms, the boy who had been barely breathing, and he held him tightly. He could not do it—he knew he could not do it—and now he held the other tightly and felt the racing heartbeat that had been pulsing wildly begin to steady.

The *bahdur* had been streaming back into him. For a wild, unfettered moment he had its full strength, pure and renewed, coursing inside him. But it had not come without a price, and with it had come another soul, as tied to its power as he was.

But he could live without it, while, losing it, Rand had plunged rapidly toward death, and so he had let it go.

There was a small hope to be gained from this failure. His *bahdur* prospered. It had been cleansed and refined beyond all his dreams. It waited for him still. One day, he might be able to regain all that he had lost and more.

Until then, there was Rand to be considered.

Stranger from another world, in his arms, rocked back to life.

Palaton.

His soul blossomed at the voice within, joy beyond any he had ever known at the Congress, and then startlement, as the two touched minds.

He answered tentatively. *I have you.* With mental irony, adding, *And it appears you have me.*

The *bahdur* had tied them together in a knot of souls, bridging the distance between flesh with that rarest of psionic abilities, pure telepathy. Only death would part them now.

Palaton was wondering what the future could hold, when the cruiser rocked under a violent assault.

"Sequencing the net matrix," the tech told Jorana. "Two inbound, one a cruiser and the other a fighter. Both unID'd at this point."

"Give me a point of origin for the cruiser." She bit her lower lip, not daring to hope.

"They're in an evasive pattern. I can't pinpoint the vector of origination."

"Could it be Sethu?" Her voices raised, vibrating with impatience and frustration.

The tech looked coldly at his screens. "It could be, choya'i, from anywhere. The fighter, however, appears to have come from the area of Blue Ridge."

Why Blue Ridge? And, if the cruiser was Palaton's, why wasn't it broadcasting its ID?

"Uh-oh," the tech said. He narrowed his eyes.

"The fighter is engaging the cruiser."

"What?" Jorana felt her throat constrict. "Scramble a flight. Get them up and see what's happening."

The tech's stony gaze wavered. "I can't, Minister. The commons have the airfield. We can't get anyone up locally. Only the deep space berths and cradles are free."

A deep space cruiser would do her no good. Jorana swore and slammed her palm down on the tech's desk. The furniture shuddered under the blow.

"Find out what the hell's going on and let me know as soon as possible." Jorana left, and broke into a run, covering the marble corridors of the palace.

It had to be Palaton, or Rufeen bringing the bodies back. The Houses were keeping their troops back now, waiting for the morning and the confusion to clear. There were no other cruisers out. It *had* to be Palaton, dead or alive.

And if he were alive, then someone from Blue Ridge was doing his best to bring him down.

But *why?*

She came to a halt at the front doors. A troop of guard in full riot gear stood just within the doorway. A similar troop was just outside, and a full line had been stationed at the sonics barriers.

She chose a Choya with approximately her build. "Soldier, hand me your gear."

The Choya blinked, then impassively began to shed his body armor and shield and vest battery pack. Jorana suited up quickly, taking every piece of gear almost before the guard could surrender it.

"Soldier, I want you to find Minister Gathon. Inform him that a ship I have reason to believe is the imperial cruiser is attempting to come in. It's under attack. I am going to the airstrip to see what I can do. I'm going alone because I think I'll have better success making my objective. Is that understood?"

The Choya nodded. "Repeat it back to me."

He did so, haltingly, with care.

"All right. Hold your station," she told the others, and stepped outside.

She was not prepared for the sight. The skies in all directions flamed and smoked. It hurt to breathe. The skyscape crumbled in blackened, falling ruins wherever she looked. The Godless had all but destroyed Charolon.

And the commons stood ringed about the palace, just as they held the Congressional Halls, determined to wreak even more destruction. They raised their voices in taunts as they saw her.

She paced to the line holding the sonics barrier. "This is Security Minister Jorana. Let me through." She put up her visor to confirm her identity.

The guard saluted, but said, "Choya'i, they'll pull you down."

"I don't think so. You have your orders. Let me through, then get that barrier back up—and take it from stun to stop."

He fumbled at the control post. The laser lines delineating the sound waves blinked and then faded. She stepped through. The barrier went back on with a sizzle behind her.

Jorana sat down cross-legged on the steps before the commons could move. She kept her visor up and said calmly, with all the *bahdur* reinforcement she could muster, "Bring me Malahki. It's time to talk."

Rand's pulse fluttered weakly in his throat as the ship veered. Palaton loosed him and fastened the safety webbing close. He gained the cockpit, almost pitching in headfirst.

"What is it?"

Rufeen said grimly, "We're under attack."

"What?" Palaton grabbed for the threshold to steady himself as she took the cruiser evasively about again. "By Charolon?"

"No . . . I don't think so. He intersected us just outside the security net. The net is down . . . we can come in, although the visual on the airstrip looks to me like the rioters have it."

"We can't land and someone is busy trying to blast us out of the sky."

"You got it." Rufeen swore as the plane rocked, catching the outer burst of another attack. "Whoever is flying is good."

Palaton thrust himself inside and sat down. He drew a harness across his chest and lap hurriedly. "What's the ID on the plane?"

"It's out of Blue Ridge."

Palaton felt as though his throat had been cut. Words left him. He reached for the controls in front of him and brought up an ID. It was a training fighter from Blue Ridge. The cruiser had no hope of continuing to elude the needle sharp form on its heels, no matter how good a pilot Rufeen was.

He thought fleetingly of Nedar. Then, as the fighter closed, he was too busy to think.

Malahki came in on a jet sled, his thick dark mane tangling with the night, the crowd parting before him. He stepped down and gave a hand to Jorana, helping her to her feet. He had answered, as she'd hoped, so quickly he must have been quartered nearby, waiting and watching.

He drew her aside. "You asked for me, to talk. Are we talking of surrendering the palace?"

"No."

Anger crossed his face. Gold glinted deep in his eyes. "Then what?"

"I want safe passage to the airstrip."

"The strip? Why? We've embargoed the city. I don't want *bahdur*-blazing Houses to come riding to your rescue. At least, not until we're ready for them."

"Palaton's trying to land."

"Palaton? Are you sure?"

She could not meet his eyes. "No. We've had no contact. But it's a cruiser, and it's the only one due back."

"And if he's dead?"

"I'll come back and talk to Gathon about surrendering the palace before anyone else gets hurt. Rindy is upstairs . . . in critical condition. I want permission to med-evac him."

"We have no quarrel with the Prelate. And if Palaton is alive?"

She looked at him then. "He'll have more control over them than you, and you know it. He'll send them back."

"Then why should I let him land?"

"Because this is not the time for revolution."

Malahki's mouth curved in a one-sided smile. "You are so sure of yourself, Jorana." He considered a moment. "I will give you passage . . . on one condition."

"What?"

He pressed a vial into her hand without words.

She looked at it.

"Use it on Palaton. Give me a child of your lineages."

She swallowed tightly. Then Jorana closed her fingers about the vial. It would not matter if Palaton were dead. And if he were alive . . . she would face the future later. Malahki knew he had his answer as soon as she closed her fist about the drug. He strode back to the jet sled and kicked it into high.

"Time is short," he said.

She mounted the sled behind him.

"Bring it about!" Palaton's voices rose above the whine of instruments.

"What?" Rufeen spared a split second to glare at him. "Are you crazy?"

"Attack back. He won't expect it. Be aggressive."

The Choya'i shook her head in despair and then said, "Oh, what the hell." She kicked the throttle loose and brought it to manual, taking it off the autopilot evasive pattern. The cruiser answered smartly to her demands on it.

Palaton's gut protested the loop of movement, but he kept his eyes on his monitors. They were just outside Charolon, within range of the strip, and its broadcast was filling his screens with electronic demands he could not answer. He could also see that most of the air lanes were blocked, filled with infrared heat that could only come from living bodies.

The commons were literally lying down on the airfield to control it.

A cruiser could not land on a thumbnail like a lifter. Nor could it continue to outmaneuver a fighter. Rufeen would have to bring it down soon. Palaton brought up his map, scanning the area, and located a maintenance field which appeared to be empty. The lanes were short. Rufeen would have to brake sharply and finesse a taxi.

Getting there in one piece would be as much of a challenge as landing in one piece.

The cruiser shuddered. Rufeen said, "He's dodging me."

"But at least you're on the offensive." Palaton brought up his coordinates. "Can you bring it down there?"

"Unless we're scrap metal by the time I need to make the approach, yeah."

"Let me take the guns."

"I thought you'd never ask." Rufeen let go of the gunfire control abruptly and applied all of her attention to maneuvering.

Palaton laced his fingers into the gunnery panel. Without *bahdur* to guide him, he felt odd, no warming tingle to let him know instinctively when to fire. The grid tracked over his left eye. He normally wore it over his right, but he normally piloted instead of copiloted. Before he could get accustomed to it, the fighter in front of him looped off suddenly, and disappeared from sight.

But he knew where the fighter was going before instruments could pick it up. "Yaw," he yelped at Rufeen and set his sights for the fighter he knew would appear there.

She did not answer. The cruiser swooped in answer to the helm. And the Blue Ridge fighter came up in his sights as he had known it would.

They fired at one another simultaneously.

Chapter 27

Smoke and flaming metal filled the sky. Palaton felt the cruiser give a shudder like a death rattle and begin to plunge downward. Shearing off the target grid, he saw the fighter tumble downward, somersaulting like a fallen comet.

Rufeen laid in the coordinates of the abandoned strip and then slumped over the panel. Palaton put a hand back to rouse her without success. The cruiser went nose-down, vainly trying to answer the autopilot. He braced himself as the cracked windshield gave way and the earth and the night tore in at him.

The impact as they hit blacked out every thought he might have had.

Malahki skewed the sled about on the road as explosions rocked the sky. "There!"

Jorana threw her helmet off to see. The two planes nearly collided with one another and shrapnel filled the air. It rained down about them as the scream of diving planes tore at her ears. Malahki did not wait for her response. He gunned the sled toward the cruiser as it hit the ground, skidding, and split in half. She had never heard anything so awful in her life. Yet as she sent her *bahdur* spiraling out, there was still life inside the wreckage. Flames died down and then flared up again.

She did not know she could move so quickly in riot gear. She reached the cockpit, which had spilled open like a cracked egg, white smoke billowing out of it and found a *tezar*. She was pale, but breathing shallowly. Jorana recognized Rufeen under the blood.

She pulled her from the wreckage, muttering, "Oh, God, oh, God," for the other Choya slumped over the controls had to be Palaton. She spread Rufeen out on her back, wondering where Malahki was, and went back for Palaton.

A wave of commons rushed toward the wreckage. Malahki secured the jet sled and saw them coming. He'd sent Chirek out to handle the airstrip and, looking for him now, was relieved to see Chirek carried among their numbers. He flicked a glance toward the downed cruiser. Jorana had brought out one body and was diving in for another. He could barely see the outline of the crowned head through the shattered canopy of the foresection, but he recognized Palaton in silhouette as flames in the fuselage section lit up the night.

She would have her Palaton, alive, if battered, he thought. And what would he have?

Chirek gained his side. Malahki waved the crowd off, shouting for calm and quiet. "Your *tezar* has come back. The Housed at Sethu did not bring him down!"

To Chirek, he said, "Damn the luck. Put them on fire control. We don't need this spreading out of hand. We need the airstrip open for emergency supplies."

Jorana stood up, Palaton across her shoulder. Dazed, he looked about and then called, in voices of sheer terror, "Rand!"

Malahki grabbed Chirek by the shoulder. "The humankind must be in the fuselage. Get him out. Get him secured. Take him to my quarters."

"Malahki—"

"Don't question me! Do it!"

Chirek gave a nod, grabbed the arm of the Choya closest to him and plunged toward the fuselage which lay shuddering and flaming yards away from the foresection of the cruiser.

Jorana put her hand to Palaton's face. "We'll get him. Now come on." She smelled leaking fuel. "We're in danger, too."

"Rufeen . . ." Palaton turned confused eyes on her.

"Already out. Palaton, please. Help me. I can't carry you out of here alone." Her *bahdur* augmented strength threatened to leave her.

He leaned on her heavily, limping and breathing raggedly. He winced as they jumped clear of the foresection, going to his knees and nearly taking her down as well. She pulled him up, struggling.

The smell of raw fuel filled her nostrils. It set her head reeling. "Come on!"

At her urging, he broke into a shambling run across the rutted air lane, putting open, torn land between them and the foresection.

The cockpit of the plane went up with a roar as they reached the sagging tree under whose branches she had lain Rufeen.

The fuselage was crawling with Choyan. Palaton leaned back against the tree, taking his weight off Jorana. He watched avidly, blinking, bloodswelling threatening to close his left eye.

"What about the other pilot?"

"I don't know. I don't see it. It went down."

"I saw the pod go. He jettisoned." He looked about, saw a dim fire. "There."

"Maybe. All Charolon is in flames tonight. The Godless have the palace and the Congressional Halls surrounded. We are all hostage."

Palaton blinked. He felt his brow, still dazed. "I need to know who it was."

"It's over."

"No. No. But it will be tonight." He patted his chest, then winced. "I think I've broken a couple of ribs," he added and felt again gingerly. Then he froze, minutely, as if distracted. His face relaxed. "Rand's alive," he said.

Jorana wondered how he knew. She watched the frantic activity of fire crew and commons working on the fuselage. "They're bringing a litter out."

"Good." Palaton lurched upright, stumbling across the wreckage-strewn airway.

Commons saw him. They shouted his name and, like a tide rushing to fill an empty shore, swelled up, blocking him from the litter.

"Palaton," Jorana took his arm. "He's out."

The fuselage gave a belch of smoke and fire and the Choyan scattered. They came back with determination, using their hands and makeshift shovels to pile dirt on the flames. The litter passed from hand to hand, and Rand disappeared from sight.

Palaton tightened his grip on Jorana's shoulder. "Who has him?"

Malahki appeared out of the furor. "I have," he answered calmly. He handed Palaton a clean square of cloth. "Have her wrap your brow. You're bleeding, hero."

Jorana took the cloth and bound Palaton's head gently. Palaton stood impassively, as if bearing her touch. He did not take his eyes from Malahki.

"Your ward is safe enough with me," Malahki said.

"Neither he nor I are the pawns you hope we are," Palaton remarked. "I'm taking the jet sled."

"Are you?"

"I have business with Congress. I understand your people have kept it in session for me."

The two looked at one another. Jorana held her breath until Malahki dipped his chin slightly and stood aside. "I advise you to hurry," he said. "The people are in dire need of the news of your arrival."

Palaton claimed the jet sled. He paused as Jorana swung up behind him saying, "I'm going with you."

Rand felt the fanning of fresh air almost before he knew that he was being carried free of the cruiser. His limbs would not obey him. His mind called out in fear and Palaton answered, reassuring him, he was alive, safe, being carried free. He lifted his head and realized he was being borne on a sea of Choyan. Not one of them shrank from touching him in his blanket sling.

They laid him on the floor of a conveyance. A Choya smiled down at him as the vehicle jolted into motion. "I'm Chirek," he said. "And you're safe."

Rand took the hand he offered and pulled himself onto a seat. His bones ached and his mind spun. For a moment, he could hear nothing but Bevan's mocking voice, "we're coming to rescue you."

He opened his eyes wide, trying to clear his mind of past and present. He saw the wreckage of the cruiser as they passed it. "Rufeen?"

"It is my understanding all lived through the crash. Emergency vehicles are being brought in." The Choya had quiet, mannered voices, yet Rand sensed something more. The conveyance was taking them from the crash site as quickly as possible.

"Where's Palaton?"

"All in good time." Chirek looked out the window. "Everything in its own time."

Rand sat back on the seat, too weak to protest, wondering if he had been rescued or imprisoned. He put his head back on the cool, slick fabric of the vehicle's seat. Images rushed at him: of Chaos, of Palaton, of Alexa and Bevan. Of Bevan piloting. Of starfighters coming screaming in. Of fire. Of Bevan.

Rand closed his eyes and tried to still his mind. When things were quiet, when he felt better, he knew he could reach Palaton. Time to wait now, until he understood what was happening and what they might be up against.

Nedar lay in crippling pain for long moments. Then he forced himself to his feet. He kicked open what remained of the shell of the jettison pod. He'd lost part of his horn crown, its jagged edge, lying before him. Nedar looked at it. It could be grafted back if he found a physician soon enough. He put a shoulder to the wreckage of the pod, letting it bolster him. He knew who had fought him in the skies, knew those maneuvers and strategy as well as he knew the palm of his hand. Palaton lived! And Palaton was destroying him piece by piece. Nedar left the bone fragment where it lay and staggered out into the night, ignoring the warm sticky stream of fluid down his face and along his neck.

A Choya came out of the night. "Sir, are you hurt? Let me help you."

A commons, but a commons with a blurring of talent. Nedar reached for him, his grasp like steel. The Choya let out a yelp and went to his knees, quivering with fear. He begged for his life but it did him no good.

When Nedar had drained him of the meager *bahdur* he carried, he let the empty body slump over and fall to the ground.

He straightened and took a deep breath. He would need shelter until he could find Palaton again. But there was havoc in the streets, and as long as confusion reigned, there would be a chance to strike again. He had not lost Palaton. Not yet. The Choya had left an idling ferry in the bushes. He took it and struck out in the direction of burning Charolon.

*　　*　　*

Bevan's skin burned as though a fever raged below its surface, threatening to crackle the delicate translucency into char. Alexa tore off the hem of her sleeve, wet it and put it across his forehead. The open shield showed her Chaos; she could not watch it, despite the drugs given her. Yet Bevan's dark eyes sank into it avidly, he would not look away, and his fingers played on the keypad of the black box which had been attached to the control panel. He muttered as he piloted, things she could make no sense or inkling of, other than, "We're coming, Rand."

The tiny instrument in her ear spoke. She listened and then said to Bevan, "Commander rrRusk wants to know how much longer."

"We're nearly there."

"So soon?" It had only been a matter of hours since they had reached FTL. She had not crossed Chaos that often, but even she knew it was a matter of days, at least. "Bevan, that can't be."

He looked at her, eyes smoldering in a death's head, and she shrank back. "I'm better at this than they are," he said. "They didn't know!" And he laughed, that high, crescendo laugh which she could not bear to hear. Abruptly, the sound truncated and Bevan looked back to Chaos. She did not cool his forehead again, afraid to touch him.

She relayed his message to rrRusk. The commander grunted in disbelief and said, "We'll be ready." She hugged her knees to her chest, feeling her dark side rising, aware of a hunt about to begin, unable to control that part of her which had become Abdrelik. Tears began to flood from her eyes, but her face stayed frozen, unaware of what it was which struck it.

Rand opened his eyes as the conveyance hit something with a jolt, and then the platform bed of the vehicle began to sink rapidly. Chirek put a steadying hand on his shoulder.

"It's all right," the Choya said.

Rand eyed him. The Choya looked common to him, without the distinct characteristics of the Housed he was beginning to learn to pick out. The horn crown was coarser, the hair and eyes light and nondescript. It was a pleasant enough face for a Choya. He looked for, but did not think he found any ill intent in it.

"Just who are you?"

"I," answered Chirek, "am a Godless. A hardworking, God-fearing commons. And you?"

"A battered and bruised Terran. And I think I have about as much cause to fear God as anybody."

"Do you?" Chirek smiled warmly. "We shall have to talk religious philosophy sometime, you and I." He crossed his legs and looked out the window of the conveyance. Rand abruptly realized they were in a shaft and dropping. "But not tonight."

"And what do you have planned for tonight?"

The conveyance came to another halt, and this time sat, shuddering. Chirek leaned over and opened the door on Rand's side. "Tonight, all plans are confounded. All hopes and all fears realized. Tonight, we wait for the end."

That did not sound as promising as Rand could wish. He stepped out of the conveyance and stood up . . . and saw himself facing the Emperor's Walk, in the ruins of what had once been Congress. A great pit from an Abdrelik bomb yawned near him. Rand looked into it, and a sudden, dizzying rush claimed him.

Abdreliks. Bombs. Again. Bevan. He began to sway and sweat broke out on his forehead, plastering his hair to his skull.

Chirek came quickly to his side. "What is it?"

He didn't know. "I—" Rand could not tell him. His voice froze in his throat. "I—I—Bombs ."

"These are old craters. Come inside with me. I'll make you as comfortable as possible. You've been through a lot."

Rand swung a hand at him, to grasp him, and fell through the other's handhold. As he went to his knees, he found himself on the rim of the crater. He wrapped his arms about the bronze railing encircling it.

"Bombs again," he got out. He knelt panting, about to vomit into the crater, his throat raw with rising gorge. "Again!"

Chirek knelt beside him, confused, dabbing a sleeve at his sweat-soaked forehead. "What is it? Are you hurt?"

Rand clutched at him. *Bahdur* ached in him. Like a volcano, it rose, lava-hot, ready to spill out. He held the oth-

er's cool hand desperately as if it could absorb the
overload. "*See,*" he begged, and put forth the visions which
came swimming past his eyes. Chaos opening, spilling forth
Abdreliks, new bombs, new horrors.

Chirek screamed. He put his head back and howled, like
a wolf of old Terra, in chilling notes and Rand in cold fear
let go of him. The Choya crawled, staggered away, and let
out another cry, of sheer, gut-wrenching pain.

Rand held to the bronze railing for his life, watching the
Choya, unknowing of what had happened, would happen, to
the two of them. He turned his head and spewed, head pulsing with the fervor, and when his stomach had emptied and
he looked back to Chirek, the Choya had crawled as far as
the dormant fountain sculpture by the Emperor's Walk.

"Chirek!"

The Choya looked at him. He reached to the sculpture
to pull himself to his feet, saying, "We must warn them.
We must tell them. . . ."

As he climbed, the fountain lit. Branch by curving
branch, fiber by graceful fiber. A silver trail of fire marked
the path of his hands. That which had not been activated
for generations came alive with a brilliance which made
Rand blink. Chirek pulled his hands away and the fountain
abruptly went out.

They looked at one another. The Choya shuddered, saying, "I do not understand."

Rand said only, "Hurry. There isn't much time."

Palaton kicked the doors of Congress down, the interior
guards taking the barricade away too slowly for his taste.
His ribs protested and he took a sharp breath in reward
for his pains. Jorana, at his elbows, said, "Careful."

The vast lobby was empty of Congressmen. It contained
only personal guards and secretaries, armed, wary, bewildered. He threw up his hands, saying, "I have no weapons."

"Heir Palaton." They recognized him with relief. He
strode through and they fell back. He entered the Halls
and a sudden hush fell on the din of conversation. His gaze
swept the rows and aisles, looking for a shock of distinctive,
snow-white hair, and the Choya which carried his Earthan
heritage as he carried his horn crown. He saw him.

"Devon of Householding Kilgalya. Come forward."

The air inside the Halls was hot, stifling, stinking of nervous sweat. These gentle Choyan had crouched here for hours, Palaton thought, while their capital burned down around them. All because they would not admit that the Godless had a voice as well as they did, and deserved a hearing as well.

All because they were craven, hovering cowardly in the shadow of their powers. They had tried to deny him Cho, they had tried to deny him his birthright. No more!

There was a flurry and then Devon of Kilgalya stepped into an aisle. His uniform was stained with sweat and wrinkled from sitting too long, but his eyes were still dangerous.

"Heir Palaton. It pleases me you were not lost at Sethu."

Palaton slipped a hand inside his jacket. Torn, soiled, bloodied, it yet carried the paper he had secured inside its pocket, and he pulled it out. He looked at it for a moment. It seemed a lifetime ago he had pulled his death warrant out of the House library. "Are you sure, Devon, that it pleases you?"

"Bring this mob to heel and it will please all of us."

The square jaw set. The white mane of hair stubbornly defied gravity, straight and spiking.

"Before all of Congress, before this *night* session," and Palaton imbued his words with irony, "I accuse you of attempting my murder. Not once, but three times. Within the sacred walls of Sethu, within the neutral grounds of Sorrow, and a third time outside the city, by the hand of the imperial guard. I accuse you, and I ask you why."

No answer could have been heard over the din which followed his accusation, but from Devon's set jaw, it was clear the Earthan would not answer.

The tiny Choya'i at Palaton's elbow yanked at his jacket sleeve impatiently saying, "On what grounds?"

Palaton let the warrant drop into her lap. She promptly put the document up on her monitor, transmitting it to all monitors on-line, across the hall and across Cho.

The document was unmistakably genuine. Devon staggered back a step, but the written proof of his deed was reflected a thousand times over at him. Nowhere could he turn and not see the warrant.

His thick, square hand slipped inside his own jacket and pulled out an enforcer.

The elderly Choya'i screamed and ducked in her seat. All about, Choyan hit the floor. In the sudden silence, Devon smiled without humor.

"I do not choose," he said, "to answer your accusation." He put the enforcer in his mouth and triggered it.

Palaton left the Halls, censureship lifted, Jorana at his side. He paused on the steps. The commons waited, gathering, so huge a crowd they could not all have possibly heard him. They filled the square from the new Congressional Halls all the way back to the palace, as far as his eye could see.

A movement caught the corner of his eye. He saw a communicator moving furtively. Palaton closed ground between them before the Choya could escape, and pulled the broadcaster from him.

He put it to his throat. "Censureship has been lifted. Tonight, you gain both an heir, and a voice in Congress. You can speak, and you will be listened to."

His crown rang with the answering vibration of their voices. He dropped the broadcaster to the steps. He saw Malahki at the fore of the crowd, listening.

They met one another on the stairs.

"Now give me Rand," Palaton said.

Malahki nodded. Shoulder to shoulder, they descended the bottom steps of the complex. The Choya led him to the Emperor's Walk, to the tunnel mouth, and they stepped on the glidewalk.

Jorana stayed silent, but she remained in her riot gear, and her palm rested on the butt of the enforcer on her hip. Malahki noticed it with humor in his eyes, yet did not remark on it.

As the Walkway opened up into the ruins, Palaton could see Rand and another Choya, walking, holding each other up, making painstaking progress toward his end of the tunnel. He broke into a run to meet them.

Palaton caught Rand up. "It's over," he said.

Rand's turquoise eyes reflected pain and fear. "God, no," he said. "Not yet. You have to let me pilot. I'm the only one who can get to the Abdreliks."

Nedar huddled at the edge of the spaceport. A launching cradle dwarfed him. The obsidian sands were slick and hard below him. The port was nearly empty, staff driven out by mobs of commons, only a few staying to protect the mechanical bays where chemicals, as well as valuable parts, were stored in abundance. He debated stealing a craft and fleeing Cho. Common sense told him it was best. Vengeance would not let him go.

He could feel his stolen *bahdur* trickling away. If he wanted to pilot, he would have to feed again, and soon. He hugged the shadows, moving cautiously, seeking out warmth in the darkness.

Berthing alarms came on. Nedar crouched, frozen, listening as bootsteps pelted past him.

"Incoming. It's a scramble." Breathless voices.

Nedar's senses knotted inside him. As much as he hated Palaton, he loved Cho. The cradle began to rock as the mechanics lowered it into launching position.

"The heir himself. . . ."

"I don't see anything on the screens," a mechanic interrupted his fellow abruptly.

"Out of Chaos—"

"Not in centuries. . . ."

"God be damned Abdreliks!"

The metal groan and clank obscured whatever else Nedar might learn. He put his back to the framework. He could not stay where he hid—this vessel would be launched within minutes. Already he could smell the beginning burn of fuel.

Out of Chaos.

Nedar broke into a shambling run. He made the lowered ramp of another starfighter, this one quiet, acquiescent, and gained the cockpit. From inside, he began the cradling sequencing to position it for launch. It rocked into motion.

Palaton was not going to do this without him. Nedar would not be left out of the acclaim and the heroics this time. He fastened his harness and brought the instrument panel up.

Palaton sat down in the pilot's chair. He frowned as the cockpit shield gave him an over-view of the launching field. Another ship appeared to be warming up. Rand sat down, distracting him. Palaton opened up the instrument console for him, and activated the black box. Rand looked at it. "Can I do this?"

"I'm here. The launch will be rough—we're not going out of a bay station. You'll have to take the G's and stay alert."

"What if I'm wrong?"

"Then we've wasted a few tons of fuel. But if you're right, GNask's finest are about to make an approach out of Chaos, and Cho has never been more vulnerable."

The starship shuddered as the final stage kicked in. The berth turned the ship into position and he lay on his back. Dully, Rand heard the call for liftoff and the cradle rocked away, freeing the ship.

For a moment, there was a sensation, not of flight, but of something stomping on him, pushing him deeper and deeper into his seat until he could not breathe. He heard Palaton's hissed intake of breath and felt, through their *bahdur*, the pain of broken ribs shifting and piercing. Long moments passed, Palaton's agony stabbing through his own fear and discomfort and then, suddenly, he could feel the flight and knew they had reached escape velocity.

The ship curved and they came slowly upright in their seats. Palaton's hands went out immediately to the screens.

"There's been another launch behind us," he said, and frowned in puzzlement.

"Who?"

"I don't know. Another *tezar*, perhaps, answering the alarm. None of us would stay aground unless we had to."

Rand turned his sight forward, through the velvet of deep space. Palaton said to him, "Reach for Bevan. A pilot can always taste the *bahdur* of another pilot."

Rand looked to him. "I'll draw him to us."

"If he's coming through anyway, an enemy we can see is better than an enemy we cannot."

Rand closed his mind. He thought of Arizar, mountainous, piney Arizar, with skies of blue and white-wisped cloud, and of the campus and Alexa and he and Bevan, like puppies, curled together after lovemaking, and at the back of his mind he realized he and Palaton were still linked, but the time for embarrassment was long past.

Bevan and Alexa, sharing and then shutting him out. Alexa and Bevan, trust and then deceit.

How had Alexa survived Arizar? How had Bevan? And why did the Abdreliks now have them both?

With a jolt, Bevan entered his mind.

*   *   *

Alexa felt Bevan stiffen suddenly. He dragged his hands off the instrument pads and thrust them to his temple, grabbing fistfuls of hair and yanking them out. He let out an ululating moan.

"Bevan!" She threw an arm about his shoulders.

He stared starkly into her face. "Get into the pod," he said.

"What?"

"Get into the pod! Now! Or you'll die with me!" He shook off her embrace.

Hands shaking, afraid not to obey him, she got out of her webbing. "Bevan . . ."

"*Now*, Alexa. They've poisoned me and they've poisoned him. The only way through is death." He put his pale, trembling hands back on the controls. He brought the ship into abrupt deceleration.

Alexa said, "Commander rrRusk, we're leaving Chaos." She yanked off her wiring and walked into the life pod. She sealed the door behind her, and sat, waiting, listening to dead silence, wondering if the pod would survive whatever Bevan had planned.

Rand's eyes flew open. Chaos ripped in front of him. Palaton let out a startled curse as the edge of it yawned, and they had not reached FTL to gain it. "What has he done?"

The Abdrelik vessel, built by Choyan, twinned the starship they rode. Behind it, he could see a wing of five more, but Chaos lipped at them, and they disappeared from view momentarily.

Palaton said, "Now, Rand. Together."

He *saw* and fed it to Palaton. Palaton worked the control panel. The starship gained on the first, as it erratically flew the tsunami-edge of Chaos.

"He's leading us *in*," said Rand.

"I've got us."

Bahdur cut a path across space, across black velvet and Chaos, bridging the two ships. It was a fiery path of destruction and when Rand saw it, he knew what Bevan was attempting to do.

"He's opening up a hole," he said. "A hole big enough to swallow Cho."

Five wingships appeared again. Palaton hesitated. Rand said urgently, "Palaton, we've got to get *him*. Or Cho is gone."

The starship behind them veered off suddenly, armament blazing. Whoever the second pilot was, the unknown *tezar* who had launched with them, he was not afraid to take on the five wingships. Palaton saluted him mentally.

Rand leaned forward in his straps. He gathered his *bahdur* even as the other spent his, following the path of fire searing across Chaos, cooling it, mending it, bringing it back. He wove light and dark and sent random segments spinning back into random sectors. He felt the heartstrings of the universe tugging through his fingers. He looked and he saw the patterns of Chaos through which he might someday pilot, the signposts of reality which impacted Chaos despite its unreality.

And they drew nearer the ship of destruction.

Palaton said, "I have a target."

For a moment, his heart failed. "Bevan," he said, and all his friendship and betrayal rode that word.

Rand.

The heavens exploded. A single white dot cascaded away, before Rand's eyes burned and he could no longer see. Blindly, he rewove the last edge of Chaos shut.

Epilogue

GNask looked at rrRusk. "It is well, commander, that out of every failure, a grain of success may be obtained."

rrRusk stood sweating. He had lost three of his finest wingships, and if he had been to the fore of the attack as he'd wished, this ship would have been lost also.

GNask sat in a vat of mud and water. "We came very close to ending the stranglehold of Cho upon us. And perhaps, with this tiny grain, we might yet do it." He smiled benevolently at the captive trussed and sitting in front of him. "It pleases me, dear Alexa, that Bevan did not take you to the abyss with him. As for, you, Nedar, I have something very useful planned for you. My intelligence reports tell me you disappeared some time ago. You are already lost to Cho. Therefore, your Brethren won't be searching for you. You are mine. All mine."

And the Abdrelik stroked his *tursh,* drool cascading from his tusks.